FREE TO BREATHE

TRACEY JERALD

FREE TO BREATHE

To my Meows.
We've laughed, we've loved, we've cried, and that doesn't begin to explain
the bond we've forged.
We've stared down demons because we've had to.
We've fought so many wars...
And we'll continue to do so.
Together.
We're stronger together than apart.
It's the meow effect.
Every day I'm blessed by the fact I have each of you.
I love you always.

THE LEGEND OF AMARYLLIS

There are variations regarding the legend of how amaryllis flowers came to be. Generally, the tale is told like this:

Amaryllis, a shy nymph, fell deeply in love with Alteo, a shepherd with great strength and beauty, but her love was not returned. He was too obsessed with his gardens to pay much attention to her.

Amaryllis hoped to win Alteo over by giving him the one thing he wanted most, a flower so unique it had never existed in the world before. She sought advice from the oracle Delphi and carefully followed his instructions. She dressed in white, and for thirty nights, appeared on Alteo's doorstep, piercing her heart with a golden arrow.

When Alteo finally opened his eyes to what was before him, he saw only a striking crimson flower that sprung from the blood of Amaryllis's heart.

It's not surprising the amaryllis has come to be the symbol of pride, determination, and radiant beauty. What's also not surprising is somehow, someway, we all bleed a little bit while we're falling in love.

PROLOGUE - CORINNA

TEN YEARS EARLIER FROM PRESENT DAY

I despise the dark with the same passion that some people reserve for hating others. Forced to surrender to the utter nothing of night, I need the light, because to me, it's hope. Something to cling to in the midst of my fear.

Tonight, at the house party Colby's housemates are hosting, a bunch of guys were looking to push things too far. When the lights had suddenly dimmed, I sought out my safe haven—Colby's room.

Knowing what I'd lived through, he swore he'd always leave his bedroom light on for me. He wanted me to have an escape for when someone would cut the lights to change the mood at one of the ROTC parties. He knew that my panic would inevitably set in.

It took a while for me to trust in him. Maybe it was the way he made me laugh or the warmth of his embrace. Maybe it was the fact that no darkness hid in his silvery-gray eyes. Whatever it was, I have faith in him. It's a wonder I trust anyone after I my parents tried to sell me for drugs not too long ago.

But there's something in me that tells me to trust Colby with every fiber of my being. Colby would never let me down. Ever.

Just ahead, the light shining underneath his door calls to me like a beacon. Quickening my steps, I reach for the key in my pocket that

Colby gave me months ago after I finally agreed to venture out to a party with him.

Within seconds, the glorious light wraps itself around me as I sit on the floor at the edge of Colby's neatly made bed. I swear, him being a ROTC boy makes him more immaculate than anybody I know. Even my sister Cassidy—who has a streak of OCD in her a mile wide—really can't compete. Not one thing is out of place. Even the boxes he's started to pack are stacked neatly in the corner. Note to self, don't invite him over for dinner before Ali, Holly, and I finish packing to head home for the summer.

On these comforting thoughts I drift off, content in the knowledge that I'm safe.

I should have known better. After all, safety is a seductive illusion created by our minds in order for us to function every day and not lose our minds in the horrific uncertainty of reality.

It could have been hours, possibly minutes when the harsh sounds of bodies slamming against Colby's door startles me awake. Heart pounding, I scramble back against the wall in the farthest corner, in the deepest shadows, while I wait to find out if I'm in any danger. I start to scream out, forgetting where I am. The tricks my mind keeps playing on me immediately throw me back into the cold dampness I lived in with Ali and Holly for a month close to two years before. I'm clenching my fists so tightly, I swear if I had nails that I didn't perpetually bite to the quick, they'd be drawing blood.

And that's when I hear it—a guttural moan.

Caught between a past that hasn't quite let me go and a present that hasn't quite caught up with my sleepy haze, my thoughts are scrambled. All I can think is don't open that door. Don't come for me. I'd rather be left alone in the dark than... There's an unmistakable sound of a key engaging each of the tumblers, then catching. The knob turns and a couple falls into the room. I let out a silent whoosh of breath. Peeking my head out from my hiding spot, I let out almost a sigh of relief. It's not the demons. It's Colby and the blonde I'd seen draped all over him earlier—Addison.

I scrunch down, trying to shrink into myself. Should I announce that I'm here? This situation is mortifying.

Colby walks Addison backward toward the bed, working her skimpy dress up and over her head along the way. "I can't wait to fuck you." His voice is raspy.

I want to vomit. Right here. Right now. What the hell am I supposed to do?

"I've wanted to fuck you since you sucked my cock dry the other night."

Addison giggles, and the noise is tinkling and grating. "Why don't you kill the lights and get on with that, then?"

The lights? No. He won't forget his promise to me, will he? I'm choking on fear so thick it's like hardened cookie batter. I'm about to gag. I haven't been without a light on in the dark since the night I was rescued from the shipping container where Ali, Holly, and I were huddled together for a month in the oppressive dark. I desperately begin to chafe my fingers back and forth against one another from where I'm wedged unseen in the corner between Colby's dresser and his closet. Just like Ali would always do to keep me calm.

As I watch the man I've been slowly falling for pull his shirt over his head, he does something he swore he'd never do. He plunges me into the pit of darkness without a lifeline.

The lack of light transform the normally spacious room into a midnight box. It takes everything in me not to howl. I raise my hands to my mouth and bite down hard enough to draw blood in order to prevent myself from whimpering out loud. I taste the metallic bitterness in my mouth as I suck on my hand. My long cascade of hair hides me better than any blanket would. It covers my drawn-up knees and disguises any brightness to my clothing. *Just breathe. You escaped a nightmare and rebuilt your life. You are strong enough to get out of this.*

From my cocoon, I can smell beer. Is Colby so drunk that he forgot everything he promised me? My anger churns inside. If that's the case, then he's going to catch the rough side of my tongue for making me suffer through this debacle.

He must have undone his belt as I can hear it clang as he makes his way across the room where his double bed sits on the opposite wall from the door. I offer up some small gratitude that I'd convinced him he'd have more space if he placed his dresser on the same wall as his door. Short of the lights coming back on, I am well out of their line of sight although I'm going to have a front seat to their show.

Lucky me.

Hopefully, they'll never know I was here.

I try to maintain my calm by taking deep breaths. "I'm going to fuck you hard this time. Then, we'll see how the night plays out," Colby mutters. Soon, the groaning escalates as Colby rams into Addison. I can't shift or I'll expose myself. I listen closely, trying to find a good time that will cloak my escape out of this new reason to hate the dark.

Addison pants, "I never thought I'd get my turn. You kept looking, but you'd always go somewhere else." Now, I'm desperate for escape, but just as I'm about to crawl toward the door, I'm frozen by her next words. "I kept thinking you were going to fuck that Freeman cow before you left instead of me."

My entire world stills. It shouldn't hurt. I've heard the whispers about how Ali, Holly, and I couldn't be related since we look nothing alike. When I sat on the couch crying about it, my family and Colby assured me I was beautiful. My heart blossomed under their gentle nurturing.

Now, it fractures when I hear Colby's breathless laugh.

Laugh.

"Cori? She's sweet. Had a rough life. I feel bad for her sometimes."

The blonde bitch laughs before saying, "You're the one who's sweet to take that on, Colby. Not many guys would."

"I can handle Cori."

Addison snorts. "I can tell. She's so huge I'm amazed even you can get your arms around her. And these are some pretty impressive arms."

"So, she's a little on the chunky side, Addison. Who cares? It's not her I'm in bed with tonight, is it?"

"No, it's not," she purrs.

The effects of their words to my heart is so severe, I fall back where I am, uncaring if I'm seen or not. I'm almost dizzy. I don't know if I can crawl, let alone stand. My soul, which had been repairing and blooming, is now shattered. This is friendship? This is what I opened myself up to? Exposed my family to? Our secrets, our wounds, our pain, and he's with me because he feels sorry for me? And as for Addison, Holly would have this chick in a choke hold. Ali would verbally flay her. And let's not mention what Phil, Cassidy, or Em would do. Then again, they're my family through the kinds of bond that have been forged in hell.

Something the two on the bed will never understand.

My heart hasn't felt like this since South Carolina when I realized there was no escaping the living nightmare I was in. The only difference is back then someone else stole me away from my home to pay off a debt. This time, I openly walked into my own hell because I saw the promise of something that maybe I was being gifted with as a reward for what I endured before.

Obviously not. People like me aren't meant to have the life they'd give their next breath for.

As much as it kills me, I wait patiently for the people in the bed to pass out from a combination of alcohol and exertion. I listen until I hear nothing but Colby's muffled snoring. Standing, my legs feeling like pins and needles. I almost lose my balance and fall to the floor. My head is throbbing from holding in my pain. Wouldn't that be awful if I toppled over now—the pathetic cow might break through the floor and disturb their precious beauty sleep.

I don't want to look over, but I'm helpless not to.

Colby is sprawled partly over Addison, his hand cradling her breast as he sleeps. How many nights did he crash on my couch with me, when I'd be snuggled into him, hoping for something like the display before me?

God, how disgusted Colby must have been.

Reaching into the pocket of my jeans, I pull out his room key and drop it right next to his shirt before I quietly make my way out the door.

Closing the door behind me, I turn and immediately slam into a warm chest. "Oomph!"

"Cori. What the hell happened?" It's Jack, Colby's best friend, whose room is across the hall.

"It's nothing. I need to go." I shove past him.

"I don't think so." Jack grabs me from behind. I take a swing at him, trying to fight or get away. "Stop moving."

I press my lips together in a firm line. I refuse to relive my humiliation. Tears well in my eyes, but I refuse to let them fall.

He shakes me. "What's your fucking problem?"

Fear and pain leave me unable to form words that will make any sense or that sound nonchalant. Anything to get me out of here. I don't want to repeat any of what just happened by telling Jack. I want to cry, to sleep, to forget.

"Did too much food go to your brain or something?" He shakes his head. "This is what we get for letting the wildlife out of their pasture after dark."

I shake my head in denial even as I back away. Turning, I race down the hall, shoving past the partygoers on the stairs, through the room, and away from Jack's laughter. Tears burn in my eyes as I hear him call out over the landing, "Holy hell, I didn't know cows ran that fast."

There's no need to keep quiet now. My sobs can likely be heard back at my own apartment. I thunder down the stairs of Colby's off-campus house and race out the front door. As I'm flying down the front steps, I vow never to speak to anyone who lives in that house ever again. Just as I think I'm clear, I stumble on my shoelace and go flying onto the pavement.

Roaring laughter fills the night air.

Wobbling to my feet, I reach up and touch my face. My hand comes away with grit and blood—a hell of a lot of blood. I turn and face the crowd. "Fuck all of you," I hiss. They go silent when they see my face.

A girl I always liked from my business classes steps forward. "Corinna..." I hold out the hand streaked with blood to ward her off.

"Just stay the hell away from me." Woozy now from my fall, I quickly bend down and tie my shoe. Standing, I turn without another word and walk alone down the lane.

When I'm far enough away, I call a campus cab to come pick me up.

THE NEXT MORNING, I manage to sneak out of my off-campus apartment I share with Holly and Ali before either of them wake up. The doctors at the hospital first assumed someone had beaten me and wanted to call the local police. It was humiliating, but I recounted the story to prevent them from doing that.

After I got home from the hospital, I told Ali and Hols about how I face-planted on my way home the night before—nothing more, nothing less. Not long after, Colby knocked on our door. It was the first of many times I had Ali or Holly turn him away, preventing him from seeing me in the next week, until he graduated.

Because Colby didn't just admit to what he truly felt about me that night. In the light of the morning, he set off a chain reaction that forced me to find out what I had.

And I can't get rid of that as easily as ignoring it.

1

CORINNA

I don't hold on to grudges because life's too short. But there are three things that to this day I hate with a passion: the dark, Colby Hunt, and my tumor.

They're constantly in my head. I can no longer separate them or get rid of them. No matter what I do, nothing diminishes their importance. I have to live with each in my life, day after day, night after night.

In my mind, the dark has become the spirit of my demons. Night —all darkness—reminds me of the humid night when sticky hands grabbed my body, waking me from a restless slumber as they stole my innocence. I was carted off into the night for my body to be used to pay a debt that was never mine.

Colby gave my demons a face when he betrayed my friendship in college. There hasn't been a time when I've seen or heard his name since that I haven't felt the betrayal his laughter about my body caused.

And my tumor is my physical manifestation, my punishment for ever believing I could truly be free.

What is freedom anyway? It isn't the choice to live my life without judgment. College and the years after taught me that. My spirit tried to live free even when my soul was dying—no, dead inside after the lies Colby fed me to believe me ten years ago.

Ever since, I've been tried, judged, and found guilty of what? Choice. Spirit. Living.

It doesn't matter anymore. None of my demons do. My demons surround me no matter where I turn. I can't get a break from them now that *he's* back.

They're everywhere.

2

COLBY

There are things I can't forget.

Like the pain that I don't want to feel each time I remember I've lost my home. Knowing my father would rather have seen me broken than bend on what he thought was best for me. My father used his fists on me once—just once— and it was one time was too many. It wasn't leaving the place as much as the memories I walked away from that I can't let go of.

I can't forget how I felt about being medically discharged from the Army. The physical pain I was in from being shot almost equaled the emotional state of mind I was in at having to resign my commission.

And I'll never forget for the rest of my life the look of hatred in the eyes of Corinna Freeman every time we're in the same room together.

Corinna hating me is the one constant that hurts me the most.

I was raised with everything I could dream of as a Hunt: a name that's uttered with some reverence; a grandfather who's a senator; a family who runs a billion-dollar empire with cars, homes, and money to burn. All I wanted to do was serve my country, to stand up for what was right for those who had fallen before and after me. To be a hero.

Maybe that's what first drew me to Corinna: I was already a hero in her eyes. That wasn't what kept me from falling in love with her, even though I knew I couldn't have her. I couldn't fall in love with her because she was too fucking traumatized by what had happened to her.

I was close to losing my ROTC scholarship when we first met. Hesitantly, she'd smiled at me during a business class we were both in as she'd slid into her seat. Later that same week, I stumbled into a pizza parlor on campus, drunk after a frat party, and saw her laughing with two girls, her golden eyes shining.

She'd given my heart a reason to beat. The same reason men like me go to war, to fight for a reason to come home.

Corinna became that reason for me even if she never realized it. With her came two sisters who were at first wary of me as a man, and later two more sisters and a brother. A new family. All of them were hesitant about my presence, and I didn't understand why. When I found out, I became murderous over what had happened to each of her magnificent family members.

When I'd finally realized Corinna had become my entire heart, I knew I couldn't do a thing about it. Not then. Maybe not ever. Because between one day and another, everything had suddenly changed.

The Corinna I had come to know was gone, and in her place was a cold shell of a woman. Her once shining eyes became as dark as the earth, like the places I would later visit in my tours around the world. Her face was closed off, desolate, and accusing.

To this day, even as I work for her brothers-in-law, her eyes are still hostile toward me. If I was reading Corinna right, I'd think she felt betrayed somehow. But how could she even think that when I'd once loved her with every fiber of my being?

I wish I knew what the hell I'd done so I could find my way back to the only thing in my life I'd want a chance at returning to.

3

CORINNA

Beep. Beep. Beep.

The sound of the alarm on my cell phone going off jerks me out of the battle I face every night—sleep. I scrub my hands down my face as I swing my legs into a sitting position, my hair falling haphazardly in front of my face.

I can't swallow due to the dryness in my throat. My memory lingers on the images from my dream of falling into the gravel at UConn. I've lived with its repercussions—finding out about my brain tumor—for more years than I care to remember. Still, despite my problems sleeping, I hardly ever dream about the past. I live by a personal mantra that has served me well over the years: Live for today, for tomorrow may never come.

I have to get a move on. The cake I need to finish decorating today won't get completed any faster, and I have a hard stop at 4:00 p.m. Tonight, one of the connections I've made by bringing people joy through my baking will be giving my family a once-in-a-lifetime opportunity.

I can't freaking wait. My siblings have no idea what they're in for.

I push off the couch that I fell asleep on last night in my master bedroom and flick off the lights that I leave on in my bedroom at night to protect me from the darkness. The early-morning sun warming my skin tells me without looking at my weather app that it's going to be a scorcher today.

I always dress for comfort in a loose tank top and baggy jeans since I wear a chef's coat on top of my clothes in the kitchen of Amaryllis Events, my family's wedding- and event-planning business. Other than quickly braiding my hair, there's no need to bother with anything else. Also, Em, one of my three older sisters who's a fashion designer, is pulling out all the stops, dressing us before we go out tonight.

Our night out is going to be incredible. I shake my head as I slip into a pair of bright pink Chucks. My sisters and brother have no idea what's really in store.

As I MAKE my way into Collyer, I munch on the banana I grabbed on my way out the door. It's early on a Friday, and I know my kitchen is going to be utter chaos. I have my standard weekend supply delivery coming in. Hopefully, my assistant got the text I sent her letting her know I need the center island clear to finish up the cake for the Martin wedding. I have about eight hours to brush on the edible rose-gold leaf before Phil decorates the top with greenery and transports it to the family's home. This will give me just enough time to get ready for tonight with my sisters.

I pull into the parking lot of Amaryllis Events and see Ali's convertible, Em's Rover, and Cassidy's new Porsche Panamera—a birthday gift from her husband, Caleb. I smile remembering how we all taunted him when he handed her the keys to the car that was as much for him as it was for her. Caleb didn't argue. Instead, he laughed and said their twins would grow up understanding they were a Porsche family.

A Porsche family. The wealth we've accumulated is a far cry from the poverty each of us grew up with. That was before we adopted each other and became a family. A family forged from the deepest horrors anyone should ever have to live through. A family that found itself in the dark but lives in the light. A family made of strength and pride.

My fingers glide over my tank top where my amaryllis tattoo rests close to my heart. As I walk around the delivery truck, I see another familiar vehicle. My back, where another tattoo rests, snaps ramrod straight.

What the hell is Colby doing here?

It's bad enough I suffer the nights Colby haunts my sleep. Ever since he left the Army and accepted a job with Hudson Investigations, he's made himself right at home with my family again.

He better not make himself at home in my kitchen. Especially not today.

My good mood soured, I stomp around to the back entrance that leads to my sacred domain. Despite Colby's presence crushing my spirits, I still get breathless every time I walk into the space dominated by spotless stainless steel and top-of-the-line walk-in refrigerators, freezers, and ovens. All told, the equipment in this kitchen cost more than my college tuition. Sometimes, when I'm by myself, I give in to the urge to spin around and dance in the kitchen, unable to hold in my emotions. I forget about the things weighing down my mind and just revel in all that is ours. Mine.

The equipment in this room helps bend things to my will, mold into the shapes I want them to. Every dish meets my critical standards or suffers getting ejected. Typically, into Phil's stomach.

When I walk into the kitchen, it's like walking into a farmer's market. There are crates of eggs covering an entire worktable. Gallons of fresh milk are lined up in crates near my walk-in refrigerator. Sacks of flour are stacked so high, I can barely see over them. Jesus, this must be twice the regular order. I sigh, realizing I don't have anywhere to decorate the cake.

Tina, the stay-at-home mom of two who comes in to help out twice a week, gapes at me helplessly from where she's signing a clipboard. "Cori, I had no idea what to do!"

Determined, I rein in my displeasure knowing there was a

massive error somewhere. And believe me, I'll find it. I sigh again. "Then let's get it put away before I kill whoever made this mistake." Since we decided to streamline ordering to go through Ali, we've cut costs significantly. But I know what I told Ali I needed for cakes earlier in the week. It was half of what's in my kitchen right now.

That means either the supplier screwed up or someone in the family did.

Every second counts right now, and I'm losing precious time as I help Tina when I should already be delicately brushing sheets of foil onto smooth fondant.

THIRTY MINUTES LATER, I've left Tina in a better state, but I'm marching up the grand front staircase, murder aforethought. I've already talked directly with the food supplier who assures me the order was correct. So that means only one thing. Based on what I just put away, I've been overbooked once again after being promised a light week.

It's been like this since I appeared on the celebrity episode of *Caketastic* on the Food Network with Brendan Blake six months ago. While the notoriety is excellent for business, I feel like there's no end in sight. I haven't had a full day off in a long time, and I have no assistants in the kitchen. Sure, I have Tina a couple of mornings, and interns from the local culinary institute, but that's not what people are paying for. They're sinking thousands of dollars for a Corinna Freeman trademark cake.

If we keep this pace up, it's going to kill me.

Not even caring who's where, I yell, "Get your asses into the conference room, now!" Fuming as I storm down the hallway, I run into a chest I know doesn't belong to any of my family members.

Of course—Colby. "Excuse me." I step aside to move by him, but he moves in front of me.

"Good morning, Cori." He smiles. God, why couldn't his face match the asshole I know who lives inside?

"Colby." I nod. That's about all the politeness I can manage for the man who once said—

Nope. Not going there today.

I hate that Colby's taken Charlie's ticket for the Brendan Blake concert since Charlie has a summer bug. Lucky me. One of the most insane gifts I've ever managed to give our family and he's going to be along for the ride. Pushing past him, I walk down the hall toward the conference room.

Behind me, I hear him mutter, "Sorry. Next time I'll get out of your way."

Just stay out of my life, Colby. Permanently. You managed to do it for over ten years after you said you felt bad for the sweet fat chick you could "handle". It's not like we had a real friendship despite what I may have thought back then.

If I was a storm before, I'm a full-blown hurricane now as I burst into the conference room.

"Shit, she's on the warpath," Holly mutters. The youngest of our adopted family holds her camera up to her expert eye, aiming its lens at each of my siblings. "Who pissed her off today of all days?"

"We all know my version of cooking involves takeout or begging for food from one of y'all, so I'm free and clear. Next?" Em pipes up.

All eyes focus on Phil. I tap my sneaker-clad foot while I wait for him to speak. He looks affronted. Finally, I snap, "Well?"

"Listen, missy, if you're pissy, don't take it out on me." Phil huffs.

"Phillip, if I'm 'pissy', it's because I just spent the last half hour sorting out a double delivery of kitchen supplies. Do you want to know what that tells me?" Without waiting for him to answer, I continue. "Someone up here fucked up, and we're about to lose thousands of dollars' worth of perishables, or I got overbooked. Again. Which means I can't cut loose the way I want to tonight because I'll be back in the kitchen baking tomorrow. You know, the first day I was supposed to have off in six damn months!"

Ali has turned and is glaring at Phil. "You said you cleared the schedule with Cori, Phil, before I had the clients sign the contracts."

Ali, our company lawyer, has ironclad contracts. Short of a death in the family, there's no breaking them.

Phil's imminent death is looking awfully tempting.

"Umm, I meant to, but then I got caught up in my floral order..." His voice trails off as Cassidy, our chief executive officer, stands up and slaps her hand down on the table.

"Enough." Her usually calm mask is gone. "Phil, you will be here at—" Cassidy turns to me. "What time, Cori?"

"I don't even know what the hell I'm baking. I haven't even seen the schedule." I'm seething.

Cassidy pulls her iPad out and scrolls through the online program. She focuses on the screen before she lets out a sigh. Handing me her tablet, she sighs. "I'm sorry, Corinna."

I look at the list and gasp. There are cakes due every day, including tomorrow.

"I have a cake to decorate in rose-gold foil by four. I now have to bake a three-tier cake and prepare the lemon curd filling to go in it for tomorrow. On top of that, I'll have to be back tomorrow morning to decorate it in buttercream roses for the Collyer Garden Club. An order—" I pause to scan the intake form. "—you accepted yesterday? *Yesterday?*" I turn to my sister. "There's nothing Phil can do, and nothing I want him to help with."

Phil flinches.

"Fine. Alison, modify payroll this week to remove Phil's percentages of any of the profits from anything he scheduled where Corinna didn't sign off explicitly accepting the work." Cassidy's voice is calm but firm.

"That's not fair!" Phil jumps to his feet. "I secured that business for us."

"If Corinna, or any of us, had done this to you, you'd be outraged. You wouldn't have tolerated a day off in six weeks, let alone six months. Since you aren't a master baker who won us the notoriety to actually make these bookings, tell me what you plan on doing to make this up to your sister?" She holds up a hand. "A sister I might add who is taking us to the Brendan Blake concert this evening. A sister who expected to be able to spend time with her friend after the show unencumbered."

Phil opens his mouth and then snaps it shut.

I don't have time for this. "Someone get me a copy of the updated schedule within the next fifteen minutes. I have to go see if my kitchen has been set to rights." I stomp toward the door. "And I'm just saying this: no lunch in the kitchen today. Keep out if you know what's good for you."

I walk into the hallway to find Colby lingering outside. "Tough break, Cori." His eyes are sympathetic.

I stop in my tracks. "Might want to be careful, Colby. Eavesdroppers typically don't hear good things. In fact—" I lean closer as if I'm about to tell him a state secret. "—they tend to hear all kinds of nasty things their 'friends' say about them. Why, is that a cow I hear? Gotta go before all the curds are gone." I head down the stairs back to set some order to the chaos of the kitchen.

And of my mind.

4

CORINNA

It's 3:45 and I'm starving. I didn't get a chance to break for lunch. If I don't get something in me, there's every possibility I'm going to end up a heap on the brick paver floor. I just don't have time. I have exactly fifteen minutes to finish the last few pieces of foil this cake needs, slice the cooled cakes, fill them with the lemon curd, and then scratch coat them with vanilla buttercream.

I don't even know if they're supposed to have vanilla cream as the frosting. Of course, Phil forgot to get that information on the intake order. "Here's to hoping no one's allergic to pure vanilla bean," I muse as I assemble the first layer. Cake, lemon curd, cake. Vanilla buttercream. Push in dowels to stabilize the cake. Begin the next layer. Repeat until the top layer is on.

Ugh.

My mind drifts as I finish the scratch coat. About six months ago, I appeared on the Food Network with Brendan Blake, country music's hottest star. That day filming was intense. The day before taping, one of the most prestigious chefs on the show came down with the flu. Since it was a baking show, they quickly scouted for local talent who could join the show at a moment's notice. I happened to fit the bill. A charismatic baker who was local and available.

It was blind luck Brendan and I got along. When we were in the green room before the show, he made me laugh by telling me he was helpless in the kitchen. After I was done laughing at his joke, I asked why he agreed to do the show. Pulling his cell out of his back pocket, he showed me a picture of his nephew who has leukemia. If he won, all of the money from the celebrity *Caketastic* would go toward a donation to help boost clinical trials at the University of Washington where his nephew was being treated.

My hand clasped his shoulder. "Mr. Blake."

He gave me a small smile. "Corinna, please. Call me Brendan."

I smiled back. "How well do you take orders?"

"According to my band, not well at all. Why?"

"Because if you want to win as much as I do, you have to do everything I tell you. And if you don't understand, say so up front. Because we're going to win for that little boy." I nodded toward the phone that displayed the photo still clutched in his hand. "And we're going to have a blast doing it to show him his uncle's doing this for him."

Brendan tipped his head down toward me and said, "You think you can beat the best the Food Network is going to throw at us?" His voice was laced with disbelief.

I tossed my long braid behind my shoulder. "I don't think it, I know it. And when we win," I said, putting the emphasis on the word we, "we'll bake your nephew a cake for you to bring home to celebrate with."

He shook his head. "I don't know why I believe you, but I do."

"Good."

We shook on the deal. And then we went out there and kicked ass.

We had three rounds to get through. In our first round, I thought Brendan was going to dive into the red velvet cake I made. I had to slap his hands away several times on camera, which the live audience ate up. When we presented to the judges, I renamed the cake Brendan's Downfall. Laughing hysterically, we accepted our accolades as well as our critique, but we made it through to the next round.

Brendan caught my fire.

The second round, while I was on camera, I engaged Brendan

into talking about his girlfriend, Dani. He told me all about their first date and how he'd written most of the songs on his first album for her. When he asked if I was married and I said no, Brendan started trying to negotiate dates for me with men in the audience.

The second cake we presented to the judges was a beautifully decorated cake Brendan helped mix, layer, and do the scratch coat. We named that one Dani's Desire since it was the same flavors as the lemon and blueberry pie they'd eaten on their first date.

The judges said it was utterly delicious, and we advanced to the finals. And that's where we both went into overdrive.

I had always planned on making Ali's chocolate sin cake for round three, which was made up of four different kinds of chocolate. All the chocolate had to be hand chopped and grated before being melted in a double boiler. During our on-air conversation, I found out Brendan's nephew loved chocolate cake.

Ali's cake was then renamed *Joey's Justice*.

Partway through the round, I thought we were out of it. Brendan's knife slipped, and he cut himself. I was alone for fifteen minutes of our precious hour, trying to be both head baker and sous chef. When Brendan came back on set, I asked how his hand felt. He shrugged as he held it up. "So I bled for my nephew a little. He's doing a hell of a lot worse to stay with all of us."

Brendan and I hugged on TV over the beginning of my dark chocolate buttercream frosting.

When the panel was judging our cake, they asked about the story behind it. He was nervous, but he explained how it was my sister's favorite cake but I'd rededicated it to his nephew who was fighting for his life. He went on to say that whether I was a celebrity chef or not, I made him feel invincible in the kitchen that day, so regardless if we had won or lost, the University of Washington would receive a donation from him.

The head judge, a snooty French pastry chef, had remarked, "Then I suppose it's good for them that you just won $50,000, Mr. Blake."

I'll never forget the look on Brendan's face when he turned to me and said, "No, the University of Washington just won $100,000 donated by myself and Ms. Freeman." He picked me up and swung me around in the air.

I felt unstoppable, like nothing could touch me. Maybe I could tackle my own demons with as much bravery as Joey Blake and as much determination as Brendan Blake. But as the weeks and months passed, and work became my primary focus again, I started to feel like Cinderella after the clock struck midnight. The glass slipper fell off a while ago. Hell, it didn't fall off—it had shattered.

It's time to face my reality head-on. And right now, reality involves laying three pieces of ridiculously delicate foil so smoothly, people would think I'd airbrushed it onto the cake.

Picking up the book of 24 karat rose-gold leafing, I match up the edge to the side of the bottom of the layer. Peeling away the delicate leafing, I pull off the paper. Almost perfect. Spinning the cake layer around, I keep going, overlapping just a bit so the lines start to obliterate. Dabbing here and there, my soft brush blends any seams. Over the top, I begin where the edge didn't quite match the height of the cake and lay the foil so it meets in the center. Using a barely noticeable patch where I know Phil will affix the ornate cake topper, I dab everything down until it's finished.

Done.

I reach under the cake layer and gently place it on top of the other layers, trying not to disturb them. It's precisely 3:58. I'm debating if I should sacrifice my time with Em and the girls to make sure this cake arrives safely at the reception, when the door to the kitchen opens and Caleb walks in. He stops dead in his tracks. "Whoa, Cori. That's..." His words halt.

"I know." It was a pain in the ass, but it's absolutely magnificent. "Let me get a picture before I head out with Phil." I pull my phone from my pocket and start walking around, taking pictures from all angles.

"No," Caleb replies. "First, you're due for a shower. Then Em's waiting on you to transform you into something more beautiful for tonight."

I snort. "That won't be too hard."

He frowns. "'Cause it's hard to improve on perfection."

I laugh as I pat his cheek. "You're sweet, but really, that was funny. I thought I'd go with Phil to make certain nothing happened with the cake."

Caleb glares at me. "I have my orders. You're to hit the shower and report to Em's studio. I'm going to help Phil with the cake." I start to protest, but Caleb stops me. "Cassidy's orders."

I shake my head. "I'd really feel better if—"

"And Cassidy would feel better making some part of this up to you. Should I assume Phil knows how to get it into the van?"

I nod. "We just need to load up from the front."

Locking the wheeled cart into place, Caleb and I slide the cake over much the same way a patient is transitioned from a hospital bed to a surgical table—carefully. Rolling my hard work down the hallway, I hear an astonished "Holy crap."

I nod, refusing to acknowledge Colby's awe more than that before I continue walking backward toward the entrance.

"Let me get the door at least."

"Appreciate that, Hunt," Caleb answers, sending me a curious look. I ignore it, as I do most things when it comes to Colby.

Colby follows us out and watches as I give instructions to Phil and Caleb about how to secure the cake and how not to touch the golden foil, and hand them the soft brush in the event they do brush anything. Despite my fury at Phil, I give him a quick kiss when I mutter, "Drive safely," before I turn to head back into the mansion.

"You're welcome," Colby calls from where he stands in the driveway. With a flick of my hand, I walk inside to bask in the warmth of a shower before my sisters descend upon me.

"CHRIST, EM. THAT HURT," I bitch a short while later as my eyebrows are being ripped from my face.

"Do you want to look and feel good?" She's merciless.

"It's not like anyone's going to look twice at me when I'm surrounded by the rest of you, so who the hell cares?" I'm dressed in a black sleeveless top, dark-wash jean shorts, and complementary black Valentino espadrille platform wedges. Okay, I look halfway decent this evening.

Em snickers derisively as she picks up her makeup brush. "Please. I was hoping that top would fit based on how much weight you've dropped since your clothes are hanging on you. Did you pick them up at a bargain sale?"

I smile beatifically. "Maybe I did."

As she dabs the waterproof foundation on my face, she leans in. "Don't get smart with me, missy. I've yet to apply your makeup. You could end up looking like a raccoon."

"Anything's better than what you're starting with."

"All right, enough. Em, give me a few minutes with Cori," Ali declares. You'd never know she had a baby less than six months ago, her body's so damn tight.

"Can it wait thirty seconds while I finish the foundation? Then she has to sit still," Em grumbles.

Ali impatiently taps her booted foot. Em pushes and pulls my face critically back and forth before muttering, "Sit still." As she slips into her adjoining office, I'm left to deal with another one of my older sisters. The lawyer, the warrior, the one who has never broken a promise to me.

Including holding my hand through the living nightmare we survived together.

"What is it, baby? Tell me." Ali crouches down next to me, her cobalt-blue eyes concerned.

"Nothing I can't handle," I assure her. Nothing I haven't handled for the last ten or so years, I remind myself.

"If Colby coming is too much, I'll have Keene call him out on some bogus work thing," Ali offers. Keene is Ali's significant other.

I shake my head. "Trust me. Once we get there, we won't be seeing the guys for a long while. Well, other than Phil." My family has no idea what's in store for them tonight. Brendan promised me tickets people would weep over, and when I found out what they were, I laughed myself sick. Brendan and I have chatted quite a bit since the show just to keep up with each other. When he mentioned he was going to be touring nearby and asked if I wanted to come with my family, I jumped at the chance. Short of singing with the band, I don't think we have a better view.

"Okay. I know what Phil did was wrong, but even though I can't bake like you, I'm willing to come in and help prep if you think it would help."

I squeeze her shoulder. "Thanks, sweets, but no. Your downtime is meant for Keene and Kalie."

"It's not your burden to carry alone," Ali argues.

Oh, if she only knew about the true burdens I carry inside. Instead, I smile at the woman who kept my mind sane for the month we were trapped together in a shipping container, when a drug consortium tried to sell us as sex slaves. We all have our scars from that time in our lives. Ali's are profound since her father was one of the leaders of the sex trafficking ring. Fortunately, she's been able to find some peace of mind over the years. Holly's are vastly different. I admire my baby sister each and every day knowing I couldn't hold the burdens she carries on my soul. Mine manifest themselves in the dark, where sleep eludes me unless I'm with someone I explicitly trust. And the last time that happened was ten years ago. Now, I don't find rest unless a light is shining because I'm petrified of the absolute darkness.

Instead, I say, "I know. Now, let's get Em back in here before we're late."

Before she can respond, I call out for our older sister. Soon, we're caught up in final makeup touch-ups. By 6:00 p.m., a limo arrives at Amaryllis Events to pick up the girls and Phil. The guys will go to will call where the tickets are being held under Keene's name since we'll already be backstage with Brendan and his band.

"Hey, Cori. There's a note for you," Cassidy says. Even my oldest sister is sporting some short shorts and a low-cut top for the evening. She hands me the note and the bottle of champagne it's attached to.

Taking both, I open the note up.

I'm singing one for you tonight. Since you deal with crowds so well, I might have you join me for it. See you soon. ~BB

I pass around the note, then work the cork out of the champagne. It bursts with a pop, and I quickly slug the overflowing bubbles. After filling glasses as they're handed to me, I lift my own in a toast. "Here's to us!"

Five other glasses touch mine before the champagne disappears.

Finally, Phil can't take it. "Holy shit! Are we really in a limo on our way to see Brendan Blake live?" He lets out a screech that would do a thirteen-year-old girl proud.

Everyone in the limo cracks up.

Sitting back, I cross my legs. "Just wait, brother. That's the least of what tonight has to offer."

5

COLBY

"Whose idea was it to leave them unsupervised?" Keene asks.

"God, did my wife actually do that?" Caleb asks. There's wonderment in his voice.

With equal parts amusement and horror, we watch the Jumbotron monitors that keep focusing on the Freeman siblings at the hottest country music show to hit Connecticut this year. Maybe ever.

"Holy hell. Who threw the bra on stage?" Jared demands.

Ryan, Caleb's younger brother and apparently a close friend of the family, just braces his hands on his thighs and laughs.

"I think that was Phil. None of the girls are wearing tops that require one," Caleb mutters.

Jason spews his beer all over Keene, whose look of disgust would fell a lesser man.

It's priceless. It's epic. It's a Freeman night out. It's been about six months since I left the Army and was hired at Hudson Investigations. But it feels like decade-old friendships with the family picked up right where they left off. My ear-to-ear grin can't be contained as I watch the shit storm near the stage keeping close to 40,000 people entertained.

Suddenly, my gut takes an elbow that's less than friendly. "Stop checking out the mother of my child," Keene yells. "It's bad enough I have to watch Blake's hired security check out her ass in those things she's calling shorts. Jesus, Alison! Will you pull those damn things down?" Keene's attention is diverted as Ali shakes her body to the music.

Fuck that hurt. The bastard may have been out of the Army years longer than I have, but he hasn't lost his moves. Deciding to mess with him, I remark, "If I hadn't met your daughter, I would never believe it. Ali's body is just as hot as it was that night at the Plaza in that dress."

Keene turns to me. "You do realize you're here because they"—he points to the girls and Phil going wild in the pit—"apparently like you. I still merely tolerate you, both here and at the office."

I can't help but keep taunting Keene. "Would it help to know I was checking out Ali and Cassidy?" Fucking with Keene about his wife and sister is something I take immense pleasure with.

From behind, I feel a slap against the back of my head right before Caleb growls, "No," from the other side of me. He wants to hear me mouth off about Cassidy slightly less than her brother since he's been married to her for two years now.

"Hey, I'm just sayin', you'd never know they had babies less than a year ago," I exclaim. Two men are suddenly in my space. "What?"

"Three other available sisters are knockouts," Keene growls. "Choose one of them."

"It's bad enough we have to watch the epic disaster occurring as other idiots... Jesus fuck, couldn't she have worn a bra?" Caleb's attention is diverted back to the Jumbotron where his wife is dancing in a top that Em decreed was perfect earlier.

I like country music. I mean, you couldn't have been stationed on a military base anywhere and not have heard it. And when my current bosses asked me what I was doing tonight, I wasn't passing up the chance to see this concert in these seats knowing we're going backstage after. Not when it came with the added sideshow caused by the Freeman siblings and their extended family.

This is one hell of a job perk that Uncle Sam's Army couldn't offer.

Cassidy, Em, Ali, Corinna, Holly, and let's not forget Phil are causing a scene in the pit, shaking it, dancing. Technically, they aren't in the pit; they are in the secure space between the stage where Brendan Blake is crooning to the masses. While typically reserved for security and the crew's videographer, Corinna's connection to the megastar had secured the siblings the special lanyards around their necks that granted them access.

All the males, save Phil, are seated in the first row behind the pit.

It's terrifying. It's a security nightmare in the making. It's a recipe for Freeman hysterics that will be reenacted for years to come.

Shortly after I ran into Ali at a party in Manhattan over a year ago, life as I know it fubared in a huge way. As the leader of an Army special forces team, my team and I were overseas on a security junket for a high-level government official when we took fire. A lot of it. I still wake up in the middle of the night trying to reconcile how things went so far out of control. How I didn't see what was happening within my own team. Peering down into the cup of cool amber beer in my hand, I take a quick drink to loosen the feeling of panic as I remember the first bullet tearing through my flesh and my gun flying out of my hand, leaving me defenseless.

I was forced to take a medical discharge from the Army. There was no way I could lead my team at less than one hundred percent. And there was no way I was going to ride a desk, so I resigned my commission. It was one of the most painful decisions I've ever had to make in my life.

It wasn't much later that I was approached by Hudson Investigations.

I was surprised to find out Keene and Caleb co-owned such a respected company. Primarily veteran hires, Hudson Investigations has a reputation for being able to compile intelligence data, provide protective details, and help in situations of missing persons where the government can't intervene. They're growing fast and need people they trust in positions of authority. I knew I had the skills and the experience, but until I sat in the chair, I didn't realize what an honor it was to be hired.

There definitely have been some fringe benefits. The salary upgrade was nothing to sneeze at—I mentally kissed my government pay goodbye. Having relatively flexible hours is excellent too. The best part was reconnecting with the extended Freeman family again, and not just for perks like tonight.

So, less than six months since I left the Army, it was more than just the tickets and the sideshow that brought me to where I'm presently standing. If I'm being honest with myself, it's a chance to get close enough to Corinna to find out where things went so completely off the rails that she abandoned our friendship.

My thoughts are interrupted by the country signing legend saying, "As you might have seen, I have some special guests tonight. She's going to kill me for doing this, but I'd like to bring her up on stage."

The Freemans are going insane in the pit as big bruisers with Security slashed across their backs escort Corinna onto the stage. God, she's fucking beautiful. Wolf whistles and catcalls come from every direction as she saunters over to country's hottest star.

When she's within touching distance, he reaches out his hand and she takes it. Since his guitar is twisted behind his back, he tugs her close for an embrace. Her arms wrap around his neck, and he spins her in circles on the stage.

Her head goes back, long hair almost touching her heart-shaped ass. The Jumbotron shows the camera zoom in on her face. It's illuminated with joy. And that's before the star says, "Thanks, Cori, for being who you are. Thank you for doing what you did, for being who you are to me, and to everyone who knows your heart," right before he launches into one of his biggest ballads with his arms wrapped around her.

Seriously?

Isn't the fucker dating some famous model? Doesn't Cori have any common sense when it comes to men anymore? My best friend tells me about Cori's exploits all the time. Where did her caution go? Jack says he heard she went wild after I graduated from college. What happened to the girl I knew?

My arms are crossed tightly across my chest as Brendan continues to croon to the audience. At the end of the song, he smiles down at Corinna, who's swaying back and forth within the confines of his arms.

No fucking common sense. This will be all over social media in less time than it will take the concert to end.

Fuming, I hear Caleb mutter to Keene, "Still think it's remarkable."

Keene says, "I know, right? All because someone got sick and she had to fill in."

I have no idea what they're talking about, and right now, I'm not sure I care.

We've been instructed to stay in our seats so we can be escorted backstage after the concert. Time and again, people come by to ask us to leave. In unison, we lift our badges.

Sheepishly, they move on.

Finally, a burly man wearing a crew member shirt and a member of security behind him walks up. It's been forty-five minutes since the show ended.

"Thanks for your patience, guys. Everyone's backstage. Ready?" En masse, we all stand and start walking. "Name's Smith. We finally got the fans out. Your people have been hanging out with the band." He pauses. "Do they always talk that much?"

Caleb looks at Keene, Keene turns to Jason, and they burst out laughing. Jason answers, "Yes."

Smith shakes his head. "Don't know what you do to get a word in. It was like a roomful of groupies when it comes to the sound. I offered to get you guys just to hear myself for a minute."

I volunteer, "You should see a family dinner. Sometimes they dance on tables."

Keene shoots me a glare.

"I can only imagine. And knowing Cori"—Smith shakes his head, and my insides freeze. He knows Corinna? How long has she known this country bootlicker? "—she's right up in the thick of it. She's a doll though. Always sending the kids on the cancer floor cupcakes and whatnot. Though, from what I hear from Brendan's girl, Dani, the nurses are beginning to intercept them and keep them for themselves."

Cori sends what kids with cancer cupcakes? And how's Brendan Blake involved?

I keep silent as Jason asks, "Smith, how's Brendan's nephew doing?"

The old-timer shakes his head. "Much better. The last trial he was in did wonders, so we're all optimistic. I'm sorry y'all won't get to meet Joey tonight, but he's still in Seattle getting his treatment. He's bummed he's still only met Cori on FaceTime. Dani flew in tonight because she wanted to meet Cori finally."

"Alison told me Cori won't take a dime from any order on any kid's cake," Keene tells the group. "Not since she met Brendan and was on that show. Now, her part of the profits are being directed to the University of Washington research programs for childhood and young adult leukemia research."

Smith chuckles. "You know, Brendan was all excited to see Cori again even before her sister let that slip earlier." He directs his attention to Keene. "He might've twirled Cori around once or twice when he heard that. I think one of the crazies—I mean, her sisters—got that on video."

Keene barks out a laugh. "For everything Cori's done? I'm sure she deserved it."

"I'm sure my husband was jealous though," Jason pipes up.

Everyone starts laughing at that. So much, they don't realize I haven't joined in.

Wait, what show? I want to ask, but I know I'll feel like a schmuck with these guys. I'm missing some huge piece to why we're here tonight.

When we turn the corner, I stop short, staring across the tent we've been escorted into.

Brendan Blake has his arms wrapped around Corinna like he's never going to let her go.

And from the look of pure joy on her face, she might not want him to.

6

COLBY

"So how was the concert last night?" Jack O'Brien, my best friend since college, asks me.

We're kicked back at his house in Darien, where he's a partner in a lucrative medical practice.

Taking a sip of bourbon, I contemplate the answer. "It was... intense? I guess that's the right word."

Snorting into his glass, Jack takes a quick drink. "Somehow, I can't imagine a country concert being intense. I still don't understand how you listen to that garbage."

I shrug. I wasn't always a fan, but there's something incredibly beautiful in the words hitting your gut when you're thousands of miles away from home. I refuse to explain it again to a man who believes in buying suits handmade in London for his office hours. "I just do."

"Whatever. Explain what you mean by intense. I'm sure there were enough women there to bang that you went home a happy man last night." His crudity rubs me the wrong way, and I frown at him.

"Actually, I was home relatively early. We were backstage for a while after the show, but—" I'm interrupted when Jack's glass clinks down on the table next to him.

"What the fuck do you mean you were backstage? And you didn't invite me? What was it, some family connections that got you back there? Jesus." His voice is bitter. Jack grew up in a single-parent household. Although we've been friends a long time, and the legacy of my family's money shouldn't matter, it occasionally bleeds through.

I begrudgingly admitted my lineage to him our freshman year, after he said I looked familiar. I'd campaigned for my grandfather a few years earlier, but surprisingly, I was recognized in the highly populated Connecticut college I'd chosen to attend on scholarship versus one of the Ivy League schools my family had handpicked for me. Jack had shrugged and moved on. Over the years, I'd shared a great deal about my past, but I'd never shared what kept me from returning to my family.

Especially the abusive, narcissistic bastard who'd fathered me.

Hunts aren't soldiers. We make the weapons for soldiers. Hunts don't do the actual fighting. We stand beside the war-torn men in photo ops to show how much our technology improved the outcome. Hunts are shallow. Hunts aren't loyal.

Except for me.

"What? Not going to tell me the details about backstage? Plan on keeping the good details to yourself?" Jack's snide comment pulls me from my woolgathering.

"Not much to say, other than we had incredible seats. Corinna got called up on stage where Brendan Blake dedicated a song to her, and—"

"Wait. Hold up. Brendan Blake called that cunt up on stage? What the fuck for?" Jack's incensed.

I can feel my temper flaring. While I appreciate Jack's loyalty, he has no real idea what really went down between me and Corinna. Probably because I don't either. All he knows is that I've been miserable without her in my life. I sent her letter after letter for years, and she never responded to any of them.

Not a single one.

While a large part of me doesn't understand how she could read my words and not acknowledge them, I have to admit, something Keene said to me last night held a lot of punch. I really don't know her anymore.

The problem is, I still feel pulled to her.

"Yeah. Turns out they're close friends."

Jack chortles. "I just bet."

I frown. "Brendan's girlfriend was there, asshole. Apparently, Corinna helped him win a charity competition."

Jack waves his hand to cut me off. "Like I care about that."

"You should," I retort. "It has to do with a kids cancer research program." Even though our past is still riddled with so many blanks, I am so proud of what Corinna managed to do.

"Oh." He swallows his drink. "I guess that's great, then." Quickly changing the subject, he asks, "So, how's the job? Pry into anyone's past you shouldn't have yet?" His bellow of a laughter pulls out one of my own.

I snicker. "Not yet, but I'm sure you'll be first on the list."

We both crack up and proceed to drink well into the night.

∿

LATER IN BED, I try to make sense of the changes in Corinna.

She was everything—beauty, grace, and a warm heart in the wasteland of my college career. Shy to the point of debasement, she never grasped how utterly beguiling she was. Is. Damn.

I don't know what changed between us. If we'd had some kind of argument, some blowup, I'd have understood the change in who we were. I broached the topic with Ali when I saw her in passing at Hudson one day. After the anger smoothed out of her expression, she said, "That's something you'd have to address with Corinna, Colby." And then she just walked away.

The only problem with that is Corinna has succeeded in avoiding me.

I just want to understand why. Why did she abandon me? Us? What did I say? What did I do? Did she finally understand my feelings for her were so far beyond friendship, and that was her way of showing me she wasn't interested?

Rolling over, I punch my pillow in frustration. I've spent years trying to figure out where we went wrong. The problem is, the person who knows the answers not only holds the lock, she holds the key too.

I think about what I didn't share with Jack with respect to what really went on backstage. Partially because I'm ashamed of myself, and he'd never accept why I was so affected by it.

My focus last night was locked on Corinna, and not the mega country star holding court with the rest of the Freeman family. I remember Brendan's girlfriend making her way over to Corinna. The two women engaged in a staring contest. What I didn't expect was for the world-famous fashion model, Danielle Madison, to grab Corinna into her arms and rock her back and forth like they were old friends.

A hand clamped down on my shoulder from behind. I turned to find Keene giving me his know-it-all smirk. "Give them a little privacy in this madhouse. They haven't had a chance to meet with Brendan being on tour and then trying to be there for his nephew's treatments."

"Treatments?" I'd replied almost dumbly, letting Keene guide me away from where the two women were talking animatedly.

"No one told you the story?" Keene had stopped, surprised. His tone wasn't condescending, which is almost a miracle for Keene. After running his hand over his dark hair, he'd inhaled sharply. "Wow. Okay. So, Cori was tagged to appear on an episode of *Caketastic* on the Food Network. It was a celebrity episode for charity. Her partner happened to be Brendan, who I might add is a horrible cook by his own admission. The rumor mill is that he went on the show to provide a spotlight for the University of Washington. He was never expected to win. I'm still not certain what happened, but I know that woman there"—he nodded toward Corinna—"doesn't give up. Ever. On anyone. She knew what buttons to push to get them through the finals. They whipped the pants off everyone. Brendan matched Food Network's $50,000 donation live on the air. I know Corinna's trying to do the same by refusing to take money for any cake she makes for children under the age of eighteen. She was really affected by the whole experience." Keene took a swig of the beer he was holding.

"From there, Brendan and Cori remained friends. She started sending cupcakes once a week to Seattle. First to the kids and then to the entire floor where Joey Blake is based." Keene finished his beer. While he looked around for a place to dispose of the bottle, it gave me a chance to process his words.

Corinna was on the Food Network? At one point, I was so close to the Freemans, someone within the family would have called and told me so I could have watched it. At the very least, taped it. Now? Nothing.

"All because someone got sick?" I'd murmured.

Keene nodded. "Bet your ass. We're so proud of not only her beating the pants off some major stars, but all the hard work she's put in since then at the office. Ali told me today that Phil double booked her for all of next week. She hasn't had a day off in six months since she appeared on TV." Keene looked over to where Dani, Cori, and Brendan were all standing. "Cori's been amazing. She's so fucking loyal to those she loves without asking for more than their respect." He shook his head. "Anyway, what did you think was going on?" Keene's a perceptive son of a bitch.

I shifted uncomfortably. "I just knew what I saw from the stage."

Keene's patented smirk appeared. "Cori and Brendan Blake?" He started laughing before he realized I hadn't joined in. His expression hardened. "You might have known her before, but did you ever really get her?" Keene brushed past me before I could speak a word in my own defense.

Taking a pull from my own beer, I felt like the odd man out. Everyone was chatting in small little groups either about the concert or genially about nothing at all. I was about to move over toward Jason and Phil, when I heard a whistle from the center of the room from the man of the night.

Brendan Blake.

"Hey, Cori! If my woman is done yakking your ear off, how about y'all come on down here for a moment," Brendan called out from where he was now sitting with an acoustic guitar in his lap.

Funny, she had no problem getting up on stage, but Dani had to drag a protesting Corinna to the center of the room to the empty chair next to Brendan, who was ignoring the shenanigans while he tuned his guitar. Something special was about to happen underneath the twinkling lights of the tent.

When the room went silent, Brendan started speaking. "It's rare when you find someone who makes magic just by existing. A person who brightens your day with just a smile."

Corinna blushed next to him. "Brendan, please. This isn't necessary."

"It is for me so, hush your mouth."

Corinna bit her lower lip, a habit she never used to have, I absently noted. Brendan continued. "The woman sitting next to me wasn't born into a family that appreciated her, but she found one that did." His eyes left Corinna's and swept the room, locking on each of the Freemans. They all nodded. Ali was wiping her eyes as she mouthed to Corinna, "Love you."

Corinna's eyes started to fill, and her head dropped before she nodded.

"Hey, none of that. You hold your head up high, girl." Brendan's voice got tight for a minute. He was having a conversation with Corinna alone in a roomful of people.

"Okay," she said shakily.

"You tell her, Brendan!" Ali shouted from the cradle of Keene's arms. Brendan's smile widened.

"I plan on doing better than that, Ali." He strummed his guitar. The room inhaled collectively, me included. "Anyone here ever hear of an amazing songwriter named Toby Lightman?"

"Oh God," Corinna whimpered. Dani squeezed her shoulders, keeping her in place.

"Before a compassionate hand drags you out of the hardest moments of your life, you sometimes forget how to do this." And without further words, Brendan Blake, mega country star, faced

Corinna and started singing the song "Breathe In" from the depth of his soul.

The only sound around the room was the sound of sobbing from various people, namely the Freemans. The song wasn't just about love; it was about hope. It was about finding the last hand in the darkness who was unwilling to let you go and that pulled you back into the light. When the song ended, the room burst into cheers. But it was Cori's reaction I'd never forget.

Even as tears fell down her perfect cheeks, the light emanating from Corinna gutted me. Her golden eyes were incandescent, not the muddy brown color I see when she looks at me. I was about to escape, knowing I had no right to be in that tent, when Corinna said, "Brendan, this is possibly the most beautiful gift I've ever been given." I turned slightly to see him lean forward and rub his cheek against hers.

It was like a punch directly to the gut. Years ago, she'd looked at me the same way when I handed her the keys to my dorm. I remember her saying something similar to me back when I felt like she was my sunrise and I was her moon—when we lit the corner of each other's days and nights. When I told her I'd keep her safe no matter what. Now, I'm lucky if I get a cryptic message like the one I got from her yesterday if she speaks to me at all.

The years we spent together mean less to her than a few months she's known a stranger she's done no more than cook and chatted with. How could the laughter we shared mean less than that? How could the secrets we told each other not be remembered? How could the nights I held her not have pumped her heart faster the way it did mine?

Fuck. Rolling over in bed, I wish I could remember the last time Corinna smiled and laughed with me the way she did with Brendan Blake.

Because I miss it. I miss her. I miss what we had.

7

CORINNA

It's the middle of the week and I'm still flying high from the concert when I get a text from Dr. Bryan Moser. I'd call him a friend, but that's a loose classification at best. Bryan's a tough person to categorize in my life. He's sinfully handsome with a runner's build that would attract most women. Too bad that he's often ordering torturous tests on me for me to like him as anything more than a friend.

How does lunch tomorrow sound?

I respond back. *That's tight for me to get to Baltimore. Phil scheduled me for cakes all week. Can we talk on the phone?*

He types back. *I'm in your neck of the woods. Where do you suggest?*

How much time do you have? I rapidly reply. Rarely is Bryan in my neck of the woods unless he's speaking at a hospital.

Little bubbles float as he types his next message. *If you can meet after 1, I'll have the entire afternoon.*

Then why don't you come to Collyer? Anything you're in the mood for? I wait for his response.

A hug. After that, I couldn't care less. We need to talk.

That doesn't sound good. *Okay. How about we meet at my house? Then we're assured of the privacy we need.*

Sounds perfect. Text me the address. See you after 1 tomorrow.

Quickly pulling up my calendar, I add in a reminder that I need to leave the office at 12:45 p.m. so I'm not late. Ugh. With the extra cakes Phil scheduled, I'm going to have to be in super early and stay majorly late to fit this in.

I let out a sigh. Not the first time I've pulled a late night.

I also send a quick note to everyone that I'll be taking an extended lunch to meet with an old friend. Looking at the cake I'm decorating in front of me, I wonder how late Genoa is open in Ridgefield. Seriously, we're addicted to that little Italian deli. As much as my siblings wish it were closer, I am glad Genoa is a hike from our office. I know if it was any closer, I'd be a little fluffier, like when I graduated college, instead of the curvy figure I've fought for and have now.

I have specific rules about working out. The main one is that I refuse to run unless things are chasing me. And hell, I might club my sisters before I caved to that level. Fortunately, Ali, who plans all of our workouts, knows better than to suggest running as a part of mine. I might have to put in more workouts each week, but at least I enjoy them. I can stop and talk to people and not drip in sweat.

While shaking my hips to Sam Hunt as I decorate a tray of cupcakes, I snicker in remembrance of the time Ali was avoiding Keene and couldn't go shopping because she had sweat through her clothes. I would never be caught in such a compromising position. Glistening, yes—I'm a baker. I work in a kitchen all day, so of course I sweat. But all-out dripping with perspiration? No. I refuse. It's why I demanded we put in a ton of money when we renovated the mansion to have true restaurant-grade AC in the kitchen. After forcing my siblings to work with me for a day—a single day with the AC turned off—they relented. Wimps.

My mind drifts, wondering what Bryan has to tell me. It's not unusual for him to be in the area, but it is odd he's taking the time to come see me. I know he's asked to consult on cases at Yale-New Haven and Sloane Kettering.

I'm lost in thought when Caleb pokes his head through the kitchen door. Looking longingly at the cupcakes on the stainless-steel worktable, he asks, "Are those for lunch or for a client?"

I grin. "What answer are you looking for?"

"I'm not entirely certain," he says ruefully, walking into the kitchen. "Those, like everything else you bake, look delicious."

"Then I'm sorry to tell you, they're for Ali's birthday dinner tonight. I had leftover batter from a cake I made yesterday, so instead of a full cake, y'all are getting cupcakes. I pulled some of the rejects aside for the crew lunch though. I just need to frost them." I wave my hand to the less than perfect cupcakes behind me.

Caleb groans. I can't help but smile at his roundabout flattery.

"Keene is coming home early so he can spend time with Ali. I forgot it was her birthday." Caleb looks sheepish, and I flat out laugh. "Thank God, Cass handles gift buying. The look she gave me when I had to admit I hadn't checked the family calendar was embarrassing to say the least, Cori. I mean, we've been married for a little over two years. You'd think I'd know better."

I reach over to the reject cupcake pile. Quickly frosting one, I hand it to him. "Here, you need this. You never, *never* admit to Cass that you didn't check the family calendar, Caleb. Didn't Phil teach you that in family orientation?" I snicker.

"I offered to pick up the kids from day care today to make up for it. That, and get everyone Genoa for lunch," he volunteers as he munches through what is easily 600 calories of processed sugar. "Actually, that's what I came down for. What do you want to eat?" he mumbles around another bite.

"I brought a salad," I tell him dismissively. "But could I ask you to pick up a few things for me? I have a friend coming up from Baltimore for lunch tomorrow. I was trying to figure out how I could get down there to get us some stuff." I wave my arm to indicate the cupcakes I still have to decorate for our family dinner.

"Not a problem. Just write it down so I can call it all in."

Caleb is a fantastic brother-in-law. Maybe I should tell him that Cass is making a fuss about him forgetting Ali's birthday because she figures their make-up sex will be phenomenal tonight? Nah.

As I reach for the pad I keep by the phone, a wave of nausea and dizziness flows through my body. I fling my arms out, desperate to reach for anything. The sturdy counter, the immovable stainless-steel work table, Caleb—anything is better than nailing my head on the floor.

"Jesus, Corinna. What the hell?" Caleb drops the rest of his cupcake on the floor as he reaches me. I clutch onto the counter for dear life.

"You'll be picking that up," I manage to get out, pointing to the cupcake on the floor.

Caleb mutters, "Shut up, Corinna. What's going on?"

I open my mouth to tell him that this could be something more. I really do. And then I see the masses of cupcakes that haven't been decorated for Ali's birthday dinner tonight at the farm. My courage ebbs away, along with my dizziness. Shrugging out of Caleb's arms, I say, "I didn't eat breakfast, Caleb. That's all. I got a bit light-headed." I'm not lying. I honestly didn't eat because I wasn't hungry. I had a few other things on my mind.

I always do.

Scowling at me, he stomps over to the massive walk-in refrigerator and comes out holding a bottle of orange juice. Slamming it down onto the counter near where I'm standing, he orders,

"Drink." He emphasizes his demand by pointing at the bottle.

I turn away without acknowledging him. Caleb snags my shoulder and pulls me around. "Don't make me force you, Corinna. I have kids." His growling at me comes from a place of fear. Concern is etched all over his handsome face.

I reach up and cup his cheek. "Two things. One, I'd like to use a glass. And two, could you get me the bottle without the rum infused in it?" I face the label toward him so he can read where I wrote *For tropical rum cake. Do not drink!*

The edges of Caleb's cheeks turn ruddy. "Oh. Well, shit."

I can't help my smile, even as I'm fighting off my internal terror. Of all the men in the world my hyperorganized sister Cassidy could trip over her prized Louboutins for, I may never have chosen this dark, tough man in front of me. That is, until I saw his heart pouring out of his eyes every time he looked at her. More than two years together, and two beautiful children, you can see Cass is still the sun Caleb's world revolves around.

Keene and Ali are more magnetic. From the moment they met, you couldn't be near them and not feel their pull. Once they stopped pushing away from each other, they'd been inseparable. Their history is so long, it's hard to imagine they've only been together officially a little over a year, with a little girl who Ali swears acts just like me.

Since Phil is still madly in love with Jason and has been since the day they met, I just want to live long enough to see my other two sisters blissfully in love before I leave this world and find my place on the other side.

Pulled from my thoughts, I see the glass of orange juice slide in front of me. "I opened a new bottle. Now, drink it all," Caleb demands.

I laugh out loud at the mason jar Caleb managed to unearth from my cabinet. "Caleb, that's about a thousand calories of juice. There's no way I'm finishing this." Picking up the glass, I take a refreshing sip of the tart sweetness.

"Corinna..."

"Caleb, I'm fine. Really. I promise I'll drink some." I pull the jar back and assess its size. "About a third of this. Then I'll have a salad for lunch. I'll be good to go." I give him a smile I hope will convince him. "Besides, you have to call in the Genoa order soon, or it's the doghouse for you with Cass."

He narrows his dark brown eyes at me. "If I ran upstairs and told her the reason I didn't get Italian was that her sister almost passed out, I'd be out of that doghouse in the half a heartbeat it would take for her to get to this kitchen. And you know it."

Unfortunately, I do. I bite my lower lip and drop my head. A sure sign of my anxiousness to those who know me well.

Caleb lets out a sigh. "I'm sorry, Cori." He brushes his lips against my head where my secrets hide. I gnash my teeth harder to fight back the tears, desperate to burst out at his care and concern. "Even with the interns you've been hiring, I know you've been under a tremendous amount of stress. I'm just worried about you."

And there. Right there is the reason I can't tell them. It's why I have to carry this burden alone. The way I've lived my life since the night my life changed. Again.

Wrapping my arms around my brother-in-law, I hug him fiercely. "Okay. What you're telling me is, you have absolutely no problem getting my Genoa order?" I drawl, trying to lighten the mood.

Caleb pulls away and searches my face before shaking his head at me and smiling.

Joining him, I tuck the memory of his care and concern for me inside my heart where it will live forever.

Even if my brain won't.

8

COLBY

I've been working with Keene on a case out of the new Hudson Investigations office in Norwalk, Connecticut. The corporate espionage case I've been working on has been challenging without my having to get shot for the adrenaline high. Earlier during a meeting in the boardroom, I said as much to Keene. He replied dryly, "Not yet, at least. It's still in the early days."

I don't know if he was kidding or being serious. It's hard to tell with his damned arrogant smirk. How Ali puts up with his ass day after day, I have no idea.

Kicking away from reading a report requiring my signature, I watch through the one-way glass overlooking the floor of analysts, seemingly pulling data out of thin air to be referenced, cross-referenced, and tagged. Suddenly, a cry goes up from one side of the room and I, along with half the floor, snap to attention. Someone just made a breakthrough on something. Hooah!

What has to be the most enjoyable aspect of my new job is the camaraderie. Even though I was hired at a higher position than the analysts sifting through lines of data on their screens, I won't permit myself to do less than an exceptional job here. Letting them down is not an option. The environment Caleb and Keene have cultivated is more than just a team, and I'm proud to take part as a member of a new unit. It's being part of something far bigger than yourself when anything can happen, and successes are celebrated together.

Suddenly, my door flies open after a brief knock. Keene and Charlie Henderson, who heads up Missing Persons and Protective Services at the firm, come flying in. Charlie's face is wreathed in a smile, and Keene's is filled with fierce satisfaction.

"We found Charlotte Collins." Keene's face explodes with a grin. "Alive."

"And unharmed," Charlie adds. I didn't think it was possible, but his smile gets bigger.

"You're shitting me." The prominent Greenwich residents had come to Hudson last week begging for help when the police and FBI were unable to find their seven-year-old kidnapped daughter. The desperate couple offered to give anything, pay anything, to get their little girl back.

"Not at all." Keene and Charlie drop into the chairs in front of my desk. "The analyst who took the tip just called in. He delivered her safely to Greenwich Hospital and plans on standing guard until the doctors check her out. Charlie has already called the parents."

"I love making those calls," Charlie mutters.

I don't doubt it. I shoot a quick grin his way before asking Keene, "Who called the cops?"

Now the arrogance reappears. I start laughing. "Enjoyed it, did you?"

"Bet your goddamned ass I did. When I think it could have been any of our girls all over again?" He and Charlie share a look, and I'm quickly reminded with a glance why the Collinses' will never see a bill for the services rendered by Hudson.

The scars left behind by what happened to each of the Freemans, one of whom happens to be Keene's sister and the other the mother of his child, are vivid reminders of why Caleb and Keene established and maintain the Missing Persons division of this company.

"Anyway. The team is celebrating tonight, so don't be surprised to get a bill," Keene reminds me only to be interrupted by Charlie.

"A large bill," Charlie adds, grinning.

Keene nods, still smiling. "A large bill," he confirms. "Randomly dropped on your desk tomorrow. We cover all the expenses for the team: dinner, drinks, transpo home if they need it. Charlie and I won't be there because of Ali's birthday, but you're welcome to go with them."

I glare at Keene now. "You know damned well I'm not missing Ali's birthday, you ass."

Keene's face is full of disgust. "At least assure me you've picked out a different sibling to fixate on tonight. I know she's the birthday girl, but for fuck's sake, Hunt, she is very much off the market."

I sit back in my chair. "I don't see you slapping a ring on that." I know damned well it's Keene for Ali, and I could not be more thrilled for her. I just can't stop giving him a ration of shit so hard, he'll be constipated for days.

Charlie chokes with laughter. "Jesus, Keene. The fuckin' new guy's calling you out now."

Keene narrows his eyes at Charlie. "I have my plan, thank you very much."

I can't hold back. "When? After Kalie's high school graduation?" Kalie is Keene and Ali's six-month-old daughter.

Giving me the finger, Keene stands. "Just for that, I'm not passing along Caleb's instructions to bounce early and come to the mansion for lunch." He pauses before leaving the office. Turning back, he says, "Feels pretty amazing, doesn't it? It's like shooting an HK MP5 for the first time."

I don't have to ask what he's talking about. "Finding Charlotte Collins supersedes that feeling, brother."

Quirking up the side of his mouth, he says, "Right answer," before leaving my office.

Charlie pushes himself up next. "Caleb is ordering Genoa. If you want to head to Amaryllis for lunch and to knock out early, better call him with your order."

I'm surprised. "I thought Keene..."

Charlie snorts. "Please. That boy knows who he takes his orders from."

Nodding, I say with complete seriousness, "Ali."

Charlie winks. "You're learning, Colby." He turns and ambles to the door. Before he makes it all the way out, I stop him.

"Charlie." He turns around. "We celebrate the successes. What do we do about the ones..." My voice trails off.

His eyes darken. He swallows convulsively. Shit. "I don't know about the others, Colby, but I pray. A lot. For their families. For their souls. For peace. And then I go spend time with some of the people I've saved."

I'm confused. "People from previous investigations?"

He shakes his head. "No, the family. Phil, Cass, Em, Ali, Corinna, and Holly. And then I realize for the ones we do save, they can make a future, a family, and have a tomorrow even if their today seems pretty fucking bleak." He takes a breath. "Call Caleb. Otherwise, you'll be fighting Phil for pizza."

I take a moment to absorb what he said before I almost blindly call Caleb.

~

As I swing my Jeep into the parking lot of Amaryllis Events an hour later, Caleb's Porsche pulls in right behind me. I jump out and make my way over to him. "Need any help?" I call out.

"That's an understatement." He walks around the back of his Cayman and opens the trunk to reveal enough food to feed a platoon. Or a pack of hungry Freemans.

"Jesus, is someone pregnant again?" I mutter as I take the boxes of pizza he shoves at me.

"Not that I'm aware of." Pausing, he says, "Not that we'd mind. But on top of our normal lunch order, Cori asked for me to pick up some food she needs for a lunch she's having tomorrow with her friend."

"Oh?" I ask blandly. "Who is it?"

Caleb carefully balances the large box he lifted. Inside the box is a plastic sack filled with sliced deli meat and cheese. Closing the trunk, he replies, "I don't know. She never said." Redistributing the weight between both arms, he juggles the one with the deli meat. "I was just asked if I could do her a favor since she's so busy."

I shake my head. I wonder if she didn't mention who it was because it's some guy she's banging.

Caleb, not one to miss much, asks, "What's the issue between you two anyway?"

I try for plausible deniability. "What issue?"

Caleb barks out a laugh. "Just to let you know, evade and diversion tactics don't work well in this family. I'm not so sure they ever did."

I snort. "There's nothing to evade." Even though I might wish otherwise.

"Right, Colby. Then why did you suddenly get all bothered when I said a friend was coming to see Corinna?" Instead of heading toward the covered front porch and the stained-glass door, Caleb makes his way toward the back of the converted mansion.

Directly toward the door leading into Corinna's kitchen.

"I'm not bothered. I'm...surprised. Everyone always says how busy Corinna is. I'm just shocked she's taking off in the middle of a workday to see a friend." I throw that lame-ass excuse out just as the back door opens.

And of course, Corinna hears me.

"You're an ass, Colby. You know that? I set my own hours. All that matters are that the cakes are made. Oh, and just for the record? I'm coming in early to make up the hours I'm away," Corinna snaps. Her eyes, which can turn gold with joy or brown when she's furious, are currently a rich shade of chocolate.

Shit.

"Caleb, you know where everything goes." Corinna nods to an available worktable along the wall.

"Where do you want your stuff, Cori?" Caleb places his box on the table, then holds up the white bag he was also carrying.

Cori picks up her piping bag and begins swirling frosting on a cupcake so fast, my eyes cross.

Moving to the next one, she tips her head to the large stainless-steel door behind me. "Any particular shelf?" Caleb calls out.

"Where the juices are is fine. Nowhere near any of the cakes," Cori calls out. Her hands haven't stopped. She's decorating cupcake after cupcake with what looks like... I reach my hand over to the bowl to get a sample.

My hand is sharply slapped. I look up in surprise. "Get your hands out of my frosting." Her voice is as cold as the air blasting us from the refrigerator.

"I just wanted to see if that was orange frosting," I protest. "You never minded before."

Her jaw clenches. "Before, these cupcakes were going to a bunch of drunk boys who didn't give two flying fucks about anybody or anything, especially the person who was baking them." My blood boils at that comment. Corinna's rewriting our past to suit her. "Now, they're going to clients who pay good money for them, or they're going to kids who need them as a pick-me-up. And even this batch for my family's lunch still doesn't need hands in them first. Even Phil knows better than to touch anything in this kitchen without permission."

"Maybe you do need time off tomorrow if this is your attitude right now," I tell her pointedly.

The sharp inhale through her nostrils is the only indication she heard me. Her hands keep flying from cupcake to cupcake until all twenty-four are decorated. Pushing away from the counter, she shoves the remainder of the icing in my direction. I don't know if she's offering it to me or aiming. "I'm done." Turning to Caleb, who has been leaning against the wall, she says, "I have to clean up before everyone comes down."

He walks up to her, touches her shoulder, and asks oddly, "Did you drink the juice, or did you make frosting out of it?"

Barking out a harsh laugh, Corinna breaks away from Caleb before reaching for a mason jar filled mostly with orange juice from under the table where the bowl of icing still sits. "I drank what I told you I'd drink, Caleb. I got inspired, so I used the rest of the bottle."

"As long as you're fine, Cori." His face is gentle, as something unspoken passes between them.

"I just need a shower and to clean up my kitchen from the crap that just got dropped in it before everyone comes down for lunch. I'll be back in a few." Walking past me without a glance, she leaves the immaculate kitchen, and my callous words, behind.

Rubbing my hand over my forehead, I catch Caleb's thoughtful look. "What?" I demand.

"No issue between the two of you, huh?" he says blandly.

No, there's no issue because I have no idea what happened to the beautiful girl I knew. What made her turn so hostile toward me from one moment to the next?

There's a breach, a chasm, a canyon that I can't get across to build a bridge back to what we were.

9

COLBY

I wander aimlessly around inside Amaryllis Events before storming out the front door. My dress shirt immediately begins to cling to my skin as I step into the summer warmth. Grateful I ditched my jacket and tie before driving here earlier, I walk to the end of the porch and wait for the all clear to head back into the kitchen.

Rolling up my sleeve, I see the keys I inked on my forearm after my heart was forever lost to me. The keys that purely represent my loss of Corinna also serve as a reminder for those who trusted their lives to me. To not let anyone else down in my life the way I was let down.

Cursing myself, I unroll the sleeve so my ink won't show.

Resting my hips against the railing that runs around the porch, I lean back against the post and close my eyes, thinking about how much things have changed between us since we were in school together. Always an open book with me, Corinna needed someone she implicitly trusted to share the tsunami of emotion building up inside of her. Our bond was forged on late nights sitting around the kitchen table in the tiny apartment she once shared with Ali and Holly.

Corinna was always baking something mouthwateringly delicious, and I became her taste tester. And her friend.

My bond with Corinna was more profound than that. I coaxed her into sharing things with me she couldn't or wouldn't tell the others. About her grandmother, Clara, who she lived with until she was four. She had taught Corinna everything she loves about baking. How she was devastated when Clara died and she was turned back over to her parents. How she worried about her major of studio art wouldn't translate to her true love of baking. How she was anxious about being able to find the money and the time to fit in summer cooking courses while working at the fledgling Amaryllis Events. She also told me why she feared the dark unless someone was holding her.

We became so close. There was no one I would have laid down my life for before Corinna. Even though we always started out talking about one of her fears, it would end up with me sharing one of my own. Was I ready to go into the Army? Was I going to be able to pull the trigger and take another human's life when they were staring me right in the eye? Was I ready to leave my friends, or watch them die if I had to? More times than not, I'd see her eyes turn gold with fierce support and devotion. Corinna had set me straight in that perfect honeyed voice of hers all the while making me fall harder and harder for her.

And I knew I couldn't do a damn thing about it.

I was leaving. She was damaged. Nothing good could come from the two of us being together. At least, nothing good for her. For me, it would have been the closest thing to heaven before I went through my rotation and likely got myself shot for daydreaming of the woman I left behind.

I found somewhere else to take care of my needs. Random chicks I'd bang who meant nothing more than releasing an ache caused by dark hair and golden eyes. I'd lose myself in the sex while thinking of what it would be like to wrap Corinna's silky locks around my fist as I pounded into her body. It didn't matter what color eyes the body beneath me had; it was always Corinna staring back at me. Corinna's smile. Something I haven't seen directed at me in more years than I care to count.

"It might be easier if you just tell her why you hurt her so badly instead of constantly beating yourself up over it." Ali's voice penetrates my thoughts, causing my head to snap up toward the door. She closes it quietly before making her way over toward me in a dark blue dress that hugs every inch of her figure.

I wasn't kidding when I told Keene and Caleb the other night you'd never know either of their women had given birth so recently. Ali looks spectacular—glowing. Pushing away from the railing, I ignore her statement. "Happy Birthday, Ali." I wrap my arms around her as she reaches me. Giving her a quick squeeze, I ask, "Happy?"

"Delirious with it, Colby. I'd like the rest of my family to be half as happy as I am." Her smile is still dazzling, which is why I don't notice her doubled-up fist that lands in my gut.

"Oomph!" The sucker punch surprises me. "What was that for?"

"That was for whatever you did to hurt my sister, you ass. I've waited long enough to do that. Be glad I didn't have a meat cleaver in my hand, or you might not be able to use certain body parts ever again." Ali's smile doesn't waver. It just hardens.

"Damnit, Ali. Don't you think I've been trying to figure it out for the last ten years?" I growl. I start pacing back and forth. "Every time I get near her, she gets aggressive. I can't get close enough to ask her about anything."

"Cori doesn't hate, Colby, with very few exceptions." Ali glares at me. "Anyway, it's time to eat. I heard Genoa is on the menu." Without adding anything further to her cryptic statement, she heads for the door. Pausing as she opens it, she asks, "Are you coming?"

"Yeah," I mutter. Mentally bracing myself, I follow Ali back down the restored hallways of the mansion toward the kitchen where the heady aroma of Italian lures us toward the kitchen. Raucous laughter can be heard long before we reach the door. Ali sweeps into loud applause and well wishes. Trailing in behind her, I go unnoticed, which works to my advantage.

Like the targeting system on a guided missile, I find Corinna in the crowd and I stop in shock.

Without the cover of the sheer shirt she wore the other night or her chef's jacket she was wearing earlier, Corinna's thin gray tank top does nothing to mask the amount of weight she's dropped.

Her once ripe curves are edged out by muscle. Corinna's arms are ripped, presumably from all the hard work baking daily requires. Where her stomach once pooched in the cutest way, her jeans barely catch low over her curvaceous hips. At least those are still there. My mind drifts back to when I'd hold her while she slept and my hand would find this certain spot on her hip. So smooth, so soft, so... Corinna. Her breasts, still ample by anyone's standards, are smaller. God knows I'd spent enough time studying them.

How have I not noticed the finer cut to her already chiseled cheekbones? Her long-lashed, catlike eyes are almost too big in her heart-shaped face. And lips that were often dusted with whatever rich concoction she dreamed up, too pouty.

She's still curvaceous, for sure, but she's now more compact. And to make matters worse, while everyone else is gorging themselves on some of the best Italian food in the Northeast, she's eating a salad from a container she'd obviously brought from home.

How did I not notice she's disappearing in front of my eyes?

Suddenly, I'm angry at myself. Instead of forcing the issues to come to a head between us long ago, I'd let her walk away. I let her become someone I couldn't talk to. Well, fuck that. I wasn't going to watch her waste away as well.

Obviously, Corinna hadn't met someone man enough for her while she was dating her way through the states of Connecticut, Rhode Island, and Massachusetts, to get through her skull she needed to take care of her body and not starve it to death. Yeah, I'd heard the talk from Jack about her serial dating one night over dinner. He laughed himself sick telling me, even though I felt like vomiting just hearing him talk about all the men she was seeing.

I'm contemplating whether or not I even feel up to eating, when I hear a sound I haven't heard up close in so long. It burns deep in my heart's memory. Corinna's laugh. It's not directed at me, but I don't care. I savor it. There were nights I was stationed in some no-named hellhole and wished I could pick up the phone and just say something, anything, to hear her laugh. To let me know the fight I was sweating, bleeding, crying for was worth it.

Randomly, I shove a bunch of food on my plate and turned around to see Phil wrestling with Corinna for a spoon filled with the frosting she made earlier. But it's the ink that wasn't there years earlier decorating her back that almost causes me to drop my plate.

The words *numquam obliviscar qui sis* are woven like a chain through an antique key in between her shoulder blades. Unobtrusively pulling out my cell phone, I pull up a page to translate the words.

Never forget who you are.

Keys. What is it with both of us and keys? For me, the set I have is a direct replica of the set I gave to Corinna, down to the key chain she kept them on. But why a key for her?

I don't know how, but I intend to find out what I need to know. When Corinna Freeman shines her golden light on you, that light becomes your reason for breathing. I just didn't realize until now I was living on life support to get back to the real air I need.

10

CORINNA

Dinner last night was a blast even if I had to see Colby's face across the farm's table for the duration of the meal.

Phil started out by saying that he should be the one receiving the gifts because he's the one who taught Ali how to give blow jobs. Keene, Ali's significant other and father to their precious daughter, Kalie, looked like he swallowed something putrid. Over the loud laughter that broke out, Keene said to Ali, "I did not need to know that."

Ali, utterly unperturbed by Phil's opening play solely made to antagonize Keene more than to embarrass Ali, nodded at Cassidy, Keene's biological sister. "On our first date, I warned you there were pictures of Phil teaching your sister about sex."

Keene's wide-eyed face resembled that of a panicked horse, and he looked like he was about to break out in a sweat. "And didn't I say it was immaculate conception?"

The whole table broke up at their byplay. Especially Caleb and Cassidy, who exchanged a kiss so heated I expected Keene was going to grab the fire extinguisher to break it up.

"Jesus, do I have to lay down the law about this shit again? No sex at the table," Keene grumbled. "It ruins my appetite." Patting his washboard abs, Keene glared at Phil first—because everything is Phil's fault—then at his sister and her husband, who has the disturbing honor of being his best friend.

Cassidy rolled her eyes at her older brother while Caleb threw him the middle finger.

Ali, never one to let Keene get away with too much crap, winked at me before dragging her fingers up Keene's chest. She was so going to mess with him. "But what if I want sex at the table, baby?"

Keene's head snapped around so fast, you'd think his neck would've broken. Keene's cheeks were flagged in red, betraying his lust for the birthday girl. His flustered state was proven when he stood up less than five seconds later and announced, "Party's over. Everyone get the fuck out."

We all cracked up. And that was before the serious drinking began.

As I'm PREPARING for Bryan's imminent arrival, I'm still laughing. I can't wait to see the photos Holly was taking all night long. At one point, Charlie grabbed the camera from her and took some of just the Freeman siblings: Em with her arm wrapped around Phil's waist, Phil's arm wrapped around Cassidy's chest, who was just in front of him. My arm draped over Em's around Phil's waist, Holly's around me. Ali tucked next to Cassidy, in between me and Phil.

It was a picture of the six of us who fought and clawed our way from hell to become the premier wedding- and event-planning business in the Northeast. The six of who held no faith but the tender bonds we had with each other. We picked each other up, rebuilt ourselves, and molded a future from the pittance of scraps life saw fit to hand us.

Now look at us. Even as I stare uncertainly into my future, I would never trade a minute of the time I spent on this earth with my family. Phil and the girls? They're my true family now. The people I'd go to war for and shed all the blood in my body to ensure darkness doesn't touch them the way it once did.

And I'm doing that.

Scooping out the antipasto from Genoa into a bowl, I hear a car pull up in my driveway. When we built our personal homes on the farm, the firm regulation we had from Collyer's Planning and Zoning was that we had to use the original foundations as our home sites. Ironically, mainly since I chose the location before things ever went down with Colby, my home is built on the site where a barn was originally.

Fate trying to tell me something, maybe? Fortunately, I love my home. Using the footprint from the original barn, the architect designed a stunning house with an enormous first-floor great room and a deck that overlooks the field of wildflowers interspersed with pine trees I often walk through when I need to escape the reality of my life. There's nothing quite like losing myself in the scents of the meadow, of waning buttercups and lavender, and blooming goldenrod to remind me there's a circle of life that started long before me and will continue long after I'm gone.

Glancing over at the wildflowers I gathered and arranged in the ceramic pitcher on my kitchen counter, I smile. I'm really a simple girl. Even in the South Carolina shit town where I was born and raised, I found my beauty in everyday things. It's why I was so devastated when the men came into my room that warm summer night, after I had been walking along creeks in the low country. I wasn't just taken and touched for someone else's sick pleasure. I had my innocence stripped as well.

My granny would have taken her shotgun and put holes in some people before she'd have ever let me be carted off. I take comfort in knowing that. Since I don't discuss my past outside the family, few know she's why I became a baker. I wanted to honor her every day by recreating the smells so imprinted on my young brain as a child.

When we were trying to ensure our past couldn't catch up with us, Charlie had asked me if I wanted to find any of my relatives. I looked at him and said if they could leave me to those monsters—my mother and father who sold their daughter as a sex slave to cover the cost of their drug habits—then no, I had no need for that kind of family. Even if they were blood kin to my granny.

I've never looked back. I never will. With the future so uncertain, I only have now.

Unclenching my jaw, I move the antipasto over to the table so Bryan and I can sit and talk. As I peek outside, I see a Mercedes pulling into my driveway and parking. When Bryan's dark blond hair emerge from the car, I grin.

Despite the fact that he really is my Bearer of Doom, he's become a close confidant. I suppose even when it's Death who's knocking at your door, you might as well invite them inside and give them respite because if they're bothering you, they're leaving other people you love alone. Granny would have been impressed with my manners.

With that morbid thought, I throw the door open. Leaning against the jamb, I wait for eyes hidden behind sunglasses to look toward me. "Did you bring me a gift? You know I love presents," I call out.

Bryan scoffs. "You forget I'm not one of those people who pander to your every whim, Cori."

I pout dramatically. "So not fair, Bryan. I've been mostly a good girl." Scrubbing the toe of my Chuck against the floor, my long lashes flutter as the corners of my lips tip up in a smile.

"Yes, I can absolutely tell." Bryan's voice is sarcastic as he makes his way around the trunk of his car toward me. "That look on your face just screams reassurance to me." He takes the stairs two at a time, and within seconds he's standing in front of me, giving me a quick scan. I don't know what my face gives away, but his raised eyebrow says, "Good, my ass. Let's go inside."

I roll my eyes at him before gesturing him through the door. Closing it, I can't help but admire him. I mean, he is gorgeous, but I wonder why Bryan is wearing a full suit.

We're just having lunch, right?

~

WE'VE BEEN EXCHANGING banter back and forth, eating the delicacies Caleb procured for me from Genoa, when Bryan sets down his fork. "I have something important to tell you." His hazel eyes are serious.

Setting down my fork with a thick piece of salami on it, I say, "I have something to tell you as well."

"You first," he insists.

I shake my head adamantly. "No, you came here for a reason. You first." Call it instinct, but I have a feeling his news is going to impact what I have to share.

He lifts his glass of water. After taking a sip, he puts it down. "I'm leaving Hopkins, Cori. I know how hard it was for you to find a program you were happy with. I didn't want you to be blindsided."

I gape at him, my mind reeling. Finding Dr. Bryan Moser was like finding a man: it was an impossible probability. He not only cares about the surgical relationship with the people he operates on, he cares about them personally. Case in point is him sitting at my kitchen table eating antipasto, telling me this versus sending me a cold form letter to notify me of his departure. "Why? Where? When?" These fundamental questions are about all I can get out while I feel like my chances of survival are narrowing minute by minute.

He reaches up to loosen his tie and unbutton the top button of his dress shirt. "There are too many reasons to name, Cori, but I have an opportunity here to do some good with the neurosurgery and neurology department that I can't do with an established program like the one at Hopkins."

I'm floundering, reeling at what Bryan is telling me. Replaying it again, my brain latches onto one word. "Here?"

"Caught that, did you?" he asks softly. "Greenwich Hospital's program is actually a branch of Yale-New Haven, but it needs someone strong in the driver's seat."

"And they just offered it to you?" I yell excitedly.

His arrogant smirk reminds me a lot of Keene's at that moment. "Would I be here otherwise?"

I jump up from my chair and give an excited whoop.

"I guess I don't need to worry about whether or not you'll be coming with me as a patient?" he asks dryly.

"No, you do not! When is this happening?" God, to not have to deflect about why I'm hauling my ass to Baltimore is certainly going to lighten my list of concerns. I think my siblings were beginning to wonder if I was banging a Ravens football player.

"We can get your next round of tests ordered for Greenwich. You're due for them soon anyway," Bryan informs me, breaking into my thoughts. "I'll work out a month's notice for Hopkins. By the time we get you scheduled and get the results, we'll know what our next play is." His words are full of confidence. He stabs a forkful of food and shoves it between his chiseled lips. Bryan begins talking about the new facility and staff and how my transition will work. But every word is like pressing on an open wound he knows nothing about because I haven't told him my news yet.

Unable to listen to his calm voice anymore, I'm unusually quiet when I interrupt him. "I had an episode yesterday."

"Excuse me?"

I open and close my mouth a few times, but I can't repeat the words. Beseechingly, I finally whisper, "You heard me."

Snapping into full doctor mode, I no longer have Bryan at my table. Now, Dr. Moser is sitting across from me. He snaps, "Describe it. Leave no detail out.'

Painstakingly, I do. I explain everything, like what I was doing right before, including baking Ali's birthday cupcakes and my increased agitation level because Colby was in my kitchen. I watch his eyes narrow before he starts asking me questions he's never asked in the five years I've been seeing him. Things like if I'd experienced any sort of numbness in any of my extremities or if I'd noticed any unexplained slurring of my speech. Was there any time where my facial muscles haven't cooperated when I've tried to blink or smile?

Finally, unable to take it, I blurt out, "You think I had a stroke!"

Rubbing his thumb along his jaw, he replies, "Truthfully, I'm more concerned the tumor may have grown or shifted, and is putting pressure along your ICAs—internal cranial arteries. Are you still having all of your tests ordered through your primary care physician?"

The tumor may have grown. The tumor may have shifted. Those words keep repeating over and over in my head. I stare at Bryan, my eyes huge. "Excuse me?" I whisper. I've known for years this could not only be a possibility, but this could be the beginning of...

I had to stay in the now. It's how I've lived my life, and I've done just fine.

"Cori, do you still go through your primary care to order your medical tests?" Bryan snaps at me. His patience is waning.

I nod slowly. I feel the oil, vinegar, and Italian spices churning in my stomach from lunch.

I think I'm going to be sick.

"I'm moving up your tests, but we'll have them done here. I need new imaging. We'll have copies sent to Hopkins so I can see them. I'll order my staff to copy Dr. Braddock at Greenwich so they can start building your case file here." Pulling out his cell phone, Bryan scrolls through his contacts. He presses a button to engage the call and meets my eyes. "Derek? Bryan Moser. The patient I was discussing with you earlier? Yes, she's on board with switching her program to Greenwich. We need to get her in for testing next week though. She's had a mild escalation of symptoms I'm not encouraged by." Bryan turns his head away and begins talking in medical jargon that involves a lot of codes.

I'm still stuck on the part where he said he wasn't encouraged. Shoving away from the table, I walk to the doors leading to my back deck.

Wrapping my arms around myself, I move directly into the wild-flowers outside, where their imperfect beauty that withstands the bitter winter and the brutality of the summer.

What if I never feel them against my skin again?

What if I never see my family again? What if I can't hold the kids?

What if I never walk again? Drive a car? Decorate a cake?

What if I can't see or speak or hear? What if I can't touch, or feel someone's touch?

What if...what if I die? I've always known it's a possibility, but now it's more like a probability.

What if all the pride I was taught to have doesn't do me a damn bit of good when I can't breathe because the darkness has decided it's time to wrap me in its cloak and mock me with laughter as

I suffer, immobile and terrified?

For the first time since they told me that long-ago day at UConn, brokenhearted and bruised, tears flow from my eyes. Why aren't I meant to live a happy life?

My spirit is finally broken. I don't realize when Bryan comes up behind me. "We've got this, Cori. You're not going to give in, not when I can fix this."

"Okay," I whisper, defeat thick in my voice.

"Okay," he says, confidence lacing his.

And for a long time, we just stand there with his hands on my shoulders, amid my field of wildflowers, both of us thinking very different things about the same issue.

My life.

11

COLBY

After I was shot, I spent more than my fair share of time in hospitals. Between surgery and rehab, the Army doctors were really good at trying to patch me together again. It pisses me off I have to knock out of work for an appointment with a shoulder specialist, including a new CT scan about a week after Ali's birthday at the farm. Unfortunately, my bosses don't give a shit. They want to make sure the Army doctors didn't miss anything when they pulled the bullets out. Things that could cause a split-second difference if I was sent into the field with my team.

Begrudgingly, I agreed. Caleb said, "Suck it up. You're not paying a dime for the tests."

"Maybe they should add in an appointment with a shrink to get the idiot flushed out as well," Keene drawled.

Charlie assured me, "Don't worry, that's not covered. Otherwise, Caleb would have sent Keene before he got his shit together about Ali."

Keene gave Charlie the middle finger, and I laughed, which earned me Keene's infamous stare.

I ended up spending the better part of the afternoon taking up space in the radiology department, flipping through year-old magazines in the waiting room and surrounded by people who have actual medical concerns.

My shoulder is mostly fine. I actively work out using the modified PT discharge routine and have had no hiccups. When Jack examined me, he couldn't tell there had been any internal damage. In fact, his last words to me were "If I didn't see the scars, I'd be hard-pressed to tell you'd been shot."

I considered that a ringing endorsement.

I stretch my legs out, trying to relieve some pressure from my lower back due to diabolically awful hospital waiting room chairs. Unfortunately, I don't see the elderly woman until it's too late. She's not looking and walking backward, intent on complaining to someone about how long she's been waiting. Her arms start to wind-mill as she falls backward. Leaping up from my relaxed position, I catch her before she falls. "Ma'am," I say respectfully.

"Oh, my," the little snow-haired angel says. Blinking at her husband, who she had just been sniping at, she gasps. "Harold! Did you see how fast he moved? It's like that Captain America we've seen in the movies." She gives me another look. "Just as handsome too."

I smile down at the little treasure as I make sure she's got her feet under her. "Just making sure you don't take any unnecessary falls, ma'am," I assure her. Resuming my seat, I hear her bickering about the hospital change into murmuring about "What a nice young man." I start to relax until her voice gets louder and she asks her husband, "I wonder if he'd be interested in Priscilla."

Shit. Elderly hospital hookup. Someone had better call my name.

As if by divine intervention, a large male nurse appears at the door. "Hunt!" he barks out.

I jump up quickly and stride over. As much as I find the task of having my shoulder scanned again tedious, anything and I do mean anything to get me out of that waiting room is more preferable.

"Name and date of birth?" the nurse asks. I respond as we make our way down the hall. The nurse pauses at one of the doors. "First stop is your IV for contrast. Then I'll be back to take you down for your CT scan."

"Got it." Sitting down in one of the soft recliners, I hold out my right arm. Quickly, my arm is punctured with the IV that's capped off after its been inserted. I'm shuffled back toward a room down a long hall. Before we veer off to the right, what I see through a one-way mirror stops me in my tracks.

Masses of hair, brown interwoven with natural blonde highlights. Hands quickly reach up to braid it before it's tied off with a band that would make her sisters cringe at the damage it's likely causing to her luscious locks. I watch in stunned silence as she lies down on the table before they lower a cage over her face.

I don't need to see her face to know who she is. I've memorized everything about that hair. I know how fast those hands move as they decorate a cake or when she's animatedly telling a story. What I don't understand is the IV similar to the one puncturing my own arm.

"No," I whisper. Frantically, I look around at the technicians moving around both in and out of the room. The ones inside the room are strapping her down to hold her immobile. She doesn't protest. Not then, nor when they take pieces of green foam and shove it in through the holes in the Hannibal Lecter–like mask to further inhibit her movement. The technician steps forward and injects her with something, then places a device with a red button in her hand. A fucking panic button. Within seconds, a blanket is lowered over her, and everyone scurries out of the room.

My chest heaves. My ears tune in to what's happening outside the room. I must be hearing things, because the technicians at the consoles are muttering about "last scans" and "size of the mass."

Before I can move my legs to brutally force one of these puny pricks to tell me why my Corinna is now being shoved into a space that's no bigger than an above-ground coffin, my technician has realized I'm not where I'm supposed to be.

"Mr. Hunt, I apologize. I must have lost you. Thank you for waiting for me to find you. Your room is this way."

Before I move, I nod toward the one-way glass. "What's that procedure?" I'm proud my voice hasn't betrayed more than a bland curiosity.

The burly man shudders. My insides wither. "Head and spine MRI. In my opinion, the worst there is. Most people can't handle the time in the tube. Depending on what images they want, they can last between sixty minutes to two hours. Your head and body are completely immobilized. Patients go in headfirst..." His voice trails off.

"Is there any light in there?" From all accounts, Corinna's fear of the dark hasn't decreased over the years.

He shakes his head. "Very little. Most patients have to be sedated. Some even have to be strapped down to avoid the panic. It's imperative they remain as still as possible to get the clearest images."

The injection. The straps.

Fuck me.

And she's going through this all alone.

Why?

I shake my head in utter disbelief. Fortunately, it's misinterpreted. "You don't have that concern, Mr. Hunt. Ten, fifteen minutes tops," he consoles me. "Worst you'll feel is a desperate need to relieve yourself once we inject the contrast."

"Great." I couldn't care less if I actually crap on myself in these stupid-ass scrubs. Just as long as Corinna comes out of her test with her mind intact.

I follow the technician down the hall, then enter my room, and minutes later, I'm done. My IV is removed. I'm assured the results will be ready within the week. I pass Corinna's MRI room on my way out.

"Jesus," my technician mutters to himself. "That's the head of radiology doing a live read. Whomever that poor person is, something serious is going on."

Come on, Corinna, I beg silently. *Get out of that damned room and come rage at me. Yell at me. Scream at me. Just tell me this is nothing.*

And as I walk away, I hear her scream over the open mic. Her voice is gasping, "Oh God, the

dark. The dark. Get me out of here!"

A male voice says, "After this series, pull her out and amp her meds. We'll have to rerun this set if we can't get the picture. Moser wasn't kidding when he said she was petrified of the dark."

"Not even close. And to have no family here to get her through this? It's a damn shame," a woman's voice responds.

And my heart shatters in the radiology department of Greenwich Hospital, knowing I could turn around and tell them they don't know shit.

Her family doesn't know. I didn't know.

But I will find out everything. God knows it's time for Corinna and me to put the past behind us. I've never let go of the promises I made to her. But first, I need to know why she pushed me out of her life.

As I'm almost dragged out of the hallway, I see the technicians roll her out on the narrow table to inject her arm again. I'm left asking myself, what the hell happened?

I'm quickly processed out once my tests are done. Changing back into my own clothes, I debate on whether I should linger for a few hours to confront Corinna here but decide against it. There's hitting someone when they're vulnerable, and then there is kicking someone when they're at their absolute lowest. I'd be doing the second if I confronted her at the hospital after she's been through something so visibly traumatic.

But the time for our come-to-Jesus meeting just became a lot shorter, because I don't know how long I can keep this from the people who love her the most, and who apparently have less of a clue of what's going on than I do.

12

CORINNA

It's the day after the MRI, and I'm in the kitchen at Amaryllis Events. I'm on edge not only because I'm waiting for the results but because I'm working all night. Yesterday while I was out, Phil took another order for a birthday cake, this time for a local leukemia patient from Ridgefield. The parents were almost embarrassed to call us for such a small cake, but they were desperate to find a baker. Phil, not having any idea other issues were weighing down my mind, immediately accepted.

It's just that today, I'm tired. So tired. Tired of handling this alone with no one to lean on but Bryan. Today, I just want to curl up somewhere comfortable and sleep. But a sixteen-year-old high school football player is relying on me, and I can sleep when I'm dead, right? Only, who knows when that day is coming. It might be sooner than any of us anticipate.

And just that quickly, I'm glaring at the phone, willing it to ring. Deep in my heart, I already know what Bryan's going to say when he calls. It's why, although my kitchen is prepped, I'm waiting to finish the last cake.

The cake and I are going to be a damned mess, one I don't want anyone to witness. I'm going to bleed my soul onto that cake before I drop the mask back on my face to deal with another tomorrow.

Hearing a rap against the kitchen door, I turn around. Holly's head peeks through, and she has her camera in hand. "Hey, Cori. Got a minute?"

"Sure, Hols." I gesture my baby sister forward. Frowning at the camera in her hand, I hold up my hands. "No, no pictures today."

Her lips turn down. "Didn't Phil tell you?"

I run a hand over my forehead. "Likely not. Phil always manages to leave out salient details about crap, Hols. What was he supposed to tell me?"

"Well..." Holly hesitates. She holds up her camera and bites her lower lip. "Phil agreed to..."

I can only guess. "Pictures? Of me decorating the cake?"

Holly nods.

I let out a long sigh. I wasn't planning on having my raw emotions caught on camera. "Okay. Sure. Fine. But not now. I wasn't planning on starting until after dinner."

Setting her camera down on one of the clean worktables, Holly hitches up on a stool. "Late night planned?"

Nodding, I reach down for the bottle of water I've been nursing all day. "I just finished the Marino wedding cake."

"Yum. The one with the cannoli filling?" Holly's smile is as bright as her magnificent red hair.

"Shh, don't say it so loud. You know Phil has a radar for leftovers. If you want the extra filling, you can have it later, after you're done taking pictures."

She jumps up and goes into the walk-in fridge for a few moments. When she comes out, she's wearing a smug smile. "What did you do?"

"I used your tape and a Sharpie to relabel it as peas. You know he'll never go after it then." We both break out in gales of laughter knowing our brother hates English peas.

"Diabolical. I love it." Leaning over to give her a high five, I start to feel a bit woozy. I quickly mask it by glancing at the clock. "Damn, is it one o'clock already? I shouldn't have missed breakfast this morning. I need to eat."

Holly frowns. "I noticed you've dropped a lot of weight, Cori. Why?"

Because I might be dying. Because I'm so self-conscious since Colby came back into our lives. Take your pick. "It was time for me to look at what I was putting into my body and determine what was healthy. I want to be around as long as possible."

Nothing of what I've said is a lie. It's just not the entire truth.

Then again, nothing since that night with Colby Hunt has been.

Crossing to me, Holly gives me a swift hug. "You're nothing but skin and bones, Cori. I'm worried. Are you sure this is healthy?"

"My doctor hasn't objected," I tease her gently. And Bryan hasn't. He also hasn't said anything about it. He's more concerned about what's inside my head than what's swirling around my hips and ass.

"Just promise me that you're not letting some stupid guy tell you that you have to lose weight," Holly threatens, cupping my face. "You're beautiful now, but you were a knockout before." She bursts out laughing. "What am I saying? You've known that forever. Seriously, even Colby had a thing for you back in school. I still don't know why you two didn't get together back then. I figure it was just bad timing with everything that happened to us."

I had just taken a drink of water and choke on it. "Please. The last thing Colby Hunt had was a thing for me. He thought I was a relative of the bovine family, Holly. I even heard him say something to that effect once." And trust me, once was more than enough.

And just that quickly, the puzzle pieces fall into place for Holly. "That's why you stopped being friends with him, isn't it?"

"One of a few reasons, yes. Colby forced me to grow up hard and fast." It feels good to let some of the steam from the pressure cooker off. Twiddling with my bottle cap, I drop it on the table. "I was nothing more than a game to him." Without waiting for her response, I continue. "In one breath he encouraged me to trust the world and that it was safe to turn out the lights." I meet Holly's empathetic gaze. "Then he plunged me into the dark all the while laughing." Finishing the bottle of water, I snag the cap off the counter and toss it into the trash. It makes a swooshing sound as it lands. "Why should I let someone like that into my life?"

Holly contemplates her camera. "Does he know you overheard him?"

I bark out a laugh. "If he didn't want to be overheard, he shouldn't have said it, Hols. Now, you asked why I doubt Colby had feelings for me? Users don't have them. He wanted something, he found a way to get it. I just happened to learn that the hard way." Too hard.

Holly moves toward me and wraps her arms around me, giving me a hug. We stand like that until we're interrupted by the phone ringing.

Crap. The phone. Bryan is calling with my results.

"Hols..." The phone stops ringing. "I really need to get back to work." The phone starts ringing again. "Why don't you come back around—" I glance up at the clock, which reads a quarter to three. "—seven, to watch me decorate the cake? I still have one more to do before then." Which I hope I don't screw up after Bryan tells me what he's going to tell me.

The phone stops ringing. He'll give it one more shot.

"Okay. But promise me you'll eat something before you start." Holly makes her way over to her camera and picks it up. Before I can answer, the phone starts ringing again. She laughs out loud.

"After you answer that call. I'm guessing they're about to receive an infamous Corinna Freeman tongue-lashing between your being hangry and your schedule."

You have no idea, sister, I think to myself. Quickly picking up the handset, I answer, "Amaryllis Events, can you please hold?"

"Yes, Corinna," Bryan's voice comes through the line, quiet and patient, giving nothing away.

Placing the call on hold, I turn back to my sister. "So, seven? I might start on the cake before that though," I warn.

She waves off my concern as she makes her way to the kitchen door. "I just need a few good shots, Cori. You probably won't even know I'm here."

Nodding, I toss her a semblance of a smile before pointing back to the phone. Hearing the swoosh of the door, I take Bryan off hold. "I'm sorry. I know you're busy, but my sister was in here."

"That's fine." His tone is flat.

I begin to pace back and forth. If I was wearing a heart monitor like Ali does when she runs, I guarantee it would be sounding off with my racing pulse. "Bryan, what is it?" When there's nothing but silence on the other end, something in me just snaps. "Tell me, damnit."

He sighs. "I'd like you to come in and meet with Dr. Braddock."

"Shit." I don't even realize the word is out of my mouth until I hear Bryan reply.

"What does your schedule look like tomorrow?" And then he starts making plans for me to meet the interim head of Greenwich neurology.

HOURS LATER, I don't know how I managed to decorate the second cake. Fortunately for me, the couple wanted a simple yellow buttercream with a seashell piping. It was beautiful in its elegance but required very little thought.

I only hope I didn't use salt instead of sugar for the icing.

For the first time in more than ten years, I reach for a spoon to taste the thin orange liquid that resembles Delsym cough syrup more than frosting. The sweet candy flavor coats my tongue. Infuriated I can't trust myself with a simple recipe, I hurl the spoon into the sink. My chest heaves as I think, *Too soon.* I know I was gifted with years, but it's too soon.

This is sheer agony. My head bows. I succumb for just a moment to the helplessness of my situation.

Maybe I should just go to the pasture behind my house where the cows used to graze and find my burial plot now, I think bitterly. At least I'll be among my relatives. Well, the relatives that don't want to sell me for drugs. The raw laugh that escapes me is cut off by Phil's voice coming down the hall.

"I swear, Em, Cori's wasting away. Soon, her ass is just going to fade away."

"Keep scheduling her for extra work, then. That gives her so much time to relax and recuperate, you jackass." Em is furious. "If Cass knew, she'd have you pinned against the wall and all your hair cut off for sure."

"I figured Cori would be more pissed at me if I didn't schedule this particular cake than if I had," Phil replies, trying to defend himself. "Now hush; I just want to peek in and see how pissed she is at me."

Taking a deep breath, I pick up the large bowl of orange I'd been stirring and check its consistency, wondering if it's ready to fly. Using the whisk in my hand, I fling a little back and forth, admiring its texture and consistency. If I wasn't planning on using it on a cake very shortly, I think it would make a terrific addition to Phil's hair.

The door cracks open a bit, and I see Phil's hand reach in tentatively waving the American flag he keeps on his desk. I can't help it. I put the bowl on the counter, which I grab to hold myself up from the giggling. "Jesus, Phil."

"I didn't have time to run out and buy a white flag." He and Em step into the kitchen.

If there were ever two people not dressed to be in my workspace, it's these two particular siblings. Em, our family fashion plate, is wearing a sheer black knee-length dress with flowers etched onto the sheer fabric. With elbow-length sleeves, a wide V-neck, and a nude underlay, it plays off her blonde hair and blue eyes encased in red-rimmed glasses perfectly. This particular dress is one of Em's own designs that can be made in any color. It's a showstopper and a huge attention grabber in the summer for garden weddings. Having a version in chocolate brown, I can also attest that it looks terrific on many different figures.

Phil looks like he stepped out of the pages of *GQ*: trim charcoal slacks, deep plum slim-fit shirt, with his blond mane swept back from his forehead. Lighter blue eyes crinkle at the corners before he looks in the bowl. "Holy hell, Corinna. Are you making a potion in there? What the hell is going on that kid's cake? Cough syrup?"

I grin. His thoughts mirror my own from earlier. "Here, taste." I grab one of the spoons I keep on hand and dip just the tip in.

Phil looks like I'm about to slip him arsenic. Em, always the braver of the two, gamely leans forward. Opening her mouth, she allows me to slide the spoon inside before closing her deep red lips over it. "Oh God, that's delicious. It tastes like...like..."

"Melted Creamsicles," I finish for her. I nod over at the cake, three imperfectly smooth mounds covered in gray fondant, just like the rocks at Lake Mamanasco in Ridgefield. Inside, the cake is a deep, dark chocolate with a chocolate-orange creme filling.

"Yes!" Em exclaims. Her navy blue eyes tip at the corners as if she is predicting Phil's reaction.

We don't have long to wait.

Phil casually begins to stroll around my workspace, and I hold on to the bowl with all my might. There's no way he's catching me with my back turned. It took me almost a damn hour to get the icing to a consistency that will fly when I throw it. If I have to spend an extra hour making him a batch, I may hold him down so Cass can do her magic with the scissors she's been threatening him with for years. "No, Phil. Not a chance."

"Just a little taste," he pleads. Sweet Christ, the man has a sweet tooth that rivals a three-year-old. You'd think he'd like salty more than sweet with the way he talks about sucking off his husband, but no. Every damn day, he's down in my kitchen begging me for scraps like a lost puppy.

"I'm about to make you work for your treats," I warn him.

He pauses. "That's not a no. What're your terms?"

"I need to tell the family something. I figure the family dinner Thursday works."

Phil laughs. "So just announce it. Now, gimme."

I hold out a hand to ward him off. "Phil, can it be just the six of us? No husbands? No significant others? No kids? No friends?" No Colby, I add silently.

The magnitude of what I'm asking for is so extraordinary, it causes both Phil and Em to drop their jaws.

Phil nods, just before he pulls the bowl of liquid icing from my arms and places it on the counter with a clatter. Some of it sloshes over the sides, and I frown. "Corinna, if you need to tell us something, just us, we'll handle everyone else. Now, take that disgustingly dirty coat off and come give me a hug."

Unbuttoning my chef's coat, I let it drop to the messy floor behind me before I move into Phil's arms. He clasps me so tightly, pulling my head against his neck.

I'm wondering how I'm going to hide the tears in my eyes and the bruise where my IV was when I pull away. I'll worry more about that in a few minutes when I can let my brother go.

Right now, I cling to him like he's the only thing in the world that's real.

13

COLBY

In our Manhattan office, Caleb and Keene are still laughing about a call to Cassidy I was privy to. Cassidy is contemplating retribution on behalf of Corinna against Phil. Due to his failure to run another scheduling decision by her, Corinna was going to be at Amaryllis Events for most of the night with the addition of a last-minute cake.

This is enormously funny because Cassidy, who would barely speak a word out of turn when I first met her, has advanced to threats about straddling Phil with scissors in hand and cutting off all his hair in chunks. Despite my worry for Corinna and what I saw at Greenwich Hospital, even I'm amused at the thought of Cassidy tackling Phil with a high-pitched "Hi-ya!" before becoming a demented stylist.

"Sucks for Cori. And it's not like anyone can pitch in for her." Keene shakes his head.

Caleb chuckles. "If you send Phil down, maybe she'll whip up a special batch of her whipped cream just for him. I hope she'll choose another color than red though. That looked so good on you."

"Fuck you, Caleb. That shit was next to impossible to get out," Keene grumbles.

"Corinna threw food coloring at you?" I'm actually impressed. "I thought the only person she did that to was Ali."

Keene corrects me. "It wasn't pure food coloring. It was dark red, strawberry-flavored whipped cream. She didn't want to hurt me, so she diluted it."

I chuckle. "Still sounds like what she did to Ali." I sober suddenly. The only reason Corinna pulled that stunt on Ali was because Corinna thought Ali had eaten part of my birthday cake before my actual birthday in college. Something I'd actually done when I'd found it beneath a box after Corinna had fallen asleep. It was either that or wake up the beautiful woman sleeping in my arms and kiss her like I'd been dying to for the two years we'd been friends.

I've been thinking hard about Corinna since yesterday. How could I not when I know what I know? I've been contemplating talking about it with Caleb and Keene. I know without a doubt Corinna would never trust me ever again if I told her family without speaking with her first. Now the trick is going to be getting a few moments alone with the woman whose eyes haunt me even if she treats me like a stranger.

"Hunt, are you even listening?" Keene barks.

"If I had to hazard a guess, I'd wager he was still thinking about dessert." Caleb's wicked sense of humor makes an appearance.

Keene shakes his head. "Colby has zero chance getting Corinna to talk with him about more than the weather."

I bristle. "What makes you say that?"

Keene waves a hand in the air. "Please. I watch everyone at those nightmares we call family dinners. Corinna strategically places herself so she doesn't have to sit next to, across from, or within speaking range of you since you started showing up. She even sacrifices herself on the altar of Phil. I swear, I owe her a personal debt of gratitude for that one."

Caleb laughs.

"We were friends," I begin slowly.

"Right. *Were* is the operative word in that statement. You must have done something you never fixed. Trust me. I've been on the receiving end of her fury," Keene concludes.

"Keene isn't wrong, Colby." Caleb stops laughing to say somberly,

"Corinna is the happy-go-lucky one of that clan. If she's mad—or, well, in Keene's case, infuriated..." Keene tips his head in acknowledgment of Caleb's words. I vaguely wonder what he did for a split second before Caleb continues. "Then your best course of action is not to let it fester. She's generally an open book." He hesitates. "I know something is hurting her deeply though. That new tattoo of hers? Keene, you saw it?"

"Oh yeah. It took me a few to translate. I hated taking Latin in school. I finally gave up and asked Alison. *Never forget who you are.*" Keene looks thoughtful. "I wonder if something from her past is coming up. Maybe I should give Charlie a call and see if there have been any flags."

"Might not be a bad idea," Caleb agrees.

"Why Charlie?" I ask.

"Charlie keeps a running tab on all of the siblings to see if their past identities have been flagged. This way, we can take steps to neutralize any threats," Caleb explains while Keene dials. "Do you need to know their history, or do you already know it?"

"I know it," I reply. Corinna told me. Not long before she stopped talking to me altogether.

The Freeman siblings lived through hell before they joined forces and became a family. Phil and Cassidy were both victims of child abuse. Em's family was killed in front of her, and she was raised by an elderly aunt. The three met in a park, where Phil and Cassidy were sleeping after they'd escaped their nightmare. Living together with Em's aunt for years, it wasn't until she passed on that the three moved to Charleston, South Carolina. There they met Ali, Corinna, and Holly, who had just been rescued from a sex trafficking ring so egregious, it rocked the national news. It was all the more devastating for the then fifteen-year-old girls because their families had either been involved in the ring or had sold them into it to pay back lingering drug debts.

When the newly formed family of six left the South, they left behind their identities and started fresh. For Phil, it was no loss since he had no idea who his parents were. Cassidy had been kidnapped as a child. In renewing my friendship with the Freemans, I knew through Cassidy falling in love with Caleb that she'd discovered she was actually Keene's biological sister. I found out Ali went back to South Carolina not too long ago and tied up her loose ends. She reconnected with some people who truly meant something to her birth mother, Katherine.

Corinna, or Elena before her name change, woke up to her bedroom door being busted in and men in masks gagging her right before they bound her in tape. They didn't physically penetrate her, but in the dark, their hands covered her body. Soon, she was tossed blindfolded and bound into a truck bed. Within hours, she was in a shipping container, desperately reaching out in the dark for someone. Anyone. It was pure blind luck she found welcoming hands that were those of Ali and Holly.

I barely managed to hold it together when Corinna told me the full story of what had happened when I asked her the meaning behind the siblings' amaryllis tattoos. Thinking of it now, I want nothing more than to break each and every bone in the bodies of the men who had touched her. Even knowing her parents are dead from an overdose, and most of the monsters are safely locked behind bars, still doesn't curb the animalistic urge within me.

It's Corinna. And in my mind, no one ever paid enough for what they did. No one ever could.

My thoughts are interrupted by Keene announcing, "Nothing on the flags."

"Maybe she'll talk during the family dinner with the siblings on Thursday, then," Caleb mutters.

That gets my attention. "Dinner was canceled?"

Keene nods. "Phil sent out an email earlier. Sibling-only dinner. No spouses. No significant others. No friends. No kids. Corinna's request."

The churning in my gut reminds me of the day I got shot. It's too coincidental. There's no way this isn't connected. I need to talk to Corinna about what I know. Tonight.

Jumping up from my seat, I ask, "Are we done?"

Keene rolls his eyes. "If we weren't, I'm assuming you are."

Caleb shakes his head. How he hasn't murdered Keene since childhood obviously means he's on the path toward sainthood. "You going to go see if you can make sense of a few things?" His voice is laced with concern.

"Yes." There's no need in beating around the bush. There are practically no secrets in this family, other than the one I'm sitting on right now.

Caleb stands. "Good luck. Knowing these women, I can honestly say you're going to need it."

Keene nods in agreement. "And change your shirt if you happen to like it. Cori's got great aim."

"Right," I mutter. Heading out into the executive lobby, I toss a wave at Keene's admin, Tony. Punching the Down button, I'm relieved when the elevator arrives quickly. The commute back to Connecticut is going to be tough enough. Even a few extra minutes might get me to Amaryllis Events so I can talk to Corinna on somewhat neutral ground instead of at her home.

14

COLBY

I pull into the parking lot and see both Corinna's and Holly's cars. I release a small sigh, grateful I caught her here. I jump out of my car and head inside through the front door. Flinging it open, I startle Holly.

"Oh, Colby!" She holds her hand up to her chest. "I was just about to lock up."

"Sorry, Hols." My eyes wander down the hall where I hear Sam Hunt blaring from the kitchen. I shake my head. Corinna and her country music. "I don't need three guesses to find her."

"Um, Colby? You might want to be careful walking in there," Holly warns me. Turning her camera, she flicks the button into display mode, and my jaw unhinges at what the small display screen shows me.

She's dressed in all white with her hair pulled back. Her arm is cocked back, and she's flinging an orange mixture at— "Are those rocks?" I ask Holly, pulling the camera closer. Using the camera's natural zoom, I lock in on Corinna's face. Her expression has me arrested.

It's anger. It's fury. It's devastation. It's Corinna's passion unleashed. I shudder, quickly going back into full screen. She's letting all her emotions pour out. Why does no one seem to notice but me?

"Sure looks like it, doesn't it?" Holly's voice is filled with pride. "By the time Cori's done, they're going to be something really fucking special for the kid with cancer who's getting this cake tomorrow. Then again, I'm not surprised. Cori just gives so much of herself." She's thoughtful for a minute, before giving me a head-to-toe perusal. "Hey, Colby. Are you busy tonight?"

I choke. I am in no way interested in Holly. I have never been. Ever since I saw Corinna years ago, her face is the only one I've compared every other woman to. And now her sister's making a play? "What?" I manage to croak out.

"Listen, I've got a date, but I hate for Cori to have to clean all this shit up on her own. She's exhausted." Jesus Christ. I let out the breath I was holding. Holly bursts out in laughter. "You didn't think I was asking you out, did you? Lord, Colby, you've always been Corinna's. I think the only two people who haven't realized it are the two of you." Still laughing, she reaches up and pats my slack jaw. "You always thought you were so cute hiding your feelings in college. But Colby? Hurt her again, they'll never find your dead body." Holly's eyes, a different shade of gold from Corinna's, holds my gaze for a heated moment. "Lock up behind me, will you? Enjoy your evening." Quietly, Holly slips out the front door.

I'm left standing in the hall, wondering why everyone thinks I'm going to hurt Corinna. It wasn't me who kicked her out of my life years ago.

Flicking the bolts on the door, I notice the music pauses. Suddenly, the country slides away and the genius of Rush's "The Pass" comes through the expensive sound system. Geddy Lee's voice is interrupted by the occasional swoosh and thwat of what I assume is frosting hitting the cake.

Making my way down the hall, I realize I have to see the magnificence of Corinna working out her emotions using her medium of choice. Back when we were at UConn, Corinna would pour everything into her art. Several of her professors wanted her to consider putting her work on display, but she'd never do it. She said it was too personal. Now she was about to serve it up on a platter for others to consume.

Cracking the door to the kitchen, I see her magnificent hair has been pulled back into a braid and is overlaid with a hair net. She's shed her chef's coat. Her back is to me, so I can see her tattooed key on full display.

Never forget who you are.

Just as Corinna lets another handful of orange icing fly, I can't help but wonder what made her get it. What hidden meaning does the key hold for her? It can't possibly be the same as mine.

"If you're going to stand at the door staring, Colby, you're in danger of getting the remains of this frosting flung at you," she says without turning around.

I move into the kitchen. "How did you know it was me?"

"Everyone else announces themselves in some way." She still hasn't turned around. "You're the only one who doesn't. You think you don't have to." Reaching into the bowl, she pulls out another handful of orange. Letting it fly, it splatters against the cake and the tarp behind it. "I don't know why you assume you have that privilege." Corinna places the bowl on the table and approaches the cake. Spinning it around, the untouched gray is now turned in her direction.

Finally, when she faces me, her face is devoid of the fiery emotion I saw captured on Holly's camera. "What do you think so far?"

"Of what?" Of our conversation? I think it fucking sucks.

"Of the cake. A teenage football player for the Tigers was diagnosed with a rare form of cancer. Caught in time, thank God. His parents called because tomorrow's his birthday. Kids at RHS have been decorating the rocks at Lake Mamanasco in tribute since he was diagnosed. The parents sent me a bunch of pictures. I'm trying to recreate it." She gestures to the photos blown up and taped to the walls.

I'm intrigued by the idea and blown away by the talent of the woman in front of me. She's not just decorating a cake; she's creating a memory. "You were always so brilliant at this," I murmur as I step forward to get a closer look at the cake and the images.

"At what?" Corinna removes her gloves and throws them into the trash before reaching for a bottle of water. Taking a large drink, she lowers the volume on the music.

"Capturing the essence of life in your art. You bring life to things all around you, Cori." I turn to find her shaking her head at me. A vile look takes over her face.

"Corinna, if you please. Cori is reserved for the people closest to me. People who actually give a shit." Corinna's voice is filled with loathing.

I'd be lying if I didn't admit how shaken I am at the vitriol in her voice. I step toward her, expecting her to retreat the way she always did back at school. But Corinna holds her ground. "You know that's not true," I grit out.

I care. I've always cared too damn much.

"Right." Her drawl is pronounced, taunting me to break through her shell. I want to throw something to break through because I know better.

This heartless woman isn't my Corinna.

Abruptly, I turn and face the graffiti images taped to the walls. They're vulgar in their beauty, denouncing the disease that racked this man/child. Words jump out at me, like loyalty, forever, light, and love. In what some would consider the destruction of something beautiful, something even more precious was built. I'll never understand how, but these kids made it happen. If they can do it, then so can Corinna and me. We can resolve whatever issues we have between us to get back what we had. Because I don't think I can live without her in my life.

Without turning, I ask, "How much longer will this take you tonight?" I look over my shoulder to see Corinna loading up an airbrush with an almost ink-like substance. Food coloring, I surmise. Knowing the damage she's done in the past when pissed off and wielding it, I have little doubt she'll fling it at me if she's angered enough. I turn back to face the artwork. Loyalty jumps out again at me. For some reason, that word makes my jaw tick.

Where was her loyalty for us?

"At least another six hours," she says, matter-of-factly.

"Jesus Christ, Corinna!" I turn fully, food color explosion be damned. "That will put you here after midnight. Alone."

"I'm a big girl, Colby. This isn't the first time I've done this," she retorts. I don't miss her subtle emphasis on the word "big." My eyes drop inadvertently to her luscious breasts. She's big all right. In all the perfect places. She always has been.

Shaking her head in disgust, she mutters, "If this wasn't the last of this color..."

I can feel the heat climb up the back of my neck. "You've always been a knockout," I admit.

The snort that leaves her lips is full of disdain. "Oh, please. Give me a fucking break and just go. I don't have time to deal with this." She waves her hand toward the back door, dismissing me, queen to a peasant.

I might have left her without trying to climb over her walls, but I need for her to know. "I saw you the other day."

"Unfortunately, I see you a lot these days. You're going to have to be more specific than that."

Taking a deep breath, I step closer to the table where she's just capped off the air gun. I place one hand on top of hers, forcing her to lower it down to the table. Infuriated mud-brown eyes lift up to mine. "Corinna, I had to get a CT scan on my shoulder for work."

Any antagonism in her features leeches from her face. "No," she whispers. Her eyes hold mine for a few more seconds before they start darting around the room. Everywhere but at me.

"Yes." I capture her chin to hold her face steady. "What happened?"

"Nothing you need to worry about," she immediately responds, trying to yank her face away. I apply the smallest amount of pressure and she stills.

"It's serious enough to have a sibling-only dinner though? Isn't it?" My hand leaves her jaw and trails down her neck to trace her collarbone. "Why keep everyone else out?"

"Maybe I want to introduce them to someone," she snaps waspishly. Corinna has never dealt well with being backed into a corner.

"Princess, the only man you're ever going to introduce them to like that is me. And it's high time we both stop playing games and admit it." I wait for her reaction to my admission of the attraction that's always simmered between us. The attraction that even her sisters have recently slammed in my face.

It's not the one I expect.

Corinna stomps over to the back door and flings it open. I'm surprised the crash doesn't shatter the glass. "After everything you did to me? After everything you said? Do you really think...of course you do! All you fucking men think you need to do is snap your fingers and any woman will drop their panties at your feet. Guess what—not this woman. Not anymore. Now get the fuck out of my kitchen before I tell the rest of the family what actually happened all those years ago to make me hate you as much as I do."

I'm frozen in shock. Of all the things I expected, this was the very last on the list.

"Now!" she screams.

Woodenly, I move toward her. Her face is turned away. "Corinna," I whisper imploringly.

"I am not kidding in the slightest. Get. Out."

"Damnit. I have to know what I saw. Something's wrong and you're not—" I demand, even as I begin to cross the threshold.

"It doesn't matter what you saw. It sure shouldn't matter to a man who never gave a damn about me," she spits at me.

Right before she slams the door in my face.

Standing outside the glass-paned door, I get my own anger under control. Suddenly, I hear a loud crash from inside the kitchen. I start to head back in, but I realize she'll never open up to me right now.

She's drowning in the pain she's in. If she won't let someone in to pull her from the water, I'll dive in headfirst to save her.

Tomorrow, there's no escaping me, Corinna.

I back slowly away so I don't alert her to my presence. Tomorrow's soon enough to have it out.

As for what she said, not give a damn about her? What a crock of shit.

15

CORINNA

After my encounter with Colby last night, I've barely slept. I stumble down my extra-wide stairs from my enormous master suite in desperate search of coffee.

Someone might die faster than I will if I can't find it.

Sliding open the repurposed barn door that hides my pantry, I lean against the jamb. There it is. Caffeine. Thank God my house-keeper stocked me back up. As I'm reaching for the pod of goodness that my industrial-strength Keurig will turn into a magic elixir to restore my humanity, I give my eternal gratitude for Mindy and her understanding of my crazy schedule.

I pad on bare feet to the maker of all wonder and drop the industrial-size K-Cup in to brew my pot of coffee. Waiting for the water to heat, I make my way over to my Sub-Zero refrigerator to take out homemade salted caramel sauce and a pitcher of cream both in their perfectly arranged glass containers. This luxury of mine may not guarantee a good day, but at least it starts it out the right way.

Without knowing what my test results are going to be, that's about all I can do anymore—guarantee my day starts out as delicious as I can make it.

After scooping a healthy amount of the gooey sauce and pouring some cream into my mug, I heat it in the microwave for a few seconds. I finish stirring just as the beeps indicate my coffee is ready. As the dark brew splashes into my mug, the combination of the steam and the aromatic smell jostle me further awake. I lift the mug to my lips and embrace the first sip. Leaning against the counter, for this moment, in the heart of my home, I feel bliss.

My house is set about as far back on the property as Ali's. Once a smaller barn, it could have held anything from large quantities of tack and carriages to smaller herds of animals such as sheep or cows. To keep my vision of an open space focusing around the kitchen and without modifying the T-shaped foundation, I built upward. My house almost replicates an actual barn. To be honest, it really is too much space for one person, but when I built it, I had hoped that someday, I'd eventually find someone to bring into it.

It's amazing how time slips away so quickly.

In the rubble of the old building, I managed to salvage a fair amount of wood which was used by the builder to make interior doors and shutters, adding warm honey wood floors and trim to the pristine white walls dotted with pictures of my family in eclectic silver frames. Unlike my workspace, where everything has to be meticulous, my home is more relaxed. I prefer to let whatever moves me to fill my space. I might have blue flowers in a red vase, just because. I found a fuzzy throw of a cute dog that I just had to have, and now, it's thrown across my favorite leather chair.

My bedroom is much the same way. Built into the eaves, it includes every woman's dream closet, and a bathroom that boasts a soaking tub for two, but the bed is awash with pillows that are there merely because they grabbed my attention. In front of my bed is a beat-up leather couch I found for a steal at a Pottery Barn outlet. Since more often than not I end up curled on it at night, I cared more about its comfort than I did what it looked like.

For me, the most important thing in my bedroom is the Edison lights I strung from the beams. Every night, they cast a muted glow throughout the room so I'm never alone in the dark.

Not by choice. Never again.

The only room where I spared no expense is my kitchen. Here, everything is top-of-the-line. I have custom cabinets with fitted drawers that are bins containing different types of flour, the largest being all-purpose and cake, of course. I have drawers filled with different sugars, and another filled with all other baking supplies like baking soda, vanilla extract, salt, and other smaller items I need quick access to. Other drawers were built with dividers so I could line up my pastry bags, decorating tips, and cookie cutters. All of my pans have a special location so they don't get scratched. Even all of my lids have a home.

We won't talk about the cost of my knives.

The last time Phil was over, trying to beg some dinner off me when Jason was working, he decided to put one of my babies in the dishwasher. I told him if he did that again, I'd ask Ali to stop his paycheck for a month to buy me a new one. The look of absolute horror on his face had him backing slowly away from me. "But it's just a knife, Cori," he'd whispered. My reply was that he was wearing shoes that I'm sure cost just as much. "But these are Gucci!" he'd screeched.

"And those are my Guccis, Phillip. Get that through your thick skull, or get out of my kitchen!" I demanded.

Needless to say, Phil will now clear the plates. He'll even wash my pots by hand. But he won't go near my knives. I feel like I won an enormous battle.

Holly has no room to talk. We joke that a third of the insurance on the mansion is because of the cost of her camera equipment, a third on Em's dresses, and a third on my knives. Ali just shrugs it off. Since her obsession is running gear, and now, along with Cassidy, baby clothes, spending several thousand dollars on a knife doesn't faze her. Cassidy demands to know how to handle the knives properly and then lectures the others if they're doing it wrong.

The only reason it drives Em absolutely batty is that I'd just as soon buy my clothes at Target so I can afford another knife. As she scores designer outfits when I need them, and I shop for cute pieces to fill in the gaps online at Luxury Garage Sale, I still hold my own when

I need to. Most of the time, I'm wearing ratty jeans and some kind of shirt that can withstand the abuse of frosting. Target holds a lot more appeal in those situations than the Valentino I wore the other night.

I'm about to make my way into the living room when my phone rings. I grab it from where it's still attached to the wall charging, and Ali's name is on the display. Punching the button for the speaker, I ask, "What's up, buttercup?" before taking another sip of my coffee. Yum. It may be a two-cup day with the caramel before I switch to regular coffee to avoid the calories.

"What happened last night? I heard you had a visitor in the kitchen after hours." Concern laces her voice. Before yesterday, Ali was the only member of our family who knew I had any sort of issue with Colby. I'd shared some of it with her when she wanted to call him after running into him at a party about a year ago. Hearing the acidic comments her significant other aims at Colby, I often wonder how much she's shared with Keene.

"It was fine. I handled it." As best as I could. What I wanted to do was take the airbrush of food coloring and spray it into his beautiful gray eyes. Bastard.

"Is the kitchen a hazardous waste zone? Do I need to bribe the cleaners to come in to get out the dye...or the blood?" It seems like Ali swallowed a mouth full of wiseass this morning. I'm grinning, even as I'm shaking my head.

"No, counselor. There's no need to defend me in any murder charges. When I say I handled it, I mean as an adult. Though I did have to throw his ass out," I admit.

"Jesus." There's a pause where I can picture her rubbing her forehead. "Do you want Keene to talk with him?"

I can't help the huff of laughter. "Because I'm Keene's favorite person?"

"You're one of them, sister. Don't you dare think otherwise," she retorts. "Red whipped cream in his face or not, he loves you."

"Right, Ali. The next thing you're going to tell me is that he and Phil are going to go out for a night together." Keene and Phil have this odd relationship. They respect the hell out of each other, but there's just something I can't put my finger on with those two. And then Ali hands it to me, like an early birthday gift. One I'll treasure and use accordingly.

"Fuck no. Keene's petrified of Phil talking about sex. Didn't you know that?"

And cash me out, I'm done. I'm outright laughing. I barely manage not to pull my coffee up through my nose. "You know there's no way I'm not talking about blow jobs or double penetration at our next family dinner just to set Keene off, right?"

Ali's now screeching with laughter as well. "Oh my God. Keene would walk out, I swear, Cori. You saw him on my birthday. He just can't take it. You know Phil will do something graphic with Em's old mannequins or some crap, and my man will be traumatized for life." Snickering, she says with mock sadness, "I'll never know the feeling of that hand slapping my ass ever again."

Our mutual hilarity can probably be heard in Norwalk, where the satellite office of Hudson Investigations is located. Even as I'm wiping my tears and gathering myself, I know Ali's going to redirect the conversation back to Colby.

"Are you ever going to tell me the full story of what happened?" Nailed it.

"Soon." Like tomorrow. Once I know the full extent of what I'm facing. "I promise."

"Good. I'm holding you to that. Oh. Hold on a sec." Ali puts me on hold to answer a call. I use the time wisely to finish off my first cup of coffee. I'm contemplating my second when she comes back on the line. "Sister, it is time to return the favor I owe you."

Reaching for the jar of salted caramel and the spoon, my brows lower. "What favor is that?"

Just as I'm about to drop a glop of caramel into my cup, she advises. "Colby is inbound. He just called Keene to tell him he wasn't coming in until the two of you talked. Keene was calling me to let me know so I could give you a heads-up, assuming you were here. We both know Colby's going to do a drive-by, not see your car here, and head to your house."

I bypass the cup and aim the spoon toward my mouth. With the sweet goo coating my tongue, I warble, "Are you shitting me?"

"No. Do you need me to warn him off?"

I close my eyes, weary over his persistent intrusion in my life. I don't understand why he just won't leave me alone like he did for so long. My emotions need to settle. It's time to deal with Colby Hunt once and for all. "Let him come. I have nothing to hold back with him anymore." And suddenly, I don't. I want this toxicity drawn from my soul before it's too late. I want to rest my head in peace. I'm tired of wondering...why? Why was our friendship expendable? Why was my pain his pleasure?

Why was my heart a joke?

I've tried to live every day of my life since that night where Colby crushed me like there was no shame or fear in the depth of my soul. I climbed into the skin of this man-eater so I don't look in the mirror and see the broken woman my family created and Colby finished shattering. I hide my rejection behind the tits and ass so many men want to grab in random bars without caring about the woman beneath. It's a coping mechanism, plain and simple.

Of course, my reputation now precedes me. Despite the few men who have actually scored, most would have sooner drunk arsenic than admit it. I was labeled as promiscuous. Funny, I never thought to the ability to count your partners on one hand was all that slutty.

I guess it's all for the best. Knowing someone loved me beyond reason the way Jason loves Phil, Caleb loves Cassidy, or Keene loves Ali, would make things worse right now. I'm preparing for the hardest battle of my life. I can't forget that.

I can never forget who I am and what I have deep inside of me.

"I'll be fine. Let me go though. I want to be dressed when he gets here."

"Call me after." It's not a question.

I smile faintly. It wasn't long ago when I was demanding the same thing from her. "I will. I promise." I'm already making my way back upstairs.

"Love you, Cori. And remember…"

"I know. You always have my hand in the dark."

"I do, you know."

Boy, do I know. "Gotta go."

As Ali hangs up, I take the stairs two at a time. I'm pulling out clothes so fast from my closet, I don't know, nor do I care, if they match. Walking into my bathroom, I throw my hair up in a loose knot and quickly freshen up before getting dressed. Just as I'm descending back into my kitchen, I see Colby's Jeep through the transom over my front door. He's passed Cassidy and Em's, driving hell-bent for leather.

Pulling open one of the double doors, I lean against the other with one ankle crossed over the other. I try to keep my expression neutral as he slams his Jeep into park. Colby jumps out before he sees me. He comes to a complete stop when he realizes I'm there waiting.

"I'd ask what you're doing here, but frankly, I don't care that much about the answer," I drawl.

His jaw clenches. I can't see behind his reflective sunglasses. "I came to get some answers."

"I really don't care that much about that either, but seeing as how I want some as well, I'll let you in long enough to get those. Then I want you gone." Turning on my heel, I lead Colby into my house.

For the first time ever.

16

COLBY

I want to spend my time prowling around, but I dutifully follow Corinna through the warm, eclectic space to a wall of windows and doors streaming the summer light into the far end of the room. Corinna throws one of the glass doors open with a flourish, gesturing me through without saying a word.

I step onto her patio and am immediately transported. Jesus. I never knew this was back here. And to think everyone thought Cassidy got the choice piece of property. There's a riot of wildflowers that make up a secret haven masked by Ali's tree line. It's an artist's dream come to life.

"How many times have you painted this view?" I murmur entranced.

"Is that why you invaded my solitude, Colby? To ask about my view?" Corinna's voice is cool behind me. It seizes my heart knowing that if I look at her, I'll see eyes the color of the earth versus the glory of the sun raining down on us. Her eyes deserve the sun streaming through them, with only the brilliance a star can display.

When I saw her laugh for the first time, I almost dropped to my knees. Her eyes were a pure golden color, framed by a fringe of thick lashes. Her smile caused my heart to clench. What I wouldn't give for that smile right now. But the woman whose space I've invaded isn't inclined to bestow one upon me.

"Why are you here, Colby?" Her frustration is palpable.

The morning light streams so brightly, it's making Corinna's old T-shirt appear transparent. It highlights the weight she's dropped. Where there was once softness, I now see edges. And for some reason, they fire me up more than what I suspect are the secrets she's been keeping. She turns her back, and through her T-shirt, I can see the faint gray color of her tattoo.

Never forget who you are.

I've never forgotten what Corinna meant to me, the feelings her voluptuous body invoked that I had to suppress. She was perfect before. Why is she doing this to herself?

Or is something else causing it?

"How much weight have you've dropped?" I ask abruptly. Corinna spins around. The way her cat eyes narrow, I can tell she's getting ready to pounce.

Then her mask of indifference drops back over her face. Shrugging, she answers, "Does it matter? No one's really mentioned it until we went to the concert. They attribute it to my working so hard."

"It's not though, is it?" Here's my chance.

Smirking, she shakes her head. "I got tired of curves. Especially the kind life throws at me. I decided to try angles on for a while to see if they were a better fit."

Frowning, I step forward. "They don't look as good on you."

"Says you."

"That's right. Says me. Says the man who worshipped every curve you had because it was real. Just like we were."

Corinna's stunned silent. One heartbeat. Then in the middle of the next, her glorious hair falls down her back from the knot it was in as she tosses her head back in a laugh so bitter, my heart blisters from it. When she finally gets control again, she reaches up to place a condescending pat on my cheek. "We weren't real, Colby." Her eyes are as dark as I've ever seen them.

I grip her wrist before she can pull away. "How can you say that?"

I rasp. At that point in my life, when I'd finally woken up to the callousness of my family, I'd found Corinna. She was never mine, but she was mine.

Wrenching her wrist away from me, she hisses, "Because if we were real, you would have been there holding my hand when I found out about my brain tumor the next week, the next month, the next year. Instead I found out about it after I was subjected to listening to your sexual proclivities—by the way, next time I'd suggest you take your belt off," she sneers. "Makes a hell of a lot of noise when you're balls-deep in someone even over the noise of a house party."

What did she say? I'm frozen by her words. Which is why her next words completely disarm me enough that Corinna's able to use all of her strength to shove me in the chest. I stumble back at least a foot. "Maybe if I moo like a cow, that night will come back to you more clearly, friend. After all, I'm just good cook who's had a rough life, right?"

"What did you say?" There's no way I ever said anything like that about her to anyone.

No way.

Visibly seething, she continues. "You should reconsider giving a friend who's afraid of the dark a key to your room for safety, Colby. Better yet, if you do, you should check to see if she's in there before you bring someone in to screw them." Pushing past me, she storms around the side of her house to the path between the trees I've didn't notice.

I've never noticed a lot of things.

"Corinna." I slowly follow her. "Are you trying to tell me..."

She cuts me off. "That I was in the room the night you screwed Addison Kaplan? Yes. That I found out exactly how you felt about me? Poor little Corinna." Her voice drops as she tries to mimic my own. "I put up with her for her baked goods." Switching back to her own voice, she yells, "I'm nobody's poor little anything! You promised me you'd never bring the darkness down on me, Colby. You promised me I'd always be safe. And what did you do?" She's visibly trembling. "You trapped me in a room with no way out in the dark. Then to hear everything you really thought about me? At least the bastards who kidnapped me wanted a onetime payment. Even if that payment was me. If I'd known friendship was so expensive, maybe I would have rethought the cost. "

"Cori..." The shame that courses through my body is devastating. She heard what was never meant for her to hear. Something I said to appease a heartless bitch long enough to sink my cock in her. For me to forget the woman I wanted, but knew I couldn't have.

"I told you never to call me that again. You want to know the truth? We're nothing because you made us that way. There is nothing you could say to me to make me believe you right now." Moving toward the gate concealed in ivy, she shoves it open. "Now, me and the ghosts of the bovine who used to inhabit this property would like your sanctimonious ass off our land."

Her voice ricochets in my mind. All of this hurt and pain over the years is because of me. I'd have said or done anything so I didn't cause pain to the one person I wanted to. Her.

I hurt her anyway. And by what I know about her lifestyle from Jack, it's caused irreparable damage.

Unable to bear the look on her face, I edge toward the gate when what she said strikes me in the chest like a sledgehammer. I freeze in place, mere feet from her. "What brain tumor?"

She waves her hand in the air. "That's none of your damn concern. Get gone."

I move closer. "What do you mean you found out years ago, Corinna? How?"

"Why are you still on my property? Do I need to call someone to have you removed?" She's shaking with fury.

"Tell me how you found out."

"You don't have the right to ask."

I play my trump card. "Tell me, or I'll go to your brothers-in-law and tell them I heard you screaming in an MRI machine at the hospital the other day."

Her face turns chalk white. "If you screw me over like that, Colby, there's no chance I'll ever forgive you."

"You were planning on forgiving me?" I'd held out a slim hope, but that hope is diminishing every second we speak.

"I forgave you for being an asshole a long time ago. I just decided to cut all assholes out of my life. I no longer have the time, nor the patience, for the people who aren't worth it. It's forgetting what happened when you're constantly around the people I love that I have difficulty with."

"Tell me, Corinna," I demand, even as my heart bleeds at her words.

She slams the gate closed before leaning against it. "Let's be clear on something. You're just somebody I used to be acquainted with. Someone whose friendship I apparently bought and paid for."

I wince.

"Right. With that understanding, I will say you upset me that night. Repeatedly. I ran into someone who made things worse. I tripped and fell in front of your entire house party, which was so much fun, let me assure you. Having people mock me when I was so upset..." Her voice trails off before she shores it back up. "Blood was still coming down my face the next day. I called the local ER, who suggested I come in. To rule out a concussion from my fall, there were tests. That's how and when I found out I have a brain tumor." She tells me this as if she's reciting a recipe. Rote. Detached. Probably because she's lived with it for years.

Flashes of that night come back to me. Stumbling in drunk. Flicking off the lights. Flinging Addison on the bed. Horror washes over me. Sweet Jesus, Corinna was in the room, and I personally plunged her into the darkness.

How many different ways did I betray her that night? Her mind? Maybe even her heart?

I broke every promise I'd ever made to the woman in front of me. No wonder she holds me with nothing but contempt.

I've held the keys to Corinna the whole time. Each tumbler of her secrets click into place, and the lock flies open. Instead of finding the way back to her heart, I see an impenetrable fortress. Instead of leaving herself vulnerable to another man, she's susceptible to no one. Instead of showering the world with her natural warmth, she hides it, reserving it for the scant few she knows she can believe in. Instead of being the Corinna I expected to find, she's both stronger and a shell of the woman I knew.

I have the answer I've been pushing for, and now I have no idea what to do with it.

Despondent, I move toward the gate. "I'll leave you alone, Corinna, if that's what you want."

She lashes out in her fury. "Absolutely. When you want someone out of your life, just tell them the truth. It's an effective way to kick them out. You taught me that."

Direct hit.

I stop right next to where she's standing. Her anger pulsates over me in waves. "I wish you would have told me."

"Why? So you could have gotten your final friendship payment of a graduation cake out of me? Sorry, I think I'll remain on the hook for that debt."

"No, Corinna. So I could have apologized then for breaking us."

"You didn't break a single thing to do with me. If anything, you made me stronger."

"By shutting down?" I ask angrily. "By letting no one in? That's not you."

"Since that's what it took, yes. I'm not that girl anymore."

"I'll bet you still sleep with the lights on." It's a cheap shot, one that's beneath everything we had shared. It's more like something Jack would say than me. I don't know where it came from other than the overwhelming bitterness I'm feeling.

With myself.

She stumbles backward in shock. "Get off my land before I find the right knife to make you."

"That was crappy, and I admit it." Where I'd normally expect to see lingering pain and fury on her gorgeous face, I see nothing. Which is worse. "I'll leave."

"Damn right you will."

I open the gate. It squeaks as I pass through. "Corinna." I pause, hoping she'll look at me.

Of course, she doesn't.

"I just wanted to say I'm sorry," I finish softly.

She doesn't acknowledge my apology. For her, the words mean literally nothing. "We're done. Is there anything else?"

"I guess not." I stare at the beautiful, creative, warm-hearted woman in front of me and feel so many emotions, with regret right at the forefront.

"Right. So glad we had this chat." Turning on her heel, she stalks across her patio to her back door. She opens and slams it behind her.

Slowly making my way down the flagstone path, I find myself back in the driveway again. I climb into my Jeep and sit for a few minutes trying to get my bearings. Never did I expect for Corinna to say what she did.

After starting the ignition, I pull out of Corinna's driveway and backtrack my way off the farm and through Collyer. I'm so disheartened and disoriented, I don't even know where I'm going until I end up back at the Hudson offices. Somehow, I power through the rest of the day without any interaction with Caleb or Keene. I don't know if I would have been able to keep any of what she said to myself.

I just know I have to.

I have to keep this promise because I broke all the others.

It isn't until hours later when I'm back in my apartment with a glass of bourbon in my hand that it clicks. I'm replaying our conversation over and over.

Who else would have heard about Corinna falling at our party all those years ago? Not me, apparently, I think bitterly. I was too concerned about getting my dick wet to have heard anything beyond the moans generated in my room. Who else knew what Corinna meant to me and could have told me what happened?

Who could have helped me figure this out ten years ago before I lost her?

When I come to the realization, I stand up and hurl the glass against the wall. Not caring about the glass shards exploding everywhere, or the amber liquid leaving tracks against the wall, I realize how thoroughly I was betrayed.

Jack was my best friend from the day we joined the same fraternity together at UConn. He lived across the hall from me. He would have been the one most likely to have seen Corinna if she came out of my room.

Like my investigations, the pieces start sliding into place. Jack was my confidant. He knew how conflicted I was about Corinna. He'd seen me downstairs drinking, and he knew I had gone into that room with Addison because I passed him on my way up the stairs.

He's known all along what happened that night. I could strangle that son of a bitch for not telling me years ago so I could have fixed this.

He knew. We talked about how much I agonized over Corinna's cold shoulder so close to graduation. For fuck's sake, it was Jack who suggested I try to contact her once I got settled on base. I sent him letters to give to her. Letters that I poured my heart into, assuming she would read them if delivered by a mediator instead of just tearing them up. I begged her to forgive me for whatever I had done. I begged her for a chance to be heard.

Now I wonder, did she ever get them?

Time to pay my soon-to-be-former friend a visit.

17

CORINNA

After Colby leaves, I wearily drag myself upstairs to shower and redress. All of his questions were finally answered, but none of mine were. Of course not. I'll probably go to the grave never understanding why the men in my life think of me as nothing more than collateral.

Dropping my clothes in the hamper near in my closet, I pad into the connecting bathroom. As the water's heating, I step on the scale and frown at the number. It's no wonder my clothes are falling off me. Even I didn't realize I've lost this much weight.

I've always been tall and voluptuous, with a body I was more comfortable hiding even before I was taken in the middle of the night to pay off a drug debt I wasn't responsible for. Let's face it. I was stacked at sixteen with oversized curves that didn't go unnoticed in the tiny South Carolina town filled with addicts where I was raised. Men had been making passes at me since I was thirteen. Puberty wasn't kind to me. It just gave license to the assholes who thought it was entirely acceptable to shove me into dark corners to cop a quick feel.

Yet another reason I hate the dark.

It takes a certain kind of immorality to agree to sell your daughter to monsters for a drug habit you can no longer control. I just wish I'd had the chance to do to my family what Holly had done to hers...but still. At least mine are no longer alive, unlike Ali's father, who was one of the people who kept us locked in the shipping container for sale. I don't have to be wary about listening to the news updates on his sentence since Judge McDonald, who passed down his conviction, was appointed to the United States Supreme Court.

It's cold and heartless, but not everyone's redeemable. And not everyone's parents sold them for their next hit. It's not everyone who's taken from the comfort of their bed and the safety of their home and told they'd be better off if they were sold by the pound, only to be thrown into a putrid shipping container in the middle of the night.

I can only hope my parents are rotting in the ninth circle of hell—treachery. I hope they're so far from light and heat, they're nothing.

After all, that's what they allowed men to make me feel like I was worth—nothing.

Even as the warm water cascades over my skin, I feel goose bumps prickle up. *Breathe in, let it out,* I tell myself. *Remember, you had Ali and Holly. And later, Phil, Cass, and Em.* Who knows what the other girls in that container went back to?

Not for the first time since I was told I have a brain tumor do I think it's my penance for being gifted a second chance. A chance to be Corinna Freeman, not Elena Baxter. A chance to live and make my simple dreams come true. Not a life forced upon me by men who think they have the right to exert their control over me.

Once Colby was out of my life, yes, I mourned his betrayal of our friendship and that final loss of my innocence. I remember Ali and Holly being in class when I sat on my bed eating Oreos and crying. I came to some hard conclusions. There's no such thing as a knight in shining armor. No man's going to pick you up when you fall. The sweet lies they whisper out of one side of their mouth are followed by the laughing, bitter truth from the other. I realized I'd better figure out how I was going to save myself because no one else was going to. That's reality.

I locked up my heart, except for those I already pledged my allegiance to: my family. I began to treat men precisely like they treated me, like junk food. Tasty for a little while, but overall, not worth the effort. Just like that package of Oreos I had been eating. Both my heart and the cookies were thrown in the trash.

Stepping from the shower, I braid my unruly mass of hair. I don't have the time or the energy to blow it out today. I needed what little I used for the confrontation with Colby today for something else. Noticing the time, I pick up my pace a little. I quickly swipe on bronzer for a bit of color on my pale cheeks and spritz on some perfume before I leave the bathroom to find something to wear.

I'm not working this morning. I have to be at Greenwich Hospital in a few hours to find out my fate.

WHY ARE hospitals always so damn cold?

I'm so glad I remembered to bring a thin sweatshirt with me. Quickly, I untie it from around my waist and slip it on. Wrapping my arms around myself, I can't seem to shake the chill I feel permeating my bones. We pass clusters of exam rooms, and I realize I should have dried my hair. Because that's what should be forefront on my mind right now, I berate myself.

Coming to the end of a long corridor, the nurse gives me a sympathetic smile and gestures me inside an office. "Dr. Braddock will be with you in just a few moments. Please feel free to take a seat on the couch."

I smile, but it's weak at best. I nod before the door closes behind me, trying to remember everything Bryan had told me about Dr. Derek Braddock other than he's an exceptional surgeon. He would have been a shoo-in for the position of the head of neurology, but he's decided to retire soon. Dr. Braddock also said throwing his support behind Bryan would be a better strategic move for the department long-term. Bryan likes him, and until he takes over as the head of neurology and neurosurgery in the next few weeks, Dr. Braddock is officially my doctor of record with Bryan consulting.

The phone on the desk rings, jarring me from my thoughts. It's a good thing the phone startled me because when the door suddenly opens behind me, I jump a good three feet. I'm positive I would have shot straight through the ceiling otherwise.

"Excuse me, Miss Freeman. I have to take that call. Dr. Moser is absurdly punctual." Dr. Braddock, I presume, strides over to his desk. Punching a button, he answers, "Braddock."

"Derek." I hear Bryan's voice come through the line. Something in me both relaxes because he hasn't left me to handle this alone, yet tightens in awareness because he's on the line. "Is Corinna there?"

"Yes, and I just got into the room. I haven't even had a chance to introduce myself," Braddock gripes.

"Not my fault you're running late with patients." There's humor in Bryan's voice.

"Not yet it isn't," he retorts.

I'm listening to the byplay, but I still haven't made a move since I initially jumped away from the door. I'm frozen by my own reality in the well-appointed room intended to relax people like me, but doing little to actually help.

"Corinna, are you there?" Bryan's concern can be heard through the speaker.

I turn toward Dr. Braddock. I don't know what he sees on my face, but his older one turns compassionate. "She's here, Bryan. And she's bracing for whatever you're about to tell her."

"You don't know yet?" I whisper. The first words I've spoken since he walked in his office.

Dr. Braddock's face softens further. He approaches me slowly. "No? Corinna...do you mind if I call you Corinna as well?" I shake my head no.

Dr. Braddock moves toward me like I'll bolt at any second, and I just might. "I don't. Even though I'm your official doctor and could have looked, Bryan—Dr. Moser—asked as a professional courtesy that I wait until we could do this together." He gestures to the leather chair next to his impressive desk , where behind it on a wall are impressive degrees. "Please, come and sit down."

Bryan's voice comes through the speaker. "Cori, we already have a plan of action. All these test results are going to tell us is the timeline. Right?"

I respond, "Right." Bryan's words should comfort me, but all they do is raise my anxiety levels to an all-time high.

There's so much I want to do in this life. It's so easy to push things off until later because nothing ever changes. The past, the present, the future, happiness, mistakes, apologies, love— everything I need to do converges together and slams into me, hitting me so fast. Later is now, and I don't have more chances. My head is spinning at the overwhelming sensation while Bryan and Dr. Braddock are talking briefly.

Suddenly, the silence in the room permeates through the fog surrounding me. I find myself pulled back in when I'd rather be anywhere else but here.

"Just tell me." I already know. In my heart, I've known since I almost fainted in the kitchen at Amaryllis the other day.

Dr. Braddock sinks to one knee in front of me and grips my clenched fists, while Bryan delivers the blow from his office in Baltimore.

"The tumor's grown. It's starting to push against your internal cranial arteries, or ICAs. We have to schedule surgery." His deep voice is direct and blunt when he delivers the kill shot.

And as the first tear falls down my cheek, I wonder how I'm able to breathe.

18

COLBY

Armed with bitterness and what I feel is righteous anger, I drive to Darien the day after my confrontation with Corinna, to the office where Jack practices general medicine with four other doctors. I time my arrival to coincide with the end of his business hours. All day, I've been hearing Corinna's voice in my head as she brutally sliced through me with her words.

Words which were worse than any wound I've suffered because there's a good chance Corinna never saw a single fucking letter I sent her from overseas, begging her to talk to me. Words that become more and more despondent before I finally stopped sending them. Giving up. On her. On us. Words that might have healed our breach so much sooner if someone hadn't intervened.

Now I want to know why. Today it all comes out. I'll find out why, even if it means having to pour him onto a stretcher afterward.

Sliding my Jeep into an open spot near the medical complex, I jump out and stride through the office building door a few minutes before five. Jack's office is on the third floor. Pressing the Up button, I'm pleased when the car door opens immediately.

I'll know everything before I leave, like I should have known everything years ago.

The door to the elevator opens. I almost smack into a familiar blonde in a nurse's uniform. Not giving her more than a cursory glance, I stride down the hallway. Her voice carries behind me when she says, "Oh my." I feel more than see her follow me down the hall.

Great. Another piece of my past I didn't want to run into. Literally.

Throwing open the outer office door, I walk up to the receptionist. "I need to see Dr. O'Brien as soon as he's finished with his last patient." My voice is polite but resolute.

The receptionist takes in my determined look but still apologizes. "I'm sorry. Dr. O'Brien doesn't have any openings today. Perhaps I can fit you in another day this week? Are you a new patient?"

The voice attached to the blonde I spied as I was getting off the elevator speaks from behind me. "It's okay, Tara. Jack will want to see Mr. Hunt." I half turn toward Addison when she continues. "This is personal, not a medical call." Addison's eyes meet mine. "Colby, if you'll come with me, I'll get you settled; then I'll let Jack know you're here."

Addison waits for the receptionist to buzz us through before gesturing down a hallway. I follow her silently past a few exam rooms that still have charts outside the walls. "You're looking at a thirty-minute wait, Colby. Jack is finishing up with one patient and has two more to see."

"That's fine."

"You can wait here. He'll be with you in a few." Addison shows me into what must be Jack's office.

At first glance, I want to laugh out loud. Jack's office looks worse than his room at our old house used to. Case files are piled every-where. Yet, I know if someone were to move a file, he'd know it imme-diately. That's just Jack.

How is it I know him so well after all these years, but he doesn't know me worth a damn? Did he think I would never figure it out? Not likely. I didn't for over ten years. The thought makes the ache in my chest tighten more. I lose myself gazing out his window at the parking lot below me.

I'm so lost in remembering my discussion with Corinna, I barely hear the door open behind me. Without moving a muscle, I ask the first question. "What did you do with the letters I sent you to give to her, you bastard?" Might as well let him know this isn't a social call.

"I must have sent you, what, thirty or more letters? What did you do with them, Jack? I begged for someone to tell me what happened between Corinna and I since she wouldn't speak to me. Anytime I could write, anytime it was safe enough to get a letter out, I sent them to you knowing you would have my back. I knew you'd get them to her for me. Since I've come back, I've been trying to pin her down to tell me what happened between us, to tell me what went so wrong. And today I finally figured out you never gave them to her. She hates me too much for that."

I finally face Jack, and for the first time since we graduated UConn, I really see him. His white doctor's coat matches the color of his cheeks since all the color has leeched out of them. "How was I supposed to defend myself when the person who should have had my back stabbed me in it?" I say harshly.

He says nothing to defend himself. But his eyes—his eyes are full of hate.

"I'm waiting," I goad him into a response.

Jack mutters, "Bastard," before he moves around the back of his desk. Removing a set of keys from his pocket, he reaches down and unlocks the bottom drawer. Pulling out a box, he drops it in the middle of the desk. "You should have left well enough alone. She was devastated that night. I handled the situation."

"You had what handled?" I can barely choke the words out.

"I was protecting you. You're a Hunt. You deserve better than some white trash wannabe slut sinking her claws into you."

"You had no fucking idea who she was!" I fire back. "But you knew what she meant to me!"

"Say what you need to, but you know who's to blame. You should never have let her slip so far out of your reach that you're here in my office, wondering what happened to these." He flips off the lids and upends the box. Hours of soul-searching lands carelessly on his desk, as each letter I wrote to Corinna lands in a heap.

The ones I wrote from the middle of the desert. The ones I wrote in the middle of classified missions I had to hide before sending. The ones I wrote from stateside bases. All of them are there. I recognize them as they carelessly land among the mess on Jack's desk.

It's taking everything in me not to dive across it and pummel the shit out of him right now. "Do you know what she told me this morning?" I ask him instead. Lifting my eyes from the letters to meet his, I tell him, "She told me she's nobody's poor little anything. She's filled with more pride and more class than you are on your best day. So, if you think you're better than her, Dr. O'Brien, you're completely wrong."

"Fuck you." Jack slams his fists on his desk.

"You'll never have the kind of honor she does. She's everything, and that just pisses you off, doesn't it? That's even with your prestigious degrees, she's still better than you."

Jack flings his arms across his desk, my letters to Corinna flying into a mess on the floor. "I'm sure as shit better than that slut."

I shake my head in disgust. "I was trying to be her friend. Not because that was all I wanted, but that was all I knew I could have. You knew this. What made you do it, Jack?"

"You said your family would never accept her." His voice is matter-of-fact.

"And in all the time you've known me, have I ever once done anything to make you think I give a damn about what my family thinks?" My voice is dripping in bitterness. "Did you think I would one day want to go back into that life and what? Take you along with me?" The twitching by his eyes gives him away. I reach over and grab him by the collar. "For a smart guy, you're a fucking moron, Jack." I release his collar, and he falls back in the chair behind him.

I start to make my way to the office door.

"Colby!" Jack calls out right before I pass through the doorway. I pause. "Don't you want to bring her the letters?"

"I think the man who held them from her for so many years needs to give her the explanation why he did, don't you?" I grate out. Lord knows right now she'd never believe me if I told her the truth.

"I...I don't know..." Jack stammers.

"I do," I say firmly. "Otherwise, that person might be wondering what kind of other things I'll find when I start digging." As Jack starts sputtering, I shrug. "The other night you asked me whose life I wanted to dig into, Jack. Now, I know the answer. Make certain she gets those letters."

Jack growls. Slowly he stands and begins gathering my letters off the floor and putting them back into the box.

I barely make it out of his waiting room before I fall back against the wall with a huge sigh. I wonder at how much of the dark I see in Corinna's eyes I could have prevented if she'd seen those letters. Even if it meant she realized her true self-worth and left me behind and found someone she could have loved.

Even if that person wasn't me.

19

CORINNA

"What do you mean, Jack?" I'm holding a heavy photo box. I'm late to the family dinner I requested because I received a call from Colby's old friend Jack O'Brien. He told me he needed to see me because of an emergency. Despite the fact I despise him, I assumed it was something to do with Colby. I agreed to meet him because I assumed my family would want to know.

What on earth is in this box that could constitute an emergency? The only crisis I can deal with is the one I'm about to face down at the farm. The one where I finally tell my family I have to have brain surgery.

Jack's face contorts as he runs a hand over the back of his neck. "Jack?" I question warily.

"There are letters in there," he bites out, pacing back and forth. I tilt my head to the side. Funny, I never noticed how many mannerisms he picked up from Colby over the years. Shaking my head from the stray thought, I tune back in to find Jack glaring at me—a typical look on his aristocratic features.

"From who?" I'm so confused. I place the box on the counter behind me and sit down on a barstool.

"Why should you be the one he chooses? Fucking bitch. Did you think I wouldn't fight to protect my brother?" Jack thumps his hand over his heart, letting it linger. Brother? Colby always told me Jack was an only child. Then again, I refer to my brother and sisters as such and we're not blood related.

Has Jack's hatred toward me stemmed from something other than just me being me?

Like a bolt of lightning, the knowledge flashes through me. "Colby. The letters are from Colby."

"Yes," he sneers.

It's a good thing I'm sitting because I probably would have fallen down. The sheer heft of that box indicates Colby had written to me for a long time. God only knows how long. No wonder why he kept trying to insinuate himself back into my life.

I jump to my feet with such force the stool I'm sitting on clatters to the ground. "How long, Jack? How long have you been hiding these?" I demand. I shove my finger into his shoulder.

Jack's face sets in a stubborn line. "A while."

Another man screwing me over. What a surprise. "It's better if you tell me the truth, Jack."

"You'll know the minute you open the first envelope." His sigh of disgust revolts me.

"Longer than a year?" He nods. "Five?" Another nod. "Ten?" I barely breathe out the word.

Jack turns his head to the side and smirks before whispering, "Maybe. Can you read well enough to find out?"

Crack!

I don't even realize my hand is flying through the air to connect with his face until the sound echoes off the walls of my home. I'm in such shock, I stumble until my back hits the counter.

"Why?" Hot tears make tracks down my perfectly reapplied makeup. "Why would you do this to me? To him?"

"I didn't do anything but protect him! Any brother would do it for someone they love!" he yells, cradling his cheek.

"What?" I barely whisper.

"God, it was bad enough a Hunt would stoop so low as to

associate with someone like you. A low-bred ingrate whose ass was so big, it should have taken two of Colby to pick you up. Jesus, I heard about you becoming this slut after we graduated. I should have sent the guys who fucked you money as a prize. Colby was fucking fixated on you. I was afraid he would come running back to you if you ever responded to him!" he shouts.

There's no air in the room when his rant is over. All that keeps spinning around and around in my oxygen-deprived head is that these letters have been here all this time.

All this time, Jack is the person who really hated me. Colby had been reaching out for years. Trying to repair something he knew was broke but had no manual on how to fix. Who knows what these letters would have done? Maybe if I read them, I would have found something in them to have forgiven him. All this time, wasted.

And there's nothing worse than wasted time.

Not to someone who might be dying.

I swipe beneath my eyes at the tears that won't stop coming. "Get out," I whisper. "Now."

"Corinna, you have to understand, you're just not good enough for him," he states matter-of- factly.

"I don't have to understand anything other than you're a liar and a thief." Isn't there some kind of law on mail fraud? I have to remember to ask Ali the statute of limitations on that.

"You were standing in the way of what is rightfully mine!" Jack shrieks.

"Colby?" There's something I'm missing. I just can't figure it out.

He nods. "I did what I thought was best."

Of course he did. "For yourself, sure. Not for me. Not for him. You have no right to stand there and act so righteous when you're the cause for so much of my resentment toward him. So much could have been healed..." I leave the thought unfinished. He doesn't deserve to hear what I need to say to Colby. He deserves my fire. Without thought to any consequences, I keep going. "What else am I going to find out tonight, Jack? Do you doctors like to talk in the locker room or something? Did you know about my brain tumor too? Before I had a chance to tell my family?" I scream.

I'm yelling so loud, I never hear my front door open. Until Ali growls, "We sure as hell know now."

I tear my eyes away from Jack and see my brother and sisters in varying degrees of shock, holding dishes.

"You were super late," Cassidy says weakly, unable to stop the tears from falling down her cheeks.

"Must have been a problem with taking out the trash," Phil remarks, right before he lands a fist to Jack's gut. Jack retches. Phil follows this with a right hook to Jack's jaw, which makes him stumble backward. Tripping on his own feet, his head knocks on the edge of the counter, dropping him in a slump on my kitchen floor.

Holly and Em cheer right before they each step over Jack to enter my kitchen.

Ali's voice is cool as a cucumber, but I can tell how angry she is when she spits out through clenched teeth. "A brain tumor?"

I nod.

"Son of a bitch!" Ali yells. She turns left, then right, looking for something to vent her anger on.

Jack unfortunately chooses that moment to groan from the floor.

Ali growls before she turns on him like fresh meat. Cassidy catches her by the arm. "Stop, Ali. This won't help."

"It will make me feel better."

Cassidy turns her tearful face toward me. "I don't think much is going to do that right now."

Ali slams her fist down on my counter. "Damn, Phil. If you don't do something about that waste on the floor, I swear to God I will. And that will mean calling Keene."

"Oh, fine." Phil looks at his now-swollen hand. "I could just hit him again, you know?"

"And Ali would have to defend you to get you out of jail," Em retorts. "Just pick him up and put him out in his car."

"Would one of you be kind enough to get his keys?" Phil's face is still etched with fury. "If I touch him for longer than I have to, I'm afraid of what I'll do."

I back away. "Not a chance."

"Cori has an excuse. Someone else find his keys and follow me out while I haul him out of the house," Phil growls.

All of us point at Em. "What? Why do I always get stuck with the shitty jobs when it comes to cleaning up Phil's messes?" she demands.

"Because, darling, normally it's your mouth spitting them at me," Holly sputters as Phil begins to haul Jack to his feet. "Get his keys now while you can."

Em curses under her breath but manages to find Jack's key fob quickly. Soon, Jack is hoisted over Phil's shoulder. He has Jack's key fob in his hand, and Em is scrubbing her hands in my sink to an inch of her life.

Seeing Em at the sink reminds me of how a doctor scrubs up. My chin begins to wobble. The wine bottle trembles violently in my hand. I sink to my knees in my kitchen. The false front I've held up for so long has left me.

There's nothing I can hide from the people who truly love me. They won't let me.

⁓

"AND THAT'S how I found out," I conclude. I'm probably on my fourth glass of wine. I can't tell for sure since I chugged a good part of the bottle earlier.

We'd tabled all talk until after Phil hefted Jack in a fireman's hold and dumped him in the back of his car. "He can wake up and get the hell off our land. Otherwise, I'm calling in your men." Phil glared at Cassidy and Ali. "Let them cart that piece of shit away."

Em and Holly proceeded to shoo me out of my kitchen to heat up trays of stuffed mushrooms and baked ziti, after slapping down a platter of white bean dip with pita chips and bruschetta to munch on. I'd just finished telling the group at large about the night with Colby in detail. How Jack had taunted me on the way out the door. And how after I fell in front of the crowd, I found out about the tumor the next morning.

"How have you been able to be around Colby without braining him, Cori?" Ali demands. Then she winces. "Sorry. Bad choice of words."

I snort into my glass. "Please. If you knew the number of times I thought about buying steel-toed boots and kicking him in the dick..."

Everyone laughs. Cassidy shifts next to me and takes my hand. "Honey, I hate this, but was Colby the catalyst for you telling us? Or is it something else?" Her perception is scarily accurate. Cassidy, for all intents and purposes, finished raising us. Now that she's become an actual mother, her skills are so sharp her twins, Laura and Jonathan, had better watch out. They will never get anything past her.

I roll my glass around between my hands. I hear heels click on the floor. "Dinner in twenty," Holly murmurs. She moves to sit next to me on the other side, while Em, who is right behind her, goes and sits next to Ali and Phil.

Here it is. The terrible moment of truth.

"Do you all remember me mentioning Bryan over the years?" I begin as I lean forward to put my wine on the coffee table.

Phil grins. "The guy I've been betting is your booty call in Baltimore? Hell, yes. Do we finally get to meet him?"

Everyone laughs except me. I bite my lip and look down.

"Shit. What did I say?" Phil panics.

"What is it, Cori?" Em asks softly.

I take a deep breath and go for broke. "Bryan exists, but not quite in the way you've been thinking."

A mild rumble of disappointment goes through the room with Phil's comment of "Damn. Who do I owe money to?"

Amidst the biggest confession I'm about to make to my family, I crack up. Of course they bet on my sex life, because that's what we do. Ali won a ton off of us when she bet Cassidy and Caleb christened our office during the planning for our biggest wedding to date.

"Honestly, Phil, I have no idea. You can settle up later though." I take a deep breath and let the words flow. "You'll get to meet him, because he's transferring from Johns Hopkins where he's been monitoring my brain tumor to take over the Department of Neurology and Neurosurgery at Greenwich Hospital." Swallowing hard, I add, "Pretty much in time to perform an essential brain surgery on me."

Silence, right before the tidal wave of pain washes over me.

"No." Holly's voice breaks into the void first. "No. This isn't happening."

"I agree," Em jumps in next. "When Mugsy had that tumor, they used radiation first to shrink it..." Em's elderly rescue dog has had about every medical issue known to the veterinary world and is still with us.

I cut her off. "They can't, Em. They'd kill me almost instantly." They collectively gasp. "My tumor appears to be sitting on top of two ICAs." At the instantly confused look on their faces, I translate. "Internal cranial arteries. If radiation touches one and it bursts..." I don't need to paint the image any further.

Ali slams her glass down. "I am so fucking pissed at you."

This was the reaction I was ready for. "I know."

"When I was so completely broken because I thought Keene had betrayed me, no one in this family had my back except for you. You were there making sure I knew I was loved, bringing me chocolate and being the shoulder I needed to lean on. No offense, Cass, but between you and your brother, I thought my heart was going to die."

When Cassidy was pregnant, she'd turned into a hormonal bitch, doing serious damage to her relationship with Ali. She waves her glass to show no offense has been taken. "Continue." She squeezes my hand hard in remembrance.

Ali continues her rampage. "Who was it who had my back? Who was it who kept me from losing myself in the process of all that damn pain? Who was it who sat on my floor and held me together when I thought I lost this family's love and respect?"

"Me." Cassidy squeezes my hand tighter.

"Then how on earth could you think we wouldn't do the same for you? That I wouldn't? Didn't I make a promise to you, to always hold your hand in the dark of any night?" Ali's voice cracks right before sobs rack her body. Em pulls her onto her shoulder to comfort her.

"I was trying to protect you," I whisper, my voice choked with the release of the burden I've been carrying for so long.

"I think what Ali's trying to say, Cori, is that we're supposed to protect each other. Didn't we learn that the hard way?" Cassidy's voice next to me holds both wisdom and sadness. I turn and meet her ocean-blue eyes that look like waves because of the tears flooding them. "Didn't we learn we're stronger together than we are apart?"

I swallow. Hard.

I feel Holly's arms wrap around me from behind. "We've got you now. We're never letting you go."

Ali kneels in front of me and lays her head in my lap. Immediately, my free hand goes to stroke her hair. "Never letting go."

Em stands and comes around behind the couch. "I hope this doctor knows what he's in for. When we decide to go to battle, anything can happen." She isn't wrong.

"I don't know what y'all are talking about. I already started the fight tonight, and my hand hurts like a bitch because of it." Phil stands from his position on the couch, taking all of us in. "I think I broke a finger punching that asshole's jaw."

"We'll be sure to tell Jason so you get a prize." Cassidy rolls her eyes.

He kneels next to Ali and looks at all of us. "You keep forgetting, little girl—I won the prize years ago when I found all of you." His eyes meet mine. "And I'm not ready to let any of you go."

Within seconds, hearts that beat because of strength and pride are tripped out of synchronization by tears of fear and anger that this could happen to one of us. It doesn't change what happens tomorrow, but for this moment it helps alleviate the burden I've been carrying alone for so long.

20

CORINNA

"So the letters in the box, Cori?" Em asks me as we finish washing the dishes from dinner.

"I honestly don't know yet, Em," I answer truthfully. "Whatever they are, Colby sent them years ago. Jack was hiding them because... well, you heard his reasons."

"Yeah, let's not mention those again tonight to Phil." She taps a perfectly manicured nail on the box. "Aren't you dying of curiosity?"

I don't know what to feel about the box. I take a deep breath. For years, I've branded Colby the betrayer of our friendship, only to find out tonight that he was also betrayed. While I had made those decisions as a young, damaged woman, Colby never gave up on me.

Don't I owe it to him, to myself, to read what's in those letters?

I dry my hands and prop my chin on my fist as I lean forward, staring at the box. "Apparently, he wrote me for years." It still is like a direct punch in the heart to find my reality shifted so drastically on all levels in such a short period of time. A tumor, Colby, Jack. The acidity of all the wine we consumed tonight begins churning in my stomach.

Em lets out a low whistle. "That takes balls."

"What Jack did? I know," I agree wholeheartedly.

"No, I mean Colby. He left knowing you weren't speaking to him, right?" I nod. "And he still spent time in a room somewhere thinking about you enough to write to you? Frankly, Cori, those letters could be about the way his socks stank up a room and they'd still be better than nothing at all. You were in his head, and maybe his heart, over some pretty long years."

Em reaches for my hand and pulls me into her arms. "How many times have we wanted to know the answers to the questions we never got a chance to ask our families? Maybe you won't get all the answers you want, but now you can ask the right questions." She brushes her lips against my forehead where she now knows the tumor hides behind layers of skin and bone. "Think about that, baby. Not all of us get that opportunity."

She quietly moves out of my arms. I know Em's parents were killed in front of her when she was young, but she never talks about it. Of all of us, her childhood from an outsider's point of view was the most stable since she was raised by a loving family member. But Em was so traumatized by the events that happened to her, it took her years to be able to speak again, even after Cassidy and Phil found their way into her life.

Regret is only the time you waste. Even my anger and fear seem worthless in every second it's stealing from the time I could be doing something worthwhile. Living.

Slowly, I pull the box toward me. Just by its weight, I know I'll be up all night reading. Gathering my courage, I lift the lid and gasp.

Stuffing the box are letters of all sizes, on different types of paper. Grazing the tip of my fingertip along the unopened envelopes, I count them. Thirty-seven. Colby tried to contact me thirty-seven times, even after I pushed him out of my life without actually speaking to him. After I ran away without confronting him. My lips begin to tremble. I can't do this with my siblings here. Slamming the lid on the box, I startle Em, who's been wiping my counters. "Sweet Jesus, Cori. What's in there? A snake?"

"No, Em. Worse. A mirror." And it's showing me the judgmental creature living inside of me. I begin to cry horrible, racking sobs.

"Maybe opening the box wasn't such a good idea," Em mutters.

"No. You were right." I wipe snotty nose with the sleeve of my shirt. Em looks horrified over my perpetual misuse of clothing before she quickly reaches for a napkin, making me laugh. "I owe it to Colby, but more importantly, I owe it to myself, don't I?" I blow my nose hard and look at my older sister for guidance.

Sighing, she brushes her fingers through my hair. "Only if you can emotionally handle it, baby. Nothing is more important than your health right now."

Maybe Em's right, but I know one thing is more important, and that's finally finding true peace in a heart that hasn't had any in eleven years before it's too late to find any at all.

It's late when everyone leaves. Each and every one of my siblings gives me fierce hugs and offers to stay, knowing the turmoil I've been through tonight would have some kind of emotional ramifications. Each one of them received the same response to their question, "Will you be okay?" thus resulting in Em ordering Holly to her house for the night and everyone leaving me alone.

Ali is the last one out the door. "You know I'm still so damn mad at you, right?"

I nod. I expected nothing less.

"But not about the tumor. How in the hell could you not tell me the whole story about Colby? I could have asked Keene do worse things to make his life hell."

I gape at her. "Are you kidding me right now?" Keene's been a jackass on purpose?

Ali cups my cheek before brushing her lips against it. "Told you he loved you, sister. Very few people have the balls to stand up to him. Or stand up for me. When I told him about Colby, he made it his mission to initiate the 'fuckin' new guy' appropriately." She pulls back and sighs. "He's going to be devastated, Cori. All the guys are. I really hope you're ready for them all to be breathing down your neck."

To be honest, I hadn't thought much beyond telling my family. The panic on my face must reflect that because Ali starts to laugh. "Oh, baby. If you thought you deserved the royal treatment before, I recommend you brace. Those men are going to carry you around on a damn pillow until we get you through this."

I grin. I can't help it. My brother and sisters have married some gorgeous men. "Now that benefit does not suck."

Ali snickers. "If I told Keene you wanted him to do it shirtless, I wonder if he'd do it?" She taps her chin thoughtfully. Suddenly, the banter turns into tears. "Damnit, Cori." Ali pulls me into her arms and rocks me. "I would have held your hand. How did you think I wouldn't have gone with you to those damn appointments?"

I blink away my tears as I rest my head on Ali's shoulder. "I know you would have. And y'all would have worried for too many years. I needed to live, Ali. I just needed to live," I end on a whisper.

"Okay." Her sweet voice is next to my ear. "You know we're going to help you fight this with everything we've got, right?" Pulling back, she mean mugs me. "No more secrets."

There's none that I can think of except Colby. "Ali," I begin hesitantly, pulling my lip between my teeth.

"Shit. There's something else? What? Dr. Bryan's an alien from Jupiter or some crap?" Ali snarks. She's really been around Keene too much lately.

I roll my eyes. "No, he's human. It's just... Colby knows already."

I wait for the explosion. Three...two...

I don't even get to one.

"How? How does Colby know before your family?" Ali seethes.

"Because he had to get a test performed at the same hospital where I had my last MRI. He saw me there. That's why he came to see me yesterday." My voice betrays my exhaustion.

Ali begins pacing, which is never a good sign. Finally, she speaks. "Were you going to tell us just about your problem with Colby before you saw him, or were you going to tell us everything?"

I lean back against a wall and sigh. "Everything, Ali, I swear. What I was waiting on were the test results. The only thing I didn't expect to tell you about tonight was the letters." I nod over toward the island where the box still sits, waiting for me. "Then again, I had no idea they existed."

Ali stops her agitated motion. "Do you want me to stay while you open them?"

I appreciate her generous offer, knowing she needs to go home to Keene and Kalie, and to release her emotions. I shake my head. "No, hon. You need to head home. I'll call you if I need anything."

Ali's gives me her best courtroom intimidating glare. "Promise?"

I reach for her hand. "I promise. I'm not hiding anything else." I give her fingers a sharp squeeze and tell her, "Go. Go give Kalie a kiss for me, and go tell your intimidating hunk this hasn't impacted my aim yet."

Ali barks out a laugh before a tear falls down her face. "Knowing Keene, he'd welcome being a target for your anger and frustration if you need it, baby." Giving me a quick kiss on the cheek, she murmurs, "I love you, Cori. Call for anything, no matter how big or small."

"I will," I whisper. I need some time to absorb everything that's happened today. Between the news of my imminent surgery, Jack's betrayal, my family finding out, and Colby, I just need to do what I can to nourish my soul.

Ali peers into my eyes one last time, then sweeps out my door. I close it softly behind her.

Finally, I'm alone—as alone as I can be with a million thoughts circling my brain for space in an attempt to make some order of the path my life has taken.

I've had my quota of life-changing events for the day, but something is pulling me toward the box on the table. The neurons and synapses firing away are telling me to open that box instead of figuring out how my part of the business will operate while I'm out on medical leave.

One letter, I promise myself as I make my way back to the counter. Just one.

Pulling the box toward me, I spin it around and rest my hands on the lid a moment.

Just one, I repeat.

I take off the lid, put it to the side, and pull out the letter closest to me, dated over ten years ago. *Well, here goes nothing.* Slipping my nail under the flap, I slice the envelope open with a flourish.

I slide out the thick sheets of paper and briefly close my eyes. *You can do this, Cori,* I promise myself.

What can be in these letters that can hurt you now?

SEVEN HOURS and thirty-seven letters later, I know the answer.

Love. Hope. Loyalty. Faith. They can hurt just as much as a betrayal.

I stumble into my office to find a pen and paper, as a batch of caramel chocolate brownies finishes in my oven. After making my way back into the kitchen, I start a new pot of coffee, having drunk a full one overnight. Hearing the timer go off, I pull the brownies from the oven and leave them to cool on a rack, knowing they need to be just right to pack up.

I'm barely awake when I sit down with the pen and paper in my hand. Taking a deep breath, I start.

"Dear Colby..."

21

COLBY

The next morning, I'm at my desk, signing off on the overtime report for the Charlotte Collins rescue, when there's a light tap at my door. Without looking up, I yell, "Come in," as I continue to mutter at the time sheet on my screen.

Seriously, I need to ask Caleb and Keene if they pay the guys to go out drinking to celebrate. Otherwise, I'm going to have a fuck load of timesheets to reject this week. Cursing rabidly, I don't even notice the door silently open or the footfalls approaching my desk.

I do notice the smell. Chocolate caramel brownies. My head snaps up, and standing before me is obviously a hallucinatory reward from staring at spreadsheets for way too long.

"Corinna," I breathe, not wanting to disrupt the fantasy in front of me. Her long hair is down around her face. She pushes it out of her face with one hand, while the other holds something containing the scent that is wafting through my office.

Since I figure I'm dreaming, it's awfully nice of me to put her in a low-cut, loose, brown knit shirt with a wide collar falling off her shoulder. One that's not covered in flour or icing. Pushing back in my chair, I notice she has on a pair of ankle boots with well-fitted jeans instead of her trademark Chucks.

Mentally patting myself on the back, I'm impressed with how good she looks in this particular fantasy of mine. I wonder how long I can keep the illusion of smell going.

It must be because I was in both of her kitchens so recently.

"Is everything okay?" the mirage in front of me asks curiously. The package in her hand shifts from one hand to another. I imagine the smell becomes stronger as it shifts closer to me, as if the real Corinna was standing right in front of me.

"Hmm?" I respond.

Suddenly, the mirage gets impatient. "Wake up, Colby! Are you watching porn on that machine or something? Do I need to get Keene in here to check? He's already pissy since I asked him to drive me here because I didn't sleep all damn night," Corinna snaps.

Holy shit. She's not a mirage. She's real.

"C-Corinna," I stammer. "Shit. I'm sorry." I power off the computer screen, likely adding more credence to her theory. Quickly standing, I smooth down my dress shirt. "This is a surprise. Please, have a seat." As she gracefully sits and crosses her legs, still holding on to the package, astonishment might be the best way to describe how I'm feeling. "What can I do for you?"

She tosses her hair over her shoulder and focuses anywhere but on me. Afforded a few moments, I peruse her to my heart's content. With the angle of her shirt cascading from so high against her neck, and so low against her arm, I catch a glimpse of the side of her amaryllis tattoo where it rests near her heart. When she told me years ago where she had placed her symbol of the Freeman family, I'd hoped one day to see it.

Hell, who am I kidding? I still hold that hope.

Her head is still facing away from me when she starts talking. "I had a visitor before the family dinner yesterday. You know Jack O'Brien, I believe."

Any semblance of ease I had been experiencing because of our calm conversation evaporates. "Only too well." I can't control the rage seeping from my voice.

The poster she's been reading about Operations Security must be fascinating. She hasn't looked away from it once since she started talking. I forget about that when her next words penetrate. "Then you might be interested to know when Phil heard Jack call me a low-bred ingrate with a fat ass last night, he knocked him out in front of the family. It was too bad it happened so fast. Holly didn't get photos. I was going to get us all something printed up with Phil's fierce expression on it for dinner next week." Her head turns, and I'm suddenly blinded by something I thought I'd never see again.

Pure discs of gold in Corinna Freeman's eyes.

"Hand to God, it was a perfect right hook, and had he landed on Phil's Guccis, I think Phil might have kicked him." Her voice is pure honey smoothing out all of the rough edges. And although the color doesn't change, the humor disappears. "Right before that, Jack admitted he stole something from me. Something from you." Her chest heaves as she tries to control the waver in her voice. "Things that should have been delivered to me long ago."

Is she talking about the letters? I stare at her, unable to say a word. I nod instead.

Corinna stands. I rise as well. "Keene's waiting to drive me back home, but...you'll see after you open the package." She pushes the box into my hands, and the smell I thought was a hallucination overwhelms my nose.

Caramel chocolate brownies. I'd recognize it anywhere. I gape at the package, then at her as she moves toward the door. "Don't wait too long to open it. It almost didn't make it here in one piece." She gives me a hesitant smile before she opens my office door and slips out.

Falling back into my chair, I would have sworn I'd just experienced the best dream of my life if I wasn't holding the living proof in my hands. Knowing Corinna's correct about the food savages I work with, I quickly open the white box.

And find a letter addressed to me on top in her beautiful handwriting. Only, it's not addressed to "Colby" or even "Colby Hunt." It's addressed to my full military address from ten years ago.

God, she got the letters.

Using the iPad Caleb and Keene showed me how to work for security matters, I engage the locks on my office door. Forgetting about the brownies, I slide the box to the side before sitting back in my chair.

What did I even say in that first letter? What did I ask her? I know I told her over and over in every single one how much I missed her in my life. I'm in shock to find my hands shaking as I hold her letter. Even though I'm scared—no, terrified—to see what she wrote, I need to read her words on the page.

The way I should have seen them so long ago.

I tear into the letter.

Dear Colby,

As you might know, your letters were a bit delayed. Next time, you might want to try a better mail carrier if you expect them to reach me anywhere close to when you send them.

I can't help the bark of laughter that escapes me. With my lips twitching, I keep reading.

Please accept the welcome home gift I should have baked for you a long time ago. We are all glad to have you home safe from your last mission. And it's to my shame I never properly let you know that.

It's early morning now. After reading your first letter from so many years ago, I have to admit, I'm baffled.

What did you want from me then?

What do you want from me now?

I think back to the night where we fell apart, and I find myself questioning everything I believed in for so many years. You broke me that night, Colby. Yes, I admit it. You did.

My heart clenches. Hard.

I haven't forgotten what happened, but when I was standing in my home last night, and understood someone else might have broken you, I realized not all of the links between us are gone.

And that is somehow both terrifying and comforting right now. Especially knowing as I write this, you could crush me again with a few ill-placed words. I beg you, if that's where your mind leads you, don't. Please don't. Right now, what's left of me needs to be focused on the battle I'm about to endure.

I close my eyes in pain. Partially because she feels she has to ask me to be gentle with her, and also knowing whatever her news was from her test, it wasn't good.

Em told me I might find questions to ask you in the letters, but there's really only one I thing I can think of for now. Would you like to be friends again?

I know I'm a risk. I've been a snot, a spoiled brat, and blamed you for things that God only knows there's no explanation for.

You weren't the best of friends to me, but then again, I haven't been a great one either. I'd think about it for a while before you answer.

Hopefully, the brownies soften you up a bit.

And Colby? Your letter might have been right at the time, but it's not right anymore. You have all of us for as long as you want us. You're not alone in the dark. Trust me. I know what that feels like.

Corinna

I clutch the letter in disbelief. Leaning my head back, my breathing sounds harsh in the empty room. There's still distance between us because we'd grown apart in so many fundamental ways, but this was so much more than I ever expected. Between whatever is going on with the tumor in her head, her crazy schedule, and me starting a new job, it'd be insanity to try to start something right now, right? And let's not forget, I don't want to be one of the crowd anymore.

I want Corinna when she's ready to be mine only.

Putting the letter on my desk, I open up the brownies and remove a few. After hiding them, I disengage the security lock. No sooner than the final tumbler opens, my door flies open. Charlie and Caleb are standing there, looking like a pack of hungry wolves. They barely glance at me before they fall upon the brownies.

"Don't you get fed at home?" I say before reaching for one in the box and taking my first bite. Jesus, they're better than I remembered.

"Not this kind," Charlie moans around a mouthful of my brownie.

"Be glad Keene had to drive Cori back to her house. You might get more than one," Caleb advises. "And don't try to hide them in your desk. He'll just pick the lock and claim it was work related."

Damn. Now I have to find a different hiding spot.

"There's no need for that," Keene's smooth voice interrupts. What the hell? Corinna only just left. "Ali came to pick her up since I have a meeting with Colby."

"Since when?" I demand.

"Since my sister-in-law baked those brownies. Do I look like an idiot? Now, fork over the chocolate and I won't kick you in the balls for knowing something was wrong with Corinna and not telling us." Keene smirks.

Caleb, his lips rimmed with chocolate, agrees. "It's worth it, Colby. If you and Cori are in a good place, she'll make you more. She can't recreate your testicles."

Damn, if the bastard isn't right. Unwillingly, I watch as my bosses devour all but the few brownies I hid right before they came into my office. As I slowly munch on the only one I'm willing to let them see, I wonder what to do next.

22

CORINNA

I hang up the phone with Bryan. It's only been two days since we last talked, but he was concerned since Dr. Braddock hadn't heard anything from me about scheduling the surgery.

My acidic reply was "Maybe I decided to go with another neurosurgeon." That had him laughing in my ear for a good five minutes. Brilliant, arrogant ass. Unfortunately, he's right.

It's what condition I'll be in once he's done that still has my anxiety spiking and delaying making the calls to learn more about the procedure.

Looking for a distraction, I spy the box of letters from Colby on the counter. I know I told him to think about whether or not he wanted me in his life, but it seems like I've heard from everyone but him.

All of my siblings have dropped into the kitchen at different times. I received hilarious pictures of Caleb and Keene with mouths stuffed full of my chocolate caramel brownies that I'm sure they had to blackmail away from Colby. Jason, Phil's husband, dragged me away from a cake I was decorating to grill me about all things medical. Since he's an ER doctor at a major hospital in New York City, I wasn't surprised. I also figure he'd translate things for Phil.

Even Ryan and Jared, Caleb's brother and brother-in-law, sent me a huge bouquet of irises. I read the card aloud when they were delivered to the office during lunch. It said, "We know you already have these, but a little more never hurts. All our love, Ry and Jared." Phil explained the meaning behind irises, which mean faith, hope, wisdom, and valor.

Damn, I have a fantastic family. But I still haven't heard from Colby.

I've long shed my chef's coat and am standing there, staring off into space, when I hear a knock on the kitchen door. "Come in," I call out absentmindedly.

"I figured I'd knock this time in the event your aim is as good as Keene claimed it was," a dark voice says from the door. I don't bother turning around. I'd know that voice it if I was blindfolded in the darkest night since he used to whisper in my ear to get me to sleep. Colby's here.

"Surprisingly, I'm not having the urge to throw things these days," I say calmly, despite the fact that my heart's beating crazily out of my chest. I turn around, and he's standing there in a long-sleeved dark maroon shirt tucked into his dress slacks. He looks positively gorgeous, but was there ever a time he didn't?

Meanwhile, I'm still in my typical tattered tank top and jeans. Both of my tattoos are on full display since my hair is in a loose knot on my head. The side of my mouth quirks in a smile as I realize we couldn't look more different. We couldn't *be* more different.

I look like you could toss me back into the trailer park where I grew up and I'd fit in just fine. Colby looks like he could be a model. Shaking my head, I approach the metal table separating us. So many regrets well up inside of me. So many wasted hours, days, years. I shove the sorrow away. "How are you?" I ask benignly.

A devastating smile crosses his face. "That's not how you normally greet me."

A laugh escapes. I can't help it. "Not lately, no. I should apologize for that."

Colby saunters around the worktable. Standing directly in front of me, he says, "No, that's not how you used to greet me, Corinna. I never received such a lukewarm greeting from you even when all you used to do was blush in business class. After we became friends, it was always a hug." Reaching up to push back a piece of hair that escaped my top knot, he reminds me, "Always."

My mouth gapes open. "You can't be serious."

His brows lower. "Were you not serious about what you wrote?"

I sputter. "Of course I was." I wrote that damned letter six or seven times before I got it right. "But, I mean, look at you. You're all dressed up from work. You can't mean you want me to touch you right now."

His face clears. "Clothes wash, Corinna."

I shake my head. "Colby..." I start to move away. I get maybe a step before I'm hauled against his chest.

"Do you really think I give a rat's ass about anything when I finally get to hold you in my arms again? Even if it's just for something as simple as a hug? You read all of my letters. Do you comprehend how much I've missed you in my life?" Colby demands.

Placing my hands on his chest, I feel my heart pick up speed. "Maybe I underestimated it a little bit," I mutter more to myself than him.

"Just a bit," he replies sarcastically. "Now, how about my hug?"

I study him for a moment, my heart beating out of my chest. I've got two choices: I can simply lean in and wrap my arms around his lean waist and give him a perfectly acceptable hug, or I can go for it. Try to bend the arc of time a little for both of us to get us where maybe we both want to be?

For just a moment, I feel like the Corinna I used to be. I'm the Corinna who didn't give a damn what people thought about the chubby girl with the gorgeous boy. I forget the old fears and the new darkness threatening me. I slide my hands over his shoulders and push. Hard.

The next thing I know, my legs are wrapped around Colby's waist, and he's boosting me around my ass as I'm laughing down at him. My arms are thrown around his shoulders, and I'm squeezing with all my might. Dark nights and lonely days disappear. Peals of laughter pour out of me as I toss my head back. My hair falls out of its loose knot and cascades down my back.

"That's much better," he murmurs, shifting me more upright. I grin down at him before dismounting. "And now, to answer you, I'm doing a fuck of a lot better than I was before I walked in that door."

"It sounds like you're having a bad day."

"Do you understand what a pain in the ass your brother-in-law is?" he gripes. "He's an anal-retentive prick with a perpetual smirk on his face."

I look around in all directions before I lean forward to whisper conspiratorially, "So was his sister when she was pregnant, but you didn't hear that from me."

Colby grins.

"Is there a particular reason you came by?" What I really want to know is are we really going to stand in my kitchen and talk about the past over stainless-steel tables?

"Actually, I came to see if you wanted to grab something to eat," he throws out casually.

"Colby! I'm a mess." I shake my head.

"You look cute. You always do. Come on, I'm starving." He grins. And because I know he's always hungry, I can't help my broad smile. It's silly because I know time can't be bent except when memories drag you back. Between the hug I gave him and his perpetual need for food, we've been transported back to cold winter days after his workouts where I'd agree to eat at places with nasty cheese and stale corn chips.

Fortunately, I have better taste now and can still appease his horrible taste in food. "Come on. I know just the place."

"Does it have—"

I cut him off. "Of course it has nachos." I let out a beleaguered sigh, even as his face lights up.

"What are we waiting for?" Moving to the back door, he unlocks it and holds it open. "I'm starving."

A few minutes later, I'm sitting in Colby's Jeep listening to Dave Matthews, feeling just for a moment like I did back in college.

Unburdened.

Digging in my purse for my sunglasses, I slip them on as I tell him how to get to Pancho's.

"Now this is what I'm talking about," Colby declares. He raises his Dos Equis in a toast as we're waiting for our waiter to take our order. "When I ran into Ali last year, she refused to get nachos. Then she barely even ate. I mean, if she wasn't going to eat, why not let me get something I wanted?"

"Likely because she didn't want to ruin a dress with your need for spicy cheese sauce?" I reply dryly.

"I was willing to risk my uniform."

"Which was replaceable."

He shrugs. I can't help but chuckle. Such a guy.

The waiter comes back with a basket of salted chips and a bowl of amazing homemade salsa. It's all I can do to avoid diving in, but I refrain. I know, life's short, but I'm trying to watch what I eat more because of the vast amount of blood work I'm going to be subject to. Once they clear me for surgery, I swear I'm eating a meal that will require me to undo my pants to sit.

And I'm not cooking a single bite of it.

"I'm torn, Corinna. I mean, you brought me to a place that has three different kinds of nachos on the menu. How am I supposed to decide?" Colby's gray eyes twinkle at me over the menu.

Without much effort, it appears we're slipping back into our old relationship. The years seem to be erased with the stroke of each of our pens. I could have lived out the rest of my days holding on to my grudge, but when the significant specter of death hangs over you, lost moments and regret seem to choke you. The anger, the harsh words, the lies you tell yourself versus the precious memories you can still have, all seem worthless.

Keeping the moment light, I reply, "You could order two of them to go."

The waiter comes up, and we give him our order: a bowl of posole soup for me, and Pancho's nachos for Colby. Once the waiter walks off, Colby picks up where we left off. "It's tragic, but no. They're never as good reheated. Not unless you're desperate for a hangover cure. Then they're fan-fucking-tastic."

I laugh and am rewarded by the smile that slashes across Colby's face. "Had a lot of those in the last few years?"

He groans. "Enough to say I should know better, and yet not too many to not be stupid with my unit." He freezes for a moment before shaking his head.

Unconsciously, I reach over and squeeze his fisted hand. "I'm certain they feel the same way about you." I'm pleasantly surprised when his hand flips over and he grasps mine.

"You'd say that not knowing what happened?" he asks quizzically. His thumb strokes the inner part of my wrist, sending my pulse skyrocketing. I discreetly pull my hand away.

"Despite the years, Colby, I know the kind of leader you are. You'd never have done anything to jeopardize one of your men deliberately," I say with conviction.

He leans toward me, forearms resting on the table. "That means a hell of a lot, Corinna. I've gone over everything time and again in my head, but..." Suddenly he's interrupted.

"Colby, nothing for years and then twice in a week!" a breathless voice says next to us. We both turn, and I see her.

Addison Kaplan.

Ignoring me completely, she reaches down to give Colby a hug. She doesn't let him up even when he stands. Wrapping her skinny arms around his waist, she pushes her breasts against his firm abs and gazes up at him adoringly.

They make an attractive couple, I think dispassionately.

Colby has the good grace to look at me uncomfortably. "Addison." He's uneasy, likely because of what I told him earlier in the week.

"I know we ran into each other at Jack's office, but I actually live here in Danbury. It must have been meant for us to see each other again. What are you doing here? Craving something?" She's practically purring.

Self-centered bitch, I think with some amusement. That amusement dissipates rapidly when the conversation takes a completely different turn. Internally, I'm wondering if this shit only happens to me.

"You know how I am," Colby says noncommittally. Then Addison lets the bomb drop.

"If I remember the last time you and I were together...what, two, three years ago at that event in DC? I do know how you are. That was a hell of a night, wasn't it?" She runs her hand up his chest possessively.

My mind goes blank. Two or three years ago? Raising my eyes to Colby's, I see he's not looking at Addison, who's desperately trying to imprint her scent on him like a bitch in heat. Appropriate. He's looking at me, beseechingly. His eyes are begging me for something I just don't have it in me to give right then.

Calmly, I reach for my cell phone and order an Uber. Pushing back my chair, I stand. "Since you two appear to have so much to catch up on, why don't you have a seat?" I offer. Tossing my hair over my shoulder, I offer, "I'll have the waiter bring you a menu."

Without even looking at me or letting go of Colby, Addison scoots in front of me and shoves my water aside. "That'd be great. And if you could have them send out some more chips too since you're off your break."

My snicker can't be contained. "Of course." Letting loose a barrage of Spanish at the confused waitstaff, I ask if they can deal with the hot mess at the table, as well as cancel my soup. I drop a twenty in the tip jar as I walk out the door to my waiting ride.

In the safety of the car back to Collyer, I ignore the persistent pings on my phone. I feel like an idiot, and I don't have time for that.

Not anymore.

It's time to be with people who accept me for who I am, and just live.

Picking up the phone, I call a number I haven't in some time. When the call is picked up, I ask, "Miss me?" Hearing the husky male laugh on the other end, I grin, knowing the night's still early.

23

COLBY

I won't apologize for having had a life in the last ten years. I won't apologize for the fact that yes, I've screwed a number of women. And damnit, Corinna and I never had that kind of relationship before. I will cede that I owe her an apology for the past being so blatantly thrown into her face without us having had any sort of discussion about it. Despite her having written a letter that put us on a more even footing, Corinna and I still haven't talked about what drove us apart.

Tonight seems to be the night to confront everything from your past though, I think bitterly. After being stuck at dinner with Addison for an hour, and trying to at first gently, then bluntly explaining to her I had no desire to rekindle what was mostly a two-time jack-off session with a live blow-up doll, I ended up with Addison's water tossed in my face.

I was irritated at the scene Addison caused, but freaking pissed and hurt by Corinna.

Once again, things got tough for and she decides to take off? As I'm making a mental list of the things for Corinna and I to "discuss" the minute she's within arm's reach, my cell phone rings. Glancing at it, I see it's Keene. I answer it using the speaker. "Hunt," I clip off.

"Whatever you did, fix it," he snaps, forcing more of my own temper to the surface.

"You don't know anything about what happened, Marshall. Now is a good time to shut the fuck up and let me get to Corinna's," I bite off.

"And apparently neither do you." He laughs darkly. "You think she's at home curled up in a ball? Hell no—that woman is at least sane enough to call her sister to tell her where she's partying for the rest of the night. And just for that attitude, do your own research to find her because she won't be alone long." Keene disconnects the call.

I let out a roaring "Fuck!" in the dark interior of the Jeep, right before I tell Siri, "Call OpsCenter-Work." My fingers tap impatiently on my steering wheel as I wait for the Hudson Investigations Operations Center to pick up.

"Good evening, Colby. Looking for someone?" Caleb voice answers. He sounds amused, which is only mildly less irritating than Keene's sanctimonious anger.

"Where did she go, Caleb?" I don't even bother beating around the bush. I want—no, I *need* to find Corinna. In part, so I can wrap my hands around her throat and squeeze it for putting me through this crap.

His laugh is so different from his best friend. "Pissed off Keene, did you? That's problematic as he's probably the only one who could have had the cover charge waived for you since he knows the owner. Unless you have a spare five C-notes sitting around?"

Five hundred dollars for a cover charge? I almost run my Jeep off the road. "What the hell kind of place requires that kind of cake to get in?" I demand.

"The kind that will allow Corinna Freeman to call up the owner and sashay her sweet ass in any night of the week she wants. A club called Redemption near the city. I'll see if I can pave the way for you to get in, but only because I'm worried about my sister-in-law."

What has she got into now, I wonder. I've never even heard of this club. "Can you send the information to my phone?"

"Sure. And Colby?" I hear Caleb typing in the background.

"Yeah?"

"Don't get shocked by anything you see inside Redemption. It's not your normal nightclub," he advises, right before he hangs up the phone.

Great. Turning my car in the direction of my apartment so I can get a dry shirt, I drop the gear and wonder what the hell he meant by that.

TWO HOURS LATER, I'm no longer wondering, and my gut is somewhere near the bottom of my dress shoes.

After following the directions Caleb sent to me, I pull up to an old warehouse on the outskirts of Manhattan in Fort Washington. If it weren't for the number of high-value vehicles in the lot or the obvious security presence, I'd have thought he'd sent me on a wild goose chase.

I make my way toward the VIP line, much to the whiny dismay of the multitude of people waiting impatiently in line. The bouncer gives me a head-to-toe look and asks, "Male, female, or both?"

Taken aback, I choke out, "Excuse me?"

He holds up two bracelets, one pink and one blue. "If you're here to pick up women, you wear a pink bracelet. If you're here for men, blue. If you don't care, you don't wear one."

I lean closer to the man who might, just might, be able to take me out. "What if I'm here for one woman?" I snarl.

He laughs in my face. "You still wear the bracelet, man. Otherwise, your ass might be a target for who knows what." His grin reveals more teeth capped in gold than not.

Snagging the pink rubber bracelet out of his hand, I hand him my ID. As he checks it against the tablet resting on the podium he was leaning against, I slip it over my wrist. Fuck, it's tighter than a cock ring. The tightness of the fit might cut off circulation later.

"And just for the record, I don't wanna have to come down and break up a fight. If the lady in question is already claimed..." He lets his words trail off.

"Oh, she's going to be claimed," I mutter, trying to adjust the stupid bracelet to give my wrist room to move. Looking at the behemoth guard, I state my intention. "By me. Just in time to spank her ass."

"We have stages for that if you want one. Just ask one of the serving staff." Quickly losing interest, the bouncer makes his way to the door.

Running my hand through my hair, I step inside the doors of Redemption's inner sanctum and freeze.

High-class sin. It exudes from everything in the club, from its patrons to the staff to the mostly naked acrobats dancing on platforms strategically placed around the room. My eyes glance off a woman in expensive black lingerie, bending in positions I didn't know were anatomically possible. Another scene I latch onto is that of a male duo, taking turns getting flogged. The waitstaff are wearing shoes that would cost me a month's salary, for Christ's sake. And the décor is so luxurious most people would need to sell a car to buy it. Fortunately, the gyrating bodies on the dance floor are mostly clad, though the way they're dancing leaves little to the imagination about what's on their mind. Those not dancing seem to be holding court lounge on chaises.

And I can't tell if anyone is wearing a damned bracelet.

I don't know if I just walked into a high-class club pandering to the über-wealthy, a sex show, or someone's fantasy. Either way, I'm surrounded by pulsating heat everywhere. It oozes from the air into my very pores.

Then the crowd on the dance floor parts just enough to see a swish of gold. I spot Corinna for a few seconds from my vantage point on the second floor. Her body sways to the thumping beat of the music before her partner leads her away from the crowd. The spotlight ripples off her dress as her hips sway back and forth.

Suddenly, I'm desperate to get down to her and get us both out of here.

24

CORINNA

"Thank you for letting me in tonight. I know it's been forever since we've talked," I yell above the thundering music pouring from hidden speakers inside Redemption.

Marco's answer is a wicked grin as he takes a swig from the bottled water in his hand. It's the first time we've stopped to talk since I sauntered onto the dance floor an hour ago. Marco took one look at my face and immediately led me there. I gulp down some water as well, because I'm scorching. On nights like this, Redemption seems to have been made for the needs pulsating through my veins. Mulberry crushed-velvet-lined walls tempered the sound from overly jacked-up speakers in the club. Crystal chandeliers are placed in lieu of a disco ball; the multicolored spotlights aimed at them jettison light into millions of different shapes and colors. Scantily clad bodies contort themselves into new positions in time with the throb of the music. This isn't just a club. It's pure elegance and raw sex.

With the world spinning out of control, I might need both of those things without any judgment.

Leaning forward to make myself heard, I ask him, "Why did we never work out?" I'm intrigued to know the answer. Enough years have passed since my affair with Marco that we've become friends and I can handle the response.

"Probably because you are far too independent, *ma chère amie*, for the things I need in a long-term companion." Marco turns his head slightly to tell me directly in my ear, "It also doesn't help when the woman you're trying to seduce is in love with another man." He shrugs his broad shoulders before turning his head away.

It suddenly clicks—the gentle letdown from the man in front of me. "Why didn't you say something?"

"How did you not know it yourself? How can you still not know? I am beginning to fear you love only once in this pathetic life," Marco murmurs, nuzzling my ear. It's too bad I don't feel anything close to what I do when Colby's merely standing in the same room.

Damn Colby, and right now, damn Marco.

"You talk as if you speak from experience," I counter, pulling away from the intimate embrace. That road between us is long past.

His entire countenance softens. "Maybe I do. It's hard when you're struck blind by the beauty of a woman, the complete acceptance you receive from her, and you can't find it with someone else." His remarkable obsidian eyes look into mine.

I guess Marco's remembering some femme fatale he met long ago, before he ever came to New York from Paris. I imagine she's as dramatic-looking as he is, with long sleek hair, pale skin, and perfect lips. I smile thinking of how perfect they would look together. Unlike Colby and me, who likely resemble a bat and a ball standing next to each other. "Yeah, babe, but that's what people who love you do."

Marco's lips twitch. "God knows, I tried often enough to get over you." My eyes bug out. *Me?* "But you are quite difficult to forget." He shrugs, as I stand there gaping like a fish. My mouth won't close. "I am content here. And I still get to enjoy your company on occasion because you are too generous not to be my friend, Cori." His lips tip in a soft smile.

I'm stunned speechless. Over the years, Marco gave me a place to just be...me. Cori. No worries. No responsibilities. No cares. Just me.

He reaches into his pocket and pulls out a handkerchief as he turns to face me fully. "Stop. There is no crying here at my club, Corinna. I built it to take all this troublesome worry away from any number of people." He frames my face with one hand. Wiping away the tears spilling over with his handkerchief, he continues. "That, and to take their money." I can't help but laugh. Leaning forward, he kisses me on the forehead. "Much better. My Corinna deserves nothing but happiness for all of her days."

I wrap my arms around him, oblivious to anything other than the music throbbing in my veins and the need pulsating in my soul to suck up every morsel of life while I can.

Stepping back and taking a deep breath, I reach for his hand. "Okay then. Make me happy. I want to get back out on your dance floor."

Laughing as he grabs my hand, he answers, "After you, *ma chère amie*. Do we require any special music?"

Grinning, my hips already swaying, I yell, "Maybe."

THE MAPLE-COLORED engineered hardwood floors are fabulous. Our shoes glide on them as our bodies fall into a natural synchronization with one another. All of my stress over Colby and my constant worry about the time bomb inside my head fades away as I shimmy on the dance floor.

Suddenly, I'm glad I wore my barely there, sexy gold velvet dress as a spotlight hits my dress and it changes into a million different hues. I raise my hands into my hair as I feel Marco press himself behind me. I'm laughing and breathless as a song by Jason Mraz ends.

"I love this place," I yell to Marco over my shoulder. He just tugs me farther into the center of the throng of moving bodies before the DJ cuts the music down.

"Welcome to Redemption! If you can't find it here, you can't find it anywhere." A huge roar goes up from the crowd. My grin must be splitting my face apart.

"I'm sure your waitstaff has told you how to send in requests to the booth. Send texts to DANCE or 32623 all night long, and I'll spin it for you." Damn, Marco didn't tell me about that new feature. I have a thousand songs I could have requested. The DJ goes on, and I stumble as his words penetrate. "I got a request a little while ago from one of the owners. Think you can keep up with him?"

Marco's breath brushes against my ear. "Ready to follow my lead?" With a dangerous smile, he brushes his lips over my shoulder.

"You suck at leading," I murmur back directly into his ear. His body starts to move against mine even as he gives the DJ a thumbs-up.

We're illuminated by a spotlight as the DJ says, "If that's Corinna with him, folks, I think we should clear the dance floor for this. It's going to be one hell of a show."

I toss my head back and laugh. "Who's in the booth?" The deep bass drops and pounds its way through the club, and we naturally sway against one another as the dance floor begins to clear.

Marco names one of his guys as he reaches down and spins me out so I'm facing the booth with the darkened windows. I snap off a quick wave before I'm expertly spun back into waiting arms. Suddenly the beat drops and Marco twirls me into a sharp turn as "Shape of You" comes on.

My body becomes liquid incandescence. An exaggerated hip roll, a pelvic thrust. My arm wrapped over my own body, beckoning as it slides between my breasts. A deep plié showing the length of my leg in my dress, twist, spin, reverse arch. My hands are continuously moving up and down the front of the soft velvet.

Heaven. Hell. Who cares? I'm redeemed.

Marco's my counterpoint. His muscles are only accented as the sweat pours off his body, making his dark shirt cling to him. He's got every female eye on him. His legs are showcased in his tight dress slacks as he squats in a pelvic thrust opposite me on the dance floor. I watch him drop his hands to his junk, and it takes everything in me not to break into laughter. I turn away from him, swinging my hips until my ass rests on top of the thin heels of my shoes before I sway back to standing.

I'm so caught up in the dance, I don't realize it's time for us to dance together until I feel him up against me. His sweaty shirt sticks against my exposed back as I toss my arm up and over my shoulder. There's nothing but seduction in our dance, and since we're us, we've been laughing at each other through the whole thing. Spinning around, I run my hand through his hair; he runs his over my back before twirling me out and back again. The song is starting to wind down when he says, "Trust me?"

"Yes." With everything but my heart. Unfortunately, that's been branded for someone who I'll end up devastating myself over. Again.

"Close your eyes."

I do, and my senses burst wide open. I feel Marco guiding the last steps to our song, his hands on top of mine running over the velvet on my dress. I feel a high letting myself out of my mind.

The song ends with me bent over Marco's arm, my leg hitched around his waist. I'm giggling, and I open my eyes with my head still upside down.

And I meet Colby's blazing eyes.

Suddenly, I'm dizzy for an entirely different reason.

One that might make me sick.

25

COLBY

I feel like I've been struck in the gut. Suddenly, the shoe is on the other foot. What she likely felt when confronted with Addison, I'm feeling ten times over. A hundred times.

And I hate it.

The man in front of me looks at Corinna much as I imagine I do —like he'd give her every star in the sky if he could. And she's oblivious to it. I stand up straighter as she pushes him aside to storm over to me on pencil-thin heels that should break under the force she puts on them. The man who held her so tightly in his arms just a few moments ago trails along behind her, a bemused smile on his face.

"What are you doing here, Colby?" Without giving me a chance to answer, she raises her hand as if that will ward me off from speaking. "No, wait. I don't care. Just leave."

It's then I notice she's not wearing a dorky bracelet like the one they forced on me at the door. I step forward into her personal space. "Where's your damned bracelet?" I ask menacingly.

She merely lifts a brow in response to what sounds like an asinine question.

"You know, one of these." I lift my wrist to show off the pink rubbery crap that's turning the skin around it purple. "Why aren't you wearing a blue one?"

Corinna smirks and somewhere the Devil is praying to God for help. "I'm so well-known here, Colby, I don't need one. In fact, if I want to do this..." She grabs a knockout redhead and pulls her close. "And this..." She then pulls the man she was dancing with near her. "No one here would think twice about it. Isn't that right, Marco?"

"*Chère*," the man behind her says, before murmuring a few words in French to the redhead. She smiles at them both before walking away. "And who is this?"

"Marco, may I introduce Colby Hunt. He works for Hudson with Caleb and Keene. Colby, Marco Houde, owner and proprietor of Redemption," Corinna bites out waspishly before turning her face away from me and into the man's shoulder.

"Ah, so he's the one..." Marco begins. Corinna's head snaps up.

"Shut up, Marco."

"I just wanted to know why I never had a chance, *chère*." Marco's distinctly amused at Corinna.

She pouts. "Just because we're only friends, doesn't mean I can't find someone else here."

He leans down and kisses her briefly. I turn vaguely murderous at the way her lips look against his. "You wouldn't because you know it would hurt me too deeply. Now go and work out whatever it is with your Mr. Hunt. I do not want bloodshed in my club."

"Fine," Corinna huffs. Glaring at me, she says, "Since you've ruined my night, you might as well take me home," before gliding off through the crowd.

Before I can follow her, I feel a tight grip on my arm. Following its path, I meet the eyes of Marco Houde. "Hurt her again, and I'll personally see to it you're left in the same condition."

I shake him off. "She sure inspires loyalty." I can't help the bitterness that seeps into my voice.

He drops a huge bomb in my lap as he shoves past me. "If it weren't for the ghost of you living in her, I'd have begged Corinna to marry me years ago."

Stunned and infuriated someone is as obsessed with her as me has me yelling, "She's not yours to worry about anymore!"

He pauses before turning around to get in my space. "She's not yours either, Mr. Hunt." Letting that sink into the lead already weighing down my stomach, his slow smile spreads. "Have a good evening." He motions to the redhead who was waiting for him before he disappears into the crowd, and I go in search of an infuriated Corinna.

I spot her in the lobby with the bouncer who slid the bracelet on my wrist earlier. Stomping over to me, she grabs my wrist and yanks it off. "Ow!" I think she took off some of my wrist hair with that little move.

"Jesus, and you were in the military?" Corinna sneers. Stomping back to the bouncer, she slaps the bracelet against his chest. "Get your kicks somewhere else, Louie. Stop tormenting all the new patrons, or Marco is going to have your nuts in a sling!"

I step closer, daring the golden dragon in front of me to turn her fire toward me instead of the bouncer. "You mean—the bracelet thing was a hoax?"

Corinna mutters, "If we're lucky, God gave you a sperm count to match your IQ—zero."

Louie grins, obviously relieved at being let off the hook. "Cori, get your fine ass outta here before you start any more trouble tonight."

Flicking her hand at him in acknowledgment, she storms off, expecting me to follow. Princess to the peasant. Maybe it's the lack of dress on that incredibly luscious body, but I can't help the stirrings in my cock. Jesus, even in a snit, she's fucking spectacular.

Before I can take a step, Louie stops me. "Sorry about that, man." He holds out a hand the size of a side of beef. Slapping mine into it, he grins. "I've only seen her this mad because of one guy. So long as you're not him, you should be safe. And hey, thanks for your service. My brother was in the Army. Made a good man outta him."

I shake Louie's hand and murmur my thanks before I set off after Corinna, because I know the truth. I am the man who drives her insane. The only man able to push her past all reasonable levels of sanity. Still, I smile at Louie before I walk out the club doors in search of a pissed-off princess who needs to get grounded in reality.

I manage to catch up to her by the time she makes it to my Jeep, the lone car in the lot that likely doesn't cost a damn year's salary to purchase. She's leaning up against the side, waiting as

I saunter up. "You realize there aren't any doors on my car, Corinna."

Raking me from head to toe with a hot look, she counters, "You realize since you decided to jack another thing up, namely your vehicle, I can't get into it without assistance." She gestures to her outfit. "I had a different sort of ride to get here."

Jealousy pounds deep. "Who is he to you?" We both know I'm referring to Marco Houde.

She turns her back to me as she says, "None of your damned business."

I spin her back around. "That dance just made it my business." Pushing her up against the hood of my car, I slide my hands over the silky smoothness of the velvet until my thumbs are just beneath her breasts. Her hands move up to my chest involuntarily. Both of our chests are heaving.

"Why?" she sneers. "You never wanted me, but no one else could either? Sorry, buddy, I had a life after you."

And just like that, the reminder of Corinna's past of a multitude of dalliances washes over me like a bucket of ice water. "Yeah, you did. Let's go." Moving my hands down to safer territory, I lift her into my Jeep before storming around the front.

Jumping in, I start the car and peel out of the lot.

How on earth did I think I could ever be friends with her?

Lunacy, that's how.

But I will support her through her upcoming ordeal. That I can promise.

～

I MAKE the regular hour drive from Fort Washington to Collyer in about forty minutes. I'm pushing the Jeep hard, much as the silence in the vehicle is pushing me. Turning onto the farm's main road, Corinna grabs the oh-shit handle, and not for the first time on the ride home. I drop the gear to slow down before the Jeep's loud engine wakes all of the residents.

Pulling up in front of Corinna's house, I start to unbuckle myself when she shoots me a death glare from eyes so dark, I can barely see the pupils. "Don't bother."

Slipping off her heels, she slides out of the Jeep before carefully picking her way across her stone driveway. My jaw locks and I grit my teeth as I see her move slowly over the stone. It isn't until I hear a hissed "Shit" that I jump out and follow her.

Shoes crunching on the stone, I reach her in a matter of seconds. I hook one arm around her waist and toss her over my shoulder. "Damn you, Colby! Put me down!" She doesn't bother to keep her voice down.

Without thinking, I smack my free hand against her ass. "Do you want to wake your family because you're being a spoiled brat?"

"Me? Me?" Her shrieking is getting louder, so I deliver another swat. It works only to lower her voice a fraction. "I wasn't the one who came in to something he didn't understand and ruined my night. That's all on you, buddy." Her voice is full of bitterness.

I slide her down my body and back her against her front door. "And what about you, Corinna? Huh? What about you?" The dam inside me bursts. "I was halfway in love with you and knew I couldn't do a damn thing about it. You were too wounded."

"Instead you and that bitch Addison decided to discuss my merits as well as my poundage while plunging me back into a nightmare you promised me you'd never put me in. Thanks for that, by the way. And what, you just like fucking that bitch so much you went back for seconds? Yeah, sounds like a perfect match. The chickenshit and the cunt. Maybe they should start a reality series after you two." Corinna's drawl is so thick with her anger I almost can't distinguish the words.

"Don't sit there and tell me you were an angel, princess. From what I heard from Jack"—I lean closer—"you were quick to get over your issues after I was out of the picture." My anger is vibrating off me. I'm angry at her for throwing away something so beautiful, something that after her past should have been cherished. Something that —right or wrong—I somehow thought might have been mine.

Corinna stills. "What are you accusing me of?"

I'm feeling so filled with wrath, I don't even know where it's coming from. "Too many men in your bed you don't even remember their names?"

"Are you saying..." She starts to back away from me, shaking her head in disbelief. "No, Colby. I know the names of every man I've ever slept with." She laughs, but I can hear her tears. "I'm just amazed that after Jack so thoroughly screwed you over that you'd still give credence to anything he's said. Especially about me."

Hesitantly, I reach out to touch her. "Corinna?"

"No. Just no. You don't get to stand there and accuse me of being some huge slut and then expect to comfort me. You get to hear the goddamned truth." Storming away from me, she walks a few steps away, but those steps are worse than a moat.

Shit.

"Four, Colby. Four men. Or is even that too much? The rest? God, after your precious Addison decided to make my life a living hell, I decided to try dating any guy who'd ask me out. Trying to fill the gap you left inside of me." Wrapping her arms around herself, she faces me. Mascara-streaked tears pour down her face. "I go out on a ton of dates. I've kissed a lot of guys, but you know what? Not one of them started to fill the space inside of me until I read those letters."

A warm feeling starts to grow inside me, right before she rips it from me.

"And then, Addison walks into dinner tonight and I'm forgotten again. How long did it take you to forget me? Seconds? How long did it take for you to remember me?" She shakes her head. "So I went to one of the few people who makes me feel beautiful just for being me. Just me. Do you know how glorious that is? Not being loved for being a Freeman, or the baker? Just because I'm me. And if you want the full truth, I was with Marco for years. He's a good man. I even contemplated introducing him to the family right before he broke things off with me. And after him, there's been no one else." Shuddering, she pushes past me to unlock her door. Leaning her head against the door, she says woodenly, "Now, go. There's nothing left of me for you to have."

My heart is somewhere under my shoes, being trampled on by my own misconceptions. There's no way Corinna's lying to me. Camouflage. It was all to hide the pain that's been buried so deep inside of her. And I was the fucking fool to believe Jack's lies and not her. "Corinna..." I try to form words.

She turns, and her eyes are a mixture of gold and brown. Typically, they descend to this color when she's ready to throw something. "No, there's one thing I want before you go."

"What's that?" I can barely squeeze the words out of a throat that's closed as tight as a clogged pipe.

"This." She reaches up and yanks my head down before slanting her lips over mine.

Incandescent. I feel like I'm being bathed in waves of pure gold energy as her sweet lips move over mine. I need more. Separating her lips with my tongue, I tilt my head, pull her head back, and take our kiss deeper.

This kiss has been over a decade in the making. I'm drowning in everything that is Corinna Freeman. Her scent, her taste, her light—it's everything I imagined it would be the first time our lips met. I tighten my arms to pull her closer, willing to go without air instead of losing her mouth.

Long minutes pass before Corinna shoves me away. "You can go now."

"I don't understand." Because I really don't. My body is vibrating with the absolute rightness of having her in my arms.

Corinna slips over the threshold with a mocking laugh. "For just a moment, I wanted to know what it would have been like if I was up to your standards. Now I do. I can die happy." Then she slams the door in my face.

I stare at the door knowing there's no way she'll open it up willingly.

I pound my fist against it in frustration with myself, before turning to head back to my Jeep. I'm so furious, I don't know what to do.

I just know that a life without Corinna in it isn't any kind of life at all.

I should know. I've been living it for the past ten years.

26

CORINNA

I'm in the kitchen of Amaryllis Events the next afternoon taking out my frustrations on a batch of cinnamon rolls we need for a bridal shower brunch, when the phone rings. Hands full of sticky dough, I elbow the button for the speaker. "Amaryllis Events. This is Corinna."

"Can you pull up your calendar?" Bryan's voice comes through the phone brusquely.

"Not at the moment. My hands are covered with—"

"I need to give you a list of dates, Corinna. Get whatever crap off your hands, find a calendar, and stop wasting time," Bryan barks.

Suddenly, I snap. I've had it. When did I suddenly become everyone's bitch and call girl? Oh, that's right. When my parents traded me in for some more heroin by selling me to a sex trafficking ring. This last week has pushed me to my limit. The tiara of peace I try to wear every day is blooming into a crown of despair.

Between finding out the tumor's grown and the hot and cold from Colby, I'm all over the place. My temper is constantly warring with my anxiety. Now Bryan wants to change the dynamic of our doctor–patient relationship just like that? Before I was a pressure cooker, where the steam was getting vented. Bryan's dismissiveness just broke off the safety valve, and I'm ready to blow.

I just can't deal with any more.

I raise my voice to be heard over his. "You know what, Bryan? Have your secretary call me back in an hour when I can talk. I'm working. I can't stop what I'm doing right now. If calling me back doesn't work, call this number." I rattle off Cassidy's direct line. "You have my permission to tell my sister who you are and what you want. Right now, I have to focus on my job. I can't do that and deal with you, this, or anything else." Even as he's starting to argue with me on the other end of the line, I hit the Off button with my elbow.

I snarl to my voice-activated speakers. "Volume seven." A hard drum beat matching my anger pulsates through the speakers. Nodding in approval, I head back over to the dough and land my next punch for all I'm worth.

I am so over people this week. Letting out a sound of disgust, I hope someone, anyone, dares to enter my kitchen. I could use some target practice.

How dare men—Bryan, Marco, Jack, goddamned fucking Colby —dare to decide what's best for me without asking me? Make a judgment about me? I may not have Ali's level of genius, but I have qualities that are just as important. I have a heart. I have a soul. And for right now, I have a fully functioning brain.

After setting the cloth over the dough to rise, I wash my hands. Reviewing the list of to-dos tacked up on the board next to the sink, I'm tapping my foot when the kitchen door opens. Phil peeks his head in and turns to someone behind him. "Oh, good. She's not holding knives."

Without saying a word, I move toward my built-in knife cabinetry. I reach into the drawer where I keep the finely honed blades and pull out my most wicked chef's knife. "That depends on who you're talking to," I threaten.

"It's just me, Cori. Lower your weapon." Cassidy breezes into my kitchen. Letting out a sigh of relief, I yell at my speakers to lower the volume, even as I slide the blade back into its slot. "Thank you. Now, do you want to tell me why your neurosurgeon called me a few minutes ago in a panic, thinking you're changing your mind about your surgery?"

Because maybe I am? The thought flits through my mind briefly. "I asked him to call you because like most men, present company excluded, Phil—"

"Though not normally, so don't get too big of a head," Cassidy interjects, punching Phil in the arm.

I nod, ceding her point. "Most men are complete fucking assholes. I have no patience to be dealing with an extraordinarily egotistical one."

"He was calling with your pre-op testing schedule, Cori," Cassidy rebukes gently. "It was important."

"All I tried to say was that I was up to my elbows in dough and it was a bad time to talk, Cass. I'm tired of being talked down to. Do people think the mass in my head makes me stupid?" I snap. "Why? Why is it so hard for people to understand I need some semblance of normalcy right now? As for it being important—don't you think I get it? After all these years, don't you think I get it?" By the time I'm done, the tears are wetting the burning fury heating my face.

Phil and Cassidy exchange a worried look. Suddenly, I feel sick. Is this what the end looks like for me? Anger and self-pity? No. I won't let it come to that—not to these people who gave me nothing but safety, happiness, and joy. At least they tried their best.

"If Bryan wouldn't talk with you, I'll call him back now," I say grudgingly.

Cassidy approaches me, inches shorter than me even in her heels. Wrapping her arms around me, she murmurs, "You don't have to, Cori. I got all of the information. It's on the family calendar." Stroking my back, she says, "Phil, if you don't mind?"

"Wait just a damn second. Maybe I can help," he argues.

"Do you have a penis?" she asks sweetly.

"A damn nice one, if I do say so myself. I'm sure Jason will happily confirm." Cassidy and I roll our eyes at him.

"If you have such a great one, then you probably don't want to be here when Cori vents her frustration against the male species. Actually, I'm sure of it. Unless you'd like nightmares, I suggest you get out," Cassidy encourages.

An evil grin crosses my face as Cassidy crosses to where I keep my cutting boards. Phil is frozen in horror. "No, that's not what's about to go on. Y'all are about to share some kind of gossip without me."

Cassidy turns to me and says, "Chef's knife bad or cleaver bad?"

I think back to Jack's debasement, to Bryan delivering the news of the increased size of the tumor, then to Marco telling me he broke things off because he realized I had feelings for another man. A man who was a ghost. And then Colby. The months of his being an irritant, making amends, running into Addison, and the scene last night at my front door. Without hesitation, I answer, "Both."

Cassidy goes into my knife drawer and hands me the first blade, a wicked cleaver I use when I'm cutting a pumpkin or experimenting with hard vegetables. I hold the perfectly weighted blade in my hand, wishing for a throwing board with every fiber of my being. I accept the equally diabolical chef's knife, sharpened enough I could run a man through.

Perfect.

"Be right back," Cassidy chirps before walking into my refrigerator.

Phil is still standing in place, jaw completely unhinged. He'd better step back or get out, lest he becomes a target of the results of my handiwork. I'm not handing out protective gear for this sideshow.

Cassidy comes out with an impressive assortment of fruits and vegetables, almost staggering under the weight of it. I'd offer to help, but I'm way too fascinated at my overly in-control sister handing me the keys to wreak havoc.

"Last chance, Phil," Cassidy tells him. Handing me a grapefruit, she says, "Think of this one as Phil's thick skull for not listening."

I don't even hesitate. I pick up the cleaver, and with a swift movement, I slam the blade down to slice it clean through.

Phil emits a choking sound.

"Again!" Cassidy demands. She shoves another grapefruit at me, and less than a second later, that one is divided in half. Cassidy promptly grabs a bowl and moves them away from the other fruit.

"Here, Cori. Phil won't leave. He's proven himself just as stupid as the others. What does he deserve for that?" In her hands is a ripe tomato. With a wicked smile at my sister, I switch knives. Not even looking at Phil, I bring the knife flat side down. Hard. Tomato chunks go flying in all directions at ludicrous speeds. I see some of it land on Cassidy, who just laughs in delight.

Phil, not so much.

"You're both fucking crazy! Do you know how much this shirt cost?" We turn our heads in Phil's direction as he pulls chunks of tomato off the lilac silk he's wearing. "Someone's replacing it."

Leaning forward, knife still in hand, I smile. It isn't pretty. "Don't say we didn't warn you."

Huffing, Phil turns and pushes the door open. "I'm just going to go see if there's something to change into in my office. If not, I'm going home." He strides through the door, which swings back and forth in his wake.

"You go home, I'm having Ali dock your pay!" Cassidy yells after him.

His middle finger coming through the door is his answer. Without hesitation, I grab some of the tomato still on my cutting board and hurl it at the door. It lands on his hand with unerring accuracy. Phil screeches like he's just been shot before yelling down the hallway, "They've both lost their minds! Don't go near the kitchen. I repeat, don't go near the kitchen!"

Cassidy and I fall on each other in a heap of laughter. Carefully, I place the knife on the counter. "If we're lucky, Holly never figured out how to wire this place up," I gasp.

Cassidy's doubled over. "She would have asked Caleb or Keene. No way that's happened yet."

"Sorry about your dress, Cass," I offer, but the smile I'm wearing contradicts that.

"The hell you are. And I'm not either." Her grin morphs into something serious. "Matt used to have me break plates."

"What?" I'm confused. What does our local coffee shop owner have to do with anything?

Shoving the still-edible food aside, she hops up on the cleanest part of the workstation. Gesturing for me to move closer, she wraps her arm around my shoulder. "I used to go see Matt for therapy, Cori. Remember he used to be a VA psychologist?" The lightbulb goes off in my head. Even as I nod, Cassidy continues. "For a long time before I met Caleb," she muses, "and a while after as well. When the pressure of everything got to be too much, he'd collect all the chipped cups from The Coffee Shop and let me hurl them at the brick wall in the back." She shrugs as if she hasn't rocked my world already by admitting she actively sought out help.

"So much has happened to you, Cori. Your foundation has been rocked by so many things. Things I would like to think we'd have been there for over the years. Thinking about it? I can't say we wouldn't have smothered you. You're too precious for us not to."

I snort. "You're the only ones who think so."

Cassidy's sad smile is like a vise around my heart. "I understand why you're feeling that way after this week, and I'm pretty certain I don't know everything. I'd be shocked if you weren't ready to explode. All I did was give you an outlet." Giving me a quick kiss on the cheek, she slides off the table. "Talk to us. It's better than wasting the food. Ali will have a conniption over the budget.

"And to that end, you'll notice I saved the grapefruits." She points at the two I cut in half. "They're next up on your to-do list for the brunch tomorrow. It's a fresh grapefruit cake." The grin that flashes across my face is because the move was pure Cassidy. Kill two birds with one stone, and keep on schedule while doing it.

"As for your doctor, I enjoyed smacking him down to reality for a few minutes." Crap, amidst traumatizing Phil, I forgot I'd given Bryan her number.

"I'm sorry, Cass. I just couldn't handle it anymore,"

"And that will be the last time you apologize for that." Her pouty lips lift in a broad smile. "When I explained who I was and that all future scheduling would come through me, he tried to give me a song and dance about HIPAA, unsigned paperwork, blah blah blah. I called Ali into my office. She explained two things. If you gave him the number to my private line, you were waiving your right to privacy. Second, scheduling typically occurs through assistants, not the surgeons themselves. He could have his call yours. De facto, that ends up being me or he could wait for a better time to speak with you. Ali just happened to have a sidebar with me about Caleb and Keene's personal donations to Greenwich while dear Dr. Moser was debating his options."

"And it didn't take long for him to decide to send the information you needed to your corporate email. Since I have access to it, it's already been loaded into your calendar," Ali says as she strides through the door. "Wow, Phil wasn't kidding. You sacrificed the shit out of some produce."

"It was one tomato. And funny enough, it was from my own lunch." My stomach growls in protest.

"Meh. Don't worry about that. We're bringing in Frances for lunch." Ali waves me off.

My ass does not need Frances, I think to myself. Or at least, I think I do until Ali smacks it. "Um, these jeans are falling off your ass. You can deal with some good ole Southern cooking. And you'll enjoy it."

"Only damn thing that place gave to us worth anything," I tease my sister, but Ali's already shaking her head.

"No, Cori. The thing the South gave us that's worth the most is each other. And we'll fight to the bitter end to keep it."

"Damn straight we will," Cassidy pipes in. "And I know I speak for the others when I say that too."

I take a deep breath. And then another. As my sisters crowd me, I heedlessly let the tears I've been holding in fall. "Damn, cutting grapefruit does it to me every time."

"I thought that was onions," Ali muses.

"Shh," Cassidy says as she hugs me. "Just go with it. Grapefruits can make you cry too."

27

CORINNA

I don't keep an office at the mansion because frankly, kitchens and electronics don't mix well. Cassidy prints out everything I need to know and tacks it up in my kitchen. Recipes are kept under lock and key on laminated sheets of paper in the same cupboard as my knives. If that's not a deterrent, I don't know what is. The only items I keep in there out of necessity are my mounted voice-activated speakers that operate my Spotify playlist, and the phone which sits in a corner.

As a result, it isn't until I'm at home that I get a chance to pull up my company email and calendar to see what was added to it by my efficient sister. Sitting with a glass of wine, I take a large mouthful before opening the message from Bryan.

To: Freeman, Corinna
From: Moser, Bryan MD
RE: Upcoming Appointments
Dear Miss Freeman,
Attached you will find the schedule of your upcoming appointments. I trust the dates and times are agreeable amidst your busy schedule. Should you have any difficulties, please contact Dr. Braddock's secretary, as I was forced to deal with yours earlier.
Cordially,

Dr. Moser.

I spew my wine everywhere. Men and their fragile egos. I hope it has nothing to do with their dick size, or Bryan's got to have some massive problems getting laid. I use the napkin I brought over with my wine to wipe off the screen of my laptop. Even though I know Cassidy's meticulously entered in my appointments, I want to get an idea of what I'm facing over the upcoming months.

Opening the attachment, I'm not surprised at my physical getting moved earlier. I make a mental note to switch primary care doctors eventually. I want no association with anyone or anything having to do with Jack O'Brien's practice. Continuing my perusal, I see blood work. Ugh, another series of MRIs, and one takes two hours? Now that my family knows, they can just drug my ass for those.

Then I pause. A psychologist? Why the hell do I need to talk with some quack? After Phil, Cass, and Em ensured Ali, Holly, and I weren't permanently scarred by what happened to us, I no longer felt the need to bare my soul to someone outside of my immediate family. What the hell are they trying to learn? Whether or not some mental deprivation caused my brain tumor?

Snagging my phone up, I quickly pound out a text to Bryan.

I just saw the schedule. Why on earth do I need to see some shrink to have you operate on my head?

The little dots move, pause, then finally his text comes through.

This is after regular business hours, Ms. Freeman. Please contact my secretary with any questions about your schedule.

And those two simple lines put me over the edge. *Five years of emotional support, and I'm supposed to trust my life to you because you get into a snit? What if there's a blade in your hand after we have a spat in pre-op?* I hit Send. I'm so done.

Furiously, I keep writing, ignoring the bubbles below my message. *Fine. Then I'll coordinate my cancelation of all procedures. If this is your attitude because of the one time in five years I couldn't drop everything to do something you wanted me to, well you and your magical hands can go whack off together.*

Hitting Send, I toss my phone aside. Shoving my computer off my lap, I grab my glass of wine and toast myself. "To you, Cori. To the end of your life, however long it is. Live it the way you want to."

Tipping the glass back to my lips, I guzzle the wine even as my phone buzzes next to me.

I ignore it. Instead, I get up and grab the bottle from the kitchen. Making my way up to my room, I decide it's as good a night as any for laundry.

"WHAT THE HELL do you mean you might not have the surgery?" Em explodes at me. I'm lying on her chaise, taking a break after having just dropped off the grapefruit cake and cinnamon buns for the bridal brunch.

Mugsy, her ancient rescue dog, whines at her tone, scooting back toward me. I shush him and rub his velvety soft ears. "You heard me. I'm not saying I'll never have the surgery." I shrug. "Just not with a doctor whose ego is as fragile as Wordsworth china, or whatever that blue and white crap is."

"It's Wedgewood. And you know all doctors have egos," Em counters.

I nod to acknowledge her point. "However, when you're used to a certain level of treatment from your doctor, and the dynamic changes in less than twelve hours because you didn't jump when they asked you to, you really need to consider if you're with the right surgeon." Tipping my head back, I whisper, "My life is going into his hands, Em. I have to trust him explicitly. If I can't, what happens?"

Em opens her mouth to argue and then closes it. "I have nothing to come back with. Absolutely nothing. You're right. If you're no longer comfortable with your doctor, and this isn't critical, then let's find someone else."

I roll to my side and curl into a ball facing my sister. "Exactly." Something else has been on my mind. "Em, would you say you, Holly, and I go on the same amount of dates?"

Em sits down across from me and grabs one of her sketchbooks.

"About that."

"Why is it that I'm the only one branded a slut?" It's not meant to insult my sisters. I'm trying to figure out the thoughts of others. The things Colby said are rancid in my gut. I still can't think of him without wanting to go back to my kitchen for more therapy.

Em lifts her head from her book before saying something odd. "You're the dream, Corinna."

I'm confused. "Excuse me?"

Resuming her drawing, she explains. "Holly's dates usually involve an intellectual meeting of the minds over some piece of art. She's friendly with all of her dates because there's no spark." She scratches against the paper continue while I wait. "My dates are all about the challenge. What will impress me enough..." Her voice trails off leaving what she wants to say unsaid, but I know how to finish the sentence. What will break through the ice around her heart?

Tucking both hands beneath my face now that Mugsy's lying down next to me, I ask, "Do you know what that is?"

"I wish I had a clue. Part of me wants the fairy tale we create day after day, yet the other part of me understands that's just for fools." I nod, understanding that perfectly. "But you, Cori? You're unapologetically sexy, outrageously funny, with a healthy dose of temper. You're basically every man's dream. Men get pissy when they can't have what they want, so they pout."

"And pouting devolves into bullying, badgering, and assumptions?" I demand.

She shrugs. "For the insecure ones, the ones whose dicks are too small to handle a woman as strong as you, certainly."

"I'm not that strong," I protest.

"Corinna, there are only five other people whose strength I would compare yours to, and we're related to all of them," Em says bluntly. Putting her sketchbook aside, she rests her arms on her upturned legs. "Now what, or should I ask who, brought this question on?"

Leaving nothing out, I tell Em about my night out, where I started out eating Mexican with Colby, running into Addison, ending up at Redemption, and the dance with Marco. When I get to the part of

Colby's accusations at my front door, I hear the hiss of breath she sucks between her teeth. "Now I'm left with another man alluding to me being a—"

"Don't you dare say it. First, because we both know it's not true. And second, even if it was, who are these righteous assholes to judge? Men who have slept with God only knows how many women before they come to us?" Em is bursting with anger. "It's okay for a man to sleep around but not a woman—not saying you have."

I pull a hand from under my cheek and wave her on.

"Right or wrong, personal decisions are just that—personal. The only moral compass you have to answer to is your own. Fuck 'em all." Em finishes her tirade. "Know what we should do tonight?"

"What?"

"Let's go back to Tide Pool. We'll force Jason and Caleb to drive. Keene too if he's not working," she decrees.

"Em, the last time we went to Tide Pool, we ended up lying on the bar while random guys did body shots off of us."

Her navy blue eyes flit away briefly before they come back to mine. "Precisely."

TIDE POOL, located on the outskirts of Collyer, is a complete dive. Jason and Caleb's protests are vociferous as we make our way over the uneven lot. "Keene's going to have our nuts for this, and I can't say I blame him," Caleb mutters.

"So, don't come with us," I tell him breezily.

"I prefer to lose my nuts over dying, Cori," he retorts. Turning to Jason, he demands, "What happened the last time you were here with them?"

Before Jason can open his mouth, we enter the dilapidated honky-tonk. My hands immediately go over my head, and my body begins swaying.

Jason sighs, coming up behind me. "Can you promise me no body shots this time?"

"Body shots?" Caleb's eyes are about to fall out. Tucking his wife closer, he asks, "Which one of you did body shots?" All of our hands, including Cassidy's, shoot up. He gapes down at his wife. "No fucking way."

Cassidy shrugs and points at Em. "Em dared me."

Em grins at Phil. "He started charging money, saying it was for charity."

Phil grins. "It was. The charity was our bar bill that night."

Ali's smile is lethal. "Remember the guy who…"

A chorus of "Oh yeahs" followed her lead-in. None of us will ever forget the man who had dreams of Holly's long red hair flying as she rode off on the back of his bike.

Caleb's looking at us like we're all certifiable. "And we're here why?"

I'll answer that one. "Because no man has a right to tell me—tell any of us—who and what we are. We're not victims. We're not doormats. And sure as shit, we're not sluts. So, stay or go, Caleb. But tonight is for family pride."

Em high-fives me. "Damn straight, sister. I'll get the tequila."

Caleb makes one last appeal to Ali. "Does Keene know where you are?"

She raises a brow. "When he finishes playing war games in his secure room and sees his phone, he will. After he gets over being pissed, he'll enjoy me this drunk. Our drunk sex gets outrageous."

"Eww. That's my brother." Cass shoves her.

"And boy, can he use his cock," Ali taunts her as they sit down around the large table. "Then again, you were there that first night."

"True. Speaking of which, you never told me…" And my two sisters are off and running.

Phil, who's dressed in a tight-fitting black T-shirt and jeans, merely says, "No one makes my girls feel less than what they are—strong and beautiful. One of us is hurting. Don't like how we fix it? There's the door. You can wait outside until the fighting starts."

"What fighting?" Caleb asks, signaling a harried waitress, who just flaps her hand at him.

"The minute all these douchebags finish texting their friends and this bar packs full of guys." Em stumbles past Phil and drops a full bottle of rotgut on the table with shakers of salt and limes.

Phil continues. "Maybe my sister will find one who won't call her a damn slut and I can sleep better at night."

I lean up to kiss my brother on the cheek. "If I die, I'll leave you my chocolate icing recipe."

Phil looks at Caleb. "Let me amend my statement. First, we're about to toast asshole doctors who have somehow convinced my sister not to immediately have a very necessary surgery. Then we're toasting all the dicks who have disparaged her this week. Stay, go, we don't care." He turns to Holly, who's meticulously pouring shots. "It's the worst tequila in the world. Who the hell cares if it gets on the table?"

Holly gives him a cheeky smile before tipping the bottle to her lips and taking a swig.

Jason picks up his phone and takes a photo.

Caleb pulls his out of his pocket before making a call. "Keene, you'd better get your ass to my location the minute you get Ali's text. I swear to God, there's no way I can control this shit alone. It's going to go bad tonight. Something happened and they're on a mission..."

Tuning Caleb out, we start the night with a toast that's all too perfect for us. "Fuck 'em all. Here's to us!" Our shot glasses clink as we lick, suck, and shoot as fast as we can.

One shot down. The whole night to go.

MY BACK ARCHES as the guy who just poured tequila in my belly button sucks it out. Holding up the lime to his mouth like a boxing coach, I give a war whoop. Holly, whose hair is intermingling with mine, is laughing. "Pay that guy over there." I wave vaguely in the direction of Phil. "It's all for charity."

"What charity is that, gorgeous?" The dark-haired biker leans toward my face.

I blink at him once, twice. "Ask my brother. He's handling the details."

"I'd rather ask you what you're doing later." Hmm. He's not bad-looking, and if I'm going to be pegged as a slut, I might as well have some fun with it.

"Later she's likely to have her head over the toilet at home, 'cause if she's not, her ass is going to be so red from being spanked it's not going to be funny." Funny. That sounds like Colby's voice...nah.

Still staring at the dark-haired stranger, I ask dreamily, "Did you mention spanking? I've never done that before."

"For fuck's sake, Corinna."

I frown. "How do you know my name? There're no names right now. I'm trying to forget who I am."

"Dude, if you don't get the hell away from my sister-in-law, there's going to be some major problems." Ah hell. Keene's here. Behind my head, I hear Holly mutter, "Shit. Playtime's over. Why'd Ali have to get with such a buzzkill? They're not even married yet."

"Dare you to say it."

"Let me borrow your orange Valentino heels sometime and you got a deal."

I shrug. I might be dead soon. She can have 'em. "Okay."

She takes a deep breath. "Keene, you're a damn killjoy! What are you doing here?"

His angry face softens when he realizes the two of us are sitting up on the bar. "Making sure my favorite sisters-in-law are safe."

Well, damn. That's sweet. Holly and I exchange glances. She shrugs. "Okay, but we were having fun."

"And Phil said it was for charity," I call back.

Keene's face darkens again before he spins around to confront Phil.

"Do you think he's mad at Phil? Hey, what charity was that for anyway?" I ask Holly, my words slurring together.

"Not so sure. S'long as it's one that helps out people like you. We had to help you tonight."

I shake my head. "Not worth helping, Hols. Didn't ya know? Just a low-class, fat slut. All the people think so." My nose itches, and my eyes start to burn.

"No! No drunk crying," Holly protests.

I sniff it back. "Fuck 'em all, Hols. We've got each other. I know—let's just get married. I know you love me. You won't call me fat or dumb, or complain if I work too late."

"Sounds perfect except for the sex."

"Vibrators!" I slap the bar beside me. "We'll be a new definition of sister wives!"

Holly cracks up.

"It's the perfect solution. See? Problem solved."

"In no way are your problems solved, Corinna," the rough voice next to me mutters. Hooking an arm around my waist, he separates me from my sister. No, wait—my sister wife—before hoisting me over his shoulder.

"Hols! Help me!" I screech.

"I hate to break it to you, Cori, but I don't think I can. Colby's got you pretty firmly in hand." Holly falls sideways on the bar before the dark-haired biker who had been standing there observing our antics rights her. Smiling up at him, she beams. "Thanks!"

"Some sister wife you are!" I yell back. Beating against Colby's muscular back, I screech, "Put me down!"

"Not until I have you out of here," Colby snarls.

Amid the confusion of Keene yelling at Phil, Ali yelling at Keene, and Phil yelling in general, no one else notices Colby making his way out the door with me. Frustrated, I resume taking my frustration out on Colby, hurling every insult I can at him as he makes his way across the parking lot. Finally, as he opens the door, I yell, "You are not the boss of me!"

Flipping me upright into the seat, he leans forward until his face is inches from mine. "The old boss was doing a shitty job. I just fired her. Now, let's see if you can avoid puking until we get you home." Stalking around to his side of the Jeep, he swings in before we peel out of the lot.

This is so not even close to the way I wanted this night to end.

28

COLBY

In the ten minutes it takes to get back to her house, Corinna questions my parentage back to the Stone Age, right up until one of her favorite boy-band songs comes on the radio. Then she starts belting it out like a champ.

I don't know whether to be pissed or laugh harder than I ever have in my life.

What on earth possessed the Freemans to go off half-cocked tonight, I have no idea, but seeing Corinna lying across the bar with her shirt pulled up, letting a random stranger suck tequila from her stomach didn't just set fire to my temper, it blew the whole thing up like an FGM-148 Javelin missile. I'm barely holding on to the small semblance of control I have when Corinna reaches over and jacks the volume up on my stereo. "Ohh, oh-oh!"

I use the controls on the steering wheel to turn down the volume. She reaches over, but before she can touch the knob, I grab her wrist.

"Jesus, what the fuck is wrong with the men I come into contact with these days? Why the hell do they have to try to control me? Just let me fucking be!" Her drawl is intermixed with her drunken slur, so understanding the words out of her mouth is a challenge.

"We're almost home, Corinna. Then you can put on whatever music you want," I try to reason with her.

"Yeah. The cows and I can get together and have a real barn burner. Get it?" She slaps her leg as if she's told the funniest joke ever. "Men. They're not worth the fucking trouble. Family, friends, lovers. They'll betray you in the end somehow." And then she starts to cry. Huge heaving sobs that I have no idea what to do with.

Shit, shit, shit. "Look, I'll turn the music back up."

Her head shakes as she curls into herself.

What the hell am I supposed to do? Grabbing my earpiece out of the console, I quickly dial Keene. "Want to tell me what the fuck happened tonight?"

"I was just about to call you and ask the same thing. Apparently, you did something to our girl to push her over the edge," Keene grates out. "Now I'm dealing with Alison riding my ass while Holly and Em are talking about marrying Corinna in a triad ceremony in my back seat."

"Give me the phone, Keene," I hear Ali demand.

"Not a chance in hell, baby," Keene growls. "Tell me, Hunt. What did you say to Corinna?"

"I can tell you that, Keene. He called her a slut. He's a douchebag, just like his best buddy, Jack. Only Jack added on she was a cow too. That's part of what sent my future wife over the edge!" Em yells drunkenly. "How the fuck is he any better though? That's what I want to know. How the fuck are any of you men any better? It's okay for you to bang anyone, but your woman has to be pure? Fuck that shit. They're our bodies. If I want a different cock every day of the week, then I should be able to have it."

"And he had no right to carry her out of that bar," Holly cries. "For once she felt beautiful. She's always beautiful, but she never believes it. We can never make her see it. I bet it's why she's talking about canceling the surgery."

"I'll bet you're right, Hols," Em agrees. "All because of fucking men."

"I'm glad I shot the assholes in my life."

"Me too, baby girl."

"Jesus, can you two keep the family secrets to, I don't know, the family?" Keene roars. Silence descends on the car. "Does that answer your question, Hunt? It sure as hell answers mine." He promptly hangs up on me.

Corinna's still crying, but her tears are quieter as we pull into her driveway. Turning off the Jeep, I race around to her side of the car. "Princess, where are your keys?"

She sniffles. "Purse."

I swing her up in my arms and carry her under the awning where she kissed me. Putting her back on her unstable feet, I pull open her purse and reach inside for her keys, then unlock the door and guide us both inside. She's still crying when I carry her upstairs to her bedroom. Wrenching away from me, she mutters, "I need a shower." She grabs a skimpy top and shorts from the couch and stomps off to the bathroom. Moments later, I hear the toilet flush and the shower start.

"You all right in there?" I yell out.

Her clothes being thrown out the door is my only response.

"I hope you'll forgive me one day, babe," I murmur, turning around the massive room, I spy a soft afghan casually tossed across the worn sofa. I touch the cashmere in electric pink, and it's like I've found the single object that represents Corinna: vibrant, soft, delicate, strong. My hand can't help but caress it as I whisper, "I'm so sorry, Cori. I never meant to hurt you. No matter what you believe." Even if it's not her, it's something tangible I can hold that represents her. Turning, I slam into a body, sending me sprawling onto the couch. I get tangled up in the throw, and her scent fills my brain, imprinting on my soul.

It will never get out now.

Corinna's standing there with her wet hair dripping down her back, her face vulnerable. "How could you not mean to hurt me, Colby? The things you said..."

I cut her off. "Came from a place of jealous rage. How could I fault you for being who you are when that's what I need in my life?"

She steps back. "Don't. Please don't. I'm too vulnerable, and you..." She presses her hand into her stomach.

I shove to my feet and step closer to her, lifting my finger to her cheek. "I what?"

"With nothing but words, you made me laugh, and you made me believe in myself when there was damned little to believe in. Then you destroyed me." She turns her back to me. Her new ink taunts me. Involuntarily, I reach out to trace it, but she jerks away. "I'll never forget who I am ever again because of you. Don't start anything with me, including friendship, unless you plan to be here regardless of whatever happens. Because, I may not be perfect, but I deserve every-thing. And you can go to hell right now if you don't think I do."

I clasp her shoulder and turn her around to face me. "I just have one question."

Her face takes on a wary cast. "Okay. Ask it."

I slide my hand through her wet hair to the nape of her neck and pull her close. "Is there room on the couch for both of us? I don't think tonight's the night for us to try sleeping in a bed for the first time together."

When the single tear slides down her freshly scrubbed face, I murmur, "We'll talk more after we get some sleep."

She sighs and relents. "Tonight, I'll let you back in. I can't guar-antee tomorrow, but tonight..." Right before she face-plants into my chest, her arms wrapping around my waist.

After Corinna's settled with her back to my front on the couch in her room, my mind wanders back to the nights she let me hold her like this, before I screwed us six different ways from Sunday. The lights entwined on the overhead beams cast a soft glow on her face. I can't sleep. I don't want to. Keene's words are replaying in my mind.

How can the woman I'm holding in my arms be ready to give in? Somehow, I've got to find the scrappy fighter willing to do anything to survive, and encourage her to come out swinging.

～

I CAN TELL by the light streaming through the window that it's late. A quick glance at my watch shows it's after ten. Most importantly, Corinna's no longer in my arms.

Shit.

Sitting up, I toss the afghan we'd wrapped ourselves in aside and scrub my face roughly. Why didn't she wake me? Getting to my feet, I stalk to the door to see if she's still here when I hear her voice behind me. "Are you always this get-up-and-go in the mornings?"

One hand still on the doorknob, I turn my head and see Corinna standing in her bathroom door with a toothbrush still in its packet. "Catch." She tosses it to me.

I cross the room in a few long strides. Corinna tips her head back to look at me. She looks good, like she got a full night's sleep, but her smile is tentative. "Hmm, let me see." I grab the toothbrush and grin. "Safety 1st Oral Care?"

Shrugging her own smile widens. "It was better than nothing. And morning breath sucks."

"True," I agree. I slide my arm around her waist. "Then again, I could have just used yours."

Corinna scrunches her nose. "Eww. Seriously? You do remember what I was drinking last night."

"Held it down like a champ too."

"That's because nothing can compare to the shit Phil used to try to make us practice on for learning how to give blow jobs." Corinna's hands come up and cover her mouth. "Crap, I wasn't supposed to ever say anything."

I sputter. "No freaking way."

Eyes sparkling with mirth, she nods.

"Do I want to know how you learned how to kiss?"

She rolls her eyes. "I was a virgin when we met, Colby. I wasn't a novice."

A growl rumbles up from the center of my chest. "Corinna?"

Laughter fills her voice when she replies with "Yes?"

"Will you please let me by to clean up before I find out if you're repulsed by morning breath or not?"

Just as I'm about to close the door, she says, "Colby?"

I lean with one arm against the jamb. "Yeah?"

She reaches up and touches one side of my cheek before kissing the other. "Thanks for the best sleep I've had since...well, you know how long it's been." Pulling away, she says, "I'll be in the kitchen getting coffee."

I can't help but watch her walk out the door, and pray we've turned some kind of corner by my shutting my mouth for once and just listening.

I MAKE my way down to Corinna's kitchen a little while later. Immediately, I'm assaulted by scents I've dreamed about: rich coffee, creamy caramel, and pancakes. "I've died. Somewhere I'm lying in the middle of a desert daydreaming again." I moan, announcing my presence.

She shakes her head, but I can't help but catch the smile flitting about her lips.

"You think I'm kidding, but if you saw what I had to eat on a regular basis, you wouldn't think I was kidding."

"Saw it? Keene made us try an MRE. I don't know how y'all don't come home and start gorging on food as fast as possible to make up for the punishment of what the Army feeds you."

I take my first sip of coffee—the Corinna special, filled with homemade caramel sauce and heavy cream—and sigh. Then her words penetrate. "Wait, Keene made you try an MRE?"

"Isn't that what they feed you guys? A bag of that crap?"

"That's what they feed you when you're in a life-or-death situation. Most of the time there's some type of a mess hall if you're stationed on a base," I explain.

"Keene's going to be in a life-or-death situation again for making me eat that shit." I grin, imagining the creative ways she'll use to get back at Ali's significant other. "I do have one question though."

In the middle of swallowing another sip of coffee that poets would write sonnets about, I wave my hand.

"Why does all the meat taste like tuna? I mean, do they have special chemists in the military that chemically alter chicken?" After I finish snickering, she places a stack of perfectly golden, fluffy pancakes in front of me. "Taste that and tell me what you think."

I put my cup on the counter and swallow hard. My hand wants so desperately to reach for the fork and to shovel the food into my mouth, but there's something I have to do first.

And she has to be sober and awake to hear it.

"Cori." Her head whips up to mine. "I know. That name's no longer mine to use, except it's Cori I need to apologize to. I hurt her when I never meant to. I need to give peace of mind to her, and if I have to piss off the woman she became to do that, I will." Standing, I move closer to her so I can lay my fingers on her heart. It's pounding beneath my touch. "I want you to know I heard you the other night. More importantly, I heard you last night. And I realized something."

"What's that?" Corinna's face is pale, and she eyes me warily.

"I owe you an apology for the present too. Your sister said something last night that struck me hard."

"Considering how drunk we were, I'm surprised. Which one?"

"Emily. She said it's your life and your body and your right to live your life as you choose. And she's right. Who am I to judge your life?" I shake my head. "No one. Even if any of it were true, the words I lashed out at you still stem from nothing other than what I said last night. I'm jealous. I'm jealous of any man whose had the chance to win this magnificent heart of yours."

Corinna tries to shove away. "Sure you are."

My other arm bands around her waist. She looks at me like a skittish kitten, not the sultry feline she so often resembles. "You give of yourself constantly. You run yourself ragged trying to be everything to everyone. You feel you owe the world for the life you've already paid the dues for. You read what I wrote to you. When are you going to understand you're everything just for being you?"

"When I can take in a breath in my darkness and know down to my soul that I'm not someone's pain, but their cure," Corinna replies. "That's when I'll know."

Wrenching out of my arms, she picks up her coffee, leaving me reeling from her words. "Is that how you see yourself?"

Taking a sip, she shrugs.

Tell her, my inner voice says. *Tell her all the things she doesn't know.* "No one is perfect, Corinna. There are dark parts to everyone's past." Including mine.

Sighing, she gestures to my pancakes. "You had better eat, Colby. Those are a spin-off of Chef Eric Greenspan's lemon ricotta pancakes. And if you're planning on telling me about your family, you'll probably want a full stomach." She mutters as an aside, "I know I would."

I'm frozen in place. "How do you know?" I wanted—no, I needed —to be the one to tell her.

"Let's just say, Addison was all too informative about her boyfriend after you graduated." Bitterness seeps into her words.

"I never told Addison either, Corinna. And let's be clear, I wasn't her boyfriend."

Ignoring me, she continues. "Then you're not the son of Brett Hunt of Hunt Enterprises. Your family business isn't worth billions?" she drawls. Turning her back to me, she stomps into the adjoining family room and picks up a familiar box. "Bet your daddy would just love it had these actually made it into my hands, Colby. Because damn you, I did read them. And I felt every word on every page straight in my heart. And I knew there could be nothing more between us but friendship because of who you are. More importantly, because of who I can never forget I am. Where I came from. What happened to me. What's going to happen to me."

"Would it help you to know I haven't spoken to them since the day my father hit me when I decided to join the Army?" The words come out so calmly, I surprise even myself. "He dislocated my shoulder the summer between my senior year of high school and my freshman year of college, shoving me into a wall because I refused to fall in line to just make the guns to kill people instead of heading out into the Jawa to serve with them. He almost cost me my ROTC scholarship, which I think was his point. I haven't spoken to my family since." The silence following that announcement is deafening.

Throwing out my self-preservation, I stalk to where she's holding the box, trembling, and give her my truth. It's time. "I don't hold regret about the lives I've taken or the life I've led. I can count on one hand the things I regret." I hold up my first finger. "One. My grandfather hasn't contacted me since I left home. God only knows what the old bastard thinks, and despite everything, I did love him. Two." I flick up another finger. "Letting you slip away when I knew damn well it was something I could fix. And finally"—I throw up the third finger—"not fighting hard enough to get through to you when I got back. Everything else will end up being a left-handed monkey wrench."

"What's that?" she asks cautiously.

"Something that doesn't exist. Why hold on to the regrets that mean nothing? Life's too precious."

Corinna drops the box at her feet. Letters fly everywhere, but she pays them no mind as she launches herself at me. I clutch her close, knowing how priceless this moment is. Knowing for so many reasons it almost didn't happen. Burying my head in her neck, I breathe in her intoxicating scent. It's sweeter than the coffee I just drank, more addicting than nachos, and more necessary than air. It's just Corinna.

I don't want to break the mood, but my stomach has other ideas. It growls noisily in the quiet room. Corinna's body shakes from the shelter within my arms. "It's not that funny. Do you even remember last night?"

"Of course I do! I wonder if it's poor form not to invite my sister wives over for breakfast?" Her voice is laced with mirth, and her face is lit with humor. "Before I worry about them, let's get you fed first."

"Best offer I've had in a long time, princess." I rub my chin against her head as we make our way back into her kitchen.

29

CORINNA

It's so familiar, and so new at the same time. I'm standing at the griddle frying up fresh pancakes, as Colby stands next to me playing with my hair like he used to do when I'd be cooking in my tiny off-campus apartment at college.

We wasted years on assumptions we have no one else to blame but ourselves for. Regardless of my missing what are now very obvious signs of Colby's interest in me then, I was in no way ready for the man he was becoming. And it's time to stop punishing him for having had a life in between.

"You know we're going to have to talk about it," I say diplomatically. Really, diplomacy's not my strong suit, so if anything should put Colby on high alert, that should.

I'm not surprised when his hand stills and he asks warily, "Talk about what?"

Turning to face him, I say dramatically, "Everything." Much more my style. But my lips can't stop twitching even as I flip the fresh stack of lemon ricotta pancakes onto a plate.

"'Everything's' a lot of ground to cover, princess." Taking the plate I hold out to him, he stands right next to me while I pour two more circles on the griddle. As the pancakes start to bubble, I glance at Colby. His face is filled with a mix of emotions.

"Colby, we have to talk about the hard stuff. If we don't, our chance for a reconciliation of any sort is doomed before it has a chance," I say softly.

"Expert relationship advice from a woman who tried to marry her sisters last night?" he says sarcastically.

"No, expert relationship advice from someone who watched two of her older sisters almost lose their soul mates before all their truths came out." I flip the pancakes over. "If we're nothing more than friends, then so be it. That's the path life chose for us. What I won't have is doubt causing us ever to question each other." His full lips part slightly at my words. Pulling back the plate from his hands, I slide the last two on top before walking over to the counter where warmed syrup, blueberries, and raspberries are waiting. Gesturing for him to sit, I continue. "We weren't saints. We aren't perfect. We're two people who refuse to let others win because they lied, and we didn't. So, we'll clear the air of the pain so no one will have a chance to come at us blind again."

"You really want to hear about other women?" he questions as he slides pancakes onto his plate. He reaches for the bowl of berries.

"About as much as you want to hear about other men," I fire back. "But would you rather hear about them from me or from someone else?" I take the remaining two pancakes before reaching for the syrup.

Colby pauses in the act of dumping half the berries on top of his dish. Quickly, I snag the bowl from his unresisting hands. "Hey! I wasn't done," he protests.

I raise my eyebrow. "Use some syrup, buddy. I want some fruit."

Grumbling, he pours the remainder of the maple syrup on top of his stack of pancakes, drowning them. It's good to see some things haven't changed. Colby still prefers to have a little pancake with his syrup whereas I want just enough to keep my pancakes soft until the last bite.

Forking the first bite into his mouth, he moans. "Sweet Jesus. These are fantastic."

I nod as I take a bite of my own.

Colby's fork clinks against the plate as he goes for another bite. He shovels it in, chews, swallows, and nabs another before he responds to my question. "You're right. I'd rather just know we both have a past and leave it where it belongs, but if the other night is any indication..."

I point my fork at him. "Exactly. And there's really only one I give a shit about anyway because, frankly, she made my life a living hell."

He sighs. "Addison." He reaches for his coffee and notices it's empty. Getting up for a refill, he adds cream and sits back down. Taking a sip, he frowns. "Why does it always taste better when you make it?"

I smirk. "There's no way in hell I'm answering that."

His leg brushes mine under the counter. "Maybe I'll just take yours." He reaches for my cup, but I slap at his hand. He just laughs.

"Give me your cup, you pathetic man." I get up and get the jar of salted caramel near the coffeepot. I drizzle in just enough to satisfy Colby's sweet tooth, then stir rapidly. This is why I prefer to melt it in with the cream before the coffee is poured. I have fewer chances of it clinging to the bottom of the mug. "Here." I hold the mug in his general direction.

Taking, he quickly takes a sip. "I want a jar of that for the office."

I snort. "Fat chance."

"Oh, come on, Corinna. I have to work with Keene all day." I give Colby a stern look, but inside I'm giggling because the idea of working with Keene sounds completely horrific. "I had to hide the brownies you gave me the other day."

I tilt my head. "Where did you hide them?"

"In the safe in my office. Why?"

I hate to break his heart. "They won't be there Monday."

Colby stills. "Why?" His voice is laced with menace.

"You're in Keene's old office, Colby. He practically built the Norwalk office while Ali was pregnant because he didn't want to be commuting to New York. Unless you changed the code on the safe, I guarantee those brownies are gone," I say with absolute certainty.

The look on his face is priceless, his muted roar more so. "I am going to use his own weapon to kill him. Ali really isn't in love with him, is she? Why the hell didn't someone tell me? This is such bullshit."

I'm wiping the tears of laughter from my eyes, I'm laughing so hard at his rant.

"You know what this means, don't you?" Silvery-gray eyes bore a hole into mine.

"Oh no. I bake when I want to or if I'm being paid." A puppy-dog look transforms his face. "Think about it this way, you're getting this for breakfast, whereas I know Ali is likely out for a run."

Colby doesn't even think about it. His "Yeah" is filled with menacing relish and lets me know Keene will be hearing all about this. Which means Ali will. Which means the family will.

I shrug any and all privacy goodbye.

"Can I bring this conversation back around to what we were talking about?" I take a sip of coffee.

Colby nods. "Honesty."

"Both Caleb and Keene hid things from Cassidy and Ali, Colby. Whatever we are, I'll have none of that. Especially after this week." My face falls.

Colby stands abruptly. "Are you finished?" He gestures to my mostly eaten plate.

I nod.

"Let's take our coffee outside and get some air. I don't want to bring the past in here."

Mentally agreeing, because I want Addison Kaplan in my house about as much as I want to contemplate having brain surgery, I leave my coffee on the counter long enough to slide on a pair of Chucks that were discarded in the entry. Colby grabs his coffee and then takes my hand. We make our way to the span of doors lining my living room.

Amazing how different this is from the last time we walked this same path a few days ago. Leaving the inside of my house, we reach the back deck and make ourselves comfortable on loungers overlooking the field of wildflowers.

Just as my anxiety begins to creep in, Colby asks me, "How do we start?" His voice holds the same wary concern I feel coursing through my veins.

I reach for my coffee but instead find my hand captured. Colby squeezes it before he caresses my fingers. "Talk with me, Cori." My eyes flash up at him, ready to protest the use of my nickname, but the protest falls before I can voice it.

But it also causes a crack in the dam of emotion I've been holding back.

"Why her, Colby? Why Addison?" It's the question that feels so good to get out. Long before she ever slept with Colby, she despised me. I still have no idea why.

"Because she's the complete opposite of you in every way possible." His answer is immediate.

That stings deep. "She's insanely beautiful," I state coolly as I try to pull my hand away.

"She's a bitch. And if you think I can't see that, you're crazy." His voice is calm. "Stop trying to pull away."

"So, because she's a bitch you slept with her not once but twice? How does that make any sort of sense?" I ask incredulously.

He shakes his head back and forth. "I fucked her both times because I couldn't have you and she was available. I fucked her to get you out of my mind. The first time, I was trying to protect you from something I now realize, in hindsight, I should have given you a choice on. I assumed you were broken, unable to handle what I wanted from you."

I nod to acknowledge his statement. "Okay, fine. I don't know what I would have done in college. But you have no idea..." My voice trails off.

His gray eyes narrow. "We'll get around to talking about what she did to you after I left later. But the second time? The time she brought up the other night?" I feel the slice in my heart again, but Colby wasn't mine. He isn't mine now. I suppress my urge to rage. "I had just written the last letter to you. I had no idea you weren't receiving them, Cori. I thought you just didn't give a damn." Letting my hand go, he slides his hand up to my face and cups my chin. "And I'm not going to lie, I was looking for a way to dull the pain. I found it in a shitload of booze and a woman."

I feel the loss of his hand when he pulls it away and sits back in his lounger. "I'm not proud of myself to admit both times I used Addison to forget it was your face I craved, your body I wanted, and your heart I needed. It always was. I'm beginning to wonder if it always will be." His head turns toward me to gauge my reaction.

My breath noticeably hitches. After all these years, it seems there was very little to heal between Colby and me. Every wall I've built up over the years to protect myself about the man sitting next to me starts to crumble.

Then he obliterates them.

Standing up from the lounger, he pulls me to my feet and begins to unbutton the wrinkled dress shirt he's been wearing since last night. I suck in a breath when I catch my first glimpse of boxed abs and let it out when he shrugs it off. I can see where they put his shoulder back together.

My fingers are raised over the puckered scars where the bullets entered his body. "Colby." The acknowledgment of the pain he'd endured is echoed in my voice.

He grabs my fingers and brings them to his lips. "We'll talk about that later. That's not what I want to show you." He takes my hand and slides it down his muscular arm until it rests on his forearm, giving it a squeeze.

My hand lifts, and I almost stumble back over the lounger. Colby's other arm comes around me to balance me.

It's a tattoo of a key ring with everyday keys on it. Two things about it make it extraordinary: the Husky key chain, and the words Never Forget in block text beneath. I immediately recognize the key chain. It's the one I left on the floor of his room the last night I was there. This ink isn't new. The ink is faded. It's got scars running through it.

My chest hurts with the need to release the pain. I keep tracing the tattoo with my fingers. My voice is choked when I ask, "When?"

"About six months after I graduated. It was a reminder to me not to let anyone else fade away the way you did." His head is lowered, his breath wafting over my face. I tip my head back and am captured by the look in his eyes. He pulls his arm away from my fingers so he can thread his through my hair. "I could never forget you, Cori. No matter where I was or who I was with. You were imprinted in my skin, not to mention my heart and soul." He brushes his nose against mine.

I stretch up a little bit. "Colby." His name comes out as a breathless moan.

"I'm sorry, princess. I should have tried harder to make you understand, then and now." His lips brush against mine as the words he says close up the wounds I've been suffering with since I was eighteen. "I can't and I won't apologize for the years in between because I just didn't understand."

"I won't either," I warn him breathlessly as his lips wander aimlessly around my face, the column of my neck.

"Then tell me this," he says, tightening his grip on my hair.

"What?"

"Why are we talking?" He crushes his lips against mine, and I lose myself in his kiss.

As our lips learn each other's taste for the right reasons, as our tongues entwine like the bands around my heart do, I lean my weight farther into him and surrender. My mind begins to fade to nothing except his kiss, but I have one last tangible thought.

Time. Do we need time to heal us, or do we just need each other?

30

COLBY

Salvation.

That's what this kiss is.

When I was overseas, I absorbed a great deal about different cultures. Buddha believed he was born into the world to be the king of truth, the salvation of the world. Hate to break it to him, but the person who was born into the world to be my salvation, my moral compass of right and wrong, has her arms around my neck, her lips parted against mine, and tastes like everything I ever dreamed of.

Incandescent light, sweet temptation, fiery passion.

I never want to let her go.

I moan into her mouth as her hands trail down my back, her nails scraping along the way. I deepen our kiss, letting my hands roam her body. I rest them on her rib cage under the fullness of her breasts. Her answering sigh lets me know she's with me.

I don't just have salvation; I'm holding a miracle.

Breaking my lips away, I bury them in the crook of her neck. "Cori," I murmur.

"Yes?" she purrs. I want to roll my eyes back in my head. That Southern accent goes straight to my cock as always.

"Princess, we still have to finish talking." I want nothing more than to spend the day running my mouth over Cori's curves, but we have so much more to discuss.

Pulling back slightly, she narrows her eyes at me. "That's less enjoyable than what we were doing just now."

Dropping a quick kiss on her lips, I pull back slightly to admire the pout forming on her swollen lips. "Agree with you a hundred percent. But baby, I want to know what your sisters were referring to last night." Sitting down in the lounger, I spread my legs over the sides to make room in between. "Sit back down and let's talk."

Eying me warily, she says, "I'm not having a foursome with my sisters and you, Colby. Our sister wives' pact involved us and vibrators."

I chuckle. "Wouldn't have even thought it. Please, Cori." I pat the spot between my legs again. "Just come and talk with me."

After nodding, she arranges herself between my legs, muttering, "I hope the chair doesn't collapse with my added weight."

I don't even think. I pinch her ass.

"Jesus, Colby." She swivels around and glares at me. "That hurt."

"I swear if you bash your curves in front of me, I'm either going to slap or pinch that magnificent ass. If you knew how many times I've dreamt of taking you from behind..." My voice trails off. I focus in on her again to find her glassy-eyed. "Are we understood?"

"That was you who mentioned spanking last night?" Her voice sounds dreamy.

"Sure as hell wasn't that asshole doing tequila shots off your stomach. Which, if I have my way, will never happen again," I growl.

I expect immediate acceptance in the wake of that kiss. Instead, I get a mild "Hmm, we'll see."

"Excuse me?" I'm irrational. I know it. We've just shared our first real kiss, but we're already so much more.

Corinna lays her head back on my shoulder. "If I unilaterally agree to what you're saying, then how are you going to have the choice of doing that in the future? So—" She shrugs impishly, making my cock get harder against her ass. "—we'll see."

I shake my head, even as a smile teases my lips. The difference between Corinna then and now is astounding. Back then, she may have had these thoughts, but they would never have left her lips. Now, the sexual innuendos are a delicious addition to her already dynamic personality.

I brush my lips over her forehead and wrap my arms around her to hold her close. My chin rests on her head as we sit for a moment, observing the breeze move the wildflowers back and forth. I bring us back around to the question burning in my gut. "What were Em and Holly talking about last night? You're not having the surgery?"

Her body stiffens. "Shit." She tries to pull away, but I don't let her.

"Talk to me, Corinna. I'm not judging." Yet. "I want to understand where your mind is."

"I need to move for this conversation," she requests quietly. I immediately open my arms, and she flies out of them faster than a bat flying out of hell.

Something's not right.

Corinna immediately begins pacing around the deck, frustration in her every movement. I sit quietly, a testament to my willpower, as I want to scoop her into my arms and get her to the nearest doctor to remove the one final barrier that could prevent me from having a lifetime to explore the feelings I have for her.

But it's not my choice. It's not my life. It's hers.

Finally, she begins talking. "There's no pain, Colby. I had a small episode that was a sign the tumor grew. Frankly, I've been in too much shock to think about it logically. Not that logic has been my strong suit." The wry look she sends me is an acknowledgment of her part of the breakdown of us years ago.

I nod, unwilling to interrupt but willing her to continue. She does. "I want to make certain I have the best medical care possible. When I was hiding this"—she faces me head-on—"I was limited in the doctors I could work with. Until this week, I never would have doubted my surgeon was anyone but the best. Now..."

"What happened this week?"

As Corinna recounts the relationship she's enjoyed with her doctor and the newfound pettiness he's engaged her in, I'm infuriated. Frankly, I don't blame her for second-guessing her medical team. This isn't a mole removal; it is a craniotomy. She has to have full faith and confidence not only in her surgeon, but the nurses, anesthesiologists, the hospital—everyone involved with the procedure from scrubbing her down to feeding her afterward.

Corinna sits down again, having spent most of her energy. "Maybe I'm tired of feeling like a fool for believing in someone so wholeheartedly, but no one else knew but my primary care. Who, by the way, is a part of Jack's practice. Did they make the best choice for me, or were they influenced? I can't trust anything after the other night," she ends bitterly.

I make a mental note to find out everything I can about my former friend, from his outstanding debt to his favorite brand of underwear, so I can make his life a living hell. I open my arms, and Corinna moves into them. "You haven't explained this to the family like this, have you?" I ask quietly.

She shakes her head against my chest. "Just Em, and well, you saw how that ended up last night." She tips her head back with a small smile.

Now, so much makes sense. While they've always had a now-or-never attitude, the Freemans were reacting to thinking Corinna was giving up. She isn't. She's trying to regroup in the wake of some pretty severe blows. "It might be possible this Moser guy is a dick, but is still the best choice of a surgeon. You just want the choice to find out."

Corinna nods. "I'm about to give someone my life, Colby. Can they give it back to me? Will I be able to drive a car again? Bake again? Make love again? Eat again? Smile again? Breathe again?" Her face crumbles. "I understand no one's guaranteed a tomorrow, but I need to know I have a chance."

The strength of the woman lying on me is equally humbling and staggering. And to have held this in for so long? "How did you feel when you first found out, Cori?"

She begins to laugh. "I was so pissed. I blamed you, unjustly."

"Is it my fault?" Sorrow and regret lace my words. I have no idea how all of this works. Maybe something I did caused this.

Corinna pushes up on my body until her face is even with mine. Her long, thick hair curtains both of us. I'm trapped, surrounded, and I never want to be rescued. I reach up to touch her face and wince. "Colby, you fucked up. I fucked up. You didn't cause the tumor. Yes, I found out that night that I had one, but in retrospect that's one good thing. It gave them time to monitor it and establish a plan of care. They suspect I had it since birth; it's that slow growing. That's a good thing." Taking a deep breath, she admits, "It was my own foolishness in not telling the family. I thought I was protecting them. The reality was, I was just holding on to my own resentment about the tumor, about you, about how this could happen to me after everything else I'd already been through."

I can appreciate her point of view, and her honesty, but still— "Nothing about this is a good thing."

"Trust me. If anything is, that is. The longer it takes to grow, the better. My problem is the placement of where it is." She shrugs. "I've always been a challenge."

I take a deep breath and let it out loudly. "That you have." Corinna smiles as she lays her head back down.

"Let's embrace the now and all of the mess we're going to create just by living," she whispers.

I can do that, so long as I have her wrapped in my arms. Brushing my lips on top of her head, I tuck her closer. "Deal."

Hours later, we've moved out of the sun and talked more freely than I think we ever did in college. Corinna has quietly been telling me about her long-standing relationship with Marco. I shudder when I think about how close I came to losing her before I had a chance to have her back.

"He was the first man who looked at me and saw me. He didn't just see a reputation or a conquest. It was just me," Corinna explains.

"He wasn't the first," I reprimand her.

She stills but then recovers. "He was after I went on a free-for-all dating everyone," Corinna says quietly. "Granted I didn't sleep with hardly any of them; the dating was apparently enough." Corinna sounds disgusted.

I feel disgusted too. With myself. I listened to the rumors and innuendos and then saw fit to give Corinna a lecture when I haven't been a monk for the last ten years. Corinna, at least, had developed a long-term relationship with someone who cared about her. I barely stuck around after I slid the condom off.

"I owe you an apology for that too," I murmur, stroking her hair.

We've moved inside and are lying down facing each other on her couch. I'd shrugged my shirt back on but left it unbuttoned. Corinna nuzzles her face against my chest hair. The sensations cause my breathing to catch.

"For what?"

I've lost my train of thought. Her uncomplicated sexuality where I never expected it years ago, and never hoped for it recently, undoes me. If she understood how completely she disarms me, I'd be a duck in a shooting gallery. "Hmm?" I slide my hand under the heavy mass of her hair and massage her neck.

A sigh passes her lips that I feel on my chest. "That feels good."

"I never understood how this tiny neck could hold up such thick hair." I slide my fingers around her throat and brush them up and down.

She snickers. "It's only tiny to you, Colby. It's pretty..." I don't let her finish.

Smack!

Right after my hand lands on her ass, I begin to rub it to soothe away the sting.

"Hey! I wasn't going to insult myself." She pouts.

"Oh, sorry. Call that one foreplay, then." Her eyes brighten. I can't resist. I laugh even as I drop a kiss on her lips.

"What else were you going to apologize for?" she asks, resuming the spike in my blood pressure by curling closer.

"I'm sorry for not believing in the person you are. For believing rumors over what I know to be true right here." I clasp her hand and place it over my heart. I slide mine over her amaryllis tattoo. It's not meant to be a sexual move; it's meant as a promise. A vow. "I had no idea you weren't getting my letters. Not that it should have mattered. I knew you. I should have just manned up and come back sooner to figure us out." I rested my forehead against hers.

She strokes my heart through my chest. "You know I've been living my life like tomorrow doesn't exist, because it might not. You accept that, right?"

As much as it churns my gut to admit it, I do. I nod against her dark hair.

"Let's put the past where it belongs, behind us. Live with me in the now, in whatever capacity you can handle. I promise to not burden you with more than you can take." Her eyes are earnest, and her mouth quirks. "Mind you, if you had any sense, you would go running through my front door as fast as you can. My ups and downs are going to drive you crazy."

"Living without you drove me crazy. I've learned to adapt to everything but that."

"Then how do we seal the deal?" I can feel the acceleration of Corinna's heartbeat beneath my hand.

"Like this." And I lower my mouth to hers to taste her once again.

Talking makes way for other types of communication, as our lips engage and our hands reach for purchase on each other.

31

CORINNA

"They're going to roast me on a spit, Corinna," Colby says as we make our way up to the main farm building holding hands.

Is it wrong I want to walk in and raise our joined hands before shaking my hips in a victory dance? In the midst of one of the most heinously emotional weeks in a long time, I'm secure about one thing. Colby's got a hold on me. He wants to hold me. And that's mighty fine by me.

We'd been secluded all day when my phone pinged with a text from Cassidy. *Family dinner at the barn at eight.* I can only assume the lack of movement from Colby's Jeep started the family rumor mill flying. I'm actually more impressed that Ali and Keene stayed away from the house. Unless Keene thought I was systematically chopping Colby to bits with a meat cleaver, and was just waiting for the high sign to come dispose of the body.

I shrug. It makes no never mind to me. I've always been an ask for forgiveness later person, which is why my news sent the family into a tailspin this week. After dealing with the blow of being sold into a sex trafficking ring, then the death of my parents, finding the brain tumor, and losing Colby so close together, I threw life the middle finger and began dancing on my own grave. Who was there to stop me but me? Suddenly I realize I no longer want that kind of life. I want the long game. And maybe, just maybe, I want it with this man.

Colby swings me around in a circle. "Where did you go?"

"Just daydreaming," I answer honestly. I'm dizzy from the speed of the spin, but I don't tell him that. I want the freedom to just be for a little while longer before the reality of my situation intrudes back in.

"Am I starring in them?"

I can't help but smile. "If I decide to share them, I'll let you know," I sass.

He drops his lips to mine. Holding me steady, his fingers tangle in mine. In my mind's eye, I'm capturing this summer moment for exactly what it is: perfection. When you realize life may cheat you out of forever, you savor each flavor of happy it blesses you with.

Our kiss is interrupted by clapping. As our lips separate, I turn my head to the side to see Ali applauding. "Damn, I've only wanted this for how many years? Keene, I told you they were working it out, didn't I?"

"He'd better treat her right, or I'll be kicking his ass," Keene threatens.

I'm oddly touched. Pulling away from Colby, I rush Keene and launch myself at him. "You were such a prick, damn you. How am I supposed to deal with all this sweet?"

Keene's arms clasp me tightly as he lifts me off my feet. "Just by being you, Cori. By loving my sister, my woman, and my daughter as much as you do. You'd better be as much of a fighter as the rest of them. I'm too damn fond of your throwing arm to let you go." Keene's alluding to my throwing a pie of whipped cream in his face for being a dick when he was courting Ali. The memory has me tossing my head back with laughter. "Now, let me off the hook to give Hunt grief."

I clasp his scowling face in my hands. "Not a chance."

He drops me to my feet. "He hurt you."

"He made it better."

"You were sobbing last night," Keene semi-roars.

"He kissed it better today," I tell him smugly.

"I'll never understand you Freeman women." Keene lets me go to take his daughter from Ali's arms. "I'm taking Kalie, baby. This way, I'll have less of an urge to punch Hunt on my way in."

"I heard that," Colby calls out. He's standing back, giving us our moment with a huge smile.

Yeah, I can see it all in those gray eyes. The long game. The question is, will I make it? Shaking my head, I turn to my sister. Ali's thoughtful expression ping-pongs back and forth between Colby and me. "How much did you really talk about?"

"Everything, Ali." I lay heavy emphasis on the first word.

"Wow. So, you talked about what hurt you so badly?"

I nod. I laid into him about that the other day.

"You talked about pasts?"

"I forced him to. I held up Cass's and your relationship as such sterling examples," I deadpan.

Ali punches me in the arm. "You're such a snot, but well done. Future?"

I get serious quickly. "Can we see if I have one first?"

Ali winces. "Right. I'm going to go remind Phil of what questions he shouldn't ask when he starts on his big-brother spiel tonight."

I roll my eyes. "Phil likes Colby."

"Baby, haven't you realized no man is good enough for us once we become emotionally involved? It's why he still gives Keene shit." Ali pauses. "That, and Keene makes it easy."

Remembering what Ali said the other day, I pale. "Tell me Phil doesn't plan on..."

"I have no idea what goes through big brother's head, Cori. I go with the flow, just like you should." She runs her hand over the crown of my head. "I love him for you. I always did." Her eyes don't stray to Colby. "I was so pissed to know my thoughts of hooking the two of you up were going awry when you told me what you did last summer."

"It worked out the way it was supposed to," I say diplomatically.

"It worked out when it was supposed to," she corrects me, hooking her arm in mine. Guiding me back over to Colby, she asks him, "Are you ready for the spotlight?"

Colby slides an arm over my shoulders. "I'm just grateful I keep a go bag in the trunk of my Jeep. Otherwise, I'd be borrowing clothes since I wasn't leaving her all day. Now wouldn't that have gone over well?

Ali shoots us both her dazzling smile. "True, because I really couldn't have controlled Keene's sterling commentary then." The three of us make our way inside, still laughing.

As always, riotous chaos is the best way to describe our family dinners. I immediately start dancing as one of my favorite songs is playing. "Someone start this from the beginning!" I call out. Phil is dancing with Cassidy's daughter, Laura, and Holly is holding Cassidy's little Jonathan. Cassidy is wrapped up in Caleb's arms. Jason, who is dancing with Em, reaches into his pocket for the remote.

I grab Colby's hand and drag him into the center of the floor as Delta Rae's "A Long and Happy Life" starts again. As he swings me out and back, I start singing along with the lyrics that echo the music bursting in my heart. I deserve this life, this love, this family. And I'm going to fight to keep them.

Whatever it takes.

I'M FEELING DELICIOUSLY STUFFED and wonderfully pampered. Grilled shrimp and steak with bell pepper and radish salad. Perfect with the blackberry-lime margarita I've been nursing for most of the night. There's a huge bowl of fresh fruit and a pan of Holly's banana pudding in the center of the table.

And I didn't have to cook a thing.

"Dare I ask what prompted this family dinner?" I drawl from the shelter of Colby's arm. He squeezes my shoulder.

"Going on the offense? Brave soul." Cassidy grins. She just settled her twins in their Pack-N-Play to calm down.

"It's better than waiting for his lordship to strike first. Remember how I handled that issue about blow jobs?" I wink at my oldest sister, who merely shakes her head in reply.

"What's this?" Colby shifts in his chair, angling toward me.

"Oh, Phil has a ritual when it comes to teaching the women of this family about how to give blow jobs. I just refused to participate. I went straight for on-the-job training." Ignoring Colby's growl, I decide to harass others instead. "You think he'll have fine-tuned his techniques in about twenty years?"

There's a pause in the conversation before my sisters catch on, realizing I'm talking about the next generation of women in our family. All the women start laughing while Keene starts sputtering. He just glares at me and says, "No. Fuck no. I'll send Kalie to a convent first."

That sets us off even harder.

"Lighten up, Keene," Phil drawls from where he's holding a sleeping Kalie across his lap. "That baton has been passed from me to your wife. It's her job to educate your daughter on how to break all the boys' hearts. I can tell you this though. You've got trouble here. She's got a bit of both her mother and her aunt in her."

Keene shoves his plate forward and begins banging his dark head on the table hard enough to make the rest of the dishes jump. "I'm so completely screwed," he declares.

All of us are laughing, but none so hard as Ali and Cassidy, who are wiping tears from their eyes.

Keene's eyes shoot daggers at me. "You. This is your fault."

I feign an innocent look. "Moi?"

"Yes. If you'd just let me tear into Hunt like I'm supposed to as your older and wiser brother..."

Phil coughs loudly.

Keene acquiesces. "Fine. As *one* of your older and wiser brothers, I would not be tormented thinking of Uncle Kama Sutra teaching my child everything she needs to know about men before she hits preschool."

Even Jason can't keep a straight face. "I love watching Keene get tortured by what flies out of your mouth, babe."

Phil leans over and kisses his husband. "I know. It adds a certain *je ne sais quoi* to dinner. Don't you think?"

"I think you're a pain in my ass," Keene retorts. He slides his arms around Ali from behind. She leans back into him, tipping her head back to receive his kiss.

"You wouldn't have it any other way," Phil says. We're interrupted by a loud banging at the front door. Kalie, who had been sleeping through the banter in Phil's arms, squirms anxiously. He begins rocking her immediately. "Shh, precious. I've got you. Nothing's ever going to hurt you. Colby, can you see who's at the door?"

"Of course," Colby looks around the room. "Are we expecting anyone?"

"No." Keene pushes back from his chair. "I'll come with you."

Figuring Keene's going to use this chance to get in his licks against Colby, I get up as well. "Since the two of you may not know everyone local, I'll come with you."

"You're no fun, Corinna." Keene's dark scowl tells me I was right.

"I'm just the right amount of fun, Keene." I stick out my tongue. Colby reaches over and snags it between his fingers. "Heeyyy!" I exclaim.

"Put that back until I can play with it later," he jokes.

"Sweet Jesus." Keene rolls his eyes while the rest of us laugh. We're interrupted again by the pounding at the door. All of our heads turn. Keene's face takes on a hard cast as Kalie starts crying. Phil starts walking back and forth to calm her down.

Colby looks ready to attack.

Caleb stands as well. "Corinna, stay here. We'll be right back with whomever it is."

I sink back into my chair. "Yeah, right. Just don't shoot anyone we can't justify it against."

Colby's not smiling. His eyes are more glittery than soft gray. Without having ever seen him in his uniform, I can tell he's ready for battle. "Go, before whoever it is knocks again and wakes Laura and Jonathan," I urge him.

The three men head off toward the door. Holly leans over Colby's seat and says, "So, spill it. We don't have much time."

All of my sisters and Jason lean in. Phil conveniently stops nearby.

"What? I told Ali outside. We talked things through."

"Bet that's not all you did," Em singsongs.

I shrug. "It's not like he bent me over the kitchen counter."

"Damn," Ali says. Reaching into her shorts pocket, she pulls out a twenty and slaps it into Cassidy's hands.

"Seriously? Y'all were betting on how far we got?" Yet even as the words come out, I realize I'm not close to being surprised by my family's audacity.

"You two have been setting off sparks for over a decade. Once the fighting gloves were off, we figured the clothes would be too," Holly explains.

While I'm slightly less offended, I wait for Em to take a drink. "I thought you, Holly, and I got married last night, Em. Sister wives and all that? How could I break my vow with y'all so quickly?"

As always, her target when she blows manages to be Phil. Since he's still carrying Kalie as he passes by, the blackberry margarita ends up dripping down his back. "Shit, that's ice-cold, Em." He squirms as the icy drink slides down his back. "Crap, I think it just went between my ass cheeks."

"He's not used to cold down there," Jason pipes in.

And we're a heaping mess of laughter. That is until the guys come back in with an addition.

"Corinna, you have a guest," Colby says tightly. "He demands to talk to you as soon as possible." His hand is cuffed behind the neck of Dr. Bryan Moser. "He was recently told by your primary care office you were no longer a patient. Since you haven't returned his messages, Dr. Moser interpreted that to mean he thought you had..." Colby doesn't finish his sentence. After shoving Bryan forward, Colby moves next to me. "Trust me, princess. There is nothing you can say that's going to prevent me from beating the shit out of Jack the first minute I get the chance."

As Bryan tries to get his bearings from the overwhelming greeting, I reply faintly, "I'm not sure I'm going to want you to."

Colby's face marginally relaxes, and he says, "Good." He presses a hard kiss to my lips.

Standing, I face my neurosurgeon and feel the flicker of anger nip at me. "Dr. Moser, before I introduce you to my family, I'd like to apologize to my siblings for your unexpected presence. In addition to interrupting a family dinner and waking their children with your dramatic entry, this isn't quite the professional setting they should be meeting you in."

"Oh, shove it, Corinna. For the last twelve hours, I've thought you were dead." As Bryan wraps his arms around me, I'm helpless to the torment in his voice. Catching Colby's eye, I mouth, "What the hell?"

He shakes his head, but I can tell he's pissed. There's more to the story he found out in the hall.

Crap.

I pull away from Bryan to see he's visibly distressed. "I'm okay."

He mutters, "And we're going to make sure you stay that way."

"Hear, hear," Jason calls.

"Listen," I say gently, "let's get you something to eat and drink, and I'll introduce you to everyone."

"I owe you an apology for being an ass."

"Yeah, but we're pretty famous for that in this family," I quip . His answering smile is shaky, but it's there. Colby slips his arm around me. "First, this is Colby Hunt. He's..." I stumble. What is Colby to me?

"Hers. I'm Corinna's," Colby interjects smoothly.

Bryan blinks a few times. "Wow, finally got your shit sorted, huh, Cori?"

I punch him in the arm. "Shut it, Bryan."

"Good. Because you're going to need a great support system for surgery."

I suck in a huge breath. "Bryan, I'm still not sure..."

"I am. That's why I was calling to notify your primary care physician to get everything scheduled. Forty-five days max." The collective inhale in the room sucks out all of the oxygen. I'm so glad Colby's holding me up because I feel my legs give out. "It's time to get that thing out of you once and for all."

32

COLBY

Corinna sways unsteadily in my arms. "Forty-five...days?" Her voice is so unsettled. She's squeezing my forearms as if her life depends on it.

And right now, maybe it does.

Jason speaks up from behind Dr. Moser. "Isn't it a bit sudden, Doctor? Typically, surgical patients have a longer time to prepare for the procedure, considering the in-depth amount of physical and psychological protocols involved."

Dr. Moser runs his hands through already out-of-control hair. "Cori, how free am I to speak in front of all of these people?"

She lets out a deep sigh, her body molding to mine. "Pull out your cell phone, Bryan." She waits for him to do so. "Can you flip to video?" His face flashes with understanding. "Let me know when it's ready."

Dr. Moser fumbles for a moment before he holds up his phone. "Whenever you're ready."

Stiffening her spine within my arms, Corinna announces, "My name is Corinna Freeman. I was Johns Hopkins patient"—she spits out a string of numbers—"I recently transitioned to Greenwich Hospital under the care of Dr. Bryan Moser. This video is to serve as authorization of the release and discussion of my medical care with my immediate family: Phillip Freeman-Ross, Cassidy Freeman-Lockwood, Emily Freeman, Alison Freeman, and Holly Freeman, as well as the following spouses or significant others as identified. This includes Dr. Jason Ross, Caleb Lockwood, Keene Marshall, and Colby Hunt. At the time this video is being made, I am of sound mind and in the presence of my doctor, Bryan Moser, as well as my attorney, Alison Freeman. Thank you." Her head drops, and I hear her mutter, "I never wanted to do that here, Bryan. You could have just trusted me."

He's sympathetic but firm. "I'm sorry, but we're running out of time."

"Why?" Jason demands again. When Dr. Moser turns on him, he steps forward. "Dr. Jason Ross, emergency room trauma specialist." The men shake hands briefly.

"Corinna's tumor has grown to a critical point in the last few weeks. In the last MRI before the images became compromised, we observed it's resting on both of her ICAs."

Jason curses before he turns on his husband. "You didn't mention that the other night."

Phil blinks at him over Kalie's head. "I honestly thought I did, Jace."

Jason rounds on me. "Cori, you realize you have to have the surgery now before the tumor grows any further. It can stop your normal motor functions. You can literally…"

"I know!" she screams, shaking. "Do y'all think I don't know this already? I'm the one who's been living with this for so many years." Corinna turns in my arms and lets loose a torrent of tears.

Corinna wipes her eyes and nose on my shirt, and I couldn't care less. "Every time they slid me into those cylinders to be scanned, I prayed, Colby. I prayed so hard the results would just be the same. I could live with the monster in my head." Her eyes fill with even more tears. "But what if I die because it has to come out?"

"This is why you have to see the psychologist, Cori. You're not going to die," Bryan interrupts.

"Shut up, Doctor," I growl. I clasp her face between my hands and duck down so our eyes are level. "He's not wrong though, baby. Even if he's not the one you want performing the surgery anymore"—I ignore Moser's gasp and continue—"we'll find the right doctor for you. You're not giving up. You're not giving in."

"Sometimes I feel like I deserve this." Her head turns away from me. "If I'd just talked to you, maybe I wouldn't be punished this way. Maybe I wouldn't be this punished. Maybe I would be spared."

Every word out of her mouth is a jagged-edged knife in my heart. Our separation is as much my fault as hers. It's only because of the letters she's blaming herself, but it was my selfish behavior that started it all. "No, princess, that's not how this works. Cori, we've talked about this. Don't let this set us back," I plead.

"Why would you want to be with someone who you know could die?" she whispers, breaking away from my arms. Looking around the room frantically, she asks, "Why would any of you?" She stares at each of us a moment before bolting for the back door.

I'm less than a second after her.

Keene catches me around the waist. "Give her a few, man. Let her get some of it out."

"Let me go, you asshole." I wrench out of his hold. "You have no idea what's happening between us." Neither do I. All I know is that I have to be with her. Holding her. Touching her.

"Colby, she needs you to have the answers to the millions of unanswered questions going through her head. She doesn't need another 'I don't know' or platitude." It pisses me off that he's right.

I push out of his hold. "I'm fine. I'm okay." I turn to a pale-faced Dr. Moser. "Hours ago, Cori was ready to start looking for a new doctor because of your attitude this week, and I can't say I'm all that impressed right now. So, start talking about what we're facing because we're all in this with her."

Keene's hand clamps down on my shoulder in approval.

"Don't you think we should wait for the patient?" Moser asks with a touch of superiority.

"Right now, you have a roomful of people who need their ques-

tions answered. Let's start with the basic ones. What kind of procedure is she facing, and how long is it?"

As Dr. Moser begins discussing the type of craniotomy Corinna
will need, I understand why she ran out of the room rather than face
this.

I want to do the same.

～

AN HOUR LATER, I drive back to Corinna's, where the lights are blazing
in every room of the house. I look up and see her moving back and
forth in her bedroom carrying armloads of clothes.

Shit.

Jumping out of the Jeep, I walk up and try the door. Locked. Of
course. I immediately ring the bell and wait. Then I ring it again.
While I'm waiting, I send a ping to Keene. *Should have let me come
after her, you dick. Now I'm locked out.*

His reply of *Shit* does nothing to ease my concern.

I call Corinna's cell phone. Direct to voicemail.

Suddenly, I get pissed. We spent the afternoon mending the
cracks between us, so why is she running scared? Why is she running
at all?

I look for the simplest point of entry. I could quickly throw a rock
through one of the massive windows in the back of her house. Effective, but a pain in the ass to clean up. Scanning the exterior, I glimpse
the fixed awning covering her front door. Following its line over the
metal roofing, I realize while the pitch is steep, the rivets will give me
enough foothold to use the open segments in her clapboard to get to
the Juliet balcony outside her bedroom.

I immediately text Keene. *She's packing to run. Need you to come
light it up. I'm breaching the perimeter.*

There's a pause, followed by, *Be right there.*

Satisfied, I slip my phone in my pocket and go around back for
the Metolius gloves I keep in my car's emergency kit. Rolling my
shoulder to stretch it a bit, I'm glad I recently had a scan to know my

shoulder isn't going to give out in the middle of this. Like I'll admit that to my bosses, I think ruefully.

After slipping on the gloves, I move over to the post supporting Corinna's awning and jump up. Pulling myself up is simple. I swing my legs over, and then my belly, and wait a few moments to make sure the canopy can support my weight when I see lights come down the drive. I turn my head away so I don't look directly into them.

A door opens and closes. "Any issues with the shoulder?" Keene calls out.

"None so far," I reply. I make my way over to the main roof pitch and carefully move over each of the lock-and-groove metal roofing tiles. Fifty-year roofs are fantastic for ensuring no leaks come into a home, but are a bitch when your feet are large and you're trying to be sneaky.

Keene shines a Maglite up when I reach the edge. "You're about four feet out," he calls.

"Got it." My adrenaline is pumping, not only from the climb but from how pissed I'm becoming.

Shut me out? After everything we finally worked through? Not for long.

Carefully, I reach out and grip with the tips of my fingers in the grooves between the clapboard. I swing my body out. The toes of my boots find purchase farther down. I hear Keene's voice cautioning me. "Easy, brother. You've got about ten feet to the balcony."

Right. I inch my fingers along, gritting my teeth at the upper-body strength required for me to shimmy across this roof due to Corinna's stubbornness. My feet slide across as I make slow but steady progress. Keene calls out, "Three. Two. I think you can swing over now, Hunt."

Gripping hard on the wall of Corinna's house, I kick my boots away from the wall, using the momentum to catch one leg against the rail. Having hooked it, I slide my hand so I can let go with the other. I latch on, gratefully. My fingers aren't used to this kind of climbing anymore.

"Do you have it from here so I can go home?" Keene asks from twenty feet below.

"Yeah, because if she doesn't open this door, I'm breaking it in," I call down.

"I'll warn the monitoring center on shift at the office. Call me if you need a rope." Keene slides back into his vehicle and backs out of the driveway.

Corinna's Juliet balcony doors are made of thin paned glass. I start pounding on them.

There's no response.

Pulling out my phone, I start sending a text. *I'm standing at your balcony door. Open them. Now.*

Before I can press Send, they swing open. "Jesus Christ, Colby, are you insane? What the hell are you doing?" I stalk into her bedroom. Jesus, it's worse than I thought. There are piles of clothes all over her bed.

Swiveling around, I declare, "You're not going anywhere, Corinna. You're not running away."

"I know?" Her voice holds a note of confusion.

"You know?" I say slowly. "Then why the hell didn't you answer your door?" I bellow.

She pulls the earbuds from her pocket. "I couldn't hear you."

Suddenly, my fury coalesces. "And why didn't you answer your cell?" It's in her hands for fuck's sake.

She blushes before admitting, "I put it on Do Not Disturb. The only person who can get through in that case is Holly. I needed some time to think, so I came home and started cleaning."

"When did Holly ping you?" She holds out the phone just as I reach her.

Holly: Hey. Figure you want to be alone, but Ali just pinged me. Apparently, Colby's gone off his rocker and thinks you're going to run. Idiot. Can you let him in your balcony door? He apparently scaled your house.

Corinna starts stammering. "I-I was putting away l-laundry, Colby. I wasn't leaving. I truly didn't hear you at the door. I forgot you're not on my breakthrough list and I—"

There's only one way I can think of to shut her up right now and alleviate the panic and fury inside of me.

I kiss her.

33

CORINNA

My head keeps screaming, *You only have forty-five days left for sure in this world. This isn't right. Move away. Let Colby move on with his life to find someone who is guaranteed in this world.*

My heart can't. It won't.

My head tilts to the side as he presses me back against the wall to absorb the fury and the pain in his kiss. And not just because of tonight. Because of so many nights. So many years we could have spent just like this locked in each other's arms.

We've both been wrong and we've both been to blame, but who the hell cares anymore? Who cares when we finally made it to where we're supposed to be, right here in each other's arms?

Colby spins me away from the wall and backs me up toward my bed. His scent is overwhelming me. It's Burberry mixed with sweat, the same cologne he's worn since college. I can't walk by a man who wears it without my head spinning, trying to find him in the crowd.

He's never been there before.

He's here now.

"Corinna, I need you to know something important." His breath is harsh in the quiet of the room.

Cupping his face, I brush my lips against his. "What's that?"

He picks me up and tosses me on the bed, causing half my clothes to topple to the floor. "You're going to have to refold your laundry." Ripping off the gloves on his hands, he also takes the time to unlace his boots before crawling on top of me.

I welcome his hard weight pressing me down into the mattress. More clothes and pillows go flying over the sides of the bed, as Colby begins devouring my body.

I laugh, unable to keep in the sound of joy.

Colby stops kissing the crevice my bra and V-neck T-shirt affords him and stares down at me. "What is it? Why did you stop?"

"Because I want to cherish this moment I've dreamed about for so damn long, and I don't want to rush through it like it's the last time. It's not. God wouldn't be so cruel as to give me the gift of you, only to let you slip away." He whispers the last as he entwines his fingers with mine. He swallows. "I know it, Cori. I know it here." He moves our entwined hands to his chest while he braces on one arm. "I need you to believe me, even if you can't believe yourself."

Tears leak out the sides of my eyes as Colby gives me his full weight again. He kisses the tears from my cheeks. "How?" I manage to croak out, tightening my fingers in his.

"How what?" he returns.

"How were we so stupid for so long?" My tears are falling in earnest. "When I think of the time wasted—"

He cuts me off. "Because we needed to be exactly who we are now to battle this, Corinna. Don't think of it as time wasted. Think of it as time lived so we know we're the only thing worth dying for."

With that, Colby rolls to the side and releases my hands. He pulls my body flush into his, drags my leg over his hip, and rocks my body into the cradle of his. I can feel the strength and ferociousness of his erection up against my mound. He's barely touched me, and I'm already primed and ready. I gasp at the contact. Tugging his head down to mine, I kiss him with years of pent-up desire. Our lips touch. Our tongues mate.

For long minutes, that's all we do. We sip at each other's mouths like we just discovered a new flavor. Decadent, sweet, savory. Addicting.

Trailing his mouth down my neck, he stretches my T-shirt over my shoulder, tasting as much skin as he can. My head arches back when he bites down on the tendon leading to my shoulder gently. I can't bear it. I want more. I want everything.

I want him never to think this was a mistake.

"Colby," I whisper in the lit room. My hands are scratching all over his T-shirt, pulling and tugging. He pulls away, far enough to grab it from behind and tug it off, tossing it over the bed. It lands somewhere amid my clean clothes.

When he looks at me, I see passion has changed his eyes from gray to a smoky black. And I begin to pray. Please God, if I remember nothing else, let me remember this look right now. Let me remember when Colby cherished and coveted me, because it might just be enough to carry me through the perpetual darkness.

While I'm beseeching a God who never sees fit to answer my prayers, I feel the catch to my bra give before Colby's hands skim up my waist. "Lift up, princess."

Suddenly, a whole new set of insecurities set in. Colby is masculine perfection from the top of his dark hair to his square jaw, down the dusting of his chest hair to his chiseled abs. His arms are so ripped, I have no idea how he managed to climb the roof of my house to my window. How is my less-than-perfect body supposed to stack up against the women he's had in the past? Even just knowing about one of them, that she-devil Addison, makes me anxious.

Before I can form a protest, in one swoop, Colby's removes my T-shirt and my bra. My breasts, no longer restrained, shift to the sides as Colby rolls me to my back. In this position, my amaryllis tattoo is clearly displayed over my heart.

"I can't wait for my fingers, my mouth, to touch everywhere my eyes can finally see." He ducks his head and blows gently on one of my nipples. It reaches for his mouth, as my anxiety melts away, and I arch toward him. "You're so soft," he murmurs. Cupping my full breast, he lifts it to his mouth to surround with his lips.

"Gah!" The sound escapes, me even as my hands scrape up his chest toward his shoulders to find something substantial to hold on to.

"I'll bet I could make you come just from sucking these luscious breasts," he rasps. Dragging his lips across the valley in between, he drops the sweetest kiss on my tattoo. "Beauty and pride. So you." Moving over to my other breast, he lashes that one with quick flicks of his tongue before settling his lips on it for a deeper suckle.

My head turns back and forth wildly. "Colby. I can't stand it," I plead. My hands weave through his thick hair to hold him closer. He slides one arm around my back to anchor me in place as he torments my body with the sweetest torture. By the time his mouth moves away, I'm pulling his hair so I can capture his lips. "My turn," I whisper as I push him onto his back.

He complies with a wicked grin. I straddle him as he reclines back against my pillows. His hands immediately go to my jean-clad hips. Mine dart into the feathering of hair that angles down his chest. His nipples are pebble hard. When my nails scrape over them, he lets out a hiss of pleasure. "God, Cori."

I can't resist biting the same spot he did—that spot I've dreamed of tasting for so long. Nor can I resist licking my way down between his pecs, where his body's scent is calling to me like an ancient potion. Soon, it's me working his nipples as I rock my hips over his straining erection.

He pulls my hair back so our lips meet. My breasts nestle themselves into his chest as we continue to rock together in the rhythm of what we'll soon be doing.

He rips his mouth away and buries against my neck. "I have to taste you, Corinna. I've dreamed of this for so long...so many nights I held you..." The flutter of his tongue where his lips are resting as he pushes his hips upward has me answering on a groan.

"Please, Colby. Yes."

He rolls me over and sits back. His chest is heaving as he delicately traces my skin from my neck to my waist, lingering on parts in between. He makes quick work of the snap and zipper of my jeans before I help him work them off by lifting my hips. Only the scrap of material of my sheer boy shorts and his jeans separate us.

"This body..." His voice trails off, and I start to freeze up. "I dreamed about it. I'd be in a desert, freezing my ass off, and somehow, I'd wake up sweating because of you. Because of the curve of these hips." His hand smooths over my hip. "Those fucking sleep shorts you'd wear didn't cover shit, but I never told you that, did I, Corinna? I'd be sleeping behind you on that couch and holding you so you'd sleep, and I never knew a moment's peace because all I could imagine was sliding my hand over the curve of this hip." My eyes flash up to his. He laughs with no humor. "Right here." His fingers trail over the spot where more often than not, my shirt rides up when I sleep, even to this day.

"Is..." I clear my throat. "Is that what you thought of last night?" Colby held me so tightly throughout the night.

"Mm-hmm." He drops a kiss on the curve of my hip. Pushing up against him, he gives me a wicked laugh. "This time, though, I was able to sleep because I knew I wasn't ever going to let you go. You know that, Cori. The minute my cock slides home inside you, I'm never letting you go."

I have to beat back the tears. Even if it's only for the rest of this life, I'll take the time he's offering.

I'm so damn selfish.

He arcs an eyebrow. "Nothing to say to that?"

Suddenly the words are flowing; I can't stop them. "I should let you go. You should be with someone you know is going to live. I should stop this now before—" And all my words are stopped as Colby slams his mouth back onto mine.

"You are who I'm meant to be with, and not just tonight, Corinna. And I'm going to make you believe that down to your very core." Colby pulls my head back so his eyes are scanning mine. "I will never regret one minute of the love we make. Will you?"

I shake my head no. I never could.

His frustration is evident. "Christ, you drive me insane." He rolls to his back, throwing an arm over his eyes.

I scramble to my knees, heedless of my lack of clothing. "Colby, please understand. I just don't want you to be hurt if..."

He jackknifes and yanks me down on top of him. Aligning our faces so our noses touch, he whispers, "I've already been dead because of losing you. Don't stop me from living when I'm only just starting to feel again."

My mouth falls open. Colby uses that to his advantage by kissing me senseless. Soon, I'm on my back again and he's skimmed off my panties. He's working his lips down my body, murmuring his appreciation for the curves he's held so close but never really touched. I can't control the keening sounds escaping my lips.

"Please," I beg as his fingers separate my lips. He's blowing on my clit, tracing a finger around the entrance to my pussy. My hips are moving up and down, trying to keep contact with him.

"Not until I taste this sweetness, Cori. Not until I drink my fill." He lowers his head. His lips surround my clit and begin to suck as not one, but two fingers penetrate my entrance.

And I detonate.

My hands reach out over his shoulders, which are between my dimpled thighs, to pull him closer. To push him away. I don't really know. I hoarsely chant his name over and over as his tongue flicks against me, while his strong fingers move in counterpart inside of me. Again and again, he brings me to the precipice and drops me over until I'm left with one foot on his shoulder, my other leg bent outward, unable to move.

I'm a wreck of sensation. I've just been destroyed in the best of ways. And I know after he slowly wipes his mouth against the coverlet on my bed, he's not done.

He's just getting started.

He stands on the side of the bed and flips his wallet out to pull out a condom before shucking his jeans. The air I was just regaining in my lungs whooshes out as I see he's been commando this whole time. All during dinner, while climbing my damn house, while driving me insane with lust, Colby hasn't had a stitch of clothing on beneath his jeans. His cock is angled toward me, with the thick head already beading with fluid.

Now it's my mouth that's watering for a taste.

I start to shift so I can reach out and capture it in my mouth, but he quickly sheaths himself. I pout, causing him to laugh. "I want your mouth on me as much as you do, but not more than I want to sink into your wet heat. Later, I'll slide my cock down your throat while you use that mouth any way you want."

I want that too. So much. I'll hold him to that promise. For now, I just open my arms and watch him prowl over me.

Even as his cock nudges against my opening, he combs his fingers through my long hair. "Give me a moment."

I run my hand over his tight flank and whisper a confused "Okay?"

"I just want to memorize the look in your eyes."

I feel him start to nudge into me. I take a deep breath.

This is real.

Slowly, inch by inch, his cock makes its way inside me. I've had sex. I've even had good sex. But this is so much more. My cheeks flush. When his pelvic bone brushes up against my clit, I gasp.

Bracing himself up on his muscular arms, he pulls his hips back and slowly moves them forward. I'm out of my mind with madness as I wrap my legs around him, giving him more of me and taking all of him.

Over and over he plunges into me. His body gleams with a coat of sweat I'm sure mirrors my own.

Then I feel it again, coming deep from within me.

"Colby..." I can't manage more as his hips are thrusting into mine. Each time they collide in the middle, I feel like he's going to throw me over an edge I've glanced at before but never really seen. Until now.

"Come for me, Corinna. I've been waiting for this moment for a lifetime," he whispers next to my ear. I don't know if it's his words or the feeling of security, but I soar over the edge. He takes flight with me.

We've made the jump together as one body.

And in the middle, I think I gave him my soul.

34

COLBY

She's asleep, tucked into my side. I smooth my hand over that spot on her hip I just can't resist. In her sleep, a small smile ghosts across her face even as she wiggles closer to my touch.

I'm a lucky bastard and I know it.

I'm also fucking petrified.

The things Bryan told us about Corinna's condition make me want to howl at the moon.

Corinna has every right to be an emotional yo-yo about this surgery.

The best outcome is that she's out of work for eight weeks and has lifelong follow-ups.

The worst...I don't know what she would consider worse. Moser told us the worst could be two things. The first is that she ends up trapped inside her own body alive but unable to see, to move, or to speak. The second is simply she'll die. Knowing Corinna and her fear of the dark, I'd say the first.

Dropping my head so I can inhale her scent, I am astounded. How has she lived with this burden for so long and not be broken? When I pull back, and the tattoo running along her back flashes at me in the dim lighting of the room.

Never forget who you are.

Corinna is strength. She is determination. She is pride. She is beauty. She is a fighter.

And she is mine.

I pull her closer to me, suddenly afraid of what will happen to us both if I let her drift too far away.

It's a long while before I find sleep.

35
CORINNA

FORTY DAYS BEFORE SURGERY

I'm ready to throw something at someone, anyone. I pray no one provides with me an excuse.

It's been a frustrating day to say the least. Unlike the last few days, where I began to believe I could do this.

The last few days with my family and Colby were not just spent solidifying his place in my life, but discussing what Bryan told them at the farm after I ran the other night. Not surprisingly, they all have their own opinions.

Cassidy, Caleb, and Holly all support whatever decision I make because I have to be the one comfortable with it.

Ali wants to find out how to perform the surgery on YouTube and have Jason do it. During the conversation at the farm Sunday, he choked when she mentioned it. After repeatedly coughing into his napkin, he said, "Thank you, but no. I have no desire to work on people's brains."

To which Keene muttered, "Too bad. You have the perfect subject with Phil."

The laughter that swept the room when Phil stuck his tongue out at Keene helped alleviate the building tension.

Relaxing in Colby's arms, my head against his broad chest, I murmured just loud enough for him to hear, "You're keeping your opinion to yourself."

"This is your family, Corinna. I'm just an honored guest."

I laughed long and hard. He has no clue. "Do you remember what you said to me a few weeks ago?"

His face got tight as he thought of all of the words we exchanged to bring us to our now. "I remember everything."

Coming to my knees, I straddled his legs.

"Hey now, we've talked about this," Keene protested.

I wiggled my fingers at him though I keep my gaze on Colby's face. Em snorted with laughter as she clarified for Keene, "Cori just gave you a flock of these," right before—I'm sure—she shoved her middle finger in his direction.

Thanks, Em. I owe you one.

Focusing on Colby, I cupped his strong chin. "You said the only man I'd ever introduce my family to was you. So, don't think you're here by accident or as a tagalong. They recognize your place here for what it is."

His arms banded around my back, tugging me closer. "What's that?"

"Mine," I said simply. "Finally."

Colby curled his abs up slowly. We were face-to-face, heart-to-heart, when he replied. "Do you know what princesses get when they act like you just did?"

A smile played about my lips even as I shook my head.

His eyes darkened to smoky gray before he leaned next to my ear. "They have every inch of their skin worshiped like a queen, Corinna." His breath next to my ear caused my body to shiver. "Not a single inch of you will go untouched later."

I found out later he meant it.

Which is why I'm more aggravated than ever. A woman should be able to bask in that kind of afterglow for weeks, not days.

Instead, I'm having to deal with doctors whose egos are compensating for the size of their dicks.

Jack decided he is the wronged party in all of this and has made it virtually impossible for me to schedule my preoperative testing with his partners. It took a call from Greenwich Hospital's neurosurgery coordinator to the general office manager at Jack's practice to get things resolved. According to the phone call I had from the neurosurgery coordinator after lunch, it was all settled. I'm now scheduled for a physical tomorrow. Gee, something to look forward to.

Not.

The kitchen phone ringing adds to the headache building behind my eyes. Without looking at the caller ID, I answer wearily, "Amaryllis Events, this is Corinna."

"You bitch!" Jack's harsh breathing echoes in my ears. "What, are you fucking the surgical coordinator now to get your way? Seems to be the only way you get the things you want."

I can't speak. Shaking, I put the phone on speaker as I pull my phone out of my pocket. Without saying a word, I choose the first app that has audio recording capabilities. Laying my phone next to the cordless handset on the counter, I say, "Excuse me?"

"You heard me," he snarls.

"Actually, I didn't," I reply in as calm a voice I can manage, with my heart trying to pound its way out through my ears.

"I should have guessed you were deaf as well as being a fat, stupid skank, Corinna." Jack's words would have had the power to gut me even just a few days ago. I was reminded as recently as this weekend that when you're made up of strength and pride, you attract the same in the people around you.

And you push away the people who have none of it.

"Is there a purpose to this call?" I'm forcing the impression of being bored, although I'm curious to see how far this prick will hang himself.

"The purpose is to tell you you're a fucking bitch. And I hope you die on that operating table. It'd sure as fuck make my life easier."

Wow. Even I'm not prepared for the strike of venom from this little snake. I decide to say nothing, and instead, I breathe in gulps of air, struggling for more oxygen.

"He's a Hunt, for God's sake. He should be surrounded by the best people in the world. You should be lucky if you're allowed to clean his cock for money. It's impossible to believe you're what he wants. I mean, he can fuck the best there is. What are you? Used. That's what you are." A tear falls from my eye that I brush away. "I mean, even your family thought injecting something was better than having you around."

I'm pissed, so why am I crying? I still don't say anything but let Jack's vitriol fly.

"He's my brother. He's supposed to take care of me—that's what family does. They take care of each other. I made sure he had everything he needed. Like Addison. He needed to fuck hard. Does he fuck you hard? Has he fucked your ass the way he did hers?"

My hand comes up to hold in the wail of pain. Its bitter taste is insidiously worming its way into my stomach. I want to wretch.

I won't give the bastard the satisfaction.

Then I feel arms slide behind me. I start to fight back instinctively. Colby presses me hard against the table, his finger lifting to the center of my lips. He glances down at the recorder. "Keep him talking," he mouths to me. I nod. He squeezes me before letting me go. Pulling out his phone, his fingers begin flying.

"Every time Colby would come home, he'd come see me, not you. See? That's what brothers do." His voice takes on an almost dreamy cast. "He'd tell me about his missions and the women. Want me to tell you about them? How their legs could wrap around his back twice before they stopped? How their breasts were so tight he could fit both of them in his mouth at once. Not at all like your body. I mean, I'll bet he could get a couple of those women in a pair of your jeans with those overstuffed sausages you stand on all day."

I try to wipe my eyes surreptitiously, even as Colby tightens his arms around me. We'd talked about our pasts enough to settle them, but having my face shoved in it like this is practically transporting me back to the night I was stuck in the room when he had sex with Addison. Jack plows on.

"Seeing your pain the night I dropped off those letters was almost as big of a high as hearing you tripped and fell the night Colby fucked Addison in college. God, it was delicious to know I helped push you over that edge." His lips smack. "Hey, since we're practically family, would you like hearing about the Hunts, knowing you'd never be accepted even now that you're famous?"

"Considering he doesn't particularly care since he doesn't speak to them, I'm not sure I give a shit." Colby nods approvingly at my response.

"Since they never acknowledge their bastard children, what makes you think they'll ever accept you? Do you really think you'll ever see Grandpa Zach walk you down the aisle to his precious grandson? Think Daddy will ever open his arms to accommodate you the way his son did? Maybe if he wants a quick fuck. Grow the hell up, Corinna. The world Colby's supposed to live in isn't where happily ever after exists. It's made up of power, and whoever has all the pieces wins."

Colby shakes his head in confusion. Neither of us have any idea where this is going.

"At least, that's what my father told my mother," Jack says, right before he hangs up the phone.

"What?" I yell at the same time Colby does.

Colby stills. "Did he say what I think he just said?" Colby lifts tortured eyes to me.

I cup Colby's face and hold on. "Just breathe."

"Cori, what if he's not just yanking my chain? What if he's..."

I finish the thought for him. "Telling the truth?" He nods wearily. "I don't know. Is there any chance he could be...?" I can't say the words.

"I don't know." His voice is broken. "But I'll be damned if I'm not going to find out. I mean, he doesn't look a damn thing like me. How the hell would I know? It's not hard for someone who's obviously gone off their rocker like he has to make a claim like this. When I was living at home we used to... Well, it's not like it wouldn't have been hard to find out information about me." He scrubs his fingers over his head. "Jesus, I'm talking about this like it's a possibility."

"Think back, Colby."

"I'd rather not. I might lose my lunch." The look of pain on his face physically hurts me.

I stroke his chest. "I know. Is there anyone who could help?"

"Yes. No. Something's not adding up."

"What?"

He just shakes his head.

I want to be calm, I really do, but there's no way I'm handling this discussion without some kind of anesthetic. I turn away from Colby.

"Where are you going?" His voice is anxious. He moves to follow me, but I hold up a hand. I just can't.

"I need chocolate."

Quickly slipping around the side of the freezer in the hall, I suddenly stop and rest my head against the cold wall. This is too much to handle. All of the emotional pain I've buried to give me and Colby a fighting chance comes back up with the force of a geyser. I slide down the wall until my butt is resting on my heels. One good weekend and here we are again, being victimized because of someone's desperation for what? Acceptance? Jealousy? Greed? Prestige? How much more are we expected to take?

As the tears fall harder and faster down my face, I don't see the booted feet move closer to me. I do feel the warmth from a body in contrast to the coldness at my back. My head snaps up. I see Colby's ravaged face.

"I promise you, Cori, I'll figure this out. This isn't the most important concern right now. The most important thing...the most important thing," he stresses, "is you. You're back in my life. I'll fight the Devil to keep you there." Reaching out to wipe the tears that keep falling, he asks, "Okay?"

"Colby, we can't just ignore..." I start, but I'm cut off.

"And I don't plan on it. Right now, my woman is on a path to eliminating the enemy from her body. That's the fight we're focusing on today."

I raise my hand to cup his jaw. "Then I wonder if I should call Greenwich Hospital to find someone else to perform my physical because there's no way I trust that office after that call."

He lets out a bark of laughter. "Good idea." Standing to his full height, he offers me his hand.

And I take it. Willingly.

36

COLBY

THIRTY NINE DAYS BEFORE SURGERY

"So that's everything." I sigh wearily, scrubbing my hands up and down my face. I've just told Caleb, Keene, and Charlie everything about my family. Including the details they won't find in any files. What happened with Corinna's and my past, and how Jack might be entwined with it.

"And Corinna knows all of this?" Keene whips out sharply.

I give him a thin smile. "She mentioned something about you and Caleb," I nod to the other man before continuing. "Almost ruining your relationships with Ali and Cassidy because of not laying your cards on the table."

Charlie lets out a bark of laughter. "She's not wrong."

Keene glares at him. "Can we keep the focus on the immediate problem with Colby and not on my mistakes with Alison which are long over?"

I stretch my legs out in front of me. "I don't know. I'd like to hear about them sometime."

Caleb laughs.

"Laugh all you want, my friend, but I seem to remember giving you the same advice you shoved back at me. And you almost lost my sister because of it," Keene taunts.

"That's different," Caleb argues.

"How?" Keene's voice is full of disbelief.

"Because it was Cassidy."

"And this is why you're not our lawyer. That argument is bullshit. At least Corinna holds a lick of sense in this family." Keene holds up his hand. "And if anyone tells her I said that after she threw a pie in my face, I'll fire them immediately."

"It might be worth it to see her smile." I can't help the faint smile ghosting my lips.

Keene's face softens slightly. "When things were all over the map for Alison and me, Corinna was the only one who stood toe-to-toe against me for Alison's sake. She has my everlasting gratitude for that." Clearing his throat, he continues. "What we're about to do, we do not only for you, but for her."

"Agreed," Caleb says. "Then again, it's family. We just do it, period."

"Let's get started," Charlie says. "No one fucks with my family."

My throat tightens. I feel the arms of yet another family wrap around me in one hard embrace. The Freemans. The Army. And now, Hudson.

HOURS LATER, Caleb has taken copious notes on his computer, while Charlie and Keene grill me within an inch of my life about my family, Jack, and even Corinna.

Their questioning is more invasive than a full-body search. As emotionally exhausting as it is, the conclusion we came to in its wake is almost surreal.

"Make the call," Keene orders brusquely.

Almost in a daze, I dial the number Caleb had one of the analysts pull up an hour earlier when the pattern started to emerge.

One ring...

Two...

The line connects, and a male voice says, "Who the hell is this?"

I take a deep breath and say the first words to a man I admired my whole life, who I haven't spoken with since before I left for college. "It's Colby. I need your help."

37

CORINNA

THIRTY-FIVE DAYS BEFORE SURGERY

"Corinna, I need you to sit down." Bryan's voice is calm on the other end of the line.

Each day seems to be getting exponentially harder as we lead up to the surgery. And to think I haven't even gotten to the fun parts that involve another MRI and spending quality time with a psychologist discussing my greatest concerns about my upcoming surgery.

Instead of voicing all of this aloud, I answer with a simple "Okay" as I ease myself onto one of the stools around my workspace.

"Your primary care doctor is claiming you've never been a patient there." Bryan lets out a sigh. "They're claiming they don't have any medical records dating back the last twelve months."

"You have got to be kidding me, Bryan. I have receipts showing I paid the bills they sent me," I exclaim.

"I completely believe you, Cori. I have the copies of the orders your doctor put in at Hopkins as well, but since I no longer work there, it could take weeks to pull those records. Weeks we don't have."

Jack. He's behind this. "So he really means for me to die, doesn't he?" I murmur.

"We're not going to let that happen," Bryan says firmly. "I don't care if we have to rerun every test in the next month, you're getting that thing out of you. First, I'm calling some friends in Baltimore." Before I can respond, Bryan hangs up.

Placing the phone on the table so I don't throw it, I get up to make my way upstairs to Ali's office.

"THE FIRST THING we're going to do is file a complaint with the Federal Office of Civil Rights and the Attorney General. Clearly, there's been a violation of your rights under HIPAA." Ali's fuming.

Jared, who's on speakerphone, suggests, "You should call Keene and Caleb, Ali. They're both on a first-name basis with the AG. It might get this resolved faster."

"Good idea, Jared. Do we know any lawyers who'd want this case?" Ali inquires.

"Salivate over it is more likely," he chuckles. "I wonder if the AMA will want to strip the practice's medical license over this."

"In enough time so I don't die first?" I wonder aloud.

Silence drops like a bomb.

"Cori, the threat of a HIPAA lawsuit, let alone the subsequent insurance fraud investigation from the highest lawyer in the nation, should be enough to produce your records miraculously," Jared assures me soothingly. "As a lawyer, I can assure you, this is not a law you mess around with. There are both civil and criminal penalties they can face. They'll try to save face as quickly as possible and claim it was an error."

As much as I hate even the idea they'll skate by this, I have to focus on my immediate needs. "How long do you think this will take?"

"Let me contact the attorney I have in mind to represent you," Jared says. "I'd say no more than a few days."

And that's a few days of worrying.

"Fine, but Jared? I want them to pay when this is over." Tears fall down my face. Ali moves from around her desk. A sob hitches in my throat as I try to talk. "I'm so stressed about this surgery already, and

to have this dick be able to pull this..." For money. Greed. For something he thought he'd get so long as he could control the people
around him, and it's unraveling around him.

Like I am right now.

"I need to bake a cake. I have to get my mind off of this." I squeeze
my sister. "Thank you both for everything."

Ali laughs darkly. "I've been looking for a good target to fight with
over what's happening to you. You just gave me the ability to help
wage war. It's me who should be thanking you."

WHEN I GO HOME SHORTLY after, I kick off my sneakers and drop my
bag in the middle of the foyer. I should kick back and relax curled up
on the couch with a comfortable blanket and sleep, but what I really
want is to guzzle wine by the gallon—glass optional. I'm debating the
merits between red or white when my doorbell rings.

I can tell Colby feels the same way when he crosses the threshold
saying, "I thought you were going to lie down this afternoon since
you haven't been sleeping well."

I shrug. "Planned on it. I was derailed a bit." I look at him suspi-
ciously. "What are you doing home?"

"I came to nap with you." His grin is quick.

I roll my eyes. "Uh-huh. Who blabbed about my day?"

Colby opens his mouth only to snap it shut. "I'll never tell."

Wrapping my arm around Colby's waist so my stomach is pushed
against his side, I explain. "See, it's like this. There are no secrets in
this family."

He scoffs. "Princess, you have no room to talk."

He's got me there. "Okay. When all the lies were taken away, no
more secrets." Melting into his body, I close my eyes. "Despite everything, I can't but help to count my blessings. In the middle of this
hell, we were left with something pretty special—each other."

"I know."

We stand together in my kitchen, just holding on to one another for a long while. Tipping my head back, I ask, "So, how was your day? Boring? Noneventful?"

"About like yours. How about we have pizza for dinner, drink wine, and do absolutely nothing but relax?"

"Sounds perfect." *Just like you.*

A normal night. It's exactly what my soul needs.

38

COLBY

There are secrets, and then there are secrets.

I don't consider the call I made earlier in the week a secret because Corinna already knows I'm looking into finding out the truth behind Jack.

I'm pretty confident she never expected me to use the connections I have to do it though.

I knew she wouldn't be angry. Far from it. But I knew it would add to the burden she's carrying.

And that's the last thing I want to do.

So, when my phone lights up with a text in the middle of watching *Chopped* with the message *We should talk. Tomorrow.* I take a quick moment to reply, *Fine.*

Corinna's cussing out the chefs while lying on my chest, and she asks curiously, "What's that about?"

I tell her without remorse, "It's work."

"Okay."

I'm not lying. Analysts in Hudson are digging deep to find out the information I need to know to close out the past so Corinna and I can move on to our future as soon as her surgery is done.

And by then, I'll know what that future looks like.

39

CORINNA

TWENTY DAYS BEFORE SURGERY

"Corinna Freeman."

Standing, I grab my coffee and bag before following a casually dressed woman down a long hall in Greenwich Hospital. The appointment I've been dreading is here.

The psychologist.

I don't need someone to poke in my brain other than with a scalpel. I don't need them to tell me I'm hanging on to emotional scars from my teenage years. Shocker, I have mommy and daddy issues. Might come from them trying to sell me. I escaped, they died. I call that a win all the way around.

Why the hell am I here again?

As I follow the woman down the hall, I find one good thing about this appointment. They don't take your height, weight, or blood pressure ahead of time. I snicker quietly.

"Right in here," she says before she steps back to let me precede her. I'm surprised to find myself in a richly colored room with over-sized armchairs and lots of throw pillows.

Hearing the door click shut behind me, I wander over to one of the pillows and murmur, "I think I saw this on sale at HomeGoods."

I spin around when the woman who escorted me in chuckles.

"You have a good eye. I couldn't pass it up. There's something about the fringe I just fell for."

My jaw drops. "You're the shrink?"

"Alice Cleary." The woman who escorted me into the room holds out her hand, and I automatically take it. "If you're surprised now, I have a feeling we're going to have fun over the next few hours."

"I think I'm going to need chocolate," I mutter.

Cheerfully walking over to her desk, she pulls open a drawer. "Dive in." I gape at the assortment of candy bars littering the inside of her drawer. Spying a bar of Godiva, I snag it. "Let's get comfortable and talk about how today's session is going to work. By the way, do you like music?"

Unwrapping the unexpected treat, I nod. "I do."

Soft music begins to play in the background. "Excellent. Let's get started."

Two hours later, I want to bring Alice home with me. "Gee, Corinna. There's nothing on your mind at all," Alice drawls as she makes notes on a legal pad. "Critical information was kept from you for over ten years, something that influenced the course of your life. Your boyfriend, the man you're falling in love with, may have a half brother with someone who's made your life a living hell. Oh, and you're having brain surgery in less than three weeks." Pausing, she looks at me, half-amused and half-astounded. "Got anything else stored up in there?"

I think about it. I really do. And then I just hand it over.

"I'm not sure which I'm more afraid of."

"What's that?"

"Dying or being trapped in the dark, unable to move because Bryan somehow fucks up what he considers"—I air quote—"easy brain surgery. I mean seriously? Is any brain surgery easy?"

"Idiot," she scoffs. "I have this completely unprofessional theory. Want to hear it?"

Since Alice is my new BFF, I totally do. "Go for it."

"Men have a Y chromosome. Therefore, as women, we get to ask ourselves why all the time. Why are they such dumbasses seems to be the leading question."

I laugh hysterically. Definitely not what I expected to do in this office.

Alice sits straighter in her chair. "What you're feeling right now is actually common before surgery."

"I refuse to admit I'm common," I drawl with a toss of my hair.

Chuckling, Alice continues. "It's the loss of control. Almost all patients feel it regardless of the procedure. Normally, the doctors can reassure them. Despite what Dr. Moser implied, with a procedure as complicated as yours, we ask you to come to speak with us. Right now, your life is so far out of control, you need to get some of it back."

"How?" I demand. I stand up, taking the pillow with the fringe I've been worrying with me. "How the hell am I supposed to control any of this?" Hurling the pillow across the room, I turn to find Alice smiling.

"That's one way. Let loose the emotions choking you, good and bad. If you need to throw things to relax, go for it."

"My sister gave me food to smash." I remember Cassidy putting the grapefruits and tomato in front of me, and the sick pleasure I felt as I saw them splatter.

Alice chuckles. "Messy, but effective, certainly. Do you remember the endorphin kick you felt after? It's counteracting the cortisol, the hormone associated with stress."

Sliding back into my chair, I ask, "What else?"

"Deal with your issues head-on, Corinna. If you think you'll feel better by preparing for your death, do it. Write letters to your family. Give them to someone you trust to be distributed in the event of something happening. Hell, write them letters for the day of surgery anyway. You're going to be out of it for over eight hours. How do you think they're going to feel?"

"Petrified."

"Take back your power as a woman, as a sister, as a friend, and let them know you're with them. Address their worries even as you address your own."

It's so simple, it's brilliant.

I jump up and give her a huge hug. "I'm not kidding, Alice. Next time you need a cake baked for any reason after I've recovered, you'd better call me."

"I'll take you up on that because you're going to recover, Corinna." She pulls back. "Dr. Moser is going to get your tumor out, then you'll recover. And then the world had better watch out for the formidable woman in its midst," she predicts.

"And to think I was scared to come in today," I say with wonder in my voice.

"People always are. It's my job to make sure you're not on the way out," she schools me. "Did I do my job?"

"You definitely gave me something more productive to think about. That's for sure," I admit.

"Then I think we're done. How about I drop by after surgery to check on you?" she offers.

With a better outlook than I've had in a long while, I say, "I'd like that. I'm sure my family would too."

"I wouldn't miss meeting them for the world. They sound fascinating."

DECIDING to take Alice's words to heart, I make a detour on my way home from Greenwich and drive to Westport. Finding off-street parking, I make my way into Paper Source. I think about what Alice said about the time my family's going to be sitting there waiting for me while I'm in surgery, and suddenly, I'm on a mission.

I find a stationery set with a black bear giving hugs, a set with sloths, and a set with peacocks. I immediately snag a set of cards with kittens giving each other a high five. I tear up when I pop the "I can't imagine this day without you!" set in my basket. I grab a mini set of boxes of "I am thankful for..." cards when I see "The Future Looks Bright" set. In it goes. I'm spending a fortune, and I don't care.

There isn't an hour that's going to pass where my loved ones are waiting for news where they won't feel me with them in the waiting room.

Just as I'm about to head to the cash register to ring up my damage, I see it. Brown leather, wrapped with a matching tie closure. I pick it up slowly, feeling the soft pebbled leather against the pads of my fingers. Flipping it open, the cream-colored pages are begging for the things I've yet to tell Colby. I clutch it to me as I make my way to the register.

"Will this be debit or credit?" the bored after-school clerk asks me.

"Credit." Pulling out my wallet, I pay the cashier, signing my name with a flourish. I take my bag and make my way to the door. Pausing before I walk out, I just have that sense of rightness about myself I haven't felt in way too long.

I feel unconquerable.

40

COLBY

Bryan ordered a final MRI for Corinna because he wants to get the best possible imaging before the procedure. Due to her extreme fear of dark spaces, Bryan's willing to have her completely knocked out for the procedure, so long as someone can drive her home. Since the entire family knows, Corinna had numerous volunteers. She smiled, thanked them all, and turned to me to make sure I could take the day off work.

Her trust in me is unequivocal. What have I done to deserve this humbling faith? The inner voice inside me says, *She loves you. You finally let her. That's all you ever need to do.*

Staggered by the realization, I helplessly watch as the technicians lift a lifeless Corinna from a gurney onto the narrow MRI platform. I helped her braid her long locks early this morning before we left for the hospital. The kiss I received after I tied it off with a rubber band that is "not Em approved" would have to carry me over the next several hours.

This is a glimpse of the hell I'll be living through in a few short weeks.

A hand landing on my shoulder jostles me from my intense focus through the windows of the MRI room. "It's going to be hours, Colby.

I got special permission for you to wait here, but are you sure you want to?" Bryan asks quietly.

"I promised her I wouldn't be farther away than this. I'm not breaking my promise." I'm firm on that.

I've already broken one she doesn't need to know about yet by keeping a secret from her.

I wince as the plastic face mask is lowered over her face. "Can you tell me why they're doing that?" I ask the neurosurgeon.

"I need her head in a certain position to get the best images. See the foam the techs are putting in by her cheeks and forehead?" He points through the window. "It's not to scare a patient, though most are the first time they use the mask." He shakes his head regretfully. "We can't have them move a centimeter inside the tube. The pictures blur and give out poor readings."

"So, it's possible the tumor hasn't grown?" I ask hopefully.

"No, that's confirmed. Before Corinna panicked during her last scan, we were able to capture the size change. I need this MRI to..." He stops himself before he finishes his sentence.

"To what?"

"I know I hurt her when I wouldn't talk with her that day. She knew my ego was out of joint. I regret that." Bryan laughs humorlessly, rubbing the back of his neck. "Time and again, I explain these procedures to patients and families alike. It's commonplace. I'm direct, concise, and I let the counselors handle the families so I don't have to."

I wait for him to continue. When he does, his words are direct and brutal, the reality slamming into my heart so painfully, I feel like I'm about to have a heart attack. "Today's scan is called a brain mapping, Colby. This way, I know where best to put the incision, where to cut when I get past the bone, and how to get the tumor out while touching as little of her healthy tissue as I can. Without it, I'm flying blind." Bryan's eyes are full of sympathy. "She's knocked out with enough drugs to keep her down for about three hours, meaning I'm going to get the clearest images I'll have seen in the five years she's been my patient. The images her former doctor had before were complete shit."

"Who did she see before?" Bryan rattles off a name that means nothing to me, but from the look of admiration on his face, it obviously means something to him. I feel better that Cori hasn't forsaken her medical care while trying to keep her condition under wraps. Seeing headsets hanging on the wall inside the MRI chamber, I frown. "Does she have music or anything in there?"

He shakes his head. "Sometimes, yes. Today, I can't have the images obstructed."

I run my hands through my dark hair. "How much assurance can you give me she won't wake up?" I'm petrified I'll hear her screaming again.

"She'll be in recovery before she even stirs. But hold her close tonight. I don't know what she'll remember." Like I'd do anything different.

Between one heartbeat and the next, Bryan morphs into Dr. Moser and starts barking orders. Moments later, Corinna is slid back into the tunnel. The technicians scurry out with her gurney. The door to the MRI room is sealed.

And the wait begins.

THREE HOURS LATER, I have a new enemy. A target for all my hatred. I just can't get my hands around it to destroy it. It lives inside the head of the woman I love.

As I wait for Corinna to wake from her tests, my knee jerks up and down rapidly as I remember what I heard.

"Clearest pictures yet, Dr. Moser."

"I agree. These images leave me very encouraged."

God, I hope so. Just seeing the mass lit up inside Corinna's brain on the screens made me want to throw my head back and scream.

I want to fix this myself, but I can't. I have to rely on someone else and the mercy of angels who may be having a bad day to save the woman I was born to breathe for.

Smoothing my hand over her head, where the offending mass lies waiting to die, I whisper, "We're going to cut you out, you son of a bitch. Then I'm going to do my damnedest to prevent anything from hurting her ever again."

Small hands touch my forearm, grazing over my ink. "Promise?" I look down into Corinna's golden eyes that are still hazy from all the drugs.

"I swear it on my life." Grazing first her forehead, and then her lips with a kiss, I mean nothing less.

She smiles briefly before her eyes drift shut, the medicine taking her under again. I sit holding her hand, keeping my promise to never be far from her side.

When my cell buzzes in my pocket, I shift so I can pull it out without letting go of her hand.

Is everything okay? Let me know when you're done at the hospital.

Typing back a quick message that it could be hours, I tell him to call Keene if it's urgent.

Right now, I have one focus.

And it's the woman in front of me.

41

CORINNA

I hang up the phone with Marco. Our conversation was much like our relationship was—sweet and full of concern. He's upset I didn't share any of this with him while we were together, but it wasn't his to know. Not before my family.

And now that family includes Colby.

How did I ever contemplate for even a moment of filling the space inside me reserved for Colby with another man?

I'll always have fond memories of Marco, unlike Colby with his history with Addison. Marco helped me look at myself differently, showing me I shouldn't undervalue the woman I am. While I know he will be thinking of me while I undergo this battle, it isn't him I need by my side.

It's Colby.

Dropping my phone on the table next to me, I feel strong arms wrap around me. "How did he take it?" Colby murmurs in my ear.

I take a moment to respond, basking in the strength at my back. Lost, found, and back in each other's arms. I offer up my thanks to whoever is listening today to my inner musings before I respond. "He's worried. Frustrated I never shared this with him. Understanding it wasn't him I was supposed to share it with." Turning within the cradle of Colby's arms, I lay my head on his chest. "He said to make sure you're taking good care of me."

Colby pulls back in surprise. "Me specifically?"

This is a little embarrassing. "Apparently, I was sleeping one night, and I might have said the wrong name when he curled up behind me." I look away. "Perhaps."

Colby captures my jaw in his firm hands. "No. Way." A slow grin spreads across his face.

I shrug, trying to play it off. "These things happen."

Walking backward, Colby pulls us toward the couch. As he falls back, I land on top of him. "That makes me feel a lot better."

Huffing, I try to push up. His arms tighten, trapping me. "It's embarrassing, Colby," I grate out. "It's not like you ever called out the wrong woman's name."

"Who says?" he counters.

My lips fall open, and I repeat his words. "No. Way."

As his dark head nods, I grin. "Okay, the only way this could get better would be if you tell me it was round two with Addison."

The red tinge that suddenly edges his cheekbones tells me I nailed it. I burst into gales of laughter. "I think you deserve a reward," I proclaim.

He guffaws. "That's not exactly what was implied at the time."

"Even more of a reason." Why I'm almost gleeful at the idea of Colby calling out my name during sex with the she-bitch, I don't know. But for me? It just further supports the idea he'd rather have been with me. "You know what you haven't let me do yet?" My voice drops as I slide my hands over his broad chest.

And down his lean hips.

"What's that?"

Reaching behind me, I drag a fingertip over his firm erection. "Play."

Colby does a crunch until our noses are touching. His hands begin to roam over my chest. "Play? You mean the things we've done in bed haven't been fun, sweetheart?"

I roll my eyes. "You know what I mean."

He shakes his head back and forth, his nose brushing against mine as he does it. "I'm sure I do, but I want to hear you say the words."

He wants the words? I'm pretty sure I can give him some filthy ones. Leaning close to his ear, I use my slowest drawl to purr, "I want to unbutton your shirt and take it off your delicious body. I want to use my hands, my mouth, and my tongue to trace every inch of your skin. I want to trace the ink you got for me while you watch."

His breath has increased. "I'm listening."

"I want to kneel on my knees. I want to peel you out of these pants that dare to mold your ass like they belong there more than my hands do. Then I want to show you how it feels when I slide your cock in my mouth while I'm gripping your hips." I take a delicate nip of his ear.

"More," he growls.

"Right before you come down my throat, when the first delicious drops of you leaks out, I want my hand between your legs so I can cup you. I want to..." I don't get to finish because Colby's pulled my head back, and he slams his mouth down on mine.

The fire of our kiss may be from my words, but the spark is from something more profound. Something I've finally grasped has been there from the beginning.

Love.

I am irrevocably in love with Colby Hunt.

And I want nothing more than to show him.

Tearing my lips away from his, I plead, "Let me touch you. Let me taste you. Let me show you."

"Whatever you want, Cori." Reaching behind him, he pulls off the T-shirt he was wearing. "Whatever you need." Lying back on the couch, he becomes a feast for all my senses.

"You," I gasp. "I just need you." If I have him, I have everything.

His eyelids drop as I press my lips against his chest for the first of a thousand times to taste him. Multiple times, I'm interrupted as he captures my lips in drugging kisses. After I've shifted down his body, my lips trace over his impressive abdomen. His hand finds its way into my hair. His moans become guttural.

I'm flying high on the pleasure I'm giving him.

I reach for the button of his pants, which gives way without any problems. And don't I just love how he goes commando. Reaching beneath, I tug his pants down, even as he lifts his hips to help me. "Tsk, tsk, Colby. What is your dry cleaner going to say?" I swipe my finger across the crown of his cock that's already weeping.

"He's probably going to be jealous as fuck." Colby's voice sounds deeper than usual. Looking up from between his legs, he's propped himself up on his arm so he can watch.

And his eyes are like the smoke right before a fire that burns out of control.

Humming a little bit, I flatten my tongue to run it up the under-side of his cock. I vaguely hear him hiss in reaction, but I'm too intent on wrapping my lips around the head for a taste to note more than his pleasure.

And when I do, you'd think I'd just told him I'd figured out a way to make nacho-flavored brownies.

"Holy fucking...fucking shit! Corinna, sweet Jesus!" he yells as I take him deep into the back of my throat. Balancing on my elbows, I play with his sack lightly while using my other hand to smear the juice from my mouth to lubricate the part of his cock I can't fit in.

This goes on for a few minutes while Colby valiantly tries to maintain control. Eventually, the feel of my swollen lips and the pres-sure from my fingertips on the sensitive skin around his balls has him pleading for mercy. "Baby, you have to slow down. I'm going to..."

I don't give him the chance to finish the sentence. With a flick of my wrist, I roll his sack in my hands, and he erupts deep in my throat. Swallowing quickly, I drink him down.

While I use my tongue to clean him off delicately, I realize now I'm always going to crave him. He's delicious. Addicting. He's every flavor I've wanted to capture and never knew the taste I needed.

Resting my head on his lower abdomen, I feel his hands run over my hair. I glimpse the brightly colored tattoo on his forearm, just as his hand is about to slide over my shoulder. Capturing his hand, I tug his arm toward me and whisper, "Never forget," before my lips cover his tattoo.

He pulls his arm away from my lips slowly before using that same arm to trace the tattoo under my shirt on back. "*Numquam obliviscar qui sis*, Corinna. Not to me."

No, Colby. There's no way I'll ever forget who I am to you. Not ever again.

He reaches down and pulls me atop of him so we're a tangle of limbs and clothing.

Tangled in each other.

Just the way it should be.

42

COLBY

Keene slams down the phone. "If I have to talk to that sanctimonious prick one more time while we're investigating this, I swear to God I'm selling the entire company to you," he says to Caleb. "Then I'm taking Ali and Kalie and moving to a deserted island. Freaking pain in my ass."

Caleb tries to coax him off the ledge. "Just remember it's for a good cause."

I have nothing to contribute to the conversation because I know what a pain the man in question can be. My encounters with him haven't been easy either as we navigate through years of bitterness.

But I need answers. And he's one of the few people who I think can provide them.

I just hope I can get them before Corinna's surgery so we don't have this to contend with when the whole family's around.

43

COLBY

EIGHT DAYS BEFORE SURGERY

It's a simple text, but it means everything.

Spoke with your father. He confirmed. Will let you know as soon as I have the lawyers make contact.

Jesus, I don't know how he pulled it off.

Yes, I do. He used all of his connections he's built up over the years to do it.

I put my phone back on the nightstand, and Corinna slides back into me. Her murmured "Colby" shakes my heart to the core.

I tighten my arms around her a little more.

I need to hold on to my world a bit tighter tonight.

44

CORINNA

SEVEN DAYS BEFORE SURGERY

Stretching, I put my pen down. Another notecard is complete. With every word I write, I'm regaining the power I didn't know I lost. Putting the small stack to the side, I pull Colby's journal closer to me. Tucking my fist under my chin, I flip through the pages I've filled with random thoughts over the last few days.

Today the blank page seems to taunt me to fill it.

Because in some ways, this is the book I dread. This is the book that could be my last chance.

Picking up the pen, I unconsciously let my brain spew through the ink.

You should know beyond a shadow of a doubt that I love you...

I finish the journal entry by scrawling my name and put it aside, just as the front door opens. Colby steps through. "Hey, princess. You ready to head to dinner at the farm?"

Pushing up from the couch, I walk over to meet him with a kiss. "I sure am. Any idea what we're having for dinner?"

"None. What are you working on?" he asks curiously.

"Just some thank-you cards," I answer ambiguously.

The slow smile that never fails to weaken my knees crosses his face. "Anything urgent?"

I shake my head. "Let's go. I'm starving."

He links his fingers in mine, and we stop at my island long enough for me to grab my purse. Soon we're driving toward the main barn where the rest of the family is waiting. Our family, I amend, because my family has become Colby's throughout this as much as they've become mine.

～

"I CAN'T TAKE ANY MORE." I'm doubled over with laughter. "I paid for your hair to be cut."

"Do you see this picture?" Alison holds up the photo Holly took of her red-streaked blonde hair. "You stuck my hair in food coloring over something I didn't do!"

"Who else could have? I didn't come home that night." Holly nods emphatically.

"Oh really?" Phil drawls.

We're sitting around the huge farm table passing around the pictures Holly took of my morning-after revenge when I realized someone had eaten a good quarter of Colby's birthday cake in college.

Keene accepts the picture and lets out a low whistle. "Damn, baby," he says, addressing Alison. He turns to me. "Every time I see this, I'm impressed by the way you dole out revenge." Glancing over at Holly, he says, "And it wasn't you?"

"Hand to God, Keene. If it were, I would have paid for that haircut myself," Holly swears.

I feel Colby's body shaking as he tries to suppress his laughter. Finally, he lets loose. Planting a kiss on the back of my neck, he murmurs, "You're going to kill me."

I still. He can't possibly mean what I think he means.

Does he?

"It was either that or do something about the raging hard-on I had pressed against your back just from smelling your skin." He drops a kiss on my shoulder. "You were so sweet, made sweeter by you spending hours in the kitchen to make me happy on a day no one else gave a shit about."

I turn around, laughter warring with indignation. "You! You ate your cake and let Ali take the blame?"

"Cori, will you miss his dick if I chop it off?" Ali says in a sugary voice. The table erupts in laughter.

"Tremendously," I assure her. Colby's grin is unrepentant. He leans down to brush his lips against mine, even as he addresses Ali.

"How about to make up for not fessing up when it happened, I treat you and Cori to a spa day once she's permitted after surgery?" The smile he's bestowing on me tells me the price he's paying now was well worth the crime. Then and now.

"Deal," we both say enthusiastically. But something's wrong. When I say the word, it comes out wrong. I shake my head and repeat it. "Deee." Frantically, I grab for Colby's hand.

My heart is out of control.

The table around us goes eerily quiet.

"Co-by." I can't say his name. Fuck. I can't say the name of the man I love! Hot burning tears slide over my lashes and splash onto my cheeks.

"Calm down, baby. You need to relax. This is probably just temporary." His voice is firm.

Jason stands up. "I'll call her doctor." He walks out into the foyer.

Guttural sobs are spilling from my lips. Here it is, the end.

It's only just begun.

And I never told Colby while I was whole that I loved him.

Jason comes back into the room. "Colby, I need you to move behind Corinna so I can do a few tests."

Colby swiftly moves behind me. "I've got you. I'm not letting you go. Believe that, Cori."

Tears continue to fall down my cheeks as dread invades every pore of my being. *How can I expect him to live with me if this might be the best of what comes out of this surgery?* I don't respond, but I'm weak. I press back into his chest.

"Corinna, I'm going to ask you to close your eyes super tight and then open them." Jason's in full doctor mode. "Good. Now, I have a flashlight; I'm going to shine it in each of your eyes." After a few seconds, he relaxes. "Good. Normal pupil response. Let's check your strength. Push my arms outward as hard as you can. Now inward." After I accomplish both, he smiles. "Now squeeze my hands. As hard as you can. Get out all your frustration and anger about this bullshit, Cori." That I can do. I use every ounce of energy inside of me and tighten my fingers around Jason's.

"You did perfectly. Let me call Bryan, and then I'll tell you what this means, okay?" Jason cups my cheek before moving back into the foyer.

Colby reclaims his seat, pulling me onto his lap, before asking "Did you almost break Jason's fingers? I saw him wince for a second there."

Without thinking, I respond. "I was trying." I sit up, stunned. "Did that sound normal to just me?"

Colby captures my face in his hands before pressing a hard kiss to my lips. "No, baby. You sound perfect." His relief is evident.

"And this isn't uncommon, Corinna," Jason says as he steps back into the room. "She's fine," he tells the greater room at large. "What you're experiencing are the symptoms you would have if you'd never known about your tumor before now. Bryan just wanted to make certain this wasn't your tumor pressing on your ICAs. It's not if my hands are any indication," he says ruefully.

Reaching over, I grab one and give it a quick kiss. "Sorry, Jace."

Cupping my cheek, he tips my head up. "I'm not. I'd rather know we're not rushing you into surgery tonight. You're under doctor's orders to take it easy the next few days. No strenuous work or lifting."

"What about sex?" I ask boldly. Colby turns bright red. The family save Keene, who begins thwacking his head against the table, all start laughing. Mostly in relief, I think with shot of pain to my heart.

"As long as you don't go crazy, you're still clear for that up to the night before you check into the hospital."

"Okay." My voice comes out shakily, but whose wouldn't? Tonight scared the living hell out of me. It also proved to me I've been blessed with the gift of time and I need to use it wisely.

I need Colby to know how I feel before I go into surgery. Love was bestowed upon me as a gift. The first time I didn't recognize it. This time, I'll cherish it until I draw my last breath.

Time shouldn't be wasted.

Neither should love.

45

COLBY

LATER THAT NIGHT

Corinna had an incident.

The text back is within seconds. *Is she okay? Is there anything I can do?*

I contemplate what to send back as I look at my heart lying next to me on the bed. *The same thing we are. Pray.*

46

COLBY

SIX DAYS BEFORE SURGERY

I leave the office early. Corinna's been home, and despite the varying family members dropping in and out, I know she must be going stir-crazy. I debate on calling to see if she wants to run out to grab some food, when something tells me to wait and see when I get home.

Home. I've barely seen the inside of my apartment in the last month and a half. Corinna and wherever she is has become my home again. We've talked about the years in between, avoiding the subject of Jack's betrayal, as it increases her stress when she doesn't need it. All we've found is those years made us grateful for having this second chance.

Fundamentally, we're the same people. Corinna is still the funny, smiling, warm-hearted, loyal woman I was falling for at twenty-one. She's also stubborn, provocative, and has a vicious temper that can drop a person to their knees.

She's everything I knew I wanted, and everything I couldn't possibly dream of because she hadn't fully come into herself yet.

As much as we both regret the time lost, especially with the specter of her surgery looming over us, it's made me realize time won't stop us. It's why we'll fight this battle and win.

There's no way the light in those golden eyes will fade.

Life wouldn't be that cruel.

Pulling in behind her car, I hop out of the Jeep and make my way to the front door. Using the key she gave me, I slide it into the lock. I'm about to call out to her when I see her hair cascading over the edge of the couch.

No...

I drop my bag and keys on the floor and race over to her, my boots almost slipping out from beneath me.

Her hands are tucked under her cheek. Her lips are tipped up turning a beautiful face into an extraordinary one.

And her chest is rising and falling.

I swallow hard, as tears come unbidden to my eyes. She's just asleep. Smoothing a hand over her hair, I choke out the first thing that comes to mind. "I love you."

When I lean down to kiss her, her lashes flutter.

"Hey, baby," I whisper.

"I must have been dreaming." She stretches. "It was such a perfect dream."

"Scoot over." She makes room for me on the couch. Prying off my boots, I join her under the blanket. "Why was it perfect?"

"It was a wish. Every wish comes true, right?"

Rolling partially on top of her, I murmur, "If you can't tell the man who loves you so he can make them come true, who can you tell?"

"That wasn't the dream?" she whispers, her lips curved in a mysterious smile.

I chuckle. "That's the reaction I get to my finally telling you I love you?"

"You know I love you too, Colby. So, so much." My heart pounds erratically as she tells me the words I already know but still celebrate hearing.

I nod, increasing the pressure of our lips against each other. I seal them together in a deep kiss where I pour every ounce of love into it. Minutes later when I pull away, I'm blinded by the blaze in her golden eyes.

My heart already begins memorizing this moment for the

upcoming days when I'll need this to comfort me and give me strength. My heart beats because hers does.

I don't know what I'll do if something happens during surgery to take her from me.

Needing to pull myself away from thoughts where our future may only be days instead of the years I want to imagine, I lighten the moment. "What do you think about going out for dinner?"

"And here I thought about making nachos," she says dryly.

I quickly open my arms and roll off the couch. Standing, I reach down and grab her hands, pulling her to her feet. "You're going to make nachos? Seriously, the woman I love making my favorite food ever? If you're up to it, I can't think of a better thing to eat."

Corinna rolls her eyes. "Of course not."

"I'll make it worth your while."

Laughing at me as she makes her way into the kitchen, she tosses over her shoulder, "I'm sure you will."

47

CORINNA
FIVE DAYS BEFORE SURGERY

"All right, no shaving my head, but what about cutting my hair?" I ask my surgical coordinator.

The woman on the other end of the line hesitates. "So many people ask me this question, Corinna. Let me ask you the question back. Why?"

I toss my thick mane of hair over my shoulder, where it cascades effortlessly to the middle of my back. It's gorgeous—probably no one in their right mind would ever think of taking scissors to it. But I need to put my affairs in order. And if I don't make it out of surgery alive, I somehow don't think they'll consider my hair an organ to donate.

I don't mention that to my surgical coordinator.

"All you people have mentioned to me is how exhausted this procedure is going to leave me for months. Months! My hair reaches the middle of my back and is as thick as a blanket. If I cut it, not shave it despite the grossness of not being able to shave within a week of surgery..." Temporarily diverted, I go on a mini rant. "Seriously, it's a good thing my boyfriend is amazing and can take my leg hair having its own five-o'clock shadow." I hear laughter in my ear as I continue. "I read the surgical materials about not shaving within so many days to avoid infection. I also understand people do things they regret later. How could donating my hair be something I'll regret? It's hair, right? It will grow back."

The silence on the other line tells me I scored a point. "There's nothing preventing you from doing this, Corinna. As long as you're sure. Surgical patients can be extremely emotional when the procedure is over. I don't want you to have distress when you will need that energy."

"Excellent. Then we're in agreement. I'll just call my salon to make sure they can fit me in as the last appointment today." I don't bother telling her I've already done that. The people I want there with me are going to take a while to reach.

MEDUSA STARES BACK at me in the mirror. With fourteen braids sticking out from all over my head, I'm certainly doing a great imitation of the Greek monster. Though I don't think she's being as pampered as I've been. So far, I've been treated to a manicure and pedicure, even though I had to decline putting on polish since it's flammable when you have surgery. I'm also getting treated to an upper back and shoulder massage as I wait for some of the most important people in my life to descend on the salon. All of the consultants at Shimmer, the salon I've been going to since we first moved to Collyer, have stayed behind to provide their services for free.

They're getting one hell of a tip tonight and dinner delivered from the local Chinese place.

I reach up and finger one of the crazy long braids. One side of my mouth tips up in the mirror as my fingers trail over the length to the ends where a piece of paper is attached. Every member of Shimmer had a hand in braiding my hair, but only my longtime hairdresser, Gail, will get to cut one braid. Just one. The rest are for my family and me to deal with. Gail will trim up what was left of my hair when it's done.

For so long, I worried so much about what people thought about my looks. I was a magnet for every dickless wonder with wandering hands. Then I fought back the systematic stripping of my self-worth during my captivity. Then there was hearing my own internal debasement from Addison's lips. I shake my head, braids with little notes attached to the ends flying everywhere.

My Colby. He paid so much for the pain he never intended to cause. My fears about my worth are what prevented me from going after the truth. There's a saying about vanity overtaking common sense. Mine did the exact opposite, it removed my common sense.

I hear Gail say, "She's in the back, but we're going to wait for the others."

It's almost time. I smile because my pride is about to be restored even as I use my vanity to take it down. Tonight, one of my vanities is about to help someone who desperately needs the reassurance I could have used years ago.

Vanity has no place in pride. Not for me. Not any longer.

～

"ARE YOU POSITIVE, CORINNA?" Cassidy says quietly, her hands resting on my shoulders. "There's no going back once we begin. They only need to shave a little bit around the surgical incision. You don't have to lose all of your gorgeous hair. You know we'll do anything you need us to while you're recovering."

I meet Cassidy's eyes in the mirror as I reach up to place my hand on top of hers. "There was no going back for me from the minute I knew this tumor needed to come out, Cass. There's no need for vanity with what I'm about to face. I need strength. Recovery's going to be an uphill battle as it is. Let's not add worrying if my hair's getting into my incision."

Her hands clench down hard. "Then who goes first?"

"Gail," I say immediately. "She needs to show you all where to cut." Leaning forward, I break Cassidy's hold on me as I place my glass on Gail's station. "Gail, where do you want this motley crew?" I joke.

All my siblings, as well as Jason, Caleb, Keene, and Charlie, have gathered around with varying degrees of shock and awe on their faces. Colby, who's standing closest to me, leans down to whisper, "Never forget, I love you."

A luminous smile crosses my face. "Gail? Show them where to cut."

Gail, who has a ridiculously small yet sharp pair of scissors in her hand steps forward. "Okay, everyone. You'll notice there's a note with your name tied around the braid you're supposed to cut. There are fourteen braids. I'll take one, show you where to cut, and take the braid after. Then you'll go in the order Corinna's card tells you."

Gail picks up the first braid, which is banded at the top about two-and-a-half inches from my scalp. "Try to cut as close to the band without actually snipping it. The braids are all measured for us to send into Locks of Love." Gail holds the base of the scissors to the only unlabeled braid. "Ready, kiddo?"

The music has switched to "Don't Give Up" by Peter Gabriel. I simply nod.

Gail begins cutting just above the top of the braid. In a few moments, it comes off in a hunk in her hands. She moves to the next station where a box lined with tissue paper waits. She lays down the braid before coming back to me with the scissors. "Hold these while I find your braid," she says. "Here it is." Handing me the card, Gail stays close to help me with the actual cutting.

I swallow the lump in my throat as my eyes meet those of my extended family. On a deep breath, I say the words I memorized earlier. "I'm not ready to leave you all." Holding the base of the scissors, Gail helps me put them in the right place, and together we cut off the second braid.

"Colby," I say softly. My boyfriend swallows as he steps up to accept the braid Gail pulls out. His voice chokes on the words "Never forget." He cuts the braid and hands it to Gail. "Ali, it says you're next on my card."

"Shit." Finding her braid, she lets loose a sob behind me. "Damn you, Corinna." I watch in the mirror as Keene steps up to hold her.

"For sisterhood." Tears flow down her face as she cuts the braid. "Keene, baby." She just hands him the scissors.

"Hell." The man who someday will become my brother-in-law glares at me in the mirror. "For the strength of convictions." He shakes his head at me as he bends down to kiss my cheek. "You're so damn strong, Corinna. Don't you ever forget it. Phil?" He hands the scissors to my brother.

Phil's eyes are overflowing so much, Gail has to step in and help him cut the braid before he can control himself enough to choke out, "For pride. Jace," he calls to his husband.

Jason steps forward. Quickly locating his braid, he reads quietly, "For wisdom." With a doctor's surgical precision, he cuts the braid. "Holly."

My sister wraps her arms around me, and I lean into her embrace. Because I know her as well as I do, I know she'll spend the rest of the night looking at the pictures of my hair and mourning in her own way. "You slay me," she whispers. Standing, she accepts the scissors from Jason. "For the strength to fight." She looks down at me, her eyes a different shade of gold than my own. "You'd better have the strength, sister. Em?"

Emily steps forward, pushing her glasses back up her nose. There are only a few braids left. She grabs hers and holds on to it as if making a wish. I hope it's the right one. Reading the card, she says, "Happiness is eternal. It's everywhere." She shakes her head in disbelief, even as she cuts my hair. "Corinna…"

"Em, just say who's next," I say gently.

"Charlie, it's your turn."

"Me?" His voice holds a note of disbelief. He looks around at the others, who are wiping their tear-filled eyes, but still nodding. "Corinna, are you sure?"

"Charlie, please," I ask softly.

He steps up to Em and relieves her of the scissors. Fumbling for his braid, he reads, "For unexpected guardian angels." Charlie's cut is precise. There are so few braids left, I can feel each and every tug against my scalp. I relish the burden being taken from my mind and body. "Cassidy."

My sister comes forward, her hands shaking. "You're so brave, Cori. I'm so proud of you."

A smile touches my lips. I just wait while Cassidy reads her card. Her hand lands on my shoulder. "No. No, this is you, not me." Her sobs are uncontrollable.

Caleb steps forward. "Cass? What does it say?"

"For the bravest person in the world. I'm just lucky she chose me as a sister." Cassidy's voice is laden with tears, her cut likely jagged with the way her hands are trembling. As soon as she passes the braid over, she buries her head into my neck. "I love you. We all love you so much."

"I know, Cass. You have to give the scissors to Caleb," I whisper.

Squeezing me one more time, she turns to her husband and places the scissors in his hand. He noticeably swallows. There are only three braids left. He finds his in seconds. Scanning the words, he murmurs, "For determination and perseverance." Brushing a kiss on the top of my head where the final two braids remain, he walks over to Colby. "Your turn again, brother."

Colby gives me a surprised look. "Two?"

"Two," I say firmly.

"I must have done something special," he murmurs.

You sure did, I think to myself. I watch him in the mirror as he reads his card. His countenance softens. He begins cutting without reading the card, handing both the scissors and the braid to Gail before pulling me to my feet. Capturing my face in his hands, he whispers, "For love," before he tenderly kisses me in front of my whole family.

The kiss goes on for some time before his lips pull away. The love sparkling between us is so bright, there's no way I'll ever be afraid of the dark ever again. Not as long as I have this man by my side.

Without moving from his arms, I reach my hand back toward Gail. She places the handle of the scissors in them. I feel for the final braid, all while holding Colby's dusky gaze. "Is it in the right spot?" I ask.

He nods. "Do you need the card?"

I smile, even as I shake my head slightly. I don't want to shift the scissors too much. Even as I hack away at the last braid, I announce to the room at large.

"This one's for the fight of my life."

THE SALON FILLS with the smell of Chinese food and wine. Where there were tears earlier, I hear laughter. Keene and Caleb quickly left to get their children. Before Gail sat me down in the chair to fix what's left of my hair, I spent time cuddling them. I'm not sure they understand who I am without the masses of hair they normally shove in their mouths, but hopefully they'll have the chance to get used to me. Now they're being passed between their fathers and uncles. My brother and my sisters are absorbed in my transformation.

I stick to cucumber water as Gail uses magic to trim what's left of my thick tresses. I now understand why she kept the hair surrounding my face out of the braids. Slightly longer in the front, the longer bangs frame my heart-shaped face, adding an almost pixie element to the cut.

Holly's taken pictures during this part of the process, more for herself than anyone else. As for me, there's no way I'll ever forget feeling as beautiful as I do right now because of the rightness of everything ricocheting inside of me.

Colby hasn't been far from my side. Every time I catch sight of him from the corner of my eye as Gail turns me one way or the other, the tidal wave of his love washes over me.

"Absolutely beautiful, Corinna. Take a look," Gail finally announces.

"You've always been beautiful," Colby says without moving a single inch. The smile he gives me steals my breath even as it promises me air.

"When I see myself through your eyes, I understand that," I tell him softly.

"Hallelujah!" Holly cries, throwing her fist in the air.

We all laugh, but I still accept the large mirror from Gail so I can see the front and the back of my new hairdo.

A hush comes over the room as I touch the back of my neck where there used to be a mane of hair. "Here, let me get the cape off so you can get the full effect." Gail quickly removes my black cape. The low V-back shirt I'm wearing displays the antique key I had tattooed to remember so many things.

Now it reminds me of nothing but that I was never forgotten across time or space.

"Why didn't I do this sooner?" I wonder aloud as I touch my short hair. My eyes look enormous in my face, even without makeup. I have to admit, "I look sexy as hell."

Colby growls. "Again, like that's anything new."

Raucous laughter spreads around the room. Keene snickers. "Are you just getting the memo on that, Cori?"

Wow. I turn to Gail. "Are you sure you won't let me pay for anything more than dinner? This deserves something. Anything. Please?"

Gail waves me off. "It was our honor to be a part of this. Between the hair and your donation, you're going to make some kids really happy."

"Hold up," Caleb intercedes. "What donation? You have to pay to donate your hair, Cori?"

"No. I'm sponsoring a child through the program so they can get a wig made," I tell my brother-in-law. I'm not immune to the swift glances around the room.

"Not without us, you aren't," Cassidy says. "And I speak for all of us." Phil, Em, Holly, and Ali all agree.

"I'm in," Jason adds. "Too many of my patients are without the funds for this kind of assistance."

Caleb and Keene just smile at Colby. "You don't even have to ask. I was going to dump a check in the box before Gail sealed it up," Colby admits.

"How much per child?" Keene asks.

"About fifteen hundred."

"Why don't we make an even fifteen kids happy. Caleb, you good with that?"

Caleb strokes his jaw back and forth. "You know who might be interested in this? Our newest client. He might want to contribute as well. Colby, what's your take?"

Colby freezes for a second before he relaxes. "Nice, Caleb. Very nice. Make it an even fifteen and add the extra donation to his bill. I'll let him know when Corinna and I talk with him later."

I'm baffled. "We're talking with one of your clients later?"

"Only because he's a pain in the ass and can't wait until you're out of surgery to meet you." Colby shakes his head. "I might be able to put him off for one more night, but longer than that and he'll be on our doorstep."

"Who, Colby?"

"We'll talk more about it privately but..." Colby takes both my hands in his before completely blowing my mind. "It's my grandfather. Senator Zachary Hunt."

48

COLBY

NIGHT FIVE BEFORE SURGERY

I never expected Cori to do what she did tonight. She let go of her shield, openly exposed who she is. With each moment that passed, she didn't shatter; she soared. Tonight cemented in my mind what I've somehow known on a molecular level since I first saw her. She's it for me. If the worst happens and we only have these few days, I'll live off the memories for the rest of my life. There will be no other who could replace her.

We've had more than most will ever experience in their lifetime. A love so brilliant, it pumps blood into the hardest of hearts. A love so self-sacrificing, she would have let herself drown before bringing others her pain. A love so forgiving, she accepted the apology, the truth, me, without reservation. Her heart is so fucking loyal to the people she loves, and she has this inherent need to make the people she loves happy.

Unfortunately, the envy and hatred of those who just can't understand that kind of beauty has left her open to a predator. But not for much longer.

Which is where my grandfather comes in.

I never expected him to be a part of my life again, not after I left. I didn't understand then, but I completely understand now.

"Are you okay, my love?" Corinna comes up behind me. We're back at her home. Lost in my thoughts, I've been staring out the long set of windows as the sun starts to come down over the wildflower meadow, saying nothing.

Turning, I see a new Corinna: peaceful, stronger, self-confident. She looks like she can take on the world, but it's my job to make sure she's protected from it. Holding out an arm, she curls beneath it. "Beyond being captivated by you, what you did tonight has me in awe. I love you, Corinna. I'm proud of who you are. You know that, right?"

She blushes. "It was just hair, Colby."

I shake my head. "It was more than that. It was a gift of strength you infused in those who so desperately needed it. You did that. You always do that." I brush my lips against hers for what was intended to be a brief kiss. Moments later, I pull away, and her eyes flutter open slowly. "You gave me that tonight, Cori."

Her shy smile never fails to kick me in the gut. Each time it's like the first time all over again. Every goddamned time.

I stroke the side of her cheek and take a deep breath. "I've never told you about my grandfather."

Shaking her head slowly, she merely says, "I knew you would when you were ready."

Pulling her close, I breathe her in. "My grandfather is a royal pain in the ass to everyone, friends and enemies alike."

Corinna's wry expression doesn't surprise me. "So, you're saying it's a family trait?"

I can't help but laugh. "Brat. And then after everything with my father, he was just gone. Gone, Cori. How could he take my father's side after I'd been hurt?" Mentally berating myself, I hiss out, "Damn, that was insensitive."

"Now I want to FaceTime him just so I can verbally kick his ass."

My lips kick up in a small smile. I can't help it. "He's a curmudgeon. He's lost even the smallest shred of decency. Even Keene's called him a sanctimonious prick more than once."

"Are you're saying I'll have a punching bag for all my frustrations? Excellent."

I can't control the laughter that wells up inside of me. Only Corinna can find that one pinprick of light and explode it into a starburst. I pull her head down on my chest. I need to purge myself of this burden.

"After I disowned my father, I never intended for it to include the rest of my family. Since I never heard from any of them ever again, I assumed they were more interested in money than anything else." I take a ragged breath. "None of them, not one, ever came to find me. Not even after I was shot."

Corinna's arms tighten around me. "Let it go." She's encouraging me to lay my burdens on her, but how much more can she take?

How selfish am I that I need this?

"I can't even tell you where I was, only to say it was unexpected." I take in a gulp of air. "When it was reported it the media, it wasn't even close to the truth."

In the silence that cloaks us, I explain the horror of the secretary of defense screaming under me as I covered her body with my own, crying in my ear after I took a hit meant for her. We were never supposed to be on the special op we were assisting with. Yet, when the accusations started flying, it was my chain of command undermining my decisions. I describe the bitterness in my soul as I sat in a hospital in Germany wondering about my future. Then the profuse apologies later as the traitor among us was revealed. Finally, my shock when Ali reached out and told me to come home.

Corinna sits quietly while I talk about Keene's jaw tightening to the point it was ready to snap, and Caleb quietly getting up and punching a hole in the wall when I revealed everything during my interview at Hudson. After all, it's not good for the Army when a traitor is found to be having an illicit affair with the secretary of defense and then sells her out for an incomprehensible amount of money while leaving his brothers-in-arms to die.

I might have come home to heal my body and my mind, but in

truth, it was my heart that needed saving. And it's the woman I'm holding close who did that.

Now, my past is threatening the peace of mind I'd finally attained. My family, my father, Jack.

Hudson Investigations has dug deep into Jack in the last few weeks without opening up the wounds I've been slowly closing regarding the events overseas. Unfortunately, it required opening up my connection to my family. I had to call my grandfather to use his influence to find out the truth.

After all, keeping this under wraps is as critical to him as it is to me.

As I'm relaying this to Corinna in a flat, controlled voice, her arms continue to get tighter and tighter around me. I'm sure pretty soon I'll have no air.

"I'm going to say this once, and I need you to believe it before I lose my shit." Corinna's voice is suppressed fury.

"Okay."

"This isn't your fault."

"How can you say that? Jack was my—" I start to protest.

"Colby," she interrupts me. "Yes, he was your 'best friend'"—she air quotes—"but he preyed upon you. You didn't know the one person you trusted implicitly was setting you up to such an extent. As for your grandfather, it sounds like he's the one who needs to grovel. I'm pretty certain he knew how to get a hold of you before now. Did you ever think about that?"

My mind blanks. "No," I whisper. She's right. The man has connections he could have used to contact me at any time.

She runs her hands up my chest to cup my face. I don't even realize I'm crying until I feel her wiping away my tears. "I don't know his motives, but I know you. Listen to me." She pulls my head around to make sure my eyes are locked on hers. "I know you, down to the bottom of my soul. You weren't wrong, not with your family. Not with the secretary. And damn sure not with the decisions you made to live. Do I love every one of them? No. I do not, but that's because some of these decisions would never have happened if the betrayals of your so-called brother hadn't been done to us. As for your grandfather, maybe he's getting old and realizes his mistakes. I just don't know."

"I'm going out on a limb to say there are probably only two things he loves enough to wade into this—his job and his reputation," I say bitterly.

Brushing her lips against my chin, she shakes me to my core. "Maybe so. But I'm going to say no, based on the amount of texts he's sending to you in the middle of the night."

I'm floored. "You knew?"

Smiling, she pulls me close. "I don't sleep much lately. I don't want to miss a minute with my eyes closed when I have you near me."

Dropping my head into her neck, I let loose the emotions that have been tangled up inside of me for the last few weeks. Harsh sobs come out until I sound like a wounded animal. Corinna holds me through it all. "Get it out, babe. I've got you."

But when do you *let it out?* I wonder. How is Corinna holding all of this together so beautifully? Before I can pursue that train of thought, my cell rings.

"Is that him?" Corinna dabs at her eyes. "How do I look?" She gives me a dazzling smile that's full of determined pride. And love. So much damned love.

I tug at her hand to lead her to the sofa, even as I connect Face-Time. "Grandfather. You just couldn't hold off for me to call, could you?"

"My grandson casually mentions he's fallen in love and you think I'm waiting to meet her? Not a chance. Hand her the phone."

I scrub my face with my spare hand.

Corinna arches her eyebrow, the light of battle firmly in her eyes. "Give me the phone, Colby."

"Suddenly, I'm not so sure about this," I mutter.

"Now," she demands. I reluctantly hand over my phone.

"Senator Hunt." Corinna greets my grandfather coolly in her beautiful Southern drawl. "Let me just lay all my cards out on the table. When I started things up with your grandson officially a few weeks ago, I never thought there would be a member of his family I'd want to meet, considering I figured they'd all look down on me for being a piece of white trash with a family of assholes that tried to sell ne into slavery." Corinna shrugs.

Watching my grandfather's face over her shoulder, he is openly gaping at my girlfriend. Corinna continues on blithely. "Now, it's my understanding you didn't give a shit after he was beaten by his father. That alone could make me hate you. Frankly, I could give two rats' behinds whether or not you like me, let alone accept me. Are we clear enough on where you stand?"

My grandfather's face is jerking on the other end of the line. He keeps opening and closing his mouth like a fish. I'm almost afraid of what's going to come out. Corinna just keeps on going, seemingly not paying any attention.

"I have to have this little thing done to my head this week. Whatever. We'll deal with it." She gives him a menacing glare. Her chest begins heaving. "Your job is to deal with Jack. The lack of support in your family disgusts me."

"Now, just a damned minute, young lady..." my grandfather sputters. Corinna smoothly cuts him off.

"I'm fairly certain anyone who knows me will assure you I'm never going to be a lady. I'm a woman. And as your grandson's woman, it's my job to protect his heart the same way he protects mine —ceaselessly." I brush a kiss on the top of her hair before plucking the phone out of her hand.

"And now that you've met the woman I love, do you have an update for me?" I ask dryly.

"Impatient thing. I was having fun with her. Let me talk with her again," the old man demands. There's a twinkle in his eye I haven't seen in far too long. My lips twitch before I can stop myself.

"Grandfather..." I warn. He waves his hand in front of the camera.

"That boy is a menace. Your father and that woman did a shit job raising him."

"Tell me something we don't already know."

I watch as the old man lights a cigar before continuing. "I did a much better job with you. Awfully proud of the way you turned out."

I choke. "Proud of me? You didn't bother to contact me for ten years."

"That was the way you wanted it, boy. You should have always known I loved you. You should have known to come to me after what your father did. It was just damn wrong."

I feel Corinna's hand as she squeezes my thigh tightly. If it wasn't for her calming presence, I might have exploded. As it is, I can't help but rail at him. "If I meant so damn much to you, if you were so traumatized by what happened to me, Grandfather, how could you allow him to keep living his perfect life? How could my father keep everything you gave to him while I fought to keep everything he almost took from me?"

My grandfather shakes his head. "I didn't, son. Not long after you left, I demanded a board meeting. He was voted out. Your uncles Gregory and Thomas took over. The majority of their children work in the firm now, but that's neither here nor there." My grandfather waves his hand in frustration. "Your father retained what shares he could, but he lost a large portion of his inheritance when I cut off his trust fund and cut him out of my will."

My eyes bug out. "What?"

His eyes harden. "No one hurts my family, even if they're family. I wasn't happy about your decision, Colby, but that's because I knew about the areas you'd be deployed to. I was scared. I couldn't have been prouder of what you wanted to do though. I was going to see if you were still willing to go Ivy and join ROTC."

"Jesus." This is freaking unbelievable.

"Senator," Corinna interjects next to me. I turn the phone so it's facing her. "What happened to Colby's father then?"

"Apparently after he ran out of money, he went to go live with his mistress and Jack in Groton."

A horrified look comes over Corinna's face. Mine must mirror it.

"That asshole fucked with my life because he didn't get Daddy's attention? Jesus, he can have it," I rail. "I just don't want him to keep popping in and out of our lives, Cori."

She shrugs. "So don't let him. Have your grandfather's fancy lawyers draw up some papers to that effect, baby. I think it's the least he would do for you."

My grandfather pipes up. "Pretty and smart. Not a bad choice, son."

I ignore the old man. "What do you think he'll want for that assurance?"

Cori smirks. "If Jack was smart, assurance you won't kill him."

"He should be so lucky."

"Then tell your grandfather a list of things you can live with, and put something you can't as last."

I brush my lips against hers. "I hate to agree with him, but he's right. You're so damn smart."

She laughs. "Hardly. Ali's just been hanging around a lot."

"No, it's your ability to read people with that enormous heart I fell in love with." I kiss her one more time before taking the phone back. "Is this doable?" I ask my grandfather.

"I'll call my lawyers tomorrow on one condition."

Warily, I ask, "What's that?"

His face suddenly looks old. "I'd like to see you again, Colby. I know I should wait to be asked, but I..." He doesn't get a chance to continue before Corinna yanks the phone from my hand.

"I agree. You should come by while I'm recovering. You can meet my family. I'm so sure they'll want to meet you." She turns to me and asks, "Do you think he'll be the catalyst for Keene and Phil to get along finally? I mean, it would just take one nasty comment and the two of them would be like the Wonder Twins, being all protective and whatnot."

If I hadn't seen what happens next with my own two eyes, I would never have believed it.

My grandfather is clutching his stomach while he's doubled over with laughter. His dove-gray eyes are crinkled at the corners, and the smile on his face sends a million wrinkles twitching. "Corinna, I should have known he'd have fallen in love with someone who's nuts."

Corinna shrugs. "Listen, he's his own brand of special. I'm not getting any sort of bargain here."

And my grandfather is laughing again.

My angel. My wonder. My love.

Uncaring if my grandfather sees, I trace her lips with my finger. "I love you so damn much."

Her eyes are shining, and she smiles at me before returning her focus back to the phone.

LATER THAT NIGHT, Corinna and I are in bed. I turn off the bedside lights and in the dim light from the overhead strands find her staring at me, her hands tucked under her cheek. "What is it?"

"Had Caleb not brought up your grandfather tonight, were you going to?" she asks bluntly.

I get comfortable next to her. Corinna immediately gets settled with her head on my chest. I stroke the skin of her tattoo, made more easily accessible now that her hair's been cut so short.

By her choice. Her need for a clear conscience.

It's time to give her mine.

"I'd hoped to get us past the next few days, Cori. I don't want to burden your mind with more than it can handle," I tell her honestly. I wait for the explosion.

It doesn't come. Instead, what she says is worse.

Much, much worse.

"What if we don't have tomorrow? What if the only time we're guaranteed is each second we breathe?" she whispers. I tense beneath her head and wandering hand. "Then tonight would never have happened. And would you know your true grandfather is inside that man he presents to the world?" As I contemplate those words, the next ones knock me over. "How would I know I could rise above my own preconceptions about you? About love? How would I know the darkness no longer is something to fear? It's just dark, but you're waiting on the other side when I come out of it?"

Bracing up on my chest, Corinna looks down at me. "The time we have is often a curse but more often a blessing. Isn't it time we stop counting our curses?"

"I know one blessing I count every day," I say hoarsely.

"Don't tell me." She slides her body on top of mine sinuously. "Show me."

And for the next several hours, I do.

I show the woman I love that she's the answer to every wish, every prayer, and every dream. I just want to know I can keep her.

Later, as Corinna sleeps curled next to me, I lie awake, held hostage by the fears that assail me, knowing I may only have a few more nights like this before I return to a landfall of days that blur together because there's nothing left in my heart to distinguish them from one another.

THE NEXT MORNING, I get another call from my grandfather. It's over. Jack was dealt with swiftly by my grandfather's attorneys when they showed up en masse at his practice in Darien.

After his initial demand they come back at a better time, their threats of their next stop being with the Attorney General scared him enough to cancel the remainder of his appointments.

As Cori predicted, Jack wanted everything he thought was due to him as the son of Brett Hunt. He asked for everything he thought was his birthright, including a stake in Hunt Enterprises. He was denied everything but his right to walk out of his office with the ability to keep his medical license, the money he would earn from selling his part in his practice, and the money from selling his house to move somewhere far away from the East Coast after he signed a document never to bother Corinna, my grandfather, me, or any of my relatives, save our father ever again.

Shaken, he realized the lawyers had him on several counts of mail fraud, where the statute of limitations was five years for withholding my letters to Cori. Cori also could have pushed a HIPAA case against his practice, which would have made his future earnings next to impossible, but all she cared about was eradicating him from our lives.

The loss of Jack in my life is like walking out of a bad movie. There are horrible images burned in my mind and a foul stench in my nose. Corinna assures me that eventually, these feelings will pass as new memories are made with people who truly love me. Apparently, these are going to include my grandfather, who is so enamored of my girlfriend he's already making plans to come up and visit during her recovery.

Seems we were all wrong. I look forward to forging new bonds back into my family fold, but the only person I plan on bringing with me is Corinna.

Not the brother I never knew I had.

49

CORINNA

TWO NIGHTS BEFORE SURGERY

"I don't know why I can't go home to get ready for a date with my boyfriend," I grumble to my sisters. We've all gathered at Emily's house because Em got a burr up her ass and wants to play dress up. "Especially one that starts at two o'clock in the afternoon."

"Listen, your idea of dressing up typically involves a new pair of Chucks and clean jeans," Em retorts as she makes her way into her closet, calling over her shoulder, "I want you to drop Colby to his knees."

With a secret smile, I open my mouth to reply, but Ali beats me to it. "Jesus, if that look is anything to go by, he's on his knees quite a bit."

We all crack up laughing. Shrugging, I let the teasing go. Why deny something that's entirely true?

Holly runs her fingers through the close cut of my hair. "I'm still not used to it."

Cassidy sits down next to me on Em's bed. Reaching for my hand, she gives it a quick squeeze. "It suits you though. Sexy and sassy."

Fingering the front of my bangs, I admit, "I don't know why I didn't do this years ago. It's so much easier to take care of."

Em walks out of her closet, her arms laden with dresses. Hoisting them onto the bed behind us, she commands, "Strip."

Innocently I ask, "But there's no music. Besides, that's Ali's thing. She's the one who took classes."

Ali rolls her eyes. "I took pole dancing classes to strengthen my core."

"Bet you're getting use out of them these days." I wink.

A dazzling smile lights her face. "True."

Cassidy slaps her hands over her mouth to stop the guffaws.

Em blows a puff of air upward to dislodge the stuck hair on her forehead. "Okay. I've narrowed this down to four choices. Let's figure out what you're wearing so we can get the rest of you ready."

I groan. "Tell me one of them is long. This not shaving my legs crap is killing me."

My sisters all laugh. "I would think not being able to shave there"—Holly makes a circle indicating my sex—"would be worse."

"I feel like Colby has to shave more often so only one of us is sporting a five-o'clock shadow," I say dryly. Screaming laughter echoes around the room. "Seriously, I'm afraid of creating a knot with our genital hair when we're having sex."

Ali falls to the floor screeching. Em is leaning against her dresser for support. Cassidy slides backward onto the bed and lands on the dresses, while Holly rips out her cell phone muttering, "I wish I got that on video."

That sends us into another round of fits.

When we finally finish laughing, Em pulls a short red number from the pile Cassidy has rolled all over. "I guess this one's out of the running. Just in case the wind blows the skirt up."

Even as Em goes to hang the dress, Cassidy, Ali, Holly, and I lose it again.

Okay, I might not have needed help getting ready for a date, but this right here defines my meaning of sisterhood. Sharing the good times and the bad with unasked support and incredible laughter.

〰

A FEW HOURS LATER, even I'm surprised by the transformation. Em's miracle closet yielded the most perfect dress: a strapless magenta silk dress with a pleated front detail that dips lower in the back. The bust line is something I've never seen before. It had an almost V cut down to the A-line seam. The material of dress seems to loop through the base, offering modesty, yet still drawing your eye.

Paired with a pair of black patent leather Louboutins, a set of dangling jet-black earrings, and a chunky onyx ring, I feel glamorous. Even the thigh-high tights I'm wearing to hide my leg hair don't detract from the look.

"Wow," I whisper as I look at my transformation. "I've never looked as beautiful as I do right now."

"You've always been this beautiful," Em counters.

Cassidy chimes in. "I agree. You're just giving yourself permission to feel it."

I twirl. I mean, how can I not? The delicate material of the dress lifts lightly before settling perfectly back in place. "Ali? Holly? What do you think?"

Ali places her hands on my shoulders from behind. "Perfect. Especially the heart that beats inside."

Holly comes up next to me and takes my hand. "Then again, you always were."

Quickly I'm embraced by each of my sisters, all taking care not to wrinkle the delicate dress. With just a moment left to myself before Colby arrives, I face the mirror one last time, catching a glimpse of my amaryllis tattoo tucked away next to my heart. It rises and falls with every breath I take. Spinning, I see my key tattoo with my reminder to never forget displayed brazenly on my back.

I'll never forget.

Not a single minute.

Leaving Em's room, I make my way downstairs to wait with my sisters for Colby's arrival.

"YOU TAKE MY BREATH AWAY."

I duck my head, thrown off by the compliment. This man has seen every square inch of my body naked, taken it to places no one ever has, and with mere words can devastate me.

"You're always beautiful, Corinna," Colby continues. "But right now, I'm fighting for air."

"Now you're just being sweet," I admonish him.

"Cupping the side of my face, he captures my hand and lifts it to his lips, murmuring, "No, I'm not.". Lifting it to his lips, he murmurs, "No, I'm not." Clearing his throat, he says to our rapt audience, "Thank you for everything."

Em speaks for everyone. "It was entirely our pleasure."

Phil, who came over to see my sisters' handiwork, deadpans, "What time will you have her home?"

Colby casts him a disparaging glance. "You'll see her sometime tomorrow."

"But doesn't she have to go to the—"

"Shut up, Phil!" all my sisters snap, cutting him off from interrupting our night of fantasy with the intrusion of reality.

Tucking my hand in his arm, Colby guides me down Em's front stairs. I'm so engrossed in him, in the magical bubble encasing us, I don't realize it's not Colby's Jeep waiting to take us to where we're going.

A gentleman is standing by a shiny black car with tinted windows, holding the door open. "Ms. Freeman? Mr. Hunt? Are you ready to begin your evening?"

I turn to Colby. "What on earth are we doing?"

He smiles down at me. "We're going on an adventure, princess. Come on." He urges me forward. "It takes a bit of time to get there."

I smile back as I step forward and accept the driver's hand. "Thank you so much."

"My pleasure, miss. Sir." He nods respectfully at Colby, who walks around the back of the car and slides in next to me.

Once we're on our way, I pester Colby with questions. "Give me a hint."

He just shakes his head, laughing. "Not a chance."

Leaning forward to brush my lips against his, I whisper, "Please?"

He returns my kiss, turning my insides out and making me forget my own name within minutes. By the time I remember my name, we're on I-84 eastbound and Colby's plying me with nonalcoholic champagne, strawberries, and cheese to distract me from looking out the tinted windows.

Otherwise, I'd have known where we were going in a heartbeat.

~

Two hours later, we're pulling up in front of a building. I'm stiff from sitting so long. Colby places his hand on my arm. "Before you jump out, I want to talk with you."

"Okay," I say slowly, reclining back in my seat.

"It started here for me, right outside this door in a room on the third floor. A girl with incredibly long hair and a shy smile walked into the room, and I felt the punch right here." He lays his hand on his stomach.

My pulse quickens. I start to look out the window, but Colby snags my chin with one hand. "The more time I spent with that girl, the punch moved from here to here." He takes my hand and puts it over his heart.

"I want to build new memories tonight over the ones that were so tainted, Corinna. I want to go upstairs and be with the woman I loved then, the woman I never stopped loving, the woman I love now, and erase the final ghosts from our pasts before we move on to our future." He releases me so suddenly my body flounders a bit. "I want to dance with you in a room where we laughed until we cried. I want to hold you where you trusted me with your deepest secrets. I want to love your body where I dreamed of touching every inch of it with mine. And then I want to do it all over again."

I sure as hell hope Em used waterproof makeup as my eyes are leaking so many tears, I can't catch them all. I can't respond verbally because of the lump in my throat. So, I do the next best thing.

I launch myself at him.

"I love you," I sob. "I love you so much."

"That," he murmurs into my neck, "is just how I feel about you."

After holding me for a few more moments, he shifts. "The surprises aren't over." Colby leans forward to rap on the window. The driver turns off the vehicle. Coming around to Colby's side, the driver waits for him to slide out before offering me a hand. Stepping onto the sidewalk, I look up at my old off-campus apartment with a mixture of fondness and amazement.

"Come on, baby. Let's go inside."

Tucking my hand back into his arm, he escorts me in.

I am in no way prepared for what I see next.

"Oh my God."

50

CORINNA

It's me. It's him. It's us.

We're everywhere.

Big. Small. Black and white. Captured in photographs. We're together.

Like we always should have been.

The room is lit only by small Christmas lights. The light casts just enough light to guide the way. It's like my hope—there's just enough to keep me alive. But Colby is looking further ahead than I am. He's getting me to glimpse our future beyond the tomorrow that may never come.

Colby ushers me farther into the tiny apartment I shared in college with Ali and Holly so he can close the door behind us. "Take your time looking around, princess. I'll be right back." Dropping a kiss on my shoulder, he leaves me to wander amidst our memories. Soon, music starts playing and the wet hits my eyes.

I'm lost in love over this man.

I stop in front of a picture of me and Colby that Holly must have taken when I was a freshman and he was a junior. If I remember correctly, a five-pound bag of flour had just exploded all over the kitchen. It had gone everywhere within a good eight-foot radius, with me being right in the middle of the blast zone. I study the picture now with a woman's eyes. Colby's expression as he brushes flour off my face while I'm laughing up at him causes my heart to clutch in my chest.

Ten years later.

"I think that was the first time I realized I was falling for you," his deep voice says from behind me. A cool champagne flute slides over the base of my neck and over my tattoo. "I never forgot what it felt like at that moment to know you were everything, and the likelihood of us was next to nothing." Handing me the flute, he assures me, "It's nonalcoholic."

"Part of me wishes it wasn't," I admit.

The side of his mouth kicks up sadly. "None of us are ready for this week, sweetheart."

Putting the flute on the nearby window ledge, I step closer to him. "It's not that. I was such a blind fool. I wasn't strong enough to see, Colby. Your love has always been there. These"—I spin in a circle —"show me how much you love me. How much you've always loved me."

Putting his flute next to mine, he adds, "How much I'll always love you, Corinna."

Suddenly frightened, I need him to understand. "Colby, if something happens..."

"Hush. Tonight's not about that. Tonight's just about love." Lowering his dark head, he ferociously kisses away the idea that something could happen to me during surgery in just a few days.

His hands soothe away the hurts of the past.

His lips sip away my fear of the future.

His body becomes my safe harbor, his body my anchor.

His "I love you" as he thrusts into me my benediction, my prayer.

As we're wrapped in each other's arms on a ratty couch he'd had brought into my old apartment, I'm at peace.

I know he's awake behind me. His hands can't stop touching me, smoothing up and down my skin, snaking over my hip.

I'm still shaking between the aftershocks of our lovemaking and the emotional upheaval in my system. Knowing someone's always loved you and seeing the evidence of it are two very different things.

Tonight, I wasn't just given my reason to live; I was shown why I'm afraid to die.

I need him to understand.

"Colby..." I start as I turn onto my back.

"Take tonight for us, Corinna. Tomorrow's coming soon enough for everything else."

We're running out of tomorrow, I want to yell. But in this sacred place, a place he built out of the love he has for me, I can't. I just can't.

"Okay," I acquiesce. "Tell me what we're going to do with all the photos," I ask instead.

"I thought we could hang them up during your recovery. We'll find frames for them and put them around the house," he says easily, but his eyes are studying me waiting to see my response.

To make sure I know he's not giving up. And he's not going to let me either.

I gulp in air so I don't burst into tears. "Okay." I have no control over anything else that's about to happen, but I can promise I'll fight.

I don't think I understood how tight his body was until it relaxes against mine. Pulling the blanket over us both, he whispers, "Get some sleep. We have a big day tomorrow."

That's an understatement.

I have to report to the hospital tomorrow morning.

51

CORINNA
DAY BEFORE SURGERY

I barely slept last night between Colby's surprise and knowing I was soon to be admitted. Today has been a whirlwind of being admitted and last-minute testing. Yet, I know I won't rest tonight either.

One more night of being strong.

One more morning of holding on.

Then, it's all out of my hands.

I feel like I've been violated in every hole available in my body, and a few new ones they created for their torturous purposes. They didn't like the temperature readings they were getting out of my ears or pits, so to ensure it was accurate, it was taken rectally. With my drawl out in full force, I advised the nurse she should have my boyfriend take care of that pesky task if we were bringing ass play into our relationship. That spawned a hearty laugh from Colby, as he was standing right there. "Roll over, princess. Let the nurse shove the probe up your butt so we can get this show on the road." I imagine our antics are making their way through the nursing staff at Greenwich Hospital with lightning speed.

A burly guy with the most sensitive hands I've ever felt put in two IVs. I barely noticed. I told him of all the vamps I've had to see over the years, he deserves a prize. As a result, he hunted up purple daisy compression bandages to hold my IVs in place. I think he scored them from the kids' ward.

Bryan came by to place the circular donut markers around my head to help guide him when he drills the head gear in place after I'm knocked out. Straddling the chair next to my bed, he began his lecture. "No food before surgery, no matter what the nurses say. Nothing but clear liquids up to eight hours before. Absolutely nothing other than IV fluids after that. For your own sanity, start tapering visitors down so you can pretend to get some rest." Glancing at the man quietly running his fingers over the back of my hand, Bryan continues. "I assume Colby will still be with you in the morning?"

"You assume correctly," Colby, who hasn't said much since the markers were added, resolutely states.

Bryan nods at Colby before returning his attention solely on me. "Then at least try to get some rest, Corinna. It's going to be a huge day for us all, you and I especially." Squeezing my bicep, he turns toward the door. Muttering an oath, he turns back to the bed and wraps his arms around me. "Fuck it. You better know I'm not letting anything happen to you, okay?"

Stunned by his outburst, I answer shakily. "Okay."

After Bryan storms out, it's just me and Colby. I need to focus on something, anything, other than that in a little more than nineteen hours, both of our lives possibly becoming irrevocably changed. I ask, "Did you remember the bag?" I sit up suddenly, frantically looking around my room. I'm unable to find it.

"Which one? The backpack you asked me to unpack, or the purple duffle you told me to throw in the closet and leave zipped or you'd hit me with your IV pole?" He's been leaning against the window ledge, but at the frantic sound of my voice he pushes off and walks toward me.

"The purple one." Relaxing back against my bed, I let out a deep breath.

"It's in the closet." Lazily, he circles the foot of the bed. "Do you need it right now?" His hand grazes my leg, fingers trailing upward over the scrubs they gave me to wear.

"Stop that. We're not supposed to...at this point."

Flicking the IV bags, he asks, "Are these hooked up yet?"

I frown. "No, why?"

"Then scoot over." Without waiting for my response, Colby wedges his way onto my hospital bed. "What's going through that head of yours?"

"Nothing," I say automatically.

"Corinna." His voice is both soothing and reproachful.

"You don't want to hear what I have to say."

"Just because I don't want to hear it doesn't mean I won't listen," he says quietly. "Over the last two weeks, this has gradually become more real to me. Today, if the kind of fear I'm feeling is anything you've been living with, I don't know how you haven't gone insane." His fingers twine with mine before he raises my hand to his lips.

"That can't taste as good."

"Kind of tastes like disinfectant. I'll get used to the taste over the next few days."

Suddenly, I blurt out, "What if we don't have a few days? Do you regret anything?"

He maneuvers us so we're both lying on our sides facing each other. "I don't need anything in the world but you, Corinna. I don't regret a thing leading me to right now."

52

COLBY

"Knock, knock." Keene pokes his head through the door. "Your next visitor worked up a hell of a lot of hutzpah to visit Corinna before surgery."

My head snaps toward the door. "Who?"

Keene smiles. It's so rare to see the real thing versus his trademark smirk. "All I have to say is, you owe me every baked good your woman bakes for you after her surgery for at least six months since he's been at my house since yesterday. He came to wish Corinna good luck for tomorrow. Oh, and Ali thinks he's the shit."

"Is the whole family out there?" Corinna's wraps her arms around me and grins.

Keene shrugs. "You try keeping them all away." Moving back to the door, he opens it to reveal a face I haven't seen in person since I left for college. "Senator, come on in. There are no flying pies, I promise."

"God, Keene. You can be such a dick!" Corinna yells as she rolls off the bed and stomps toward him with her fist raised. Keene laughs. Meanwhile, I'm frozen in place as my grandfather hesitantly moves into the room. It's the first time we've been in the same space since I left for college over fourteen years ago.

A quiet hush settles, other than the beeps and pings of Corinna's hospital equipment.

Without hesitation, I stand as well. Somehow, his presence still commands it even though I'm no longer a young boy. I hold out my hand to the man I wanted to emulate at one time. The man who I thought didn't stand by me. "You just couldn't wait, could you?"

Shaking his head, my grandfather swats away my hand and pulls me in for a hug. "It's so good to hold you, son. So good to have my arms around you again."

"Damnit, I'm going to cry," Corinna mutters. Keene wraps an arm around her shaking shoulders and squeezes.

A nurse pokes her head in. "Ms. Freeman, you need to keep your blood pressure under control. If you can't, we'll have to ask all but one to leave." Spying something in the hallway, she frowns. "And nachos are not on your approved diet."

"Don't worry, those are for me," I assure her with a charming smile.

Corinna looks at my grandfather and mutters, "He's such a pain in my ass. He knows I can't eat anything, so, of course, he orders nachos."

The senator moves from my arms. "Ali tells me you throw pies when you're angry, you yell at my grandson, and from all I've been hearing have a heart of gold." Studying Corinna for half a second, he moves toward her with his arms open. "Welcome to the family."

In the midst of the worst anxiety I've ever faced, every moment leading up to witnessing this is suddenly worth it. The shit-eating grin I'm wearing isn't going away anytime soon.

The man I love, respect, and thought I lost is holding the woman I love, found, and reclaimed. For this moment, for this perfect moment, everything is right with the world.

HOURS LATER, Corinna and I are lying in her bed. Everyone has left, including my grandfather. He wished he could stay longer, but he carved out only a short amount of time to be in Connecticut before he had to head back to DC. Playing the political game as long as he has, he knows he can't stay for Corinna's surgery, lest we want a media storm outside the hospital tomorrow.

We politely declined.

Corinna's night nurse has already popped in several times to check her monitors and IV. Each time she's frowned at us curled up on her bed, but I'm not budging an inch until I absolutely have to.

That's not right now.

"Zachary's not what I expected." Corinna runs her fingers lightly over mine.

"He's fairly incredible," I agree. We have so much to work through, my grandfather and I, but it's good to know the old bastard hasn't really changed even if his phone manner has become more crotchety over the years. My eyes bore into hers. "Just like the woman I love."

"Colby." Golden eyes turn into sparkling pools as tears begin to fall. I blurt out something I've been thinking through for weeks. I've left it to almost the midnight hour before asking her.

"I need you to tell me now if you want me to fight Bryan with everything in our combined arsenal to be in that room with you tomorrow," I blurt out.

She yanks her head back. "What?"

"During your surgery."

"You want to be in the room while I'm being operated on?" She's confused.

"I want to be there if you need me, Cori. If that means—" I swallow hard. "—being in the operating room, then yes."

Her eyes close. I see her lips move, but I can't make out the words. Long minutes pass where she doesn't say anything, so I begin to fill the silence. "You haven't said anything about how you're handling the pressure of this, Corinna. And I'm scared. So fucking scared. If I'm scared, what the hell must you be feeling?"

"I'm...complete." Sitting up, she leans over and kisses me softly. "Go grab the purple bag from the closet and bring it to me please?"

Confused and hurt, I grab the enormous duffle bag from the closet and put it on her bed. She reaches into the outside pocket and pulls out a leather journal. "This is what I needed, my love. Come sit with me?" Patting the bed next to her, her eyes are glowing softly.

After I get settled next to her, she turns the journal over and over in her hands. "This is what I'm feeling, Colby. I've been able to explain a lot of what I'm feeling here. In moments. Bursts. Random thoughts. When I saw the psychologist, she said I was spiraling out of control. That bag and this book were my ways of taking it back. Now it's for you to read tomorrow," she adds, placing it back in the bag.

"Cori, I can't," I immediately protest.

"I need you to understand what I haven't been able to articulate so you can be my voice when I can't be. Even if everything goes perfectly, I'm going to need that from you." Her lips twitch. "It's not only my guide on what's been going through my head, but it's also an insider's guide on how to handle the family. It's every dream and all the wishes I've had since we've met." She rubs her hands over mine. "There just weren't enough hours for everything, Colby. There were too many things to say. This book says what I didn't have time to."

"You make it sound like you're giving up," I rasp.

She shakes her head. "Quite the opposite. This gave me the clarity to fight the right battles."

"Have you won?" I ask.

The smile that crosses her face is a glimpse of a solar eclipse, a rare gift you want to stare directly into. "I'm sitting in my hospital bed with you. If this isn't considered winning, I'd say it's the championship round, and I've got amazing odds."

I cup the nape of her neck and pull her toward me until our foreheads are touching. "Never forget who you are to me, Corinna."

"Never, Colby."

"And you're not going to give up if I'm not there?" I persist.

"All I'll need to hear is your name," she whispers. "That's all I'll ever need now. Tomorrow, read the book. I promise it will become so clear."

53

COLBY

DAY OF SURGERY

"You warm enough, baby?" I ask Corinna.

It's not even 5:00 a.m. and we're already down in the pre-op area. Corinna's been scrubbed tip to toe with surgical soap, wiped down with sanitization wipes, backup IVs are in, and she has a surgical cap on over her short hair that will be removed once she's in the operating room.

Anesthesiologists, members of her neurosurgery team, and nurses have all been by. She's said her legal name and date of birth so many times, I'm beginning to recite it with her when people come into the curtained area.

We're waiting on two things before she's wheeled back in for the estimated eight-hour procedure: a quick visit by her immediate family, and Bryan's orders to move.

"Knock, knock," a familiar voice says suddenly. Ali peeks her head around. "We have to come back two at a time. I drew the short straw and have Phil with me."

Corinna laughs. "That's because Holly is too emotional, Em would just yell at him, and Cassidy's going to be asking questions of all the doctors." It's incredible how she has her sisters pegged.

"That might be true, Cori, but I'll bet their knives don't cost as much as yours do," Phil drawls.

Am I really hearing this?

"But I'll bet they get more vicious when they're not handled properly," Corinna retorts.

Yep. Definitely happening.

"She's got you there, Phil. Hospitals tend to get sued over stuff like that," Ali chimes in. I look at my friend and wonder if she's lost her mind as she turns her back and discreetly wipes her eyes.

And it's in that moment that I understand their gallows humor. By not dwelling on the real reason for standing by Corinna's bedside, they won't completely lose it in front of her. Adding to the levity, I ask, "I wonder if Bryan makes custom adjustments. We could make Keene forget the combo to my safe, permanently."

Phil snorts. Ali grins, and Corinna laughs.

"Listen, I'm still bitter about my brownies being eaten. Don't kid yourself."

"You're practically living with the master baker of the universe. Can't you figure out a way to earn some more?" Ali rolls her bright blue eyes.

Corinna laughs. "Can you imagine how bad this is going to be during recovery? He's going to have to eat"—her voice lowers to a whisper—"store-bought cookies."

"Hold on. You haven't been baking stuff and freezing it? What type of sister are you?" Phil says indignantly.

"The kind with a sex life," Corinna replies dryly.

We all laugh before quiet settles over us. Ali's holding Corinna's hand so tightly, it's got to hurt her IV. Phil's squeezing her shoulder. They don't want to let go.

I know the feeling all too well.

"I hate to break this up..." I begin when the curtain whooshes open.

"But Corinna's doctor is on his way up," a sympathetic nurse finishes for me. "I understand you have a few more siblings who need to come back?"

Phil and Ali lean over to kiss Corinna, murmuring words of encouragement. Soon, they're being whisked away. "This is harder for them now," Corinna muses quietly. "Promise me, no matter what happens today, you won't ignore anything unusual that happens."

Her words don't quite make sense, which worries me. Her fucking tumor needs to come out so I know I have my Corinna safely back by my side. I lean over and kiss her before murmuring, "I promise," just to appease her.

The nurse guides Holly, Em, and Cassidy back, making an exception on the two-person visitor rule because of the time. The girls are trying to joke with Corinna in much the same manner Phil and Ali did when the curtain flies open again.

Only this time, it isn't just the nurse coming to escort the girls out. It's Bryan.

This isn't the friendly doctor whose visited the farm several times in the last few weeks. This is the surgeon barking out orders left and right to his team. My faith and confidence skyrocket as I see the man behind the mask of geniality come out. It's like Clark Kent has stripped off his suit and his alter ego is flying around with his cape now. Superman is in the house.

Thank God.

Bryan sits down at the computer at Corinna's station, clicking through screens before he even says a word to any of us.

The clock on the wall reads a few minutes before six.

"Corinna." Sharp hazel eyes snap to her. "Are you ready?"

She barks out a laugh. "Sure. I guess that's what you call it."

"Are you sure?"

She nods.

He abruptly stands. "Okay. Then there are too many people here. Family, it's time for you to go. Say your 'see you laters' so we can go to work."

Em comes forward and kisses Corinna on the forehead. I don't know if the noise in the pre-op has dimmed or if I've suddenly clued in, but this time I hear the murmured "This one's for happiness."

Cassidy comes forward and kisses her on her cheek and says quietly, "For whatever bravery you need, take it."

Holly is the final Freeman to kiss her sister. Unlike the others, she can't control her tears. "Use all my strength. All of our strength. Just get through this. We need you." She kisses her other cheek, and then the three sisters are rushed out.

Corinna wipes her eyes using the sheet draped over her. "Hey, that's my job." I reach forward and swipe my thumb beneath them, forgetting about the hustle and bustle around us. "You have to let me do my job."

She lets out a watery laugh. "Okay. Think you can manage a tissue?"

I kiss her lips softened by the tears. "Sure, princess." When I stand, I bump into Bryan.

"I hate to break this up, but it's just about time. The sooner we get started, the sooner we'll be done." In his scrubs, he's ready to run through a final check with his team.

They're ready to take Corinna back to the operating room.

Another choked sob escapes her, and I reach over and take her hand. "Can you give us one minute alone, Doc?"

"Just that, Colby. Then we need to do the final check. Until we start wheeling her, you can remain with her." He steps outside the curtain and pulls it closed to give us an illusion of privacy, even though there's none.

I'm grateful for whatever we've got.

"Corinna, look at me. Baby, see me." I cup her jaw. "Please?"

Wet eyes stare into mine. I know I'm crying too. I feel the hot salt burn tracks down my cheeks.

"You have every right to be scared, but know this: I love you. Forever. And that isn't going to change." I trace around her temple where in a few hours an incision will soon be. "Not because of a scar, or what you can or can't do other than love me. Do you love me?"

"For always," her strangled whisper comes out.

"Then know I'll be with you in that dark to pull you out. I love you so damn much." I lean down and kiss her with every intent on giving her my own breath for her to come back to me. When the curtain is whooshed from behind me, I murmur, "For love." Standing, I move back but don't release her hand as the surgical team quickly checks her.

All too soon, they're unlocking her bed. I hold her hand until we get to the final doorway where I can't pass. "You have to say goodbye her here, sir," one says politely.

I lean over and kiss her one last time. "Never forget."

She reaches up with an IV in her hand. "I never will."

And within seconds, she's pushed through the doors for the fight of her life.

54

BLACK BEARS

"Is she out?"

"Yes, Doctor."

"Good. Let's move her on three. One, two...lift. Make sure she's centered before you strap her down. I'm going to let Moser know we're ready for him."

~

"COLBY, why do you have Corinna's Vera Bradley bag with you?" Holly asks curiously.

"I honestly don't know," I admit. "All I know is that she told me I had to carry this with me all day."

We've taken over a private waiting room at Greenwich Hospital. Over the years, Caleb and Keene's families have donated an insanely generous amount of money to the facility, so they arranged to secure the space for our private use for the duration of Corinna's surgery.

Eight fucking hours.

I don't know how I'm going to handle it.

I get up and begin to pace.

"Jesus, if you're this bad and we're only a half hour in, I can't imagine what you're going to be like at hour seven," Ali mutters. I turn to blast her, but I catch the glint in Keene's eye.

Suddenly, an annoying alarm goes off on a cell phone. Everyone starts checking their devices. Comments of "Nope" and "Not mine" pepper the room. Halfheartedly, I grab my phone. I'm shocked when I see a reminder going off.

6:50 AM: Purple Bag—Ziploc 1. Love, Corinna

"Holy shit," I gasp. I quickly take a screenshot of it before silencing the alarm.

Caleb shoves his chair back. "What is it?" He's not as calm as he'd like to pretend he's being.

None of us are.

"It's Corinna."

The room lets out a collective gasp, so I quickly correct myself. "No, I mean it's Corinna who did this." I heft the purple bag onto the table.

"What do you mean, Colby?" Cassidy tilts her head.

I hand my phone over to her husband, who lets out a slow smile. As they pass my phone around, I dig around in the bag for a Ziploc with the number 1. It has a bunch of neatly addressed envelopes and a single sheet of paper.

Colby,
Make sure everyone gets these. I think they'll need them.
And don't forget to read your journal.
All my love,
Corinna

After I pass out cards to everyone in the room, the family starts tearing into them. Laughter turns our frustration into a moment of shared joy as large silly brown bears open their arms to be giving us hugs from the woman we so desperately need them from. "When did she find time to do all of this?" I murmur.

Phil pauses in his attempt to use his bear to fornicate with Jason's. "I don't know, but I'm damn glad she did. Aren't you?"

"Yeah." Remembering the rest of her note, I reach in the bag for the butter-soft journal and sit back to open it.

I thought I could write something about black bears, tie something prophetic and meaningful into my surgery, but really, I just thought they were cute.

How incredibly shallow of me.

I laugh out loud.

I know everyone - mainly you - has been worried about how I am handling this. Frankly, I was too. And then I met Alice. (BTW, she's really cool and she'll be down to visit y'all later.)

Alice made me realize what I needed in my world, which was spinning out of control, was to regain some of it. Between the insanity of work, the insanity of my brain, and the one insanity I never want to change which is falling in love with you, I was spiraling out of control.

The way I prepared for my surgery was my way of taking it back.

From the way I CHOSE to prepare for today, including cutting off my hair, to the things in the purple bag, and maybe a few others not in the bag (no, you're not getting any more hints than that), these were things I could actively partake in, not watch happen to me.

By now, there should be someone knocking at the door. If not, they may have gotten stuck in morning rush-hour traffic.

Know you're buried deep in my heart, Colby Hunt. I chose to put you there.

Now, go give one of my sisters a hug. I'm pretty sure they can use it.

Love,

Corinna

PS - Stop reading now. Mark the page with your bear hug. The next time your alarm goes off, you can keep going XOXO

Smiling, I do what she says. After all, she's in control of the situation. Standing, I move over to Holly, who looks like she can use Corinna's hug the most. "Can you believe she did this?" My arms wrap around her tightly.

Holly shakes her head. "And I thought she needed our strength? I think she's giving us hers."

My jaw unhinges slightly at Holly's profound words. "Maybe you're right." Before I can explore the thought any further, there's a knock at the door.

The room snaps to attention.

"Relax," I caution them. "Corinna said this might happen." They relax marginally. Throwing open the door, I reveal Matt and Ava from The Coffee Shop on Main Street in Collyer, holding huge boxes. "Holy crap. What are you doing here?"

"Early-morning breakfast delivery from Ms. Corinna Freeman," Ava announces cheerfully.

"Are you kidding me?" Ali exclaims, laughing. Keene's arm slides around her waist and squeezes.

"Charlie has all of your kids. He'll be down with another round after he drops them off at daycare," Matt announces as he ambles into the room. "Cori asked if we minded opening an hour late today, apologizing for being a burden. As if." Matt snorts. "I can't guarantee your coffee's hot, but I know it tastes better than the shit they serve here."

The Freeman siblings rush him en masse.

Keene comes up behind me and clasps my shoulder. "Corinna's strength might get us through this."

I shake my head, disagreeing with him. "We'll get through this because of her love."

"Better answer," he agrees. Stepping away, he calls out, "Did someone bring normal coffee? Not this froufrou crap?"

Ava laughs before handing him a large to-go cup with his name written on it. He kisses her cheek before moving to go stand next to Ali.

Carefully, I put away the journal I've been holding this entire time. I slide the purple bag under the table so nothing will get spilled on it before I go claim my own drink.

Courtesy of the woman I love.

55

BLANKETS

"Good, she's in place."

"Yes, Doctor."

"You're certain she's out?"

"Yes, Doctor."

"Then get the frame attached. I want to get this fucker out of her head before it can wrap around her ICAs."

"WHY THE HELL are hospitals always so cold?" Holly rubs her arms up and down.

Cassidy's teeth are chattering. "I don't remember it being this cold when I was stuck in here."

"You were too busy healing." Caleb's face takes on a dark cast, even as he wraps his arms around his wife. "Besides, they give the patients warm blankets. Why do you think I snuggled next to you so much?"

Cassidy laughs. "Yeah, that's the only reason why."

"When were you a patient?" I ask just for something to talk about. It's been more than an hour. We've heard from the patient liaison things are progressing smoothly—whatever the hell that means. Em and Holly are cuddled together in a corner, talking, while Jason and Phil are running their mouths about what Corinna will need when she gets home.

Cassidy replies, "Three years ago, Thanksgiving weekend. I was shot at a wedding."

I'm floored. "When the hell did the wedding business become so dangerous?"

"When my family decides not to let old ghosts rest where they should." Caleb frowns at me.

Warning received. I nod and continue to do nothing. Nothing but wait for more news that tells us nothing.

"Seriously, Keene. Go and donate another wing or something to get us a heater. Why is it so damn cold?" Ali complains. I can't help but huff out a laugh. The request is so ridiculous.

"Sorry, everyone. Hospitals are notoriously cold to keep the germs away," Jason explains. "Do you want me to run back to the farm and grab everyone some jackets?"

I'm pretty sure everyone's about to jump on that suggestion when the door slams open. Alarmed, we all look up.

What the hell's going on now?

Charlie comes stumbling in with an awkward-size box under one arm, while trying not to drop a tray of coffee on the floor. "Freaking hell—can someone grab the coffee? I'm running low on caffeine already today."

Holly jumps up and snags the stacked trays, as much to hold the warmth to her as to help out the avuncular figure to the Freeman clan. "Got it, Charlie." And from the blissful look on her face as her hands wrap around a cup, he'll have a hell of a time getting it back.

"Three under the age of one children have been dropped off. Sweet baby Jesus, do I have a new appreciation for the mothers of this world."

Dropping the box right next to where Em had just dropped off in a nap, she jumps up yelling, "I'm up! What's happening? Where's Corinna?"

"How the hell am I supposed to know, girl? I just got here." He shakes his head at her.

"Jesus, when did it get so cold in here?" Em asks the room at large. We all groan.

Suddenly, the alarm goes off on my phone, and a stillness permeates the room.

7:50 AM: Charlie should be there with a brown box. Have him play the video in his email after you open it. Love, Corinna PS - You have something to read.

"Charlie, open that box." I snap a picture of the entry and then hand it directly to him.

"Email?" he asks, confused as he tears into the box. "I don't have any..." I hear a discrete ping. "Well, I guess I do have a new email." Then he starts to laugh. "What the hell do we have here?" He pulls out a bright magenta square and shakes it out.

It's a fleece blanket with "I Love You" stitched on the edge. My eyes fill with hot tears. Judging from the number of hands reaching up to wipe beneath their eyes, I'm not the only one. "Charlie, shove the box over. Pull up her email," I say roughly.

There are enough blankets for everyone in the room, plus a few extra, as if she knows there will be others coming by later. Soon, people who were complaining a few moments earlier about being cold are wrapped in the warmth Corinna provided.

And then I hear her voice.

"Hey, y'all." My head whips around so fast because it's like she just stepped in the room.

I know you have to be freezing by now. Every hospital I've ever been to has been like this. I get the reason why, but I figured none of you all dressed warmly despite my warnings. I'm hoping the blankets come in handy.

Think of them like a hug.

That's your assignment for the next hour. Give everyone in the room a hug from me.

Okay?

I love you all.

And then she's gone.

I don't hesitate a second.

I clasp the shoulder of the person closest to me and pull them in for a hug. It just so happens to be Keene. "That's from Cori, man," I manage to choke out. Before I can pull away, Keene's arm hooks over my shoulder.

"She's everything to us too, Colby. You're not alone in this room," he murmurs. "You just can't be alone as a member of this family." Pulling back, Keene meets my eyes for a second before he nods and moves over to Ali. Picking her up, he twirls her around and kisses her soundly. Before I can smile at the spectacle, I'm pulled into an embrace by Holly, then Em, then Jason.

I nab Cassidy and Phil in a three-way hug. Charlie and I meet as we're crossing around the room, him to Cassidy and me to Caleb. Finally, I'm back in my chair with her blanket wrapped around my shoulders, and I pull out the journal. Opening it to where I left the bear bookmark, I start reading.

Hello, my love.

I need you to calm down.

I snort out loud. Good luck there, Cori.

No, seriously. Everyone's going to take their cue from you. They probably suspect I've told you more than I've told them (which between us, I have, but shhh...).

Close your eyes.

Don't keep reading. Shut them, Hunt. For at least a full minute.

She knows me too well. I shake my head, but do as she asks.

In my head, I see her as she was the other night, in a dress that almost perfectly matches the blanket I'm wrapped in. Glorious color dancing between the black-and-white memories of our history. Finding beauty in facing our past pain before digging in to fight for our future.

I don't realize I'm crying until I taste the salt of my tears against my lips. Opening my eyes, I reach for her, for her words.

I need her. I'll never be complete without her.

Now that you've let some of the pressure go, you can be there for the others. *Just know my arms are holding you tight. Every time you think I'm slipping away, wrap the blanket a little tighter around you.*

Because I'm not letting you go.

Never letting you go.

Not ever again.

Love,

Corinna

Now, stop reading. Mark your page with the bear. You'll get another alarm later. XOXO

56

SLOTHS

"Perfect incision."

"I agree. She'll barely be able to see the scar once her hair grows back over it."

"Skin and muscles are moved back nicely. Clip it. I'm almost ready for the drill."

~

IT'S TOO QUIET.

If someone were whispering in the room right now, everyone would hear it.

We're united in our misery of waiting. Everything is so damn slow. I don't know how I imagined it would be otherwise. Every time footsteps pass in front of our door, I suck in a deep breath, hoping it will be news.

I'm reliving every moment I've spent with Corinna. In my heart, I'm feeling her pain. Where she's bleeding from her head, I'm bleeding in my heart. I despise myself for not forcing our issues sooner, for every ounce of pain I caused her. For the stupid choices I made for her instead of giving her.

Scrubbing my hands over my face, I let out a harsh sigh. Did I do enough to let her know I'm irrevocably in love with her? Does she feel that in the darkness she's surrounded by?

A gentle hand lands on my shoulder. "She knows, Colby." Holly sits down next to me. "Stop tormenting yourself."

"How can you know? Everything I did for years was wrong. I let her go when I should have held her close. What if I was supposed to stand by her side now? She hates the dark." I swear viciously.

Ali drops into the chair on the other side of me. "I held her hand for a month in the darkest, nastiest conditions you can imagine, Colby. We weren't living in filth by the time they let us out of the shipping container—we *were* filth. Remember, Holly? We'd barely been hosed off once a week from that old garden hose going full blast."

Holly shudders. "I still can't stand cold water to this day."

Ali nods adamantly. "Right? I had to move. I just couldn't sit still. A lot of days I still feel that way. Cori needed to be in the light, but Colby? We all survived without it. All of us. In comparison to that darkness, she's got this beat." Ali squeezes my arm. "Try to focus on all the ways she's going to make you wait on her after instead."

Horror washes over me. "Oh God. She's going to be a nightmare."

Holly gives me a quick grin. "That's the spirit."

"Who wants to take bets that she asks for a bell as a get-well gift?" Ali says dryly.

Before I can respond with threats of bodily harm to the sibling who buys it for her, the alarm on my cell phone goes off.

"She has a fucking sixth sense about gossip. I swear, it's uncanny." Ali's voice is filled with mirth.

I look down. *8:50 AM. Purple bag. Ziploc 2. Then you have something to read and listen to. Love, Corinna*

I grab the purple bag from under the table. Rooting around in it, I find the bag with a big 2 marked on it. "Corinna mail!" I call to the room at large.

"Let's wait and open them up together," Phil suggests.

"I love that idea," Em agrees.

When everyone has their envelopes, we all tear into them and find sloth cards. Cassidy points at Phil and says, "She must have been thinking of you, brother."

Phil sticks his tongue out at Cassidy. "Very funny." He flips open his card and bursts out laughing. "Oh my God." Pulling out a sloth on a stick with Corinna's face superimposed on it, he dances it around.

"Did y'all really think today was going to move any faster than normal? It's me after all. Love, Corinna," Holly reads aloud.

Everyone bursts into hysterical laughter.

"Priceless," Em declares. She's bouncing her Corinna-on-a-stick around and cracking up.

Ali's using hers to fling an envelope spitball at Keene. "Hey, it's not pie, but it works," she says cheekily.

"Knock it off, Alison." Keene shakes his head, but the wide grin on his face belies his reprimand as he uses his Corinna to bat away the spitball.

Before these cards, our energy was like that of sloths themselves. Short of hanging upside down, the mood in the room was low, so low. Bryan told us these would be the toughest hours with little to no information from the operating room. Seeing the energy filling the room, I take a minute to reach for Corinna's words.

The minute I touch the journal, I feel peace within the newly launched chaos. I untie the string and find where I last left off.

Hello, my love.

I'm okay. I know they're taking good care of me. I'm worried about you though.

I'm sorry. I just don't know if I should be apologizing for not being strong enough to hold off on falling in love with you or not admitting it sooner.

Is she crazy? I'd have been infuriated to know all of this after and not have been there to support her. Clenching my jaw, I keep reading.

If I'm honest with myself (and I'd like to think I have been lately), I've been falling since you first came back home. Much like the sloths, I had to camouflage myself, only I was doing it with my anger. I fed myself off the bitterness of the past. The injustice I felt. It's easier to keep doing the same thing day after day than to look beyond yourself and change.

From the moment you were hired at Hudson, I should have known you weren't what I thought you were. We should have had it out then, but I was afraid. Buried beneath all of my harsh words was a woman who was hurting from the past who had no idea how to open her mouth and scream out her sense of betrayal.

You tried to hold on. Those letters—when I read them, my heart died... and then it was reborn, Colby.

Did I have a chance? Was it too late? How is it you don't hate me?

I still don't completely understand why you held on. Looking at this from a distance, I can't discern what makes me so special in your eyes. From mine, I'm a hot mess. But I guess I'm your mess, just as you'll always be mine.

Through thick and thin.

I swore I was living my life, but now I know I was just merely existing until I opened my heart to loving you.

I'm so sorry, Colby. Just like the sloths, I moved slowly to eradicate the walls between us. So much time lost because of my fears.

I hate that time's moving so slowly, isn't it?

Soon, my love, you'll hear the news you're waiting for. Then time can stop for both of us.

Love,

Corinna

Pull up Spotify. I made you a mix. Pop in the earbuds I packed for you. Get away from the family for a few. Put the journal away for a while. I'll be back soon.

Reaching for my phone, I launch my Spotify app. Fucking hell. She must have loaded this last night when I dozed off. "Corinna's Surgery Mix," I mumble. Digging around in the massively packed bag, I find the case with my earbuds. Popping them in, I push Play. I grab my Corinna-on-a stick and lie back. Closing my eyes, I listen to the first song, clutching my paper Corinna to my chest.

57

PEACOCKS

"Take the craniotome, please."

"Yes, Doctor."

"Let's get the flap covered quickly. Hand me a scalpel so I can start to peel back the dura."

"Are you ready for the loupe, Doctor?"

"Damnit. Someone get me a retractor. I need to be able to see what the fuck I'm doing here. Goddamnit, Corinna, where the fuck are you bleeding from?"

~

"WHAT DO you mean they're a little behind schedule?" Cassidy demands.

"What causes that to happen?" I'm right on her tail with my question.

The surgical coordinator is agitated. "Any number of things can cause that. I wasn't given more information than that from the OR. I'll call up and come back to you with information as soon as I have it." And then she scurries from the room.

A thunderous slam from the far side of the room surprises us all.

We all turn, shocked to see Jason having slammed a chair into the far wall in frustration. Jason, who never loses his cool no matter the situation, is throwing chairs.

I'm going to be sick.

I shove past everyone and run down the hallway, barely making it to the men's room in time.

I hurl everything that's in my stomach into the toilet. I'm heaving tears and snot and profanity against the walls in between.

I never loved before now, so I could never hate quite like this.

My father, Jack, Addison, the enemy I was taught to fire on in the Army—none of them deserved the hate I feel right now. This tumor deserves it because it could steal my heart from my body. My head hanging down between my arms braced on the toilet seat, it's hard to reconcile that it's possible I could end this day breathing but completely dead inside.

And then my watch goes off. *9:50 AM. Purple bag. Ziploc 3. Then your journal. Love, Corinna*

I punch the side of the stall. The sound reverberates all around me before I unlock it. I stagger drunkenly over to the sinks to splash water in my mouth and all over my face. It isn't until I lift my head to stare at my face in the mirror that I glimpse Caleb leaning against the wall behind me.

"I'm a fan of that particular stall. When Cassidy was shot, she was unconscious for days. I was petrified she wasn't going to wake up." His opening salvo has my attention.

"How did you deal with it?" I rasp.

His laugh is dark. "I did a lot of that." He nods to the stall. "I also prayed a hell of a lot. Corinna wasn't kidding when she said Cass and I had a lot of unresolved issues between us. I kept a lot from her, and even if she woke up, I still wasn't sure she was going to take me back.

"There are three things you can't forget today, Colby: the power of doctors, the miracles of prayer, and the strength of these women. Together they're unstoppable." With that sage advice, Caleb leaves the men's room.

I'm not far behind him. I have a bag to open.

I open the door to our waiting room, determined to be what Corinna needs me to be: the strength to get her family through the day ahead. Without a word, I walk over to the bag and pull it onto the table, ignoring to the concerned glances being passed from family member to family member.

I find the next bag of cards and pass them out. Opening my own card, the glorious peacock preening at me makes me smile. Flipping it open, I read, *Find us a vacation spot where I can see a peacock after I've recovered. I hear Florida has some. XOXO, Corinna.*

I reach for my journal. She wants to go on a vacation? I'm ready to go wherever and whenever Corinna wants. Unwrapping the leather tie, I turn the page and freeze. The words are so simple. So profound. So perfect.

Don't give up. I'm not.

I love you.

Corinna.

Put the peacock here. I'll be back soon. XOXO

I take a deep breath and let it out. Closing my eyes, I do something I haven't done in years.

For all my loved ones, and even my enemies, I begin to pray.

58

KITTENS

"Do you need the aspirator?"

"No. Now that we clipped off that bleeder, we're fine. Fuck, she had me scared for a few minutes. How's her drainage?"

"We're just about done draining naturally."

"Did you put in the monitor for her ICP?"

"Yes, Doctor."

"Then let's get started."

～

"I DON'T KNOW a damn thing I'm not telling you." Jason's yelling. I tend to believe him as he's being cornered by everyone, including his husband. "I swear to God, I tried to get more information, but they're not saying a word."

"Shit. I believe him," Phil grumbles.

"Thanks, baby," Jason says sarcastically. Shoving away from the pack of desperate Freemans, Jason stalks over to a chair and throws himself into it.

Phil goes to open his mouth, but I clap my hand on his shoulder and shake my head. "Jason," I call to him. His head snaps up. Glaring at his husband standing next to me, he raises his eyebrows. "Thanks for trying," I say before I let Phil loose to go grovel at his husband's feet.

We're in hour five of Corinna's surgery. Our last update consisted of things were still "going well." Jason volunteered to try to find out more specifics, but that failed. We're barely hungry, yet we're starving. We're exhausted, yet we can't sleep.

We need some kind of reassurance Corinna's still with us.

As if she hears us, my cell phone alarm goes off. *10:50 AM. Purple bag. Ziploc 4. Then your journal. Love, Corinna*

The cards feel thick as I pass them around the room. We tear them open, and the exclamations of "Where the hell did she find these?" begin. Even Jason can't hold on to his anger as Phil rubs the furry card against him and makes kitty noises.

"Jesus, can someone please get me eye bleach?" Keene mutters over my shoulder, as he's unable to look away from the train wreck that's Phil curled up in his husband's lap pretending to purr like a cat.

"So, I take it you and Ali don't plan on being furries anytime soon?" I ask innocently.

"Bite your damn tongue right off."

"You know that if you just ignore him, his antics stop faster." Ali slides up next to Keene, wrapping her arms around his waist.

"They never stop. It's like watching bad internet porn," Keene bemoans.

Ali arches an eyebrow. "Have much time do you have to do that these days?" She stalks away to talk with Cassidy and Em.

"Shit. How is it I always end up in the doghouse?"

I snicker. "Don't you mean the cathouse?"

Keene gives me the middle finger before he goes to coax Ali back into a better mood. I drop down into a chair and open my own card, and slap a hand over my mouth before the snicker can escape and draw any attention.

It's going to be all about playing with the kitty for a while. Sorry, baby! XOXO

Reaching for my journal, I open it to where the peacock marker rests. Turning the page, I start reading, and suddenly, I can't control the laughter.

This is the kitten checklist. If I'm right, can I have a real cat?

Doesn't she realize she doesn't need to guess? She can have whatever she wants.

Phil is rubbing the card (and likely himself) all over Jason. Keene is complaining about being traumatized. Ali is wondering why Keene can rock her world in bed, but is such a prude around the family. Holly and Em are trying to stay sane by scoping out hot doctors when they escape the room for a few minutes. Caleb and Cass are cuddling more than usual to bear up under the strain because today is bringing back too many memories of when she was a patient here, and Charlie is trying to get some semblance of order by bossing you around?

How did I do?

Seriously, y'all needed to lighten up for just a few minutes, and I just knew that giving Phil a card like this would be set off a chain reaction.

Consider this the meow effect!

Love,

Corinna

In case you didn't figure it out, my love, stop reading. But don't use my kitty to mark the page. It will just stretch it. And what good is a stretched pussy?

I'm laughing so hard, I can hardly breathe.

"Do you think we need to get him a doctor?" Holly says worriedly.

"If you go to get one, I'm coming with you," Em replies.

Clutching the journal to my stomach, I laugh harder.

"Hunt, get it together! You're losing it and scaring people," Charlie barks at me to get me in line.

Just like Corinna said.

"Can't breathe," I manage to get out. "Knows...you...all...too well."

I flip the journal over and howl like a lunatic.

"Colby, are you okay?" Cassidy, sweet Cassidy. I spin around in my chair and grab hold of her. Just to offer her a moment of peace, I press the journal in her hands. "I swear I'm not losing my mind. Just... here. See what she did and you'll understand." Watching Cassidy closely as she absorbs Corinna's words is almost as good as me reading them for the first time.

"Oh, Colby." Her face loses its tension. "This is priceless. And so utterly Corinna." Cassidy's tension has been replaced with something different.

Hope.

"I know." I accept the journal she hands back to me, sliding the peacock card in place again as a bookmark before sealing it closed.

"I've always said she has the biggest heart of us all," Cassidy murmurs. Dropping a kiss on the top of my head, she continues. "How fortunate she chose to give it to you for safekeeping."

"I'm not just fortunate, Cassidy. I'm blessed."

59

WITHOUT YOU

"Scissors? It's too big to get out in one piece."

"No, not yet. I'm going to try to massage it out."

"Seriously, Moser? Are you fucking kidding?"

"It's not large enough to be a problem, and it's too close to the ICAs to try to use anything sharp to go after it. If I nick something, I risk her bleeding out. Ah, there you are, you little bitch. Come to Daddy..."

"NOT EVEN GENOA IS APPEALING." Em shoves her sandwich away from her. "I'm too damn worried to eat."

"I never thought I'd ever say that." Holly eyes her slice of pizza tragically. "It's almost making me nauseous."

Caleb winces. "Sorry, guys. I thought asking Charlie to make a run would be a good idea."

"It was a great idea, my love," Cassidy consoles him. "Maybe if we heard some kind of news that was substantial, Caleb."

"These hourly updates aren't telling us dick," Phil bitches.

"Lord knows if we wanted to talk about dick, you're the guy we should go to," Ali jokes weakly.

"Alison, must you encourage him?" Keene throws down his sandwich in disgust.

"Yes, because I need something to distract me, and I didn't prepare for this kind of agony, Keene." Ali's face crumbles. "What if we get this far and they walk in that damn door and she's not Corinna anymore? What if she can't walk or talk or speak?" Jumping up from the table, she runs to the door.

"Shit, I was waiting for this to happen," Keene mumbles, racing after her.

Charlie sits down next to me. "Don't have much of an appetite myself."

My sandwich sits untouched before me. The idea of eating is nauseating, to say the least. The closer we get to the end, the more anxious I'm starting to become. Stomach beginning to churn, I wonder if something's going wrong in the OR.

And it's been more than an hour and a half since Corinna last told me to locate something in the big purple bag. My cell phone hasn't gone off. I've checked my alerts; none have been missed. I need her "voice" right now. I'm going crazy wanting to protect her, and unable to fight against the vortex trying to take her from me.

As my morose thoughts consume me and desperation sets in, my cell phone alarm goes off. *12:45 PM. Purple bag. Ziploc 5. I didn't forget about you. You guys needed to eat! By now you should know the drill. Love, Corinna*

Finally. My chin drops to my chest in a silent prayer.

There she is.

Standing, I pull the bag from under the table and plop it in my chair.

"Cori sent another message?" Holly exclaims excitedly.

"Yes. She said she wanted us to eat first."

Ali catches the tail end of what I'm saying as she and Keene come back into the room. "Not even for her could I eat her chocolate cake right now. Gimme," she demands as she rushes over.

"Such patience." I hand her the card with her name on it. Keene saunters up more slowly. "Here's yours." Lowering my voice, I ask, "Is she okay?"

"About as okay as the Apollo 13 crew was knowing they wouldn't touch down on the moon."

"Right," I mutter, ripping into my own card.

The colored card stock seems innocuous enough. It's the scrawled words, "I can't imagine this day without you!" in the center that grips my heart in a vise so tight, I can't breathe.

There are no options without Corinna.

I open the card with dread.

The best parts of me don't work the same way without you in my life. I should know. I tried for too many years. Love, Corinna

Holding the card to my lips, the closest I can get to kissing her right now, I think, *Neither do mine, princess. That's why I need this day to hurry up so I can know all our parts will work right together.*

Forever.

INSTEAD OF REACHING for my journal right away, I give myself some time. It's getting harder and harder in between Corinna's words. I don't know if this is what she wants me to do. I just know it's what I need. Other than random comments here and there, I'm so disjointed from the rest of the occupants of the room. The person I need to talk with is fighting through the dark for her life, my life, our love.

And her words are the only thing keeping my sanity anywhere in this stratosphere.

I manage to hold back until the patient advocate comes in and says the words we've been waiting for.

The tumor has been isolated and is in the process of being removed.

The minute she leaves, my knees collapse and I flop into the chair. My feet bump the bag under the table, and suddenly, I need her voice in my head holding up her end of our ongoing conversation.

I reach for the journal and the last place I left off.

My Colby,

You should know beyond a shadow of a doubt that I love you.

The woman I was before is eclipsed by the one I am now because of your love. Maybe I needed to go on without you to know I could survive, but I'd never be alive without the gift of you now that you're indelibly buried in my heart. Where I can't picture a day without you in my mind? Perhaps.

Now, I can appreciate the honor you wear isn't just a word but part of your soul. Much like the tumor that sits in my head. And with that honor comes truth, loyalty, and love.

I know you love me too. And because of that, I will fight the darkness to come back to you.

Know that.

Believe in that.

Because it's your name that will bring me back from the abyss. Your lips that will give me air I need to breathe. Your love that will keep my heart beating.

Love,

Corinna

Without reading any further, I take my newest card and place it in the journal. Whether or not she meant for me to move on, I don't know.

I'll never know.

60

THANKFUL

"It's labeled for pathology?"

"Yes, Dr. Moser."

"I want a rush on it. I don't want to wait longer than absolutely neces-sary for the results."

"They're waiting on the mass, sir. We'll get it right to them."

"Do you want me to begin to close the flap?"

"Not quite yet. We have to perform the motor tests."

~

IT'S ALMOST 2:45 and we haven't heard anything new. My phone hasn't buzzed. I'm going to tear the hospital down until I find her OR suite soon.

Everyone has taken a quick break outside the room. Cass, Caleb, Keene, and Ali stepped outside to FaceTime their children, who Ava agreed to pick up and keep at the main farmhouse until at least one of them could get home later. Matt would be going over to help her.

Holly and Charlie are walking around the grounds with Phil and Jason.

And Em is somewhere, getting more drinks, I think. To be honest,

I really don't care. I have the room to myself for the first time since very early this morning.

My grandfather called a few minutes ago, expecting we'd have heard more definitively from the surgical suite by now. He couldn't entirely conceal the concern lacing his voice when I said we were still waiting, and ordered me to call back as soon as I knew anything before hanging up. As much as the little boy in me wishes he could be here, I can't fault him for not offering. I know he took a considerable risk by showing up last night to provide us with his support. If he'd stayed, news broadcasters would be waiting for us when we stepped outside the front doors.

I'm just hoping we have the chance to make up for the missing years. Somehow, deep in my soul, I know if Corinna doesn't make it, there will be nothing left of me. My heart's beating only because hers is.

Maybe I need to take a page out of Corinna's book and write my grandfather a letter letting him know that. Letting him know that if something happens to Corinna, my heart will never be the same. I will never be the same. It will be the end of me and not because I gave up, but because how does your heart continue to beat when your soul is so gone? It's crucial for him to know I'll never be the same again if she's gone.

Over the course of the day, I've put together the pieces of the cards and notes she's left me.

She thinks she's going to die.

Pressing the heels of my hands against my eyes, I feel my stoicism crack, and misery floods every available space. The sounds coming out of me when I finally cut loose are wretched. Deep from the bottom of my soul, I howl my rage. How could she love me and expect to leave me at the same time as telling me she's fighting for me?

"Because it offers her an ability not to break, Colby." An unfamiliar feminine voice answers the words I didn't know I said out loud.

I face the doorway and see a middle-aged woman wearing a

comfortable sweater and jeans. "Who the hell are you?" I rasp, not the least bit embarrassed by the tears on my face.

The woman steps forward and offers her hand. "I'm Alice Cleary, Corinna's psychologist."

I'm taken aback. "You're Alice?" I ask dumbly, even as I take her hand.

And then I smell something familiar. Chocolate caramel goodness.

"Do you know I was expecting to come down here and club you in the head so I could steal what's in this package and run?" Alice jokes as she hands me a familiar white box.

I gape at her, then roar with laughter. "She swore I'd be eating store-bought cookies while she's in recovery."

Alice's laugh is like an ancient car coughing to life—rusty, and in need of some oil. "Of course she did." Nodding at the box, she asks, "Are you planning on sharing while you tell me what's wrong?"

Before I can open my box, my cell alarm goes off. *2:00 PM. Alice is bringing you your next card. There isn't one for the family. I suspect the brownies will be enough. Love, Corinna*

Showing Alice the text, I explain, "This is what's been getting me through the day, until about twenty minutes ago."

"What changed?" Alice asks as she sits.

I shake my head as I open the box. Inside is a card. Ignoring the overwhelming scent permeating the room, I open it.

Colby,

I know you too well, so stop being pissed. You're thinking the wrong way. (I should have Keene slap you upside the head, but I figure you having to fight to hold on to your brownies is punishment enough.) Controlling today and telling you all how much I love you isn't about giving up.

It's about being thankful.

I've been introspective in the last few weeks. What would have happened to me if I never found Ali and Holly? Cass, Em, and Phil? Charlie? Caleb? Keene? You? I'd have died in my soul long before the tumor had any chance at me.

This was the best way I could think of to keep you all going and to finally get a chance to show my gratefulness by making you all laugh, making you smile, and holding you close in the place that's the most important—my heart.

I'm in the other room fighting for our lives - the family's for sure, but most especially yours and mine.

We're so close to the finish, baby.

You'll get to hold me soon, and I. Can't. Wait.

I love you,

Corinna

My arms drop to my knees, and my head falls in between them as I clutch her letter in one hand. "God, baby, I love you too. Keep fighting."

I'd forgotten Alice was in the room until she says, "I know she will, Colby. She has more fire in her than half of the patients I see."

My head snaps up. Alice smiles. "I see she took my advice to get her life under control." She nods at the letter in my hand.

Suddenly, I can't talk fast enough. "All day. Every hour or so. It's like just as I was sinking, she knew how to bring me back up."

Standing, Alice tells me, "People with huge social support go into surgery with less anxiety and depression. Their odds are better than those who don't have that backup in their lives, Colby. Corinna already had a much better chance because she's so remarkable. Everyone gravitates to her."

I need to tell Alice what Corinna didn't know for sure when they met. "I'm crazy in love with her."

Alice grins. "There's nothing crazy about love when it's the right person."

I smile, my first genuine one all day. I'm about to reply when the door opens.

It's Bryan. Dr. Moser's take-charge persona has been left in the surgical suite it seems.

And my anxiety slams back into me, freezing me in place.

"Alice." He nods at the psychologist. "Colby. Where's the rest of the family?"

I swallow hard to clear the vomit hovering in the back of my throat, waiting to expel itself. "Around. They're around."

He nods, exhausted. "Let's get them up here. I'll go over everything."

I reach in my pocket for the phone. "Bryan, can you tell me..." I can't ask. I'm petrified to know the answer.

He drops himself into a chair. Scrubbing his hands harshly over his face, he looks up at me wearily before a huge smile breaks out. "She's alive. The whole fucking tumor is gone. Now, text the family and give me a goddamned brownie."

I shove the box over at him as I collapse into Alice's waiting arms, crying. It takes a few minutes before I can compose myself enough to walk around the table and grab him up from his seat. Slapping him on the back several times, I start to express my gratitude but stop because the words won't come out.

Soon I've texted the family, and they've raced back in. We're a mess of tearful, hugging, and kissing lunatics. But I can't say my eyebrows aren't the only ones that don't shoot up to the top of my head when Dr. Bryan Moser grabs Em by the waist and lays a kiss on her that expressly says he's interested in more than gratitude from the willowy blonde.

When he lets her up for air, she gazes up at him for just a moment before pushing up her glasses. In pure Em style, she mutters, "Holy hell."

Bryan laughs.

I grin right before asking, "How long till I can see Corinna?"

Bryan comes over and clasps my hand. "Another few hours. I'll send someone down to bring you up. I don't want everyone in tonight to confuse her, but I know you'll want in there. In the meantime"—he reaches over and swipes another brownie and eyes Em up and down —"I need to finish some paperwork. I'll see you all soon."

Bryan leaves the room, and Phil pounces on his sister like a lion with raw meat. "Well, well, well."

Em tries to ward him off. "That was as much of a surprise to me as it is to you!" she exclaims.

Leaving the Freemans to fight it out, I turn to Alice. "Thank you," I say with the utmost sincerity.

"It's been my pleasure, Colby. Take care of her."

I plan to. For the rest of our lives. Which I can now begin to plan beyond today.

61

LOOKING BRIGHT

"Corinna, wiggle your toes."
 "Move your fingers."
 "Now open your eyes. There you are..."

"CORINNA, baby. Please open your eyes. Bryan said you can. I need to see those beautiful eyes to know you're okay. I need to know you're with me."

I can hear Colby through the soupy haze. I'm not sure what I'm on, but it's like swimming in a foggy swamp to get to him.

But he's doing what I knew only he could do.

He's pulling me back from the abyss.

I try. I struggle to beat back the feeling of wooziness every time I get too close to the edge of reality. My brain is screaming at me to relax, but he's asking for something so small in comparison to what I put him through today.

I manage to slit my eyes and part my lips.

It's enough.

I'm finally enough.

He lets out a gush of air that I feel across my face. It's quickly followed by dampness. I hope it isn't an IV bag leaking.

"There you are."

62

EPILOGUE

CORINNA - ONE YEAR LATER

There are three things in this life I love with a strength I would never have believed existed inside of me.

The dark, because it represents the closure of another day I'm here, blessed to be surrounded by the people I love who love me best.

The scar that bisects my hairline is a permanent reminder I'm standing here. Alive. Whole. Healthy. A year after my surgery, I hardly notice it unless I brush too hard. A minimal price to pay for the rest of my life.

And the thing I love the most with all my heart and soul is Colby Hunt. The man who never gave up on me, despite all the perceived roadblocks. He fought for me. For us.

Recovery wasn't easy. I was an emotional yo-yo between purging the anesthesia from my system and my physical weakness. I was so out of it at the hospital, I didn't remember any of my discharge instructions. Especially the ones about getting confused and distressed easily.

Thank God, Colby did.

The first night we were home, I panicked because I couldn't remember where I put an old UConn hoodie he'd given me. It took a call to Ali to remember I'd packed it away long ago. The pain that settled in my heart when Ali told me was devastating to my befuddled mind. I gave myself a brutal headache from crying. It hurt so badly that I thought I might have to go back to the ER until the meds kicked in.

Colby held me through that first storm, reassuring me with soft words, all while he had someone run to his apartment to get one of his sweatshirts that smelled like him to slip over my heaving body.

Through the weeks that followed, Colby centered me. When I began to get restless halfway through my recovery, Colby carefully carried me into the field of wildflowers behind my house for a surprise picnic amid the fall foliage.

Colby arranged for me to call Brendan—something I'd forgotten to do prior to the surgery. I felt so bad that I'd forgotten all about Joey's cupcakes. I figured Brendan would be pissed. He was, but for a completely different reason. "All this damned time, you were fightin' for everyone else but yourself?" His fury was a living thing over the line.

"B, it wasn't intentional. I just ran out of time," I whispered helplessly. Colby rubbed my shoulders as I sat on FaceTime. Through the camera I saw Dani doing the same to Brendan.

Brendan ran his hands through his hair, visibly agitated, before freezing. "Wait. If you haven't been working, who's been sending the cupcakes?"

"I...I don't know."

"Cori, they've been coming in every week like clockwork. Granted, Joey said they're not as done up as usual, but I figured that was due to them just gettin' dinged in the mail or something."

Colby crouched down beside me so he could peer into the camera. "She was never supposed to know, Brendan."

I must have looked like a fish. "You...?"

He shook his head. "Not me, baby. You have a whole family who knows what this means to you." I emitted a choking sound. "You know the rest of your cake orders had to be directed to other bakers." I nodded. Colby brushed his fingers against the back of my neck. "Well, Phil, Cass, Em, Ali, and Holly just couldn't let this go to someone else. They figured if you could coach Brendan through your recipes, maybe between the five of them they could figure cupcakes out on their own. Though they admit, they're shit with decorating," he joked.

Overwhelmed, I buried my head in Colby's shoulder, and I remember him telling Brendan we'd call back. Strong arms held me as I wept over my family's constant support, love, and understanding. Over Colby's.

During my time away from the kitchen, when I was banned from lifting more than a container of milk, Colby was there. When I was frustrated over trying to remember a recipe, he told me I'd remember them. When I felt like I'd break, he'd remind me I was invincible. And so was our love.

Throughout this experience I learned I'm here by a blessing. I've had a lot of time to think in between watching episodes of the Food Network On Demand. I realized the past is what it is. So, it's time to forgive the most important person in the fiasco of the last ten years.

Myself.

Why should I hold a grudge against the girl I was, or the woman I am, because I was built differently than everyone else? This body of mine—this fucking beautiful body of mine—just survived one of the most harrowing experiences a human can live through. Each breath I take is a damned miracle. So, I have more curves than the woman walking down the street. Who cares? If the way my man worships every inch of me when he makes love to me is any indicator, he loves it too.

What matters is that I'm healthy. I'm alive. And tomorrow, I'll wake up from another night to see the bright sun in the sky. I'm strong enough to put in a full day of hard work and then some.

What matters is family. Mine. Colby's. Zachary came to visit during my recovery, making good on his promise to start getting to know his grandson all over again. Now he's a frequent visitor at our farm table. And just like I'd predicted, his belligerent attitude forged a truce between Keene and Phil, as they took on the cantankerous senator as a united front in verbal warfare. It adds a whole new dynamic to our family dinners when he's visiting.

What matters is love. If love could be measured like a recipe, the love I have for my family would need to have the Earth on one side of the scale to balance it out. The love I have for Colby couldn't be measured, even if the universe could be placed on the other.

This life, this family, this man—they are my everything.

I need nothing more.

∾

BRENDAN'S PLAYING at Madison Square Garden tonight. This time, Jason, Caleb, Keene, and especially Colby argued there was no way they were letting us get away with the antics we pulled at last year's show.

I laughed but agreed to ask Brendan for extra VIP passes. When I think back to that long-ago night, all I can remember is being overwhelmed with so many emotions. Now, I'm in such a different place, it's like there was this invisible plane I passed through where I found the strength in myself I was missing to make me complete.

Tonight, we stand as one family, while Brendan's singing his heart out to his fans. His latest ballad about loving someone as fiercely as the sun just made it to number one on the country charts. He strums his guitar a few times at the end before the arena erupts.

"Thank you!" Brendan calls into the mic. Just as he starts to talk, a member of his security team walks directly over to me. I experience a moment of déjà vu. "Ms. Freeman, can you come with me please?"

Here we go again.

Turning in Colby's arms, I give him a lingering kiss before yelling in his ear, "I had no idea!"

He grins. "I know. Go on up. I'll see you soon enough."

I smile and follow the beefy security guard up the side stairs so I'm hidden in the wings. I run a hand over my short hair and take a few deep breaths. Someone approaches me with earbuds so I can hear Brendan over the noise of the crowd. They quickly help me slip them in, just before I hear Brendan say in my ear, "...my good friend Corinna Freeman. Let's bring her out here!"

"Be careful of the cords, Ms. Freeman," the roadie warns me as I'm about to step out on stage. Nodding, I step out with a huge smile on my face. I catch a glimpse of Dani's beaming face in the other wing. I give her a quick wink as I make my way in dark-wash jeans, a black low-cut shirt, and pumpkin-colored, studded Valentino heels toward her boyfriend.

Just like last time, Brendan holds out his hand, and pulls me close but doesn't spin me around. "You know, I think we should bring up another one of my friends too. Colby? You up for joining your woman up here?"

Shock almost has me falling as my gorgeous boyfriend strides out from the same place I was standing just a few moments before. What on earth is going on?

"Surprise, baby," Colby says into his own microphone as he reaches me. I feel Brendan step back. Fumbling, I lean over into Brendan's mic.

"I call shenanigans." The crowd roars. I'm frozen by Colby's words though.

"I call it love," Colby counters.

My head whips back toward my boyfriend to find him holding a small velvet box in the palm of his hand. Suddenly, the world disappears. Brendan. My family, who are likely jumping up and down in a frenzy. And the almost 21,000 people in Madison Square Garden.

The world has narrowed to me and the man who has moved to stand next to me. I stumble before I catch myself. The tender look on Colby's face stabilizes me like nothing else. Pressing one hand against my stomach, the other lifts to my mouth. I shake my head back and forth.

Is this really happening?

"I was born to love you, just as you were born to be mine. I need to know you're going to be in my life for the rest of our lives, Cori." He doesn't get down on one knee, and I'd never expect him to. He did enough of that during my recovery to tie my shoes, shave my legs, or just give me a hug. Instead, he cups my chin in his hands. "Wake up with me every morning. Give me the first breath I need to start the day. Come home to me and go to sleep in my arms. I can't promise it will be perfect."

I drop my hand from my mouth so I can touch him. "I don't need perfect," I say shakily.

"I can promise I'll love you and whatever family we create more every morning we're together."

"That's all I need."

"Tell me you love me," he demands. "Tell me you'll love me forever."

"I've already loved you forever. That will never stop." The tears are pouring down my face.

He opens the box. Pulling out the ring, he tosses the box behind him. Hopefully, one of my family members catches it. Sliding the symbol of his love on my finger, he lowers his head to seal our engagement with a kiss. "Then, soon-to-be Mrs. Hunt, get ready for the rest of our lives." Colby pours every ounce of his love into a kiss that seems to go on forever until Brendan breaks it up despite the screaming crowd so the show can go on.

I'M STILL WALKING on air as we make our way into our suite at the Hilton Midtown. I'm keeping the party going in my head by humming every tune from the concert that comes to mind. Colby's shaking his head, laughing as we move farther into the suite, smiling the entire time.

"I want to keep dancing," I announce as I kick off my shoes. They fly through the air, and I hear a thunk and a crash. Oops. I'll worry about that tomorrow. "I want to celebrate us."

"I think that can be arranged." He shrugs off his jacket, casually tossing it on the low-lying couch. His smile is nothing less than predatory as he makes his way toward me.

"I think there's a music channel on the TV, fiancé." I tack on the last word just to try it out. He just shakes his head with a smile.

Colby turns on the first music station he finds. Turning, he tosses the remote back on the table. The slowest, sexiest version of "Time After Time" begins to play. Tears prick behind my lids as he slides his arms around me and begins to sway.

I lay my head on the chest of the man I'm going to love forever and let out a small sigh. "All those years ago, in your wildest dreams, did you ever believe we'd be this happy?"

The man I love, the man I'm going to be with for the rest of my life whispers, "It's terrifying to realize the love I had for you back then isn't comparable to the love I have for you now. Every morning I wake up shaken because the intensity of my love for you causes me to stop breathing."

Shaken, I pull back. My mouth opens and closes, but no words come out. My chest feels like it's going to explode. Not long ago, I wasn't sure if I'd live to see another year, and now the years stretch ahead with nothing but promise. I choke on my tears.

Pulling me close, he says, "I've got you, baby. Just breathe."

How do I explain this? How do I make him understand how beautiful it feels to have been broken inside for so long and to have been healed. My head. My heart. My soul.

"Every time I take a breath, I inhale your love into my heart. Of course I'll breathe."

THE END

WHERE TO GET HELP

The medical issues Corinna went through are real. According to the National Brain Tumor Society, nearly 700,000 people in the United States are living with a brain tumor, and approximately 79,000 more cases will be diagnosed in 2018. Brain tumors can affect men, women, and children of all ages, races, and ethnicities.

In the story, Corinna made difficult decisions based on her definition of "living" under the watch of her medical care team. It is not, nor is it ever my intent, to advocate certain medical decisions. If you are ever diagnosed with a medical illness of this magnitude, the steps you'll need to take for your well being are what you as an individual must be able to live with to survive. Physically. Emotionally. Spiritually.

It's what I did when I was diagnosed with my own personal medical issues — different than Corinna's — but those which I called upon when writing this book. I, however, was incredibly fortunate I was guided toward a fantastic support group to lean on.

Founded by a brain tumor survivor, Stupid Cancer offers a lifeline to the young adult cancer community by helping those in need feel normalized and connected to their peers. They end isolation and educate about the age-appropriate resources people didn't know they needed, to navigate the crap they're about to endure with dignity and on their terms.

Their mission is to empower, support, and improve health outcomes for the young adult cancer community. Just as their manifesto states, it's not a contest. Even benign tumors can be as devastating as malignant ones. I'm thankful to them for the support they gave to my family and to me.

I could go on about hospitals and doctors and other crap, but I'm not. There's just one last thing I want to say.

Take a deep breath and live.

COMING SOON

I've experienced the ways love can change a poor man into a rich one, a sinner to a saint, and make people beg for redemption.

Yet nothing I'd ever done was as profound as marrying the woman I love.

Every mission I took was a risk worth taking knowing I'd go home to her loving arms.

What I didn't know was in my quest to right all the wrongs of the world, I was destroying the only part of it I'd die for - my marriage.

The ripple effect of miscommunication and the sin of my omissions would change all of our lives.

And it would be my wife who would pay the price.

Ripple Effect by Tracey Jerald
February 3, 2020

Amazon/Kindle Unlimited
Add to your Goodreads TBR
Sign up for Go Live Notice

ALSO BY TRACEY JERALD

Amaryllis Series

Free to Dream

Free to Run

Free to Rejoice

Free to Breathe

Free to Believe

Free to Live

Glacier Adventure Series

Return by Air

Return by Land (Pre-order - October 12, 2020)

Return by Sea (Coming Winter 2021)

Standalones

Close Match

Ripple Effect

Lady Boss Press Releases

Easy Reunion

CBY - Title to be released soon!

(Coming August 2020)

ACKNOWLEDGMENTS

To my husband, thank you for supporting me through this and through my own wars. Through sickness and health, I will always love you.

To my son, no matter what, I love you. Remember, just take a deep breath and know Daddy and I are here to support you. Always.

To my mother, I never meant to turn your hair gray early but... You had to listen to things no mother should ever hear about their child. Then, my real battles began. Just remember, I'm still here to finish turning your hair white. I love you.

To my father, first for doing step aerobics with me as a child and then for being guardian angel after you died. I didn't appreciate one then, but I cherish both now. I just wish I could tell you I love you one more time.

Jen, when we were on vacation in Montana, the feeling came over me this would be something special after I saw the look on your face. Thank you for confirming what I was already feeling. I love you always.

Chapter 58 — The Meow Effect. Jen, Tara, Greg, Alissa, and Kristina — my Meows. We've lived through too much together, but damnit, we've LIVED! We've held each other up through the worst (and I do mean the worst), but together, we are an unconquerable force. I love each of you so much.

To Jennifer Wolfel. You have my eternal gratitude for always telling me like it is, never holding back, knowing I can take it, and for making me better than I thought I could be.

To Alessandra Torre, Jenna Jacob, and Rebel Farris. Each of you has offered incredible wisdom, support, and strength to me. I hope one day to be able to be able to pass it on. All my love and a million hugs.

To Sandra Depukat from One Love Editing. If someone asked me to describe you in a single word, it would be flawless. I will never forget the "love notes" you left me in the margins as you read Breathe.

To Trifecta Editing Services - Amy, Lyndsey, and Dana. My full appreciation for the hard work each of you put into this book is unable to be expressed. Thank you for everything you've done!

My cover and brand designer, Amy Queue of QDesigns, you once again spun your magic for me. I wish you a rainbow of joy every day.

To my team at Foreword PR. Linda Russell – only you could handle me getting a concussion right before the marketing of this book occurred. I love you to the moon and back! Alissa Marino - working with you is knowing I'll never fall. Here's to a fantastic year!

For my Facebook group — Tracey's Tribe. I'm sending my love to you and the home we created amid the madness.

To all of the bloggers who continue to read my books, thank you from the bottom of my heart.

To my readers, I love each and every one of you. Thank you for your love, for continuing to follow me on this journey, and for choosing to read my words.

ABOUT THE AUTHOR

Tracey Jerald knew she was meant to be a writer when she would re-write the ending of books in her head when she was a young girl growing up in southern Connecticut. It wasn't long before she was typing alternate endings and extended epilogues "just for fun".

After college in Florida, where she obtained a degree in Criminal Justice, Tracey traded the world of law and order for IT. Her work for a world-wide internet startup transferred her to Northern Virginia where she met her husband in what many call their own happily ever after. They have one son.

When she's not busy with her family or writing, Tracey can be found in her home in north Florida drinking coffee, reading, training for a runDisney event, or feeding her addiction to HGTV.

To follow Tracey, go to her website at http://www.traceyjerald.com. While you're there, be sure to sign up for her news-letter for up to date release information!

Made in the USA
San Bernardino, CA
29 June 2020